Jesus H. da Vinci

An Adventure of Spirit

DK Creative
12400 State Hwy 71 W
Suite 350-413
Austin, TX 78738
info@dkcreative.com

Editors – Carolyn Roark, L'aura Terry
Cover Design – Kelly Hunter
Photography – Heather Johnston

Jesus H. da Vinci: An Adventure of Spirit

ISBN – 978-0-9825449-1-4

Printed in the United States of America

Library of Congress – 2015900376

Jesus H. da Vinci

An Adventure of Spirit

D.K. Stanley

Published by DK Creative
Bee Cave, Texas

Table of Contents

Dedication

To the unflinching, persistent spirit of humanity,
in its pursuit to know God.

Acknowledgements

I'd like to thank the following people for their effort and time to make this book possible. Without you, I would never have finished it.

Carolyn Roark, Dave Wieckowski, Kay Ellen Shores, Keith Baker, Laura Terry, Miriam McCarron, Patrice Sullivan and Phillip Tien.

Thanks go to Kelly Hunter for the wonderful cover.

Much appreciation also goes to the gang at H&L, especially Nathan Hawkins. Your support and encouragement have been truly helpful.

I'd also like to thank all my teachers and mentors over the years. To list all of you would fill this page. Thank you.

Introduction

We've all had our own rollercoaster ride through life. No matter what our religion or spiritual beliefs, the Universe tests us over and over again. Without regard to convenience or what we think we want out of life, it continually presents our lessons, whether we're conscious of them or not. We can avoid them, we can distract ourselves, we can even deny the existence of an almighty being, but eventually we have to address our lessons or be faced with the "dark night of the soul"—the ultimate test.

For thirty years, I've been on a conscious spiritual path—and the Universe has definitely insisted that I learn my lessons. However, it has provided inspiration in the form of books like *Illusions: The Adventures of a Reluctant Messiah, Way of the Peaceful Warrior* and *The Celestine Prophecy.*

I know I'm not alone. I know that you've had your challenges and could use some encouragement as well. With that in mind, I offer to you *Jesus H. da Vinci: An Adventure of Spirit.* I think you'll be able to identify with much of what the protagonist goes through. I'm sure you'll laugh, you might cry, and it is my hope that you'll be inspired. Enjoy!

Jesus H. da Vinci

An Adventure of Spirit

Chapter 1 – Arrival

Emerging from the light, darkness enveloped him and his awareness resumed anew. *Am I alive?* As he breathed in, the air was so cold the naked man gasped. *It feels like I'm alive. Are my senses functioning?* Vision—blinking several times, he saw nothing but total darkness. Hearing—he only heard his pounding heartbeat. Touch—cold raindrops struck his skin and pebbles hurt his feet. Smell—inhaling, he detected something; could it be the rain?

Leaning his head back, he stuck his tongue out to take a sample. It was almost sweet. Taste—check. Some twinkling stars caught his attention. A loud pop from overhead startled him and as he looked up a bright light blinded him. Hearing and vision—check, except for those dots in front of his eyes. *Let's see...two arms, two legs, ten fingers and ten toes.* The transmogrification had been a success!

Why is it so cold? This location was supposed to be more temperate. He crouched down, grabbing his knees to stay warm, and fell over. Balance—shaky. He struggled up into a squat, shivering. *Am I dying?*

He fell over again at the sound of a high-pitched noise nearby. Bright, flashing lights approached and stopped about a hundred feet away. Within moments, a narrow white light shone in his face and he instinctively covered his eyes.

A human approached. "Are you okay? Where's your clothes, buddy? Stand up and raise your hands!" The naked man struggled to his feet and lifted his arms overhead.

"What's your name?" Trembling, the naked man said nothing. "What's your name? Speak up!" The naked man stood silently.

A second human emerged from the darkness. He was just as concerned about the lack of clothing as the first. "Where's your clothes?" He glanced at his partner. "Roy, go get him something to cover up with."

"On it, Rick." Roy walked into the darkness and returned with a blanket. As he approached, the naked man recoiled slightly.

"Assault? Were you attacked?" asked Roy, wrapping the blanket around him. The naked man shook his head no. Grabbing his arm, Roy pulled him toward the flashing lights—possibly a type of conveyance. Opening a door, Roy guided him inside and then got in himself. There was some kind of metallic netting separating the front seat from the back seat.

"Whaddya think? Jail or state hospital?" asked Roy. "He doesn't appear inebriated."

"The state hospital is on lockdown," said Rick.

"Really? Why?"

"A stabbing, and the perp still isn't in custody."

"Our shift's almost over and the game starts in forty-five minutes. What are we going to do with this guy?"

"Hmm, he doesn't seem dangerous and the only crime he's committed is indecent exposure. How about that church soup kitchen? He can get some food and maybe some clothing there," suggested Rick.

Food sounded pleasing to the naked man and he certainly wasn't getting any sustenance from his leg terminations. Gathering up his courage, the naked man spoke for the first time, "Good." He enjoyed the vibration of speech in his throat and chest.

"He speaks! Do you have a home or an apartment we can take you to?" asked Roy.

"No," the naked man replied.

"What's your name?" asked Rick.

The project group for this mission had put significant thought into this. They studied human communications for several years and concluded that they wanted to choose a name that humans could identify with, that wouldn't stand out too much. The group picked the name of a well-known human prophet, thinking that there would be many humans with that name. For a surname, they picked one of the most creative humans to ever live. "Jesus H. da Vinci," the naked man said.

"What does the H stand for?" asked Rick.

His stomach growling, Jesus said, "At present...hunger." The humans laughed. Jesus smiled as he experienced his first feeling of connection.

"All right, let's get you some food," said Roy.

"And some clothes," added Rick.

The car sped up and did a U-turn. It was the fastest that Jesus had ever gone in his life, not including the space flight, and he found it exhilarating. Even though it was night, everything was lit up. Glowing signs were everywhere. He concluded that humans must be afraid of the night considering the effort they put into making it less dark.

The car stopped and Roy got out. He opened the back door and helped Jesus out. The growling in his stomach had turned to pain. They approached a large building on a hill, making their way along an ornately landscaped path to a side entrance. Jesus was surprised how many plants there were on this planet.

Several humans milled around the poorly lit entrance. They grumbled and moved out of the way as Roy, grasping Jesus's arm ushered him inside. The room was too bright with ugly fluorescent light that bathed the beige walls and lime-green linoleum floor with an irritating glow. Rows of tables, inscribed with initials and depictions of human body parts, filled the room, and scattered on the walls were posters and pictures. The smells caught Jesus's attention—they didn't remind him of anything in particular, but his mouth began salivating.

Leading Jesus to an empty table, Roy told him to sit down. "Where's the pastor?" Roy asked no one in particular. For some reason, this human seemed to command everyone's attention.

Through a swinging door in the back of the room, an elderly man emerged. He trudged towards them, his gait slowed by his girth. "How can I help?"

"Pastor, me and my partner found this man in the middle of the road, naked and with no identification. We thought that you might be able to help him with some food and hopefully some clothing," said Roy.

"Certainly, Officer, certainly. Jack! Jack!" the pastor cried out. A short, stocky young man with blue eyes and blond hair parted in the middle came scurrying over.

"Yes, Pastor?"

"Bring this man some food...and don't skimp on the portions. I can hear his stomach growling."

Jack scampered off to the kitchen. "Thanks for taking this man in, Pastor," said Officer Roy, as they walked to the door.

"Did you get the young man's name?" asked the pastor.

"He said his name was Jesus H. da Vinci," Officer Roy said.

"Seriously?"

"Yup."

"Do you know where he lives?"

"Nope. Good night."

The pastor approached Jesus with a look of purposefulness and solicitude. "Now son, what is your name?" he quietly asked.

"Jesus H. da Vinci."

"Don't you mean 'Hey-Zeus'?" the pastor asked condescendingly. Jesus stared at him, not answering. "In this country, we don't name children after our Savior. Where are you from?"

"I'm from France."

"I see. Do you have a place to stay? Do you have any money?" The pastor's questions sped up. "How old are you? Are your parents alive? Do you have a job?"

Jesus blurted out, "I have amnesia! I think." His project group had come up with that explanation as a catch-all response when he needed some distance, and it did put an end to the barrage of questions. Jack returned with the food and distracted them both.

"Eat, my boy, eat," coaxed the pastor.

Jesus looked at the plate of food momentarily and then scooped up a handful of mashed potatoes and stuffed it in his mouth. It tasted exquisite and his body shuddered briefly.

"Pause please." In a fussy sort of manner, the first judge asked, "Humans eat with their mouths? They don't take in nourishment through their leg?"

"That is correct, Your Honor," said Jesus.

"Continue with your testimony," said the fussy judge.

"A little decorum, my son," the pastor said emphatically. "Here's a fork and spoon," handing Jesus two utensils. He stared at them blankly. Grabbing the spoon, he gobbled up more mashed potatoes.

Exasperated, the pastor said, "No, no. That's not how you use a spoon." He demonstrated which utensil to use with what food and how to hold them.

"I'm sorry. Like I said, I have amnesia...I think," Jesus said. He quickly finished the food. The pain in his torso subsided and he felt satisfied. Suddenly and simultaneously, an emission of gas and a loud noise issued from his mouth.

"What must have happened to you for you to forget your manners?" the pastor asked.

"I...I don't remember," Jesus said, and that seemed to satisfy the pastor.

"I don't suppose you have a place to stay?" the pastor asked. Jesus shook his head no. "Jack, don't you have an extra bedroom?"

Quietly standing beside them, Jack had been cleaning his glasses and listening to the conversation. His face contorted and the pastor said, "Now Jack, it's important to do good works, and sheltering this young man would be a good thing for you to do."

"Pause," said the second judge. "I'm curious how the pastor knew what Jack was thinking without Jack communicating it through speech?"

"I found out later, using their global electronic memory they call the Internet, that 90 percent of all communication on their planet is physical or nonverbal. They call it body language. It's not taught, it's picked up through experience. There are some exceptions—there are many helpful websites when one is having a difficult time obtaining a sex partner. I was unaware that I needed to learn about body language before my mission."

"What's a sex partner?" asked the curious judge.

"I explain that in detail later in my story, Your Honor."

"Continue please," said the curious judge.

"You look tired, my son," the pastor said. "Jack, why don't you get this young man some clothes from the donations box." Jesus realized he was feeling fatigued. Returning with some clothes, Jack led him to the restroom so he could dress.

Jack laughed when Jesus came out. His shirt was on inside out and his pants were on backwards. By pure luck, he had managed to get his shoes on correctly. Jack pointed out the errors and Jesus reentered the restroom to make the necessary changes. When he emerged a second time, Jack nodded his approval.

"Let's head for *mi casa*," Jack said. As they headed for the exit, the pastor came over and asked Jack to bring "Hey-Zeus" by the church the next day. "Sure thing, Pastor. Good night."

"Thank you, Pastor, and good night," Jesus said.

"I'm parked over here," said Jack, as they exited the church. His conveyance wasn't as smooth or shiny as the officers'. They got in and after several attempts, it started.

"Yes!" said Jack enthusiastically. "The pastor is a good dude, but a bit old-fashioned, if you know what I mean. I've been looking forward all night to getting out of there and going home to smoke a doob. What's your name?"

"Jesus H. da Vinci."

"Seriously?"

"Yes," Jesus said, beginning to doubt the project group's choice.

"That is one unusual name, dude."

"Is 'home' the same as 'mi casa'?" Jesus asked, with some confusion.

"'Mi casa' is Spanish, man," Jack said.

"Oh."

"Are you cool, dude?"

"No. I'm no longer shivering."

"Nooo," said Jack. "Do you get high?"

"Higher than you can possibly imagine."

"Excellent. I have a little bit of killer weed left," Jack said gleefully.

"Pause," said the third judge. "There are deadly plants on this planet?"

"No—well, yes," Jesus said, "but in this case, that's slang for 'outstanding.' What's more interesting is that they burn plants and inhale them."

Surprised, the third judge asked, "To what end?"

"To alter their consciousness. About half a billion humans take legal and illegal drugs to alter their consciousness. Add two billion people that drink alcohol, which is legal almost everywhere, and that brings the number up to almost 40 percent of the total population on Earth. The country I lived in uses 80 percent of their world's pharmaceutical opiates even though only 4 percent of the population live there."

"Great merciful Goob! What drives them to do that?" the third judge asked empathetically.

"Emotions...to deal with their emotions. It's incredibly challenging and my story will reflect that, Your Honor," Jesus said.

"Proceed," said the empathetic judge.

Jack's home was a small two-bedroom apartment. Upon entering, Jesus smelled a wide variety of competing odors—a combination of dust, dirty socks and underwear, pot, rancid food, and urine. With a two-hour-old human body, he was still adapting to its senses. The combined sight and smell was too much, and Jesus collapsed shouting, "Great Goob!"

Taken aback, Jack helped Jesus to his feet. "Yeah, I know it's a little ripe, but there's no need to go all Meryl Streep on me. Hold your nose if you don't like the smell. Remember, I'm doing good works by letting you stay here."

Picking up fast-food wrappers and pizza boxes off of the furniture and floor and going to the kitchen, Jack grumbled something that Jesus couldn't make out. He stood there unsure what to do next.

Reappearing, Jack said, "Okay, kitchen...this is the living room. Follow me. This is the bathroom. I'll clean it tomorrow. This is my bedroom. Don't go in there. And down the hall is your room."

They entered a small room with only a twin bed and a wooden chair in the corner. "Sorry, I only have one set of sheets and I'm using them." Jack paused as Jesus stood there saying nothing. The silence growing uncomfortable, Jack asked, "Are you tired? Do you want to watch some TV?"

"I'm tired. I think I need to rest."

Jack stepped out, closing the bedroom door behind him. "Good night, man."

Jesus's brain ached from the intensity of his situation. Every single moment was fraught with stress, new experiences, and the possibility that he would do or say something that would risk exposure. He was grateful for some time to process the events of the last two hours.

His chest was tight and his breathing seemed restricted. Something was going on in his lower abdomen. It felt like it was moving up his body towards his heart, throat, and head, making him feel weak. It was more than just the physical exhaustion he was feeling. It had to be some form of not-love. He didn't understand why he was feeling this, because the mission was going well. Everyone he had met so far assumed he was human. Not only that, he had a place to stay, too. None of that made any difference to what he thought must be fear, and slowly, he became conscious of another feeling. Was it loneliness?

"That's enough for today," said the fussy judge. "We'll continue tomorrow. Put the defendant in the hole."

Chapter 2 – The Trial

On a planet unknown to Earth, the morning sun shone dimly through the glass ceiling of a triangle-shaped courtroom. The door opened and the three judges filed in slowly. They made their way to podiums in each corner, carefully climbing onto conical perches. They are Goobers—a race of three-legged beings with peanut-shaped bodies and limited emotions. Two arms that can move in any direction, terminated by three-fingered hands, hang at their sides. They have two eyes—a large one in front and a smaller one in back—which affords them a 360-degree view.

A report detailing the scant particulars of the case lay before them. This was day two of a secret trial convened in a case of treason—practically unknown on a planet where stability and caution are paramount.

The fussy judge, in a low monotone, asked for the defendant to be brought in. Jesus entered, escorted by two court sentinels. He walked down a ramp, moving his front leg and right leg clockwise then his left leg and front leg counterclockwise, snaking his way to the defendant's floor. He gently climbed onto his perch.

"All Hail Goob," the fussy judge declared. "Wake up!"

Everyone in the courtroom responded in unison, "I am in the moment."

"State your name for the court," the fussy judge ordered.

"Jesus H. da Vinci, Your Honor."

"No, no. Your real name...not the name you took for your mission," the fussy judge insisted.

"That is the name that was chosen for me and I intend to keep it for the rest of my life, Your Honor."

"Immaterial," the fussy judge said in an emotionless tone. "You are charged with treason. Do you want to continue with your original plea, keeping in mind that a plea of guilty could mitigate your punishment?"

"Yes, Your Honor. I am not guilty."

"Really?" said the fussy judge, as nonplussed as a Goober can be. You exposed the existence of our planet to an alien race. How could you possibly be not guilty?"

"There were extenuating circumstances, Your Honor."

"What possible extenuating circumstances could there be for you to expose your home planet to possible annihilation?"

"Emotions, sir. And it's impossible to give you a simple explanation of them. You would need to know the specifics of my mission to understand my actions."

The curious judge said, "I think that we would like to hear those specifics, since the information we've been given is meager at best."

"If it please the court, would you like to hear the account of how and why this mission was launched?"

The judges exchanged glances. Prior to this trial, they had no idea that Gooberia had the technology to visit another planet. "Yes, begin there please," said the empathetic judge.

"Fifteen years ago, the first attempt was undertaken. The cosmogoobs returned safely, but something unexpected happened during the space flight. The spaceship disappeared into a 'wormhole.'"

"A wormhole? What's a wormhole?" the curious judge asked.

"You can think of it as the circulatory system of the galaxy, or maybe even the universe. It transported the spaceship far away in just a few moments. We don't even know where yet. The cosmogoobs found themselves close to the third planet in a star system with eight or nine planets. We began to monitor this planet and discovered that it supported life."

"Life? What kind of life?" asked the empathetic judge.

"Advanced life comparable to our own."

The judges reacted with surprise. "Well, there is advanced life out there. We are not alone," said the empathetic judge.

"True. And the incredible opportunity to visit this planet was too great for the project group to ignore."

"So, you arrived on the planet and were immediately recognized as a member of an alien race?" asked the curious judge.

"No. A process of transmogrification was performed during the transport to the planet."

"Trans-what?"

"Transmogrification. It's a process that transforms a being into another type of physical being, leaving the mental makeup intact."

"How is this done?" asked the fussy judge.

"I am not entirely familiar with all the technical details even after going through this process, but the basis of it is that all three-dimensional beings, including ourselves, appear on the physical plane via light passing through a matrix formed on one of the spiritual planes."

"How did our scientists even know how to do this?" asked the fussy judge.

"A long time ago, there was a discovery of ancient sacred texts by our scientists that explained the technique. They've been working on this for many years with some success."

"Weren't you afraid that you might be transmogrified into something else, like an insect or back into a plant?" asked the curious judge.

"I had read about their research and observed the process in several simple tests and concluded that the risk was not that great."

"How come *you* were chosen to visit this planet?" asked the empathetic judge.

"I was chosen from amongst the other scientists because of my high SAP—Stability and Persistence—score," said Jesus, without a hint of pride.

"Not according to our report. It says here you were chosen at random," said the fussy judge.

"Really?" asked Jesus. "Why was I told otherwise?"

"It says here that it was to keep you from feeling not-love," said the fussy judge.

"Excuse me, but how did the scientists even know what to transform you into?" interrupted the curious judge.

"The next flight to Earth placed a space buoy in geosynchronous orbit and subsequent flights gathered information from it. We were able to collect sufficient data on their physical makeup to execute the transmogrification process successfully."

"I'm having a difficult time understanding all of this. You appeared on their planet in their physical form. How did you know how to behave to remain inconspicuous?" asked the fussy judge.

"We collected other data besides physical information. I studied for two years prior to my space flight."

"So, the trans-so-and-so process was initiated from our spacecraft?" asked the fussy judge.

"Yes, that is correct."

"So, what do they look like?" asked the curious judge.

"They are about one-third taller than us and are bi-pedal," said Jesus.

"Hold on, they only have two legs? How do they remain upright?" asked the empathetic judge.

"The terminations of the legs protrude forward about one-sixth the length of the leg."

"That still seems unbalanced," said the curious judge.

"It is but they learn. It takes them several thousand attempts to master walking. They become proficient at it after about twelve to eighteen months as children."

"What's a children?" asked the empathetic judge.

"It's the plural of the word child. You see, they do not come into manifestation full-grown like us. They start out small in stature and achieve maturity about one-quarter of the way through their life. About that time they are able to procreate."

"How do they procreate?" asked the empathetic judge.

"I'll explain that later," said Jesus. "They have two eyes like us, but they are both in the front of their head. They are the most advanced predators on their planet."

"What's a predator?" asked the curious judge.

"Many animals on their planet prey on or eat other animals."

"How barbaric!" the empathetic judge exclaimed.

"Maybe so, but that was God's plan for them."

"You mean Goob, don't you?" asked the fussy judge.

"God or Goob, what's the difference?"

"'God' is not whom we believe in. Goob is whom we believe in. And you will use Goob in this courtroom," the fussy judge said sternly.

Jesus, ignoring him, continued, "We have the same set of senses—sight, hearing, smell, touch and taste, but since they are predators their senses are much more enhanced than ours. They also have, and this is an understatement, amplified emotions that cover a much greater range than our own."

"There's love and not-love," said the curious judge. "What else is there?"

Jesus, nodding in agreement, said, "True, but there are many gradations in each of those with human beings. There are more than twenty specific feelings they identify with love, and many more than that identified with not-love."

"Why so many more gradations involving not-love than love?" asked the empathetic judge.

Jesus pondered this question for a moment. *Indeed, why?* The very question had consumed him during his visit to Earth. "Because human development is generally driven by a feeling of dissatisfaction, and that generates the pursuit of happiness."

"Immaterial," said the fussy judge. "What does this have to do with you, disguised in an alien body, revealing the existence of our race?"

"It was emotions that led me to that revelation. It was emotions that guided all my actions and decisions during my mission. It was emotions that made me feel more alive than I have ever felt before. Without them I felt—feel—dead inside. Feelings and emotions are the key to my story and my defense, though I feel no need to defend myself. My actions were based on trying to fulfill my mission, and to do that I needed to stay sane. Only through revealing my true nature to a human being was I able to keep my sanity and fulfill my mission. My explanation is that I had no choice."

The fussy judge exclaimed, "Nonsense. You're guilty without a doubt. It is time to consider the punishment and execute it."

"I would like to hear his story," said the curious judge.

"Me too," said the empathetic judge.

The fussy judge mumbled something about the other two judges being nothing but plants, and then said in a loud voice, "Continue."

"Come on sleepyhead, time to get up!" yelled Jack.

Consciousness resumed and Jesus's mind was fuzzy and dull. With some effort, he opened his eyes. Slowly, memories of the previous day emerged. He jumped unsteadily to his feet. "Ow!" he said, loud enough for Jack to hear.

"What's wrong? Did you stub your toe?" asked Jack, coming into the room.

"That chair is not very comfortable."

"You slept in the chair? Was there something wrong with the mattress?" Jesus began to realize that this mission wasn't going to be easy. Even with all his preparation, he was still unaware of many of the basics of human life.

"No. I'm sure the bed is fine. I must have fallen asleep in the chair. My neck hurts."

"That'll pass. Let's eat and head on over to the church," Jack said impatiently. Walking to the kitchen, Jesus felt the presence of hunger again, plus a new sensation that brought him to a stop. Observing his hesitation, Jack said, "The bathroom is in there."

Jesus, having studied the human body, thought he knew what was happening, but wasn't really sure what to do next. He stood staring at a seat with a hole in it and water below. From the next room, Jack yelled, "Hurry up! I've got things to do after dropping you off at the church."

When Jesus didn't respond, Jack came to see what was going on. "Dude, shut the door. You're not an animal and this isn't the woods. Sit down and get to work," he said in an irritated tone.

"Yes, I will do that," Jesus said, shutting the door. He pulled down his pants and sat down on the seat. Convulsions began in his abdomen and solid materials and liquids emanated from his body.

"Pause, please. What were these solids and liquids?" asked the empathetic judge.

"Fertilizer, Your Honor."

"Really? These humans carry around their waste products?" asked the curious judge.

"Yes, they carry their waste inside their bodies. The solid waste can be carried around for days. The liquid is expelled several times a day. It's far less efficient than our own process."

"Fascinating!" exclaimed the empathetic judge.

"Even more interesting, is that the male's third leg is used for pleasure also."

"What's a male?" asked the empathetic judge.

"Humans have two genders—male and female. Both are necessary to reproduce."

"And this male third leg is used for reproduction, elimination and pleasure? Do these processes ever get confused?" asked the curious judge.

"Just on fetish websites, Your Honor."

"What?"

"It's unimportant, Your Honor. May I continue?"

"Yes, please continue," said the curious judge.

Jesus stood up and inspected what he had eliminated. A roll of paper hung next to the toilet and he quickly figured that out. What now? Was his waste just going to sit there all day? Noticing the silver handle, he gingerly pushed it down, turning away in case the toilet spewed its contents back at him. It did not.

He went to the kitchen where Jack had prepared a bowl of cereal; as he ate, Jesus copied each move. The food was sweet and pleasurable, giving Jesus a rush of energy. Eating on this planet was a delight and he looked forward to trying out different foods.

Putting his cereal bowl in the sink, Jack said, "Let's go, Hey-Zeus!" while jingling his keys. Jesus felt uncomfortable with Jack's pronunciation of his name, but decided not to mention it, and followed him out the door.

The sun was shining brightly, but it was chilly and windy. The air smelled sweet and pure. It was exhilarating and an improvement over Jack's apartment. As they got into the car, Jesus decided to test his knowledge of human aesthetics. "This is an ugly car."

"Your mama!" Jack shot back, amused by his comment. He inserted the key and turned it. The car started and he sang, "Can I get a hallelujah, brother?" Jesus stared at him, not sure how to respond. Jack sighed, "Amen," and they left for the church.

Jesus got his first look at the church in daylight; it was imposing. He knew from his research that this was where humans worshipped their God, but it didn't look particularly inviting. As Jack pulled up near the front entrance, he said, "I'll pick you up in about an hour," and drove off. Jesus walked up to the huge, elaborately carved front doors. Either there were humans much taller than he was aware of, or the entrance was supposed to be intimidating. He wondered if he should ask the pastor about this and entered the building.

It was much nicer inside. The windows were made of stained glass. It smelled pleasant, too. There were rows and rows of benches, much nicer than the benches in the soup kitchen, and they appeared to be made of wood like the chair he had slept in the previous night. Rubbing his neck, he surmised that they must be used to keep the parishioners awake or, as a stabbing pain shot down his neck, to chastise sinners.

"Pause," said the fussy judge. "What's a sinner?"

"That's a difficult question, Your Honor. A sinner is someone who doesn't follow the laws of God; in almost all of their religions, everyone is a sinner."

"How long have the humans been practicing these religions?" asked the empathetic judge.

"That depends on what you call a religion or a belief. A human temple recently discovered is estimated to be 13,000 years old."

"Do they sin less?" asked the fussy judge.

"I'm not qualified to answer that, Your Honor. That would be for their God to determine."

"Goob!" exclaimed the fussy judge.

"Of course, of course. Let's put it another way. Has their behavior improved?" asked the curious judge.

"Yes and no, Your Honor. A specific behavior might be acceptable in one religion and a sin in another religion. Even within the same religion, there is disagreement. The most predominant religion where I lived is called Christianity. There are 34,000 separate Christian groups. All of them identify themselves as followers of the prophet Jesus Christ, yet they are divided by the specifics of their beliefs. And to finish answering your question—yes—overall, the human race has matured."

The pastor emerged from a door to the right of the pulpit. "Welcome, my son! How are you feeling today?"

"I am satisfactory, Pastor. Why did you want to see me?"

The pastor put his arm around Jesus's shoulder and guided him towards the pulpit. A huge cross with the prophet Jesus Christ nailed to it hung high on the wall above. The violence depicted was unsettling. "Son, since you're obviously making some kind of transition in your life, I would like to offer my help."

"Pastor, you've already been a great help with the food last night and a place to stay."

"You're welcome. There are other considerations, though. You can't stay at Jack's for free. Do you have any money or a job?" asked the pastor.

Jesus wasn't sure what to reveal to him. Should he tell him that he had money? He decided that it was all right to say, "This morning I remembered that I have an account at the Profit Bank."

"So, your memory is starting to come back?" asked the pastor. Jesus nodded yes. "Maybe seeing a doctor would help." The project group had concluded that seeing a doctor would be inadvisable. They weren't sure if he would be completely human internally.

"I will consider that."

"All right, my son, but what about a job?" asked the pastor. Before Jesus's arrival, his project group had accessed various databases and placed his name in the birth records at a hospital, the Department of Motor Vehicles, at a bank with enough money to fund his mission for a year and the Social Security Administration.

"Pause, please," requested the curious judge. "What is the Social Insecurity Administration?"

"Social Security," Jesus corrected. "Since human names can be similar or exactly the same, they are identified with numbers—many, many sets of numbers. Seeding sets of numbers in the appropriate databases would prevent any legal ramifications that might result in the exposure of my mission. I didn't need the money, but a job was a splendid way to observe human behavior. They spend half of their waking hours at work."

"What do they do with the other half of their waking hours?" asked the empathetic judge.

"Mitigating their experience of work."

"I see. Please continue," said the empathetic judge.

"Um, I think I need a job," Jesus lied.

"Maybe there's an opening at the grocery store Jack works. We'll ask him when he returns," said the pastor. "Let me take you on a tour of the church."

The tour ended with the pastor's office. The only window faced a wall outside; little daylight entered the room. Unlike Jack's apartment, almost every inch of wall space was covered. There were lots of photographs interspersed with a few diplomas and crucifixes. The pastor sat down behind a big, dark, wooden desk and asked Jesus to take a seat.

"We offer many activities here at the church that all are welcome to attend. We have singles dances, a basketball league, AA meetings, and the soup kitchen you know about." He paused momentarily, "Oh, and monthly roundtable discussions."

"What's that?"

"We gather together and discuss whatever anyone wants to talk about. Events of the day, religious questions, whatever is on one's mind. You might enjoy it."

"That does sound interesting," said Jesus, encouraged at the prospect of being able to ask any question in a format where it's allowed.

"May I ask you a personal question, my son?" asked the pastor. "Do you believe in God?"

Not expecting the question, Jesus haltingly answered, "Ab...solutely."

"Excellent! Maybe you would like to join our church?"

"I promise to give it some thought," Jesus said, wondering if this might be an additional opportunity for insight into human behavior.

The pastor paused before he asked his next question. "Have you been baptized?" Jesus shook his head no. The pastor frowned. "You might want to consider that."

"Why?"

"To purify your soul, my son," the pastor said. Jesus didn't yet know that all humans were sinners, and the pastor's statement seemed offensive. *Who is he to think I'm not pure?* Before Jesus had a chance to respond, there was a knock at the door and Jack stuck his head inside.

"Ready to go?"

"Jack, come in and sit down," said the pastor. "Hey-Zeus needs a job. Are there any openings at the grocery store where you work?"

"Sure, we're always short-handed. I don't have to work until four, so I'll take him right after lunch."

"Perfect! Then Hey-Zeus would be able to pay you rent for your extra bedroom."

Jack looked at Jesus with an indecipherable facial expression. He raised a finger and opened his mouth, but before he could respond, the pastor dismissed them. "I think we've made some progress here. I'll see you boys in church Sunday." Jack and Jesus looked at each other, exhaled and left.

"Don't I get to choose my own roommate?" Jack grumbled, as they walked to his car.

Jesus wasn't sure how to respond, but he tried. "The pastor was correct. I would be willing to pay and help with the maintenance of the apartment."

"You'd be willing to clean?" Jack asked, in disbelief. "None of my previous roommates even bothered. Hmm, this could get interesting...."

Sizing Jesus up for almost a minute, he finally said, "Okay, if you get the job, and you should because Grains for Brains will hire anybody, then you can stay. Rent will be $500 a month plus half of the utilities and cable."

Jesus decided to be bold and practice some humor. "If I get the job, since I am an 'anybody,' and I agree to pay $500 rent and half the utilities and cable, do you promise to drive this thing to the junkyard and return on foot?"

Jack held up two fingers. "I have two things to say to you. One, get in the car." He retracted his index finger, leaving his middle finger in the air. "And two, your mama." Jesus wasn't sure what the fingers meant, but since Jack was smiling, he smiled back.

"What's next?" Jesus asked.

"I've got three errands to run and then we'll get some lunch," Jack said. "Are breakfast tacos okay?"

"I thought we already had breakfast."

"Breakfast tacos are for anytime, day or night. They're God's food."

"Your God eats food?"

"Shut up, ya goober!" Jack said playfully.

Goober! How did he know? "What do you mean, 'goober'?" Jesus asked.

"All right then, is 'dumb-ass' better? How about 'moron'? What is your preferred put-down?"

"Besides 'your mama'?" Jesus said. "Believe it or not, 'goober' is definitely most appropriate."

"Goober it is, then." Jack put the key in the ignition. "Oh Heavenly Father, I beseech thee to reanimate this car." After a halting, grinding sound, the engine begrudgingly started.

"Hallelujah!" Jesus said. Jack smiled and for a moment, Jesus felt like he was fitting in.

Chapter 3 – The Job Interview

At a Tex-Mex restaurant named Blondie's, Jesus and Jack gorged themselves on breakfast tacos and chips and salsa, giving Jesus's new taste buds a workout. After a few belches, Jesus was ready for conversation.

Jack's father was a colonel in the Air Force and had been stationed in nearby San Antonio. When Jack graduated from high school, he moved to Austin to go to college. He liked riding his bike, but hadn't ridden much lately. He loved video games and seemed very interested in having sex anytime and anywhere. Their conversation was peppered with, "Yowza!" or "There is a God!" almost every time a woman would walk by.

Jesus deflected each of Jack's questions with one of his own. When there was a lull, Jesus asked, "Do you have a computer?"

"Yeah, sure. Who doesn't?"

"Would it be possible to use it this evening?"

"Yup. I'll be playing on my game console anyway."

"Good," Jesus said. He had a number of topics he needed to research and it had grown to the point that he would have to make a list to keep up with them. Plus, it was time to make his first status report.

"Pause, please," said the empathetic judge. "How did you make these status reports?"

"A common tool for communication on Earth is electronic mail or 'e-mail,' and I would send status reports to myself. The space buoy scanned my e-mail account—RealGoober@me.com—daily, and when our spacecraft returned, it would download the information."

The curious judge asked, "So, initially you did make status reports?"

"Yes, Your Honor."

"But at some point you discontinued these reports?"

"Yes, Your Honor. I will explain that later in my story."

They finished their lunch and as they left, Jack said, "You can get the next one." Jesus agreed and asked what was next.

"Are you ready for your interview?"

"What interview?"

"Yeah, even though the store will hire anybody, you still have to go through an interview."

"What do I have to do?"

"You've never been through an interview before?"

"I worked at my family's cheese shop in France. I didn't have to interview."

"That makes sense. Hey, why don't you have a French accent?"

This never occurred to the project group. "Uh, it must be the amnesia," Jesus stammered.

"Uh-huh. Are you sure you're not a criminal on the lam?"

"Why would I want to sit on a lamb?"

"Never mind. For the interview, you have to answer a bunch of questions about your work history and your qualifications, plus you have to provide documentation and tell them that you're not a rapist or serial killer. Let's head to the store," Jack said, as they got into the car. With much pleading, it started.

"Documentation might be difficult," Jesus said. "I have to replace all my papers."

"Don't worry. There's probably a way around that. The boss's name is Clara and she's pretty good as bosses go. She has lots of theories on how to improve things, but don't slack off too much around her or she'll rip you a new one."

"A new one what?"

Looking at Jesus peculiarly, Jack said, "An asshole, duhh."

"I wouldn't want that. I'm having enough trouble getting used to the one I have now." Jack snickered and alternated between glancing at the road and Jesus. Uncomfortable with the scrutiny, Jesus remained silent the rest of the trip.

As they entered the store, Jesus was briefly overwhelmed by the abundance of sensory input and he froze. Jack grabbed him by the arm and dragged him to the office. Anxiety swept over Jesus and momentarily, he considered bolting for the car. Composing himself, he said, "It looks like an entire forest was sacrificed to decorate this place."

"Yeah, it *is* a little nouveau-riche hippy, isn't it?"

As Jack opened a door with a sign saying "Front-End Office," Jesus asked, "Why is it called that?"

A stout Hispanic woman with a French manicure answered, "Because in it resides the Front-End Department Head at the front end of the store. I'm Clara," she said, sticking out her hand.

Jesus had studied this ritual before his mission. He moved his hand slowly towards hers, taking a deep breath as he gauged its trajectory. He was on course—engaging, docking complete, grasping, two pumps and release. Success!

"Ah, good handshake. Please have a seat," she said. Jesus smiled with pride as he sat down. He knew how important it was to get this human ritual correct.

The office would hold at most five people sitting down. Ordinary shelving lined two walls and was filled with register tape, broken baskets, empty tills, and personal belongings. Another wall served as paper bag storage and the last wall had a bank of lockable, wooden slots for the tills.

"What's your name?" Clara asked, as she looked him over.

"Jesus H. da Vinci."

"Seriously? Jack," Clara barked, "I told you no more practical jokes."

"That's his name, Clara. He's in a bit of a tight jam and is looking for a job. Have you hired a new bagger yet?"

"No, I haven't," she said, facing Jesus. "Sorry about the 'seriously' comment. You have a very unusual name. Are you interested in working here? The only position we have open at the moment is bagger."

"Yes, I am. I need a job. Even an entry-level position would suffice."

"Well then," she said, "let me get you a job application." As she was looking for the form, Jack winked at Jesus, giving him a hand signal of one thumb up. Jesus calculated that together with Jack's grin it was a positive sign.

"Here's the form and a pen. I have to step out for a moment. Why don't you just hang out in here and fill it out. If you have any questions, I'm sure Jack can help you. I'll be back in about fifteen minutes," Clara said and left.

"Okay, put my address in there," Jack pointed out, as Jesus sat down at the desk. "Yes, you're legally eligible for employment."

"Is it possible to be illegally eligible? Does that make any sense?"

"Not at all. Are you twenty-one or older?"

"Yes."

His gaze narrowing, Jack asked, "Just how old are you?"

"I'm twenty-nine."

"Previous employment?"

"I worked at my parent's cheese shop in France. That's the only job I've ever had."

"Okay, what about education?"

Jesus immediately said, "I'm for it!"

Jack snickered. "Nooo, the level of education you've completed. Did you go to college?"

"I finished high school and then went to what you call a community college of sorts."

"All right then. How many years completed, degree attained and name of institution?"

Jesus replied, "Uh, two years, an 'ecole de la vie' degree at Bonaparte Polytechnic."

"You seem a little tall for Bonaparte Polytechnic. Did you study military history there?"

"No. I majored in business...and minored in empire building," Jesus said. He was enjoying the banter with Jack. It seemed to magnify that feeling of connection that he had been experiencing intermittently.

Jack chuckled, "Dick Cheney must have studied there, too. That's an American education if I've ever heard one. You could run for president, that is if you were born in America."

"I was born in America. Goobertown, Arkansas. We moved to France when I was two."

"No wonder you're sensitive about the word 'goober.' Okay, next section. What are your skills and qualifications?"

Jesus listed his skills. He was knowledgeable about computers, he knew how to type and, of course, he spoke French.

For references, he listed Jack and the pastor, who was also his contact in case of emergency.

"Good choice," Jack said emphatically. "Sounds official."

He began to go over some of the benefits the store provided. Jesus wasn't interested in the least. He scanned the room, noting four sets of calculators and chairs. Papers were stacked everywhere, even though there was a file cabinet.

The door flew open and a young woman entered. "I'm sooo bored!" she exclaimed. Jesus looked into her green eyes and instantly felt an attraction.

"This is Barbara," Jack said. She smiled at Jesus and dimples appeared. He immediately felt the urge to touch her.

"I'm Jesus," he said, standing and offering her his hand.

"Beg your pardon?"

"Jesus. Jesus H. da Vinci."

"What a fascinating name!" she said, brushing back her black hair. He didn't know why or how, but her eyes were sparkling.

"Pleased to meet you, sir," she said, taking his hand. He instinctively enveloped her hand with his free hand. She did the same. For some reason, the two-pump rule for handshakes didn't apply with her. "Barbara, Barbara Kaminski," she purred.

After several more seconds of pumping, Jack said, "Okay you two, break it up. Jesus is applying to be a bagger."

"Grains for Brains will hire just about anybody," Barbara said, "not that you're just anybody."

The door flew open again, almost hitting Barbara and Clara walked in. "Finished with the application?"

"Yes," Jack said, "here it is."

"Barbara, back to your register," Clara said. Barbara silently walked out, looking back at Jesus with a smile.

Clara shut the door and looked over the application. "Let's see. Hmm, speaks French, computer skills," she murmured. "Okay, the job pays $10.50 an hour. Are you interested?"

"Yes."

"Can you start tomorrow?"

"Umm, yes."

"Now, what about your documentation?"

"I seemed to, uhh…it's a long story. It will take about two weeks to gather up replacement identification."

"That'll be satisfactory," Clara said. She stood up and offered her hand. "You're hired."

Jesus smiled, relieved. He didn't know why, but it seemed important to him that she approve his application.

"Your shift starts tomorrow at three thirty. By then, I'll have a better idea what the rest of your schedule will be. Are there any days that you can't work?" she asked.

"Well, I did want to visit the pastor's church."

"No Sunday mornings. Got it. See you tomorrow then."

"Let's go," Jack said. "I've got to get ready for work." Jesus nodded and they left.

Back at the apartment, he asked, "How am I going to get to work tomorrow?"

"Don't worry. I'll check the new schedule and if we have the same shift, I'll drive you. Otherwise, it's close enough to walk. It only takes about 20 minutes."

"Okay. I think I need to get some more clothes," Jesus said, as they entered the apartment.

"I've got to get ready now. We'll run whatever errands you need to do tomorrow morning," Jack said, disappearing into the bathroom.

Jesus hadn't gotten a good look at the living room the night before. It was disgusting—mismatched furniture, stained carpet, a few torn and wrinkled posters on the wall, and a couple of half-dead plants. On the coffee table in front of him was a big ashtray with a pile of butts in it. Next to it was the television remote. He knew from his research that he could learn a lot about humans from watching television. Pressing the power button, it instantly came on, which was surprising considering that almost everything else in Jack's possession appeared to be in disrepair or dying.

A few minutes later Jack emerged from the bathroom. "Okay, if I don't see you tonight, I'll see you in the morning. Take care."

There were so many things Jesus needed to do and it felt overwhelming. He decided to acquire a birth certificate since he needed that to get some of his other documentation. A last-minute decision by his project group to provide him with a credit card made it easy. Next, he accessed his e-mail and wrote a short update on his situation. Then, he made a list of things he needed like clothes, toiletries, a bicycle and a computer.

He felt hungry, but he had no idea what to eat or what he would like. He had studied human nutrition in preparation for his mission, but learned later that eating on Earth is generally more about what you like than nutrition. Rummaging through the refrigerator and pantry for about fifteen minutes, he finally decided that he would have a bowl of cereal and some pickles. The meal eliminated his feeling of hunger. Already organized for the next day and momentarily feeling in control, he decided to watch television again.

He had been on Earth thirty hours and had already obtained lodging and a job. He was learning how to take care of his human body. Things couldn't be going better...yet, he felt incomplete. Maybe it was fear? He couldn't identify this particular feeling and decided to label it "discomfort."

"Pause, please," interrupted the curious judge. "'Discomfort'?"

"During my research, I had read about emotions. It was surprising to me that given my initial success, I didn't feel happy or comfortable. With humans, it is reasonable to assume that success produces some measure of happiness, and I felt none at the time. In fact, I felt uneasy. I attributed this to anxiety about working at the grocery store the next day. I discovered later that it was more than that. Shall I continue?"

"Yes," said the fussy judge.

The television had a wide range of choices, and Jesus selected a cop reality show.

"Pause," interrupted the fussy judge. "What is a 'cop'?"

"Humans find it necessary to have a segment of their population monitor another segment of the population that misbehaves. In the country where I was doing my fieldwork, nearly 3 percent of the population were incarcerated or under correctional supervision the previous year."

"You mentioned that word before, 'country.' What is that?" asked the curious judge.

"A country is a collection of humans with their own government. At the moment, there are 189 to 196 countries on Earth, depending on the criteria used. The country I resided in is called America. On Earth, it is widely accepted that it is the freest country, yet it has the highest incarceration rate on their world."

"When you say 'freest,' what do you mean? Isn't Earth a 'free will' planet like ours?" asked the empathetic judge.

"You are correct, Your Honor. However, they don't see it as such. Humans believe freedom comes from without, not within. They view it as something to be earned, and in some ways they are right. Essentially though, they are wrong. Everyone on the planet has freedom of choice, it's just that some may be incarcerated or put to death for their words or actions. For each individual, it is a moment-by-moment decision on how they should use their free will. I found it fascinating that the country acknowledged as the freest has the biggest problem with individuals making, shall we say, poor choices. I don't know, but maybe that should be expected. In any event, it is also interesting to note that humans enjoy watching the failures of others. There is a wide variety of 'entertainment' based on the foibles of humankind."

"Was that the basis for choosing the location to observe from— freedom?" asked the empathetic judge.

"Not entirely, Your Honor. The city I lived in is called Austin. The city motto is 'Keep Austin Weird.' My project group realized that it might take some time to learn human culture so it seemed appropriate to pick a location where my behavior would probably not be questioned."

"Let's get back to the 'foibles of humankind.' Why do they find that entertaining?" the empathetic judge asked.

"I think it comes from their animal nature as predators. As their saying on Earth goes, 'What's bad for my enemy is good for me.' Their society has evolved with predatory instincts intact, so far. Watching other humans fail seems to be a part of that."

"That doesn't seem very spiritual," said the curious judge.

"If you consider that God's plan for them is—"

"Goob, Goob, GOOB!" the fussy judge exclaimed. The other two judges glanced at each other.

Jesus, ignoring the interruption, continued, "...to progress from an animal nature to a spiritual nature, it seems normal. There are some signs that the predatory nature of marking one's territory, having already been established with almost 200 countries, is beginning to change. But we've gotten off topic here. May I continue my story?"

"Proceed," said the empathetic judge.

"Excuse me a moment, I have another question," interjected the curious judge. "The humans view each other as enemies?"

"That is a complicated question. Rarely do they view themselves as one interconnected entity called humanity. They mostly view themselves as individuals. As individuals, they compete for resources. They do not trust their God to provide for them, so when making decisions in their lives, they do not usually consider what's best for humankind. They consider what's best for themselves, then their families, their friends, their place of employment, their country, et cetera. The hierarchy I've stated is a generalization, of course."

"Thank you for the clarification. Please continue," said the curious judge.

While watching the cop reality show, Jesus felt several emotions he had yet to experience. The first was compassion. Seeing these humans struggle with their choices in life was quite moving and this led to another feeling— sadness. He even shed a tear or two.

"Pause. What's a tear?" asked the fussy judge.

"A secretion of fluid from the eyes. Most often this is generated from feelings of not-love. However, after the cop reality show was over, I watched a movie, a visual story if you will, called *Sister Act*. When the main characters, a group of spiritually oriented women called nuns, sang and had fun while doing it, I started sobbing."

"'Sobbing'? What is that?" asked the curious judge.

"When one sheds tears it is called crying. Crying to the extreme is called sobbing. Interestingly, it shares most of the same physical characteristics as laughing, such as the convulsing of the navel point. I determined that this was another way that humans clear their emotional body."

"What is your point?" asked the fussy judge.

"I'm getting to that, Your Honor. Here was an example of what humans call 'tears of joy.' I was responding to the spiritual exuberance exhibited by the nuns. In fact, it is also possible to laugh in the face of misfortune."

"So, they react inconsistently to stimuli?" asked the curious judge.

"No, their reactions are based on their experiences and beliefs, but that's not what I'm getting at. I'm just showing the wide range of emotional responses. Now I want to introduce you to the concept of conflicting emotions."

All three judges stared blankly. "Conflicting emotions are where one feels more than one emotion at a time," Jesus pronounced.

The fussy judge grimaced, which is very unusual for Goobers, and exclaimed, "That's not possible. There is love and not-love. One or the other; you cannot feel both simultaneously."

Jesus said solemnly, "On this planet, you can." He paused to let this sink in.

"How confusing that must be for them," said the empathetic judge.

"Indeed, it is. I can attest to that and I will give many examples as I continue," Jesus said.

"Proceed," said the fussy judge.

Chapter 4 – Getting Settled In

Emotionally drained from watching the movie, Jesus went to bed. It was definitely more comfortable than the chair, but it still took a while to fall asleep.

He awoke the next morning to noise coming from the kitchen. Getting up and with eyes barely open, he went to see what the racket was.

"Dude! Put some clothes on!" Jack said.

"Sorry," Jesus mumbled, shuffling out.

When he returned, Jack exclaimed, "Pants, man, pants. Put on some pants!" Apparently, a shirt wasn't enough. Finally, fully clothed, Jesus returned to the kitchen and found Jack cleaning.

"Thank you for washing dishes. So, what's your concern about wearing pants?" Jesus asked.

"You *need* to cover up your manhood."

"What's wrong with my manhood?"

"Nothing. You have a handsome penis, I swear. But, in this country, we're sort of ashamed of our private parts. Americans aren't nearly as comfortable with our bodies as the French."

"Okay, I'll wear pants from now on." During his research, Jesus hadn't come across any pants-wearing protocol. He made a mental note to add this to his list.

"I'm about to fix some eggs. Want some?"

"Sure." The hunger feeling had returned. *Human bodies need a lot of fuel*, Jesus thought. "Are we going shopping after breakfast?"

"Yup. Have you got a list of stuff you need?"

"Yes," Jesus said. "Clothes, toiletries, a computer and a bicycle."

Looking up from cracking eggs, Jack said, "You've been doing some planning, haven't you?"

"Uhh, yup," Jesus said, trying out some slang.

"We don't have time to do all that today. Let's stick to the essentials. You should add sheets and a pillow to your list. And towels, too. Hurry up and shower before I finish fixing breakfast. In this instance and *in this instance only*, you can rub your handsome penis on one of my towels."

Jesus laughed out loud. "I look forward to it."

Jack yelled after him, "And remind me to do some wash tomorrow. Especially the towels." *Human males sure are peculiar about their third leg*, Jesus thought.

They ate quickly, and as they left Jesus asked, "How am I going to pay for all of this?"

"Hmm, I could cover it, but if you get canned at the store then I would be shit outta luck." Jesus wasn't sure what that meant, but it sounded like a bad thing.

"No, I have more than enough to pay for these purchases, Jack. Last night, I started the process of replacing all my identification."

"Okay, I'll cover you, but I better get a good seat in Heaven for all this."

"Pause, please," said the empathetic judge. "What is Heaven?"

"That differs from faith to faith. The religion that I had the most experience with, Christianity, does believe in a Heaven. After death, one will be judged on the quality of life that one has led. Generally, it's 'pass/fail,' but in some religions you can get an 'incomplete.' The reward for passing is that you get to go to the heaven of your choice for an eternity of lawn bowling and badminton. In this spiritual playground, you are surrounded by dead humans of the same color, holding the same or mostly similar beliefs."

"Humans are different colors?" asked the curious judge.

"Yes. They encompass a spectrum of colors. Humans identify strongly with the color of their skin."

"Are there any specific benefits to any of the skin colors?" asked the empathetic judge.

"Like invisibility?"

"Yes," said the empathetic judge.

"No, all skin colors have the same strengths and weaknesses."

"Now, what is lawn bowling and badminton?" asked the curious judge.

"Those are games and I was just being humorous, Your Honor."

Banging his gavel loudly, the fussy judge said, "I will not tolerate jocularity during these proceedings."

"I'm sorry, Your Honor. I picked up the habit on my mission. I'll do my best to contain myself in the future."

"See that you do. Proceed," the fussy judge ordered.

Jesus found the shopping bewildering. There were endless selections of types, styles and colors of each item. How was he supposed to make an informed choice when he had no experience at all? He tried to rely on Jack's preferences, but several times that invited ridicule. "How does this look on me?" produced a response of, "You look fine, lady," or, "Just great, ma'am!" After several hours, they finished and returned to the apartment and had lunch.

Jesus found the food Jack prepared unappealing and realized he was going to have to try many different types of food to be able to determine his favorites. He decided that he would take one bite of anything offered to him.

Jack finished eating and started a session of video gaming while Jesus logged on to the computer to continue gathering his documentation. When he finished what he could, he did some research. He couldn't find anything on pants-wearing protocol, but he did find some articles on what colors to wear at what time of year.

"Time to get ready for work," Jack abruptly announced. As he headed to the bathroom, Jesus went to his bedroom to change into his new clothes. They met in the hallway and Jack laughed.

"Dude, you don't leave the tags on your clothes. Let me get some scissors," he said. Jesus stood motionless as Jack cut the price tags off. "And put on some deodorant, Frenchy. You stink."

Jesus emerged from the bathroom smelling like a summer breeze. Jack walked up to him and grabbed his arm, peering at it intently. "Did you put deodorant on your forearm?"

"Yes," Jesus proudly replied, "and on my hands, face and tongue." Jack fell to the floor laughing, curled up in a ball, and continued for at least a minute. Jesus concluded he had applied the deodorant incorrectly.

Jack finally got to his feet, wiped his eyes, and panted. Trying to catch his breath, he wheezed, "No, you moron. You apply it to your armpits and maybe a dash across the chest for flavor."

Nodding, Jesus said, "Okay." The mistake produced an uncomfortable feeling, but he was glad that he didn't have to use it on his tongue. It tasted odd. From now on, he would read the instructions.

At last, they left for work and Jesus experienced some anxiety when Jack said, "Man, you're full of surprises, Frenchy." He was sure to meet a variety of new situations at work and he hadn't even put on deodorant correctly. He resolved that he would ask as many questions as necessary to avoid further embarrassment.

They arrived early for Jesus's shift. The store was just as busy, noisy, and confusing as the previous day. When they entered, Clara said, "There's my novice. Welcome! Come in and sit down. There are a few things I have to review with you."

As Jesus sat down, Jack left. "Here's your button. Put your name on it and cover it with a piece of tape so it doesn't wear off. I'm going to give you a quick store tour to show you where everything is. You're going to be paired with Brad, one of our head cashiers, actually, one of our best cashiers. You'll bag only for him until he thinks you're ready. Have you bagged groceries before?" she asked.

"No, I haven't."

Clara explained the basics of bagging. She completed the lesson with, "Do a cart run every once in a while. And remember that Grains for Brains prides itself on customer service. Umm, what else? Oh, you'll go on break when Brad goes on break. Got it?"

"One question," Jesus said. "Do I actually have to run with the carts?"

Clara blinked several times. "No. A cart run is when you go outside, collect the carts and bring them inside. Understand?"

"Yes, I understand," said Jesus slowly.

"Good. Let's take a quick tour of the store."

Jesus jumped up out of his chair and held the door open for Clara. She studied him for a moment. "Such manners," Clara said, smiling. "You'll fit in nicely here."

They quickly walked through every department, and several times, she exhorted Jesus to keep up. As they reached the back of the store, she stopped in front of two metal doors. Pointing straight ahead, she said, "Meat and seafood." She turned left through the doors as Jesus was trying to catalogue all the aromas, and the door sprang back and hit him.

"Oh, sorry about that," she said. "This is the backstock area. To the right is the main office. To the left are the restrooms and over there are the mop buckets." She turned and walked back to the front of the store rapidly. Jesus made sure to follow close behind and catch the door this time. "Let's go and pick up my coffee, and then see if Brad is here."

They reentered the front-end office where Brad was pulling a till out from a wooden slot. *He's much thinner than most of the humans I've met so far*, Jesus mused. "Brad, you're here. Good. This is our new bagger, Jesus."

Jesus looked up at Brad as he stuck out his hand. Staring at it a moment and scratching his head, Brad said, "Nice to meet you," and shook his hand.

"Brad, I'm going to pair Jesus with you," Clara said. "He'll bag for you until you think he's ready to move around on his own."

"Good enough."

Jesus, already feeling tired, sat down. *There is so much to learn!* He was going to have to research all types of food when he got back to the apartment.

"Oh, one other thing," Clara said. "After thirty days, our department votes on you. Until then, you're on probation. Okay?" Jesus nodded yes, noting this was another thing he needed to study.

Brad was busy rummaging through his till. "What are you doing?" Jesus asked.

"Making sure my cash drawer is accurate. You'd be amazed how often one of these can be off."

Clara was pinning a piece of paper up on the wall. "Here's the schedule for the next week," she said, groaning as she stretched up. "Jesus, I've got you working both Friday and Saturday nights for now. I hope that doesn't put a crimp in your social life," she said, grinning.

A social life? Jesus hadn't given that any thought at all. "No, that will be fine," he said, adding to his research list.

His counting finished, Brad said, "All right, I've got to hit the head and then we'll start."

Clara was busy with paperwork as Jesus sat there. For some reason, he felt like he should say something. "Clara, what happens once I get voted onto the department?"

"I like that confidence," she said. "Bagger is an entry-level position. Most baggers become cashiers. The good cashiers become head cashiers. Next, on most teams, comes the Assistant Department Head. Then comes Department Head; that's me. Store management begins with Squad Leader, who pilots the shift. Then comes the Assistant Unit Leader, unit being the store, then the Unit Leader."

"Sounds kind of governmental or military-like."

Nodding and sighing, she said, "What can I say...Grains for Brains," and took a sip of coffee.

There was a slight lull in the conversation until Jesus asked, "What's the Unit Leader's nickname? The *Kernel*?"

It took a moment for Clara to get the joke. She choked and laughed as coffee spewed all over her desk. Jesus smiled at the reaction. Brad walked in and asked, "What's so funny?"

"Jesus came up with a nickname for Bob—'The Kernel.'" Brad smiled and snorted, trying to repress his laughter.

"That's good," he said. "I'll have to remember that one."

When Clara finally got herself under control, she said, "Now Jesus, don't go spreading that around. You're new here and Bob's somewhat sensitive."

"Somewhat?" Brad said, as he grabbed his till. "Come on, newbie. Let's go to work."

Brad led Jesus past two registers and stopped at the third one. "Patsy, you're free. Time to go home," Brad said.

"You're my Moses," replied Patsy, with a smile. "Who's this?" she asked.

"This is our new bagger, Jesus," Brad said.

"So, that must make you one of his disciples," Patsy giggled.

"Now Patsy, you can make fun of the customers, but not your coworkers," Brad said flatly.

"Yes sir! I'm sorry. Nice to meet you," Patsy said, sticking out her hand. Jesus shook it and nodded. "Nice handshake!" she said, dashing off to the front-end office.

The till made a loud jingling sound as Brad dropped it in the register then shut the drawer. He quickly typed in something and the drawer popped open. "What are you doing?" Jesus asked.

"Typing in my cashier code," he said. "That way only I have access to my cash drawer plus the register gathers information about my performance."

Immediately, an elderly woman approached with a cart full of groceries. "Hello ma'am. Did you find everything you were looking for?" Brad asked.

"Yes, yes I did," she said, as she unloaded her cart onto the counter.

"Ma'am, do you have any special bagging instructions for our new bagger?"

The woman turned and looked at Jesus with a critical eye. "Oh my, yes. Please bag the cold items separately. Don't make the bags too heavy. Double-bag everything and please put the eggs on top," she said.

Nodding, he started to bag her groceries. The woman barked, "No, no, that's not double-bagged!"

With a meek look on his face, Jesus said, "I was going to do that after I finished filling the bag." She grimaced and shook her head slowly.

Brad jumped in. "You have to double-bag first. You'll never get the second bag around the first bag if there are groceries already in it," he said quietly, demonstrating the technique.

"Ah, okay. I understand," Jesus said. "Thank you."

He finished bagging the items as Brad finished the transaction. After placing the bags in the cart, the elderly woman looked inside every bag inspecting his work.

"This one is going to be too heavy."

"Yes, ma'am. You're my first customer, ma'am," Jesus said. He picked up the offending bag and split its contents into two.

"How's that?"

Inspecting the two bags, she said, "Okay. I'm going to need help to my car."

She walked quickly towards the exit with Jesus following. "Jesus! You're supposed to push the cart for her," Brad said emphatically.

"Oh! Of course." Jesus doubled back, retrieved the cart and headed towards the exit smiling at the elderly woman. She shook her head again and continued on.

"Don't tell me you've never seen double-bagging before."

"Where I'm from ma'am, people generally purchase groceries for a day at a time."

"Where are you from?"

"France, ma'am."

She shook her head once more, "Wait!" she cried, coming to a dead stop and abruptly spinning around. Jesus jerked the cart to a stop to avoid hitting her. "You're name is Hey-Zeus?"

"No ma'am. It's Jesus," he replied, smiling at her.

"That's blasphemy!"

"It is?"

"Jesus is our Savior," she said. "We don't name our children after our Savior." As they arrived at her car, she asked, "Why on earth would your parents name you Jesus?"

"My parents were hippies."

"Oh! I see."

As he started loading the groceries into the trunk, she asked, "Have you thought about changing your name?"

"No, ma'am."

"Well you should," she said, her voice hinting at anger.

"Don't you think it would be inspiring to be named after arguably the greatest person ever to grace this planet?" he asked. "It's better than being named Adolf, don't you think?"

Standing there, slightly shaking, she said rather loudly, "No, I don't. Jesus was not a man. He was—is—the Son of God!" With that, she climbed into her car, slamming the door. Jesus stood there, stupefied. As he headed inside with the cart, a small black hole of fear pulsated in the pit of his stomach. His name could become a problem, if this was a typical reaction. Maybe to blend in, it would be better to change his name. At the very least, he should study the prophet Jesus and his teachings to find out why everybody was reacting so.

He returned to Brad's register. "Did you get a tip?" Brad asked.

"Yes, to change my name."

Trying not to laugh, Brad said, "Don't let it get to you. Mainly, we get liberal types in here, but we do get some fundamentalists, too."

The next few hours became routine; he bagged groceries, put away carts, and did the occasional carryout. At one point, he asked if he should restock the bags and Brad agreed. At another point, Brad sent him outside for a cart run. The air was crisp from the north wind and the sky was a beautiful blue. Jesus inhaled deeply. This planet was so much prettier than Gooberia. After gathering the carts, he returned to Brad's register.

"Why is that planet so much prettier than ours?" asked the curious judge.

Jesus paused a moment to choose his words carefully. "Well, it is much more colorful. There's such a variety of plant life. Most of the time there is a breeze that feels marvelous on the skin. The birds and insects chirp. There are so many aromas. When you compare sensory experiences, theirs is at least a hundredfold greater than our own when it comes to variety and intensity."

There was an awkward pause as the judges considered this. "Continue," said the fussy judge.

The head cashier, Julia, arrived with a look on her face that suggested she wasn't enjoying herself at all. "Time for your break. Be back at..." she paused looking up at the store clock, "six forty-five."

Punching in his code and carefully lifting out his till, Brad said, "Come on, newbie," and headed to the front-end office. Jesus dutifully followed, and looked forward to the quiet of the office. He suddenly realized Brad hadn't called him by name since his first customer. *Maybe I should change my name*, he thought.

Silently, Brad locked up his till. He turned and walked back out onto the sales floor. Jesus followed him to the prepared foods department where Brad picked out a sandwich. Not knowing what to choose, Jesus picked the same item. Brad got a bag of chips and a drink; Jesus did the same.

As they reached the register to pay, Brad frowned when he noticed that Jesus had picked out the exact same things he had. As Brad was paying, Jesus realized that he didn't have any money. Fortunately, they were in Jack's line. As Brad walked to the front-end office, Jesus looked at Jack. "Of course, you don't have any money...yet," said Jack. He reached for his wallet, grabbed a bill and handed it to Jesus—a twenty. "Now you'll have money for tomorrow, too." Jesus thanked him earnestly and quickly walked to the office.

Brad sat facing the wall so Jesus did, too. There were several minutes of silence as they ate, until Brad asked, "So, where you from?"

Jesus paused for a moment to swallow before answering, "France."

"Never been there."

There was another couple of minutes of silence before Jesus asked, "Where are you from?"

"Here...Texas."

"Have you lived here all your life?"

"Yup."

The door to the office flew open. It was Jack. "I need some quarters, quick," he said. Brad produced a key and retrieved a roll of quarters from his cash drawer, trading Jack for a ten. Dashing out the door, Jack said, "Oh, I almost forgot. Jesus, if you want to buy a bicycle this is the guy to talk to."

"A bike? You want to buy a bike?" Brad asked.

"Yes, I need some transportation. Do you know anything about purchasing a bicycle?"

"Yeah, I used to work at a bike shop. What are you looking for? Mountain bike, racing bike, cruiser?"

"What do you have?"

"A top-of-the-line racing bike."

"How much do they cost?"

"With tax, about five grand."

"Grand?"

"Thousand."

"Is that a lot of money for a bicycle?"

"Not for a racing bike. You can get cheaper racing bikes for sure, and used ones, too."

"I think a grand is about my limit," Jesus said. "I don't want to get more bike than I can handle."

"I'll tell you what. We'll go to my old bike shop; you can test-ride a few models and see what feels most comfortable."

"You would help me?"

"Sure, why not?" Brad smiled.

"Great! But it's going to be a few days before I have the documentation necessary to get my replacement credit card."

Staring at him, Brad asked, "Why do you need a replacement?"

"I don't know. I think I have amnesia."

Dumbfounded, Brad sat silently. Finally he asked, "What's the first thing you remember?"

Jesus related the story about being found standing naked in the street by the police, the pastor and the soup kitchen, and rooming with Jack.

"So, you don't remember anything before two days ago?" Brad asked.

"No, not entirely. I remember I was born in Arkansas. My family moved to France when I was young. I worked in a cheese shop with my parents," he said and paused a moment. "And I remember most of my numbers—Social Security, state ID card, bank account and credit card number. But that's all."

"That is so messed up," Brad said emphatically, striking the table, startling Jesus. "The memory is a funny thing. My dad has Alzheimer's. Not that you do, but I've seen the toll it takes on someone when they don't have their full memory." They sat in silence for a couple of minutes. Brad slumped in his chair and Jesus recognized what he thought might be sadness.

Looking at his watch, Brad said, "Break's almost over. Time to hit the head and get back to the register." He slowly got out of his chair, took a deep breath and put his hand on Jesus's shoulder. "Everything is going to work out just fine," he said, walking out the door.

Jesus sat quietly for a few moments. He wasn't sure what he was feeling, but he certainly was feeling a lot of it. His eyes watered and it felt good that someone sympathized with his predicament. He felt fatigued; his life essence seemed completely gone. Struggling to his feet, he tried to breathe deep, but even breathing required more energy than he had. His neck ached and it was stiff. Steeling himself for the second half of the shift, he hurried out to the registers.

Brad stopped ringing up groceries. "Hey Jesus, you're sharp enough to be on your own now. You can bag for the other cashiers. Just don't forget your old buddy, Brad," he grinned.

"Brad who?" Jesus said, smiling back at him. He felt energized by that brief conversation.

He went to Jack's register. "Brad decided to let you roam, eh?" he said, out of the corner of his mouth.

"Yes, free at last."

Jack repeated with extra emphasis, "Free at last. Just remember, you owe me money, so I want to see you down here often."

Jesus moved to the next cashier, an African-American woman, in bright red lipstick named Wanda. "'Bout time I got some help, newbie," she said. She finished ringing up her customer and asked what his name was.

"Jesus." Peering at him for a moment, she exclaimed, "Praise the Lord! Just yesterday, I prayed for a man in my life and look who showed up today. Are you the man I'm looking for?" she asked, hands on her hips.

Considering her intensity and feeling a bit intimidated, Jesus replied, "Probably not."

"Too bad for you," she said. Jesus bagged for her and moved to the next register.

The next couple of hours were a blur of bagging, stocking bags, and cart runs. Around nine o'clock, the pace slowed and Jesus sat down at the end of Brad's counter. He calculated that he had walked more that night than in one month on Gooberia.

His exhaustion must have shown, because Brad said, "You look bushed. Maybe you can leave a little early."

Jack, at the next register, overheard this and chimed in, "I'm his ride, so I'd need to leave early, too."

Brad smirked. "Of course. Let me go run this by Julia."

Excitedly, Jack said, "All right! Off first, then home for some herb and a righteous session of gaming." He paused and looked at Jesus. "Man, you really *do* look dog-tired." Numb from head to toe, Jesus didn't respond.

A few seconds later, Brad emerged from the office smiling, "You're done for the night, Jesus. Head on home. You too, Jack. I'll count your till, if that's okay."

Jesus felt like crying as he searched for the energy to stand up. *How do these humans do this day after day?* he wondered.

Brad and Jack walked over and helped Jesus to his feet. "Come on, goober. Time to go home," Jack said. Safely in the car, Jesus fell asleep immediately.

"Wake up! We're home."

"I'm in the moment." Jesus rubbed his eyes. "Oh, all right." He half-staggered into the apartment, and headed straight to his room.

"Don't you want a little weed?" Jack called out.

Jesus mumbled, "No," as he fell onto his bed. He was asleep before his head touched the pillow.

Chapter 5 – Anger

Jesus woke up in the middle of the night from a dream. Or maybe it was a nightmare? In his three nights of sleep, this was the first dream he had remembered.

He didn't recall all of it, just the part with his first customer. She kept yelling over and over again, "You're not my Jesus! You're just a weed! You're not my Jesus! You're just a weed!" He found it unsettling. He had studied dreams a little prior to his mission. Why would she think that he was trying to be her Jesus? He was here to study humans and Earth.

"Pause, please," said the empathetic judge. "What is a dream?"

Jesus explained the division of the human mind into the conscious and the subconscious, giving examples of the functions of each.

"Sounds complicated," said the fussy judge.

"It is very complex. A dream is the subconscious mind's attempt to process the conscious mind's experiences. My research led me to conclude that I was trying to make sense of the confrontation with the elderly woman in the parking lot. The other issues provoking this dream were my insecurity about my mission and the unintended significance of my name."

"You mean the name you chose for this mission," corrected the fussy judge.

"That my project group chose, Your Honor."

"Continue," said the fussy judge.

Jesus eventually fell back to sleep until a skillet fell to the floor in the kitchen. He got up and put on a pair of pants. Jack greeted him with, "'Bout time. Geez, you slept eleven hours."

"I guess I needed the sleep," Jesus said, as his stomach growled loudly.

"Nice! But you'll have to make your own breakfast and I'm adding it to your tab," Jack said, teasing. "I've got to run some errands. Are you going to need a ride to work?"

"Yes, please."

"Okay, but you'll have to find a ride home."

As he had already started his search for appealing food, Jesus mindlessly responded, "Okay."

"See you at two!" Jack hollered as he left.

His mind was thick and slow and Jesus wondered if it was like this for all humans when they awoke. A knock at the door startled him. Setting down the box of granola, he went to answer the door, his stomach complaining about the interruption.

"Two packages for Hey-Zeus H. da Vinci," the deliveryman said.

"It's Jesus."

"Sign here," the deliveryman said, looking at him in an odd way. Jesus signed his device and handed it back and smiled. The deliveryman was still staring.

"Thank you."

Jesus opened both packages. They were his birth certificate and credit card. Sitting down to eat, his mind began to extrapolate what this meant. The credit card would allow him to buy things. The birth certificate would allow him to get a state ID card. In turn, he could get money and repay Jack. Suddenly recalling the earlier comment about "adding it to his tab," Jesus's jaw clenched, and his face felt warm. *What is happening?* he wondered. It dawned on him that he might be angry.

He was familiar with anger from his pre-mission study of emotions, but it never occurred to him that he would actually feel it. Even though he was participating in a normal life, he was still just an observer. Why would remembering Jack's comment produce this sensation?

Jack had taken him into his home—Jesus truly felt grateful about that and yet, he didn't like being teased about the debt. He promised to return the money. Did Jack not trust him? Was that causing this sensation?

"Pause," interrupted the empathetic judge. "Is this an example of conflicting emotions that you mentioned in your earlier testimony?"

"Yes, Your Honor, and it was confusing."

"Proceed," said the empathetic judge.

Though he still felt perplexed about his reaction, Jesus surmised that if he paid Jack what he owed him plus rent then the feelings of anger would dissipate.

The rest of the morning, Jesus did research online, wrote a status email for his project group and watched TV. Jack was late to pick him up. As soon as he got in the car, Jesus told Jack that he would be able to repay him by the following week.

"Outstanding!" Jack said with genuine warmth. "With interest, you must owe me thousands by now."

Jesus glared at him. "Hey, I'm just kidding. Whenever you can get the money back to me will be fine and I'm *not* charging you any interest," Jack said.

Jesus found his anger flaring again and the rest of the trip was made in silence.

After arriving, Jesus found Clara in the office. "How'd your shift go last night?" she asked.

"It seemed to go well, but it left me exhausted."

"Bagging is very physical."

"I'm sore here and here," Jesus said, pointing to the tender spots.

"Oh, we call those the bagging muscles. It's from lifting all those heavy bags. By the way, Brad said you did a good job last night. Don't forget to clock in and be sure to add your time from yesterday, too."

"Thanks. Just to let you know, I left early last night."

"Understandable," she said, smiling. "Okay, I think I have everything, so I'm leaving. Bye."

His shift didn't start for fifteen minutes so Jesus wandered around the store. As he looked at shelf after shelf of products, he began to appreciate the wide variety of sustenance available to humans. *This will be far more interesting than the dirt we ingest on Gooberia*, he thought.

He got an urge to check out the main office. Approaching the double-doors, he wondered if there was a correct...WHAM! The door hit him right in the face and stunned, he fell backwards to the floor.

"Are you okay?"

"Yes, I think so," he said, articulating his jaw, blinking rapidly and squeezing his nose. Above him, Barbara stood grinning. "That's the third time in four days I've hit the ground," he said, slowly rising from the floor. "Are you smiling at my misfortune?"

"No, no, no!" she said. "It's just that it's nice to see you, that's all."

"All right, you're off the hook...unless bleeding resumes," he teased.

"Are you working tonight?" she asked.

"Yes, I am."

"Okay," she said, walking away with her hips swinging back and forth in an exaggerated fashion.

He stepped through the correct door, preoccupied with the thought that Barbara had seemed more interested in seeing him than concerned about causing him physical pain. The main office was empty of people, but filled floor to ceiling with boxes and papers. It sort of reminded him of a recycling center he had seen on the Internet. *Nothing interesting to see here*, he thought, heading back up front to begin his shift.

All night long, Barbara smiled coyly at him. He felt uncomfortable by the way she was behaving towards him even though he felt some level of attraction to her. But due to his lack of experience, he wasn't sure what that meant.

Jesus mentioned the new credit card to Brad. "Time to check out some bikes, is it?" Brad asked.

"Absolutely. I could definitely use your expertise."

"How's next Wednesday for you? I'm taking my car into the shop on Tuesday."

"Wednesday would work just fine," Jesus replied, pausing. "Since you have a car, is there any way I can get a ride home this evening?"

Brad nodded and then greeted an approaching customer. "Hey, Martha! Namaste."

"Hey Brad, Nama-ain't it a great day," Martha said, as she set down her basket.

"Martha, I'd like you to meet, Jesus, our new bagger."

Grinning, Martha said, "We can always use some more Jesuses on the planet." Pausing and looking up at the ceiling, she said, "What is the plural of Jesus? Never mind."

"Nice to meet you," Jesus said.

"Martha and I go to the same yoga class. You might want to try it out. It could work the soreness out of those bagging muscles," Brad said.

"Plus, it will help quiet the mind and soothe the emotions," Martha added. That caught Jesus's attention. He was aware that his negative emotions and thoughts had been increasing, almost matching the time he had been on the planet. Besides, his neck and shoulders were sore. Maybe a yoga class would help.

"I would be interested in attending a yoga class," he said. Brad cocked his head to the side, and studied him. Jesus began to wonder if he was saying or phrasing things correctly. To make sure he was going to fit in, he would have to do some research on casual speech and slang.

Paying for her groceries, Martha said, "Oh goody, I love introducing newbies to yoga. Come here and let me give you a hug," she said, walking around the counter with arms outstretched. Jesus took a step back. "It won't hurt...I swear."

The hug lasted for at least five seconds. When she finally let go, she had an odd look on her face. "Well, nice to meet you, Jesus. See you at yoga!" she said, leaving with her groceries.

Jesus noticed her puzzled expression, but if Brad had seen it, he said nothing. "Hey, would it be possible also to go by the DMV next week too, so I can get my replacement state ID card?"

Brad, watching Martha leave, answered distractedly, "Yeah, sure."

After he finished his work, Jesus waited outside for Brad to finish his closing duties. It was a clear, cold night with the stars twinkling. He felt insignificant looking out on space, wondering how many more planets might have intelligent life, and where his own was.

Brad emerged from the store walking quickly. Seeing Jesus staring at the sky, he quipped, "Trying to find your home planet?"

The question startled Jesus, who decided the truth was a better strategy than denial. "Can't find it. Wormhole travel is much faster than a return signal from our space buoy. My planet has yet to locate your planet," he said. Stopping in his tracks and trying to repress a laugh, Brad said, "That's good. You should write." Jesus smiled and nodded.

On the way to the apartment, they talked about bicycles. When they arrived, Jesus asked for one more favor: a ride to church in the morning, so he could speak further with the pastor. Brad agreed since that was his church, too. Alone in the apartment, Jesus did some research on the computer for a while, but he tired quickly and went to bed.

The next thing he knew, Brad was shaking him and telling him to wake up. Jesus inhaled deeply and asked what time it was.

"It's almost nine thirty. We're going to be late. You sleep in your clothes?"

"How did you get in here?" Jesus mumbled, his brain in a fog.

"Jack let me in."

"What do you sleep in?"

"Pajamas," Brad said, as if Jesus should already know that.

"So, clothes, but a different kind of clothes?"

"Yes. Now hurry up," Brad said, walking out of the room. Jesus got out of bed, stretched, yawned, and thought, *Add to the list—research pajamas.*

"And put on some deodorant, too," Brad yelled back.

"Right. Underarms. Must apply to underarms."

Sticking his head around the corner and giving him one of those questioning looks again, Brad asked, "What?"

"Must apply to underarms," Jesus repeated. "Where do you apply it?"

Brad's gaze narrowed, and it became apparent to Jesus that he had said the wrong thing. "Sorry, I'm a little groggy this morning," he said. "I don't think my brain is 100 percent yet."

Brad seemed to accept that explanation and went back to the living room. Jesus soon pronounced he was ready.

They arrived late and sat in the last pew. The pastor had already begun. It was the last sermon in a series on the seven deadly sins—today he was covering anger. He went on about the subject for some time. He gave examples and differentiated between the various types of anger: irritation, annoyance and indignation. He explained how humans use anger to control their environment. He was very thorough, except he never mentioned how to heal or release anger.

When the sermon was over, Jesus stood up and spoke. "Excuse me, Pastor. How does one heal or release one's anger?" Every parishioner turned around and stared at him. Scanning their faces, Jesus interpreted that they were not pleased.

Pausing to take a deep breath, the pastor said, "My son, there are many approaches to healing anger, but my favorite is to ask for God's help to heal my anger and forgive my sin."

Jesus thought about that for a moment. "Okay, but is there anything other than prayer to alleviate anger?"

"My son, that is an extensive subject and there are many opinions. Why don't we meet after the service and we can discuss it further?" he patiently replied.

"That would be nice," Jesus said, sitting down. Brad turned to him and glared. Jesus realized he had probably committed another faux pas and he resolved to research proper church behavior. Once the service was over, Brad told him he would wait outside and quickly left. Jesus got up and started wading through the exiting congregation. A few people smiled, but he quickly found himself nose to nose with an elderly gentleman who exclaimed angrily, "Why would you do that?"

"Do what?"

"Interrupt the church service. Don't you have any manners?"

Jesus paused a moment. This was the second time he had faced anger. "I'm sorry if I've offended you, but I thought church was the place to get one's spiritual questions answered."

The man looked shocked. Jesus pressed, "Did it occur to you that maybe someone else in the congregation might have that same question?"

"Humph," the man snorted and hurriedly walked off. Jesus felt triumphant. He had met anger, did not respond in kind, and outwitted it. A little more practice and he'd have these emotional waves he was experiencing under control. Feeling proud, he headed to the pastor's office.

At the door, it suddenly occurred to him that if the elderly gentleman was upset with his interruption, the pastor might be also. His door was open and Jesus tapped on it.

"Come in, my son. Please have a seat. This will only take a moment." After some shuffling of papers, he looked up. "Done. All right now, what was your specific question again?"

"First, I'd like to apologize for interrupting your service with my question," Jesus said contritely, though he really didn't mean it.

"Possibly in the future, you can save your questions for after the service," the pastor suggested.

"I'll do that. So, what are my options to alleviate anger or anger-like feelings once they have commenced?"

"You mean besides prayer?"

"Yes. Well, in addition to prayer. I have no problem asking for Goo—God's help. It's always the first option, but it seems a tad...passive at times. They're my emotions. I'm responsible for dealing with them. You know, 'God helps those who help themselves' as the Greeks said. What can I do to cope with them better, in the moment?"

"In the moment," the pastor hummed. "Well, you can always take a deep breath and count to ten. That does actually work."

"Okay. I can do that," Jesus said, nodding. "What else?"

"There are a number of, shall we say, psychiatric techniques or approaches that deal with a specific type of anger. You wouldn't deal with feeling jealous the same way you would deal with volatile or unpredictable anger. Just what kind of anger are you feeling, my son?"

"Ohhh," Jesus groaned, "I owe Jack money. Sometimes he makes jokes about it and I get angry. It's very uncomfortable."

"Perfectly understandable," the pastor said. "New people, new situations, your medical condition, all of these things would lead you to feel extra-sensitive. I'm sure that your skin will thicken up, as it were, the more comfortable you get in your new surroundings. By the way, how are things going for you?"

"Satisfactorily. I've been on the...I've been here five days. I have a place to stay. I have a job. Brad has offered to help me buy a bicycle and gather my documentation."

"Remarkable," the pastor said, leaning forward, "and your physical condition?"

"Physical condition? Oh, right...my amnesia. You know I almost forgot I had amnesia."

The pastor chuckled, "You know, at our roundtable discussions, we talk about all sorts of things including how to deal with emotions. You might consider attending."

"When's the next discussion?"

"The week after this Thursday at 7 p.m. in the basement."

"I'll check my work schedule to see if I can make it," Jesus said. He stood up and shook the pastor's hand. "Thank you for seeing me."

"Anytime, my son, anytime," he said with a smile. "My door is always open."

Jesus was surprised how good he felt after talking with the pastor. He met Brad outside. "So, how did it go?

"It was beneficial," said Jesus. "I've got something to test now."

"Test?"

"It's the scientist in me. I love the process—make an observation, ask a question, form a hypothesis, conduct an experiment, interpret the results."

"Oh, okay. You want to go get some lunch?"

"I can't. I'm working the mid-shift today. I'm supposed to be at work in thirty minutes. Can you drop me off at the store?"

"Sure," Brad said. "Let's go." On the way to the store, they made plans for a bike ride after Wednesday's errands.

Jesus thanked Brad for the ride and went inside, grabbed his button and headed to the registers. Barbara and Wanda were working with three cashiers he hadn't met yet. He made a point of introducing himself, and all three had some reaction to his name. George, a medium-sized man with sad-looking eyes, asked, "Did your mama give you that name?"

Carol wondered aloud if it wasn't sacrilegious to be named Jesus.

Pete thought it was cool. He asked, "So, are you still a Jew or did you convert to Christianity since returning?" Jesus responded yes to conversion, but to Islam instead. Pete collapsed onto his counter, laughing.

As Jesus began bagging for Wanda, she winked at him suggestively, "Hello handsome! Have you come to give me some help?"

"Is there something wrong with your eye? You seem to have a tic."

"I'm fine honey. You're a little off though," said Wanda, putting her hands on her hips.

Jesus decided to attempt some humor. "I came to give you a hand," he said, putting out his right hand, turning and covering his eyes. "Do with it what you will."

Giggling, she grabbed his hand and massaged it. "Mmmm, that's a mighty fine hand you have there. Can we go to the back for a little privacy?"

I think this is flirtation, he thought. Retrieving his hand, he said, "Maybe on break." He moved to Barbara's register where she had been observing them.

"Having fun?" she asked, slamming a can of beans down on the counter.

"We were just playing around," Jesus said, bagging the can.

"Maybe not everybody is having fun," she said emphatically, this time slamming a jar down.

"Hey! That's a $20 jar of organic raw almond butter. Be careful!" the customer said, leaning forward and catching Barbara's eye. "If you two are going to fight, wait until I leave."

The comment surprised Jesus. He wasn't aware that Barbara and he were fighting. He had discerned her discomfort; from her comment, he was pretty sure it had something to do about his contact with Wanda. This was too complicated to think about while working, so he made a mental note to create a flowchart of this episode and his other interactions with Barbara once he got home.

The rest of the shift, Jesus avoided her. He bagged for her, but he didn't make any further effort at conversation. It felt uncomfortable even thinking about talking to her. She left work early, complaining of a headache.

As Jesus restocked the bags at the registers, he suddenly remembered he needed a ride home. The store was closed and the cashiers were counting their money in the front-end office. He went in and asked if someone could give him a ride.

"Oh honey, let me give you a ride," Wanda said, batting her eyelashes.

Finishing up, Pete said, "I'll give you a ride home, Jesus. Wanda, you're so aggressive, I swear you've got a penis under there." Everybody laughed, including Wanda.

Raising her right hand, Wanda said, "I do solemnly swear I am not hiding a weapon of mass destruction down there...and I am available for inspection."

After it quieted down, Jesus added, "Well then, Wanda, I'm sure you'll be receiving a call shortly from the Department of Homeland Purity." That started another round of laughter and as he walked out the door, Wanda called out, "They're going to be disappointed!"

A few minutes later, Jesus and Pete met up outside and walked towards his car. They had the usual get-to-know-you conversation and Jesus told Pete his cover story. He was fascinated of course. It turned out Pete was a Muslim from Lebanon and had just gotten married.

Thanking Pete for the ride, Jesus fumbled to open the apartment door. Once inside, he found Jack was not home again and felt irritated about that. *Why isn't he here?* He tried to ignore the feeling and got on the computer. He made another progress report and did some research. Then he made a flowchart of his interactions with Barbara and concluded that she must be attracted to him...a lot.

That deduction brought up a variety of emotions for Jesus. The scientist in him was excited about a possible new experiment—intimate human relationships. But would that hinder his objectivity? He was supposed to observe rather than participate.

This was too much for him to digest. He thought it best to rebuff her advances and keep his distance. He'd had energy when he got home, but this deliberation had drained him. He turned on the TV, and realized he was getting used to it always being there. It gave him something to focus on besides his feelings and it helped alleviate his loneliness.

Chapter 6 – Learning to ride a bike

Jesus walked to work the next day. He had been over the route enough times to feel comfortable that he wouldn't get lost. Barbara wasn't working and he was thankful that he didn't have to deal with her. Late in the shift, he spoke with Brad to confirm their ten o'clock start the next morning.

"Do you mind if we go by the bank after the DMV so I can pay Jack back?" asked Jesus.

"Most definitely," said Brad.

Feeling like he had things under control, Jesus began the walk home contemplating his mastery of the human experience so far. But there was something unnerving about walking after dark; it brought up the fear that he experienced his first night. Humans were supposed to be the predators, but now it became apparent that they could be the prey, too. *No wonder they make so much effort to light up the night,* he thought.

His heart was racing by the time he got to the apartment. It was empty once again and he felt disappointed. He hadn't seen Jack at home in a couple of days. Where was he? Jesus still relied on him and he wasn't around to help. Feeling alone and disconnected, he retrieved a pillow from the bedroom. The old apartment building creaked when the neighbors walked upstairs and every little noise caught his attention. He turned on the TV, clutched the pillow to his chest, curled up in a ball on the couch and fell asleep.

He awoke early the next morning. Struggling to get up, his body was stiff—especially his neck—and it was painful to move. It seemed that every day he was on this planet, his physical condition worsened. *Maybe my body is deteriorating faster than a native human body? Maybe the transmogrification process is reversing? Am I physically changing back into a Goober?* he wondered. There had been several instances where it appeared that his third leg was growing back...but that had been episodic and only in the company of females.

"Pause," said the fussy judge. "Let me see if I understand the steps taken to ensure the stability and safety of this mission. You studied their communications for two years. That seems reasonable. What did you test transmongrelization on?"

"Transmogrification, Your Honor. The process was tested on Gooberian plant life."

"You hadn't tested the process on animal life until you yourself tried it?" asked the fussy judge.

"That is correct, Your Honor."

"Why not?" the fussy judge said, his voice rising.

"There was no guarantee that the process could be reversed. And there was no guarantee that a human could survive on Gooberia."

"You could have done it on the spaceship, correct?" the fussy judge asked.

"That is true, but again, the spaceship provides an environment for the Goober life form and we were uncertain that a human could survive in our environment. Even if the process were successful in our environment, if it couldn't be reversed and with no human food available on the spaceship, the test subject would have starved. To put as few lives at risk as possible, the decision was made to send someone to Earth without further testing."

"So, you were willing to risk your life?" the empathetic judge asked.

"Yes, Your Honor, I was."

"Why?" asked the fussy judge.

Taking a deep breath, Jesus said, "I don't know why, Your Honor. I've thought about it a thousand times. I simply do not know why except to say that at some level I was drawn to attempt this. Maybe it was a sense of adventure. Maybe I'm a gambler at heart, I don't know."

His face puckered in disbelief, the fussy judge said, "And breaking our first commandment? Continue."

Brad picked up Jesus the next morning and they drove to the DMV first. It took ninety minutes before he was called on. They didn't chat because sitting there, it seemed the life was being sucked right out of them. Now that Jesus had something to compare the store's energy to, a feeling of gratitude spread over him. Fortunately, the process went smoothly and he got his "replacement" state ID card.

The trip to the bank didn't take long and Jesus had already calculated how much he owed Jack. After getting the money in his hands, he felt a sense of relief. *This should put an end to my anger towards Jack*, he thought.

He was looking forward to the bike shop. There was something like a bicycle on Gooberia, so he expected the process to be simple. Unfortunately, the reality was somewhat different. On Gooberia, balance wasn't necessary as the vehicle was really a tricycle...and the speed topped out at three miles per hour. The pedal clips on the shoes were another surprise.

Wearing his new cycling shoes, Jesus prepared to mount the first model to test out in the parking lot. Getting his foot attached to the left pedal was fairly easy, but propelling himself forward and staying balanced while trying to clip his shoe to the right pedal was not.

The next several minutes involved Jesus practicing his limited knowledge of cursing as he fell first to one side and then the other, alternating falling forward and then back.

It was after falling over for the fourth time that he wished he knew more swear words. The salesman wondered out loud whether Jesus knew how to ride a bike at all. Brad thought the same, and said so as he helped Jesus up.

"It's been a while, okay?" Jesus said, with a bit of irritation in his voice.

"Don't give up!" Brad encouraged. "At least you're beginning to learn how to fall properly."

"You're kidding, right?"

"No, I'm not. It's an important skill. Everybody crashes. Now come on and get up. This time if you have to put your foot back down on the pavement, bend your knee. That'll help your balance. And maybe you should buy some cycling gloves to protect your hands as you get the hang of this."

"Why didn't you suggest that before?" Jesus complained. "And how about a first-aid kit and some bubble wrap, too?"

Laughing, Brad said, "I'm sorry. I didn't know you didn't know how to ride...yet."

"I appreciate the encouragement. I'll master this...eventually. Hopefully without too much more blood loss. I'm leaking everywhere," Jesus half-groaned.

Laughing again, Brad said, "I'll show you where the gloves are."

Jesus found cycling gloves that fit, and as he walked around in the cycling shoes, he started to get the hang of their slipperiness. Back to the parking lot they went for another attempt.

The fifth attempt was unsuccessful too, but Jesus stayed upright. He turned to Brad and proudly said, "I didn't fall!"

Brad laughed, "Step one complete—not falling. Step two—getting both your feet in. Point your toe down. Make contact with the pedal. Push down with the ball of your foot."

Jesus followed Brad's instructions exactly and it worked. Remembering an expression he had heard at work, he yelled, "Yee-haw!"

Brad doubled over. "You did it! I told you that you could do it."

Next Brad taught Jesus how to shift gears and brake properly and explained what to look for when testing a bike. He added, "You gotta have a toolkit and a bike pump in case you get a flat. You need a couple of water bottles, a helmet, and you'll need at least one pair of bike shorts. The more you're prepared, the more you'll enjoy yourself."

"Bike shorts?"

"Yeah, they have a chamois crotch to prevent abrasion. It feels like a velvet glove cradling your balls," he said, almost wistfully.

Laughing, Jesus said, "Yeah, yeah, I could go for some velvet-gloved ball-cradling. Let's get two pairs."

After test-riding several bikes, Jesus made his selection. He didn't know why, but paying for it with his credit card was exciting. Was it the act of making a purchase or what the purchase represented? He wasn't sure, but made a mental note to study this.

They loaded the bikes onto Brad's car and headed for the apartment. After they parked, Brad asked, "Do you want to ride today, or do you want to get a little first aid and rest?"

"First aid first, then ride," Jesus said dramatically.

"I like that confidence. Let's ride!"

While Brad was getting the bikes down, Jesus went inside to change and apply a little first aid. The bike shorts felt so good he thought he just might wear them to bed.

He left the apartment and locked the door. There was still no sign of Jack. "All right! Let's ride!" Jesus uttered in a deep voice.

"Take this slow in the beginning. Get into your lowest gear first," Brad said.

Jesus did as instructed as they began riding through the neighborhood. "Start looking over each shoulder to get used to it," Brad said. He could look over his right shoulder, but his neck was still stiff and it hurt to look over his left shoulder. Even though it hurt, the stretch felt good.

As Brad decelerated to get alongside Jesus, he said, "Okay, you want to stay with a comfortable cadence and use your gears to speed up. Shift to second gear." As he did, the pedaling got a little harder but he sped up. "Okay, now it's time to practice proper pedaling technique."

"What's that?" Jesus asked.

"Visualize pedaling in a circle. It's called spinning. It's easier on the knees and a more efficient use of your energy," Brad said. Jesus tried this technique but to no effect, and told Brad so, making a mental note to do research on every facet of bicycling. "Don't worry. Keep practicing. You have to program your body to do it."

They kept riding and the breeze felt magnificent on Jesus's skin. Compared to walking on three legs this felt like utter liberation.

"Shift into third gear. We're coming up on a downhill stretch so get ready to shift your left gear shifter," Brad yelled as he sped up and got in front.

Moments later, they came to the crest. Jesus heard a couple of clicks from Brad's bike and he took off. Jesus shifted the left gear shifter and accelerated rapidly. Brad had already put fifty yards on him and was continuing to pull away. He wasn't able keep up, but he didn't care. He couldn't believe how fast he was going! It was rough and bumpy and excitement and fear welled up deep inside him, when he suddenly shouted, "Oh my Goob! Oh my Goob!" But the fear didn't keep him from pedaling faster as he closed in on a car in front of him.

Brad had already reached the bottom of the hill and was coasting. Shortly, Jesus caught up to him. "Pretty awesome, eh?"

"Awesome isn't the word. Stupefying would be more accurate," Jesus exclaimed breathlessly.

"Shift down. Slow up. Return to a normal pace and catch your breath."

Jesus did just that and they rode silently for a while. "Keep practicing looking over your shoulder," Brad said.

"It hurts to do that. My neck is stiff."

"Well then maybe it's about time for a yoga class. Yoga will help you keep limber and fresh."

"Isn't that a religion?"

"No, not at all. Try a class and see how you feel. There's one I go to on Mondays."

"Okay," Jesus said, since Brad's advice had been accurate so far.

"Besides, tomorrow you're going to be sore from all those falls you took. I swear it will make a difference."

"All right, I'm willing to give it a try."

They rode for another fifteen minutes when Brad said, "Let's head for home. By the time they finished, Jesus was tired but he felt good, not just physically, but mentally and emotionally as well. "You may want to take a hot bath to soothe those muscles. You're probably not going to feel like riding for the next few days. Maybe we could get in a ride after yoga on Monday?"

"That sounds good," Jesus said, wondering how sore he was going to feel.

"Fifteen miles is a very good first day. See you tomorrow!" Brad said, getting into his car.

Jesus dragged his bike inside. He sat down for a while and watched some TV. He fell asleep after ten minutes and didn't awaken until Jack walked through the door.

"Hey."

"Where have you been the past few days?" Jesus asked.

"I've been enjoying some female company."

"You have a girlfriend?"

"Better. A friend with benefits," Jack said, with a smile.

"What kind of benefits?"

"Sex. Glorious sex. And lots of it."

"Lots of it?" Jesus asked, groaning to a standing position and walking to the kitchen to get something to eat.

"Yup. She has got to be the best I've ever had. She gives incredible head," Jack said, with an enormous grin.

Peeking around the corner, Jesus asked, "Head?"

"You know. Oral sex. A blowjob. You've had one, haven't you?"

"Oh sure," Jesus said, trying to picture what Jack was talking about.

He popped a burrito in the microwave and got a glass of water. Returning to the living room to eat, he asked, "Why is 'friends with benefits' better than a girlfriend?"

"No attachment. No girlfriend demands," explained Jack.

"What does a girlfriend demand?"

"You know. No 'Are you thinking about me?' or 'I'd like you to meet my parents or friends' or 'Let's got to the museum on Saturday' crap. You know, girlfriend stuff. You've had a girlfriend before, right?"

"Oh yeah, but apparently I don't find it as onerous as you do," Jesus said smugly.

"Yeah, yeah. Judge me if you want, but this was a fantastic couple of days. Maybe the best couple of days of my life."

"Okay," Jesus said, moving gingerly to his backpack. He retrieved the money and shuffled over to Jack. "Here's what I owe you with a little interest," he said.

Jack's face lit up as he took the money. "Thanks, dude!" he exclaimed. "I can get some killer weed with this tomorrow."

"You're welcome," Jesus responded, sitting down with a groan.

Jack sat staring at the money with a silly-looking grin. After a couple of moments, his expression changed. "Why are you walking around like an old man?" he asked.

"I went bicycle riding today," Jesus replied, getting up off the couch cautiously to get another glass of water.

Spotting the new bike, Jack said, "Sweet ride, dude. How many gears does she have?"

"Honestly, I don't know."

"Let's see. It's looks like sixteen." After examining it thoroughly he said, "It doesn't look like you wrecked it."

"I didn't wreck that bike," Jesus said irritably. "It was the first bike I was test-riding that I crashed on...repeatedly."

"Repeatedly?"

"Four times."

"Four times? FOUR TIMES!" You don't wreck four times on a bike unless you're learning how to ride."

"It's been a while since I've ridden. It must be the effects of whatever caused the amnesia," Jesus said, trying to end the conversation.

"Maybe you should consider training wheels," Jack laughed.

Jesus needed a comeback but knew nothing that applied. Making a mental note to look some up on the Internet, he finally grumbled, "Well, you keep a messy apartment."

"Oooh, burn. Did you at least enjoy riding?"

"Yes, very much so. I think I experienced an adrenaline rush. Brad and I are riding again after yoga next week."

"Maybe I'll go with you guys."

"Talk to Brad."

There was a lull in the conversation. "Hey, want to go get some food? I'm buying...with your money."

"No. I just ate and besides, I'm worn out. I'm going to get on the computer and then go to bed early."

"Don't you mean 'crash'?" Jack cackled.

Jesus scowled at the comment. "Don't be so sensitive, dude! I'm just teasing," Jack said.

"Must be a reaction to the pain," Jesus said with a groan as he got up off the couch.

"You're such a drama queen," Jack said, going to his room.

Jesus was too tired to muster any concern for Jack's feelings. He did some research and wrote a brief status report and went to bed. It took less than a minute to fall asleep.

Waking up early the next morning, it would have been quicker to list what didn't hurt than what did. *How do humans deal with these bodies? Is physical pain a natural state for them? Maybe I haven't learned how to use it properly yet,* he thought. After about five minutes, he finally made it out of bed and went to the bathroom. As he stood in front of the toilet, he tried to look on the bright side...at least it didn't hurt to pee.

Shuffling to the kitchen, he noticed Jack wasn't home, which this time produced a feeling of relief. He wandered around the apartment most of the morning, and the pain eased some. But when he realized he was due at work in an hour, a feeling came over him that he later he identified as dread. He found it paralyzing. After contemplating the situation, the scientist in him decided he should think of this as an experiment, even though his pain was making a persuasive argument against it.

When he arrived at work, Brad greeted him with, "How's it going, buddy? How you feelin'?"

Jesus responded by plopping down in a chair with a moan.

"Come on. Get up," Brad said, waving his hands, "I'm going to show you some stretches. You'll feel better afterwards, I swear." For some reason, Jesus felt like punching him in the throat, but he went ahead and stood.

Given the look on Jesus's face, Brad repeated, "I swear you're going to feel better. Now lift both arms over your head." Jesus's eyes widened.

"You won't die. Try it."

He did, and repeated the action several times. He found his shoulders loosening up. It must have shown because Brad said, "See, it works. You just need to untie those knots. Stretching is just a part of exercise. Now, bend over and touch your toes."

Jesus looked down at his feet. "But they are so far away," he complained.

Brad laughed, "Both hands, both feet." Jesus reached, letting out a very loud groan.

It must have been loud because Clara walked into the office and asked, "What's wrong with you?"

Jesus mumbled, "Exercise, bicycle riding, crashing," as he struggled to reach his toes.

Clara asked, "Am I going to be down a bagger today?"

"He'll be fine. He's just not used to this. They must not exercise a whole lot in France," Brad said.

After researching comebacks that morning, Jesus responded, "Takes one to know one!" in a voice strained by effort.

Both of them laughed, and Clara said, "Okay when you're done groaning, it's time to start work."

Straightening up and red-faced, Jesus said, "Stop groaning? That'll be sometime next week...or month," as he attempted to touch his toes again.

Laughing, Brad said, "He'll be right out but first, left hand to right foot and vice versa."

Jesus complied, and after a few attempts he stood up and said his back felt better. "Of course. You're doing a few rudimentary yoga positions. You'll feel even better after class next week," Brad said.

"I look forward to it," Jesus said sincerely, heading out to the registers. "See you tomorrow...buddy."

48

"Ten-four," Brad said.

Work wasn't too difficult, but by the end, Jesus felt exhausted. Fortunately Pete was there to lift his spirits. "I hear that test-riding bikes didn't go too well yesterday," he said.

"Yeah, it took a while to get my footing," Jesus said, "but I finally stayed up and we got a ride in."

"Did Brad not explain the importance of staying up initially?" Pete asked, suppressing a chuckle.

Jesus stuck his tongue out at him as another newly attempted comeback.

Pete laughed, "I'm glad to see you're persistent."

"Hey, I scored high on the persistence part of my...uh, uh, college entrance examination," Jesus stammered.

"They test persistence in France?" Pete asked, with a surprised look on his face. "Hmmm, that must have started after World War II."

"Hey! Don't be knocking France. If it wasn't for France there wouldn't even be a United States."

Pete looked skeptical and Jesus continued, "France was the main financier of the American Revolution, which oddly enough caused sufficient financial hardship in France to kick-start their own revolution."

Pete nodded and changed the subject, "What was your major in college?"

Pausing, Jesus said, "I majored in wine and minored in napping." Pete laughed, and as they continued their banter the shift went quickly.

Barbara was quiet and seemed to make an effort to touch him whenever the opportunity presented itself. He did his best to ignore her efforts.

On Monday, Jesus met Brad at the yoga studio. He realized he was a little bit nervous and excited. Reduced physical pain and participating in another human activity? Who wouldn't be excited?

The teacher began by announcing, "We're going to tune in with the Adi Mantra to connect with our inner teacher and help set up our vibratory fields." She closed her eyes and began rubbing her palms together.

Jesus was not aware of having an inner teacher, but physical energy fields were known on Gooberia. He mimicked the teacher, but couldn't quite pick up the wording of the mantra. "Let's warm up with some Breath of Fire," the teacher said.

Jesus eyes widened as he whispered to Brad, "Am I going to expel fire through my nose?"

Brad erupted into laughter and tumbled onto his side. Even the teacher laughed. "I take it you're new to Kundalini Yoga?" she asked.

"Apparently."

"Breath of Fire is a breathing technique that brings *prana*, or life force, into the body," she explained. The class continued with the teacher explaining the details of breathing techniques, hand positions, eye focus, positioning of the body, and more mantras.

By the end of class, all his nervousness had disappeared. His breath had deepened and standing up took much less effort. His brain felt clearer, too.

Taking into account his physical, mental and emotional states at that very moment, Jesus felt the best he had since he arrived on the planet. Up until now, every activity he had engaged in seemed to have some potential for pain and he was beginning to wonder if that was consistent with all human endeavors. Could he have found something that was safe and pain-free?

After class, Brad was talking to a short, redheaded woman and motioned for Jesus to come over. "Jesus, I'd like you to meet Alice. She helps run the soup kitchen and, of course, she loves yoga."

"Jesus? Well, if you've returned, that shoots my belief system all to hell," she said, smiling. "Is that a chosen name or a birth name?"

"What's wrong with your belief system?" Jesus asked innocently.

"Nothing, nothing at all."

Brad jumped in, "Alice is an atheist."

"Oh, I get it. Good joke," Jesus said, sticking out his hand.

Alice shook it hard. "Brad tells me that you're a member of the Megalithic Church."

"I've attended but I haven't joined."

"Maybe you'd like to do some service work and help us out in the soup kitchen. It would get you in good with...well, *you*," she said, chuckling.

"Isn't that a sin of pride—trying to impress yourself?"

As they laughed, Jesus considered that working in a soup kitchen might be a good opportunity to check out another segment of human society.

"The pastor has been of great help to me and I would like to do something in return."

"Do you work nights or days?"

"Mostly nights right now, but that can change weekly."

"Perfect! We need people for the lunch shift. How many days a week can you help?"

Thinking on it a moment, Jesus said, "Let's start with two."

"Geez, most people only say one when I ask that."

"What can I say...'service' is my middle name," Jesus joked.

"Come to think of it, what *does* the H stand for?" Brad asked.

"Why, help, of course!" Jesus replied.

Brad and Alice laughed as Jesus headed for the restroom. Brad called after him, "Hey, you feel like a bike ride?"

"Yeah, I think so. Maybe only ten miles instead of fifteen."

They changed into their bike clothes and left the yoga studio and rode to Jesus's apartment to drop off their backpacks. It seemed like spring had arrived early in Texas with the temperature in the mid-seventies. Yoga had helped, and although he was still a little sore and stiff, it was not enough to impact the pleasure of the ride. It was glorious to work up a sweat, filling the lungs up completely, the breeze he created cooling him down. The ride took about forty minutes and Jesus felt invigorated when it was over.

Brad suggested a twenty-five mile ride on Wednesday to which Jesus agreed, provided his body held up.

Smiling, Brad said, "Keep up with your stretching and you'll be fine."

"Okay."

"Take care, buddy," Brad said, as he rode away.

Twenty-five miles sounded like a lot. Jesus went inside and did some stretching and got ready for work. He arrived twenty minutes early and ran into Barbara in the front-end office.

The first words out of her mouth were, "So, we're finally alone."

Jesus exhaled audibly as he sat down and his discomfort must have been apparent because her demeanor changed immediately. After a long pause, she asked, "What have you been doing today?"

"Yoga class and a bike ride with Brad," he replied quietly.

"That sounds nice. I've haven't ever tried yoga."

He nodded, trying to avoid any further conversation, but she was persistent. "How was it?"

"What? The yoga class or the bike ride?"

"Both," she said, smiling.

"Yoga was outstanding. I'm going to try to go every week, I think."

"That good, huh? Why was it outstanding?"

"My body felt so much better afterwards and I seemed sharper mentally."

"Well then, it sounds like you should definitely continue," she said. "How about the bike ride?"

"Other than falling, I love bike riding," Jesus said, "plus I get a tremendous sense of freedom when I ride."

Barbara had smiled and nodded until she heard Jesus say that he fell and her countenance changed. "Falling? Did you fall today?" she asked, standing and reaching out towards him.

"No, no, not today. When I was test-riding bikes I fell...several times," he said sheepishly.

"Ohhh," she said, sitting down and patting his arm. "Poor boy."

"It was the shoes. I wasn't used to how slick they are," Jesus rationalized.

There was a long awkward pause. He felt uneasy and realized keeping her at a distance was going to be hard work. Standing quickly, he said, "Time for work."

"Thank you," Barbara said, as he was walking out the door.

Jesus turned around. "For what?"

"For sharing," she said, with a kind smile.

Jesus inhaled deeply and nodded. "Yeah. Sure." He left for the restroom, and thought about that interaction for the next several minutes. Yes, there was an attraction, but he had to be cautious because of his mission. His pre-work tranquility was oozing away.

During the shift, every time Jesus and Barbara's eyes met, she would give him this look that he couldn't identify and it made him uneasy. Towards the end of the shift, she surprised him with, "Maybe we could get together and do something?"

Unprepared to respond, Jesus racked his brain, but before he could come up with a response, she asked, "Are you doing anything special this week?"

Breathing deeply, he said, "I'm going to the church's roundtable on Thursday and I am attending services on Sunday.

"The Megalithic Church?"

"Yes."

"I'm a member!"

"Are you?" he said, frowning.

"Yes, I am. The pastor has been a great help to me," she said. I've never been to one of the roundtables before though. Maybe I should check that out," giving him a sideways glance and a raised eyebrow.

"Maybe you should. Excuse me. I need to start my closing duties," Jesus said flatly and walked away. *It really is going to be tough fending her off,* he thought.

Jesus finished up and rode home. He made a status report and searched the Internet about emotions and other subjects. He wanted to be ready for the roundtable the next night.

Chapter 7 – The first roundtable

The next day at work, Jesus asked Jack if he was going to the roundtable that night. Eyes twinkling and with a big grin, he replied, "No can do. I've got some fun in store." With a lecherous chuckle, he threw his head back and then uttered, "Ahhh." Not knowing what to make of this, Jesus walked away.

All day long, he contemplated what to ask at the roundtable. He had so many questions—what was important? There were big issues that he wanted answers to and there were minor issues to get clarification on. He decided that since there would be ten or eleven of these roundtables during his mission, he could pace himself.

Getting online, he found a bike-safe route to the church. Making several wrong turns, he arrived after the group had already started. Barbara, Brad, Alice and the pastor were there. Jack was there as well, and he didn't look happy.

"Hey-Zeus! I'm glad you could make it. Let me introduce everyone. This is Ralph," the pastor said. Ralph, picking at his bald scalp, rose stiffly and shook Jesus's hand.

"Hello," Ralph said in a gruff tone.

"This is Jane."

Twirling a lock of her platinum blonde hair and smiling, Jane said, "Hello, young man."

"And this is Juan." Jesus caught himself staring at the scar on Juan's face.

Glancing across the table, Brad asked, "'Hey-Zeus'? Isn't it Jesus?"

Jesus nodded yes and glanced at the pastor. He, Jane, Ralph and Juan looked uncomfortable at this clarification, so Jesus said nothing.

"Uh, let's get started," the pastor said quickly. "What do we want to discuss?"

"How about emotions and how to deal with them?" Jesus suggested.

"That's an excellent subject, my son," the pastor said. "Would you like to begin?"

"Uh, how do humans deal with anger? Or how do you get rid of anger?"

The pastor said, "I count slowly to ten and then ask God to forgive me of my sin."

Barbara said, "I do that too, but I add in something. I count zebras—one hysterical zebra, two hysterical zebras and so forth. If that doesn't work, I scream." Her face reddened when everyone stared at her.

After a pause, Brad said, "I do yoga and that helps keep me more tranquil. I'm less likely to react to something in the first place, but if I'm still reacting, I go for a bike ride. If it's really bad, I imagine the face of the person that I'm angry at underneath my pedals, like I'm squishing them."

Several people smiled and Jack laughed out loud. "I sort of do the same thing, but with video games."

"I'm not sure that imagining violence towards what or whom you're angry at is very productive. However, I like the idea of exercise to work off emotions," said the pastor.

"I ask Jesus," Jane said, pausing and looking across the table, "uhh, to forgive me of the sin of anger, too."

"I don't understand that," Jesus said. "God gave us emotions to deal with. Humans have them so it must be part of His plan, right?" Everyone nodded in agreement. "So, is feeling any emotion actually a sin or is it how we *deal with* the emotion?"

"Well my son, there are types of anger that aren't a sin. Righteous indignation for example, is not a sin," said the pastor.

"I can understand having passionate energy about something that is despicable, but on this planet it would seem that we have to learn how to deal with our emotions. I think that's what God expects of us. I mean as God, He would know that we would need to practice, so it wouldn't really be a sin, but natural growth," Jesus said.

There was a pause in the conversation as everyone reflected on this hypothesis. The pastor spoke up, "I think we're getting off-topic here. Let's get back to dealing with certain emotions and not discussing whether certain emotions are sins."

"I keep my anger inside. I think it's undignified to show emotion," Ralph said.

"I do, too," said Juan.

Exhaling audibly, the pastor said slowly, "Actually, that is a sin. It's a sin to repress anger."

"It says that in the Bible?" asked Ralph.

"Yes it does. In Ephesians," said the pastor.

"Really? Why?" asked Juan.

"I think it is because repressed anger can lead to depression, irritability, and being over-sensitive, especially letting little things get out of hand. Making a mountain out of a molehill," said the pastor.

"Well, I'll be. So, what's an appropriate way to express anger?" Ralph asked.

"I think it's the way it's phrased. Using 'I' statements," Brad said.

"'I' statements?" asked Ralph.

"Yeah. Like, 'I feel angry when you leave your clothes on the floor and I have to pick them up' or 'I feel upset when you talk about so-and-so like that because I understand their situation.' Talking about how you feel rather than putting the blame on someone else is an acceptable way of expressing yourself, or so I've heard," said Brad.

Silently, the group contemplated their struggles with anger. The pastor asked for a new topic.

"I don't understand greetings and salutations," Jesus said.

"What do you mean?" the pastor asked.

"I mean they seem so limited. Good morning, good afternoon, good day. Why limit one's good intentions to just a few hours?" Jesus asked.

Laughing, Jack said, "Live long and prosper!"

"Hey, that's a good one," said Jesus.

"That's from a TV show for nerds," Jack said.

"So? That seems much more encouraging than, I hope you do well till noon, but that's all."

Chuckling, Brad asked, "What would you recommend, Jesus?"

"We used to say 'Wake up.'"

"Why?" Barbara asked.

"Because the only place for us to find God is in the here and now. It's a way of stopping thought and getting back to the present," Jesus said.

"Was there a response?" the pastor asked.

"I am in the moment."

"Really? Intriguing. I don't think I've ever heard that before," said the pastor.

Everyone nodded in agreement and before anyone could say anything else, Jesus asked, "And what's up with the word 'fuck'?"

Jane gasped. Jack laughed. Ralph's face reddened. The pastor said, "Oh my! Son, we don't use that word around here."

"Why not?"

"Because it's vulgar," the pastor said.

"I read somewhere that it came from the sound that intercourse makes."

"Nevertheless, we don't use that word in church. If you must make reference to it, say 'the F-word'," the pastor said.

"Sure. I don't understand why humans reference the act of procreation with what are considered vulgarities. Are they ashamed of it? Isn't it a perfectly normal act for all animals?"

"Well, yes it is. However..." the pastor paused, "it's very complicated as you well know."

"From what I've learned so far, for more souls to arrive on this planet, it must be a part of God's plan that there be...animal-on-animal action."

Brad lowered his head and shook it slowly. Jack was laughing so hard that he fell out of his chair. Barbara's chin was on her chest. Jane excused herself for a drink of water.

"Like I said, my son, it's complicated," said the pastor, placing his head in his hands.

"It just doesn't make any sense to me. There seems to be so much judgment on this planet about absolutely necessary learning experiences."

"I think you have a point. I just don't know what to do with it," the pastor said.

Jane returned and sat down. There was idle chitchat for a while and then the pastor said, "We have time for one more subject."

Everybody looked at each other and then back at Jesus. "Okay. I've got one more question."

The pastor took a deep breath and braced himself. "Yes, my son. What is your question?"

"It's along the same lines as my previous question."

"Oh, good Lord," said Jane.

"This oughta be good," said Jack.

"It's the slang word mother—uhh, effer."

"I knew it!" Jack said.

"What about it?" the pastor asked wearily.

"It doesn't make any sense as an insult."

"Why not?" the pastor asked.

"Because it implies that once a woman has a child it's wrong or bad for her to attempt to have another. And if a woman were restricted to having only one child per lifetime, humanity would become extinct. Every family with two or more children has a father who's a mother-effer. If anything, men who are mother-effers are heroes, perpetuating the species. Once a woman has a child she's untouchable? I don't get it."

Half the room was in shock and the other half shook with laughter. Finally gathering himself, the pastor said, "I think that's enough for this evening."

"Hey, we have a Mother's Day and a Father's Day; maybe we should have a Mother-effer's Day, too," said Jack.

"Jack! That's enough!" said the pastor.

"Yes sir," Jack said, looking down.

"All right then," the pastor said, clearing his throat. "The next roundtable will be in four weeks. Thank you for coming," he said with a smile. "Hey-Zeus, could you stay for a moment?"

"Sure."

Standing, Jack whispered, "Someone's in trouble."

After everybody left, the pastor said, "My son, it is obvious that you have a sharp and inquiring mind. Possibly in the future, you can limit your suggestions to more culturally acceptable topics."

"You wish to restrict my free will?" Jesus said, moving to the edge of his seat. "I'm not sure I'm comfortable with that."

"That's not my intent. I'm just asking you to keep in mind other people's feelings when bringing up your questions," said the pastor.

"Just so I'm clear on this, are we talking about the vulgarities?" Jesus asked.

"Yes, the vulgarities. This is a house of worship and a certain level of behavior is expected."

"I see. You've drawn a line you expect me to walk and I understand why. It's just I have many questions and topics to explore and I may inadvertently stray from culturally accepted norms. I want you to know that I in no way wish to insult anyone. I'm just gathering information."

"I know that, my son. That's why I welcome you to attend the next roundtable," the pastor said.

"Have you ever unwelcomed anyone?"

"You're going to be a trial, aren't you, my son?" the pastor said. "Good night, and see you in church on Sunday."

"Good night, Pastor." When he got outside, Barbara, Brad and Jack were waiting for him.

"Awesome, dude!" Jack said. "I can't believe you said 'fuck' in church and in front of the pastor. That was awesome!"

Frowning at Jack's comment, Brad said, "Jesus, you've got to be more careful."

"I know, I know. The pastor made it clear to me to consider other people's feelings," Jesus said, as they walked towards the bike rack.

"I can't believe you even think of such things," Barbara said, looking at him with a bit of awe.

"I'm a scientist at heart. What can I say," Jesus said, his pride showing.

As Jesus unlocked his bike, Brad asked, "Are we on for yoga Monday?"

"And maybe a ride afterwards?" Jesus said, grinning.

"Definitely," Brad said.

"I'll see you at work tomorrow, Jesus," Barbara said.

"Okay."

Jesus and Jack rode home together. He kept chuckling and shaking his head. When they arrived, he said, "Wow! That roundtable almost made up for missing out on sex tonight. This calls for a massive doob. Want to join me?"

"Why are you so excited about me saying 'fuck' at church?" Jesus asked.

"I love seeing 'the man' brought down a peg."

"The man?"

"You know, 'the man.' Authority figures. Cops, pastors, the IRS, the M-A-N."

"What have you got against authority figures?"

"They're always telling people what to do, how to live, where to take a dump. I hate that."

"Isn't that their job? It's not like you have to obey, you know."

"Awww, I don't want to talk about this anymore. Let's get wasted."

"No thanks. I've got a morning shift tomorrow. I'm getting online to do some research and then going to bed early."

"Suit yourself. I'm imbibing and playing a video game."

Jesus got online and looked up how to deal with anger. There were fifteen to twenty different ways to deal with it, some of which they had covered at the roundtable. It was evident that it would require practice. He still felt some irritation at Jack and he wanted to work that out as quickly as possible.

The next day at work, the store was abuzz about what Jesus had said at the roundtable. As he walked through the store to the front-end office, his coworkers stared at him.

"I heard there was a little excitement last night," Clara said.

"There was?"

"You have an interesting perspective on things."

"Oh. I like to study the human condition."

"Would you like to become a cashier?"

"Really?" Jesus said, thinking that bagging would be his only job during his time there. He quickly mulled it over and decided it would give him a better opportunity to speak to customers. "Yes, I would like to become a cashier."

"Wonderful! I'll start you training tomorrow. Oh and also, when you complete your training you'll get a raise."

Jesus smiled and said okay. Clara excused herself and left. Barging into the office, Wanda said, "What's wrong with you? You can't be swearing in church! How would it look if Jesus went to hell?" She started laughing and slapping her thigh.

"If my Father and I were playing hide-and-seek...it would be one helluva hiding place."

"You got that right, sinner," she said with a chuckle. "Just be careful."

"Careful?"

"Yes, careful. We need all the good people we can get on this planet and I want you, Jesus, to be on our side," she said.

"Oh, I am." As she started to walk out the door, Jesus asked, "Hey Wanda. How come you, a religious person, don't have a problem with my name?"

"Everything happens for a reason, baby, everything happens for a reason," she said, her voice trailing off as she shut the door.

Jesus's emotions stayed fairly balanced over the next few days, until he allowed the unsettling, intense scrutiny of Barbara to bring him back down. He did his best not to provoke any conversation with her.

Jack wasn't doing well. His "friends with benefits" situation ended with a denial of service. Three nights in a row, Jesus arrived home to a haze of pot smoke and Jack repeatedly yelling at his video game, "Die, you pile of crap, die!" He was not happy and Jesus did his best to avoid him, too.

Monday was yoga and he was looking forward to it. His body had improved every day since the last class. He didn't know what he liked better—stretching his sore muscles or the focus on breathing. The teacher brought up practicing yoga at home. Jesus hadn't considered that, but it made sense. She said that it would increase one's peace, and that sounded right to him.

Martha was there and she stopped to talk afterwards. "I thought you were going to be at class last week," Brad said.

"Yes, but I had a last-minute client. He was going through something very difficult."

"Ah, physical pain?" Jesus asked.

"No. Emotional pain."

"You heal emotional pain? I thought you were a masseuse and acupuncturist," Jesus said.

"I am. But the mind and the emotions are the essence of what the body experiences. What we think and what we feel manifest in our bodies."

"Interesting. So, you could help someone who has issues with anger?"

"Most definitely. In several ways, actually."

"I just might have to schedule a session with you," Jesus said.

She reached into her backpack, pulled out a card and handed it to him. "Here's my number. Call me anytime," Martha said, smiling and walking away.

Brad looked after her for a moment or two. "Brad?" Jesus asked.

"What? Oh, ready to ride?"

"Let's pound those pedals," Jesus said.

It was a cloudy day and there wasn't much wind to impede them. They took turns leading and then falling back. Jesus's shifting had improved and it made climbing and descending hills much easier and faster. Brad led them into a quaint neighborhood, where he dove into the corners as close as possible to the curb and then accelerated out of them. Jesus followed suit and it was great fun, until he caught a pedal on the pavement and went down.

Brad heard the crash and circled back. He dropped his bike on the curb and asked Jesus if he was okay.

"No, I'm not okay," he said, face down. His elbows and knees felt like they were on fire.

"Roll over onto your back," Brad said, grimacing when he saw Jesus's face. His nose had scraped the pavement.

"Is anything broken?"

"I don't think so," Jesus said, slowly sitting up. He looked at his elbows which had tiny rocks embedded in them. They were both bleeding, and it was the same for his knees, too. A welling of emotion began bubbling up inside him. Without warning, a loud honk came from behind them, startling them both. Jesus leapt to his feet swaying, and looked around. He stared at the driver for several moments and the driver honked again.

Jesus walked unsteadily over to the car and yelled, "What?"

"Get out of the road!" the driver said, with his window rolled up.

"Hey! I just had a bike wreck! Cut me some slack!"

The driver responded by honking again. Jesus had read the phrase "seeing red" and assumed it was just a colorful description, but he now understood that it was an extreme physical reaction to anger. Seeing red and nothing else, he screamed, "You motherfucker!" and started pounding on the car window. The driver extended his middle finger and honked again. Jesus kept yelling and then got creative. With his bloody elbow, he started writing "fuck you" on the car window. When his right elbow ran out of blood, he continued writing with his left elbow, until the driver honked again and floored it.

Brad dove out of the way, grabbing Jesus's bike at the last second.

"Sonuvabitch! Sonuvabitch!" Jesus screamed. His heart pounded and he was sweating profusely. Wobbling slightly, he felt woozy.

"Come on. Come on over to the curb here and sit down," Brad said, guiding him. "Breathe deep. Close your eyes. Relax. Hey, there are insane people on this planet."

"Apparently, I'm one of them."

"The guy's a dick. He'll get his, I'm sure," Brad said.

Jesus looked at his elbows and knees. "I think I'm running out of skin. That may not be a good thing."

Laughing, Brad said, "Relax, you'll heal. If it makes you feel any better, I've probably put elbow to pavement at least fifteen times."

"Really? Actually, that does make me feel better."

"Let's just sit here, rest, and catch our breath. Then we'll ride home and get you some first aid."

They sat there for several minutes, just breathing. Jesus had calmed down quite a bit when Brad said chuckling, "Well, now I know why you're so interested in emotions."

Jesus frowned at him and stuck out his tongue. Brad laughed and asked, "Why did you keep calling him a hero? Are you sure you want to encourage him to procreate?"

Jesus doubled over, laughing. "He certainly doesn't deserve his own special day."

A car stopped in front of them, honking. It was the same driver as earlier and he was flipping them off. He pulled away, looking over his shoulder and continuing his finger salute—until he ran into a parked car.

Brad and Jesus glanced at each other. "That's a fairly quick turnaround on karma," Brad said, standing.

"What are you doing?" asked Jesus, as Brad walked over to the car.

"I'm going to see if he needs help."

"Really?"

Brad nodded yes and continued over to the car. Jesus couldn't help admiring Brad for his actions and at the same time wondered if he could ever be capable of the same.

Just before Brad arrived at the car, the driver jumped out and yelled, "Get away from me! This is all your fault!"

Holding up both hands and walking backwards slowly, Brad said, "I was checking to see if you're okay."

"Sure you were," the driver said, as he walked to the front of his car to check the damage. "Ha, my headlight isn't even broken." He turned to get back into his car.

"Wait. Aren't you going to leave contact information?"

Menacingly, the man approached Brad and growled, "If you say anything, I'll make your life miserable."

"Too late," Brad said, smiling.

The man stopped in his tracks for a moment. "Fuck you," he said, getting in his car and speeding off.

Brad peered at the man's car as he drove away then walked up to the door of the house where the damaged car was parked.

A woman came to the door and they talked briefly before walking out to the car and inspecting it. She went inside and returned with pen and paper. Brad wrote something down and handed it back to her. They shook hands and Brad sauntered back over to Jesus.

"What happened?"

"I gave her his license plate number and my phone number," Brad said.

"Aren't you afraid that man will make your life miserable?"

"It was the right thing to do. Come on, let's get you home and get you fixed up."

60

The ride to Brad's apartment was tedious and painful. Jesus's body stiffened quickly and several trails of blood had reached his socks. When they arrived, Brad brought both bikes inside. His apartment was much nicer than Jack's. It was tidy and didn't smell at all.

"Sit here," said Brad, pointing to a stool. It sort of reminded Jesus of home, but it had four legs. "Let me get the supplies." Brad returned with gauze, tape, ointment, a washcloth and some pills. "Take a couple of these arnica pills. They'll help with the swelling and bruising," he said.

Jesus took a couple and handed the bottle back to him.

"Nope. Keep them and take them per the instructions."

"Thanks."

"If you get on top of this, you can be back on your bike in a couple of days."

"I'm not sure I want to do that."

"Hey. When you fall off the horse the best thing to do is get right back on and ride again."

"Hmm, what do horses have to do with—owww! That hurts!"

"Sorrryyy. I've got to get the gravel out. Let me use the tweezers. Also, you should definitely get some work from Martha, when the swelling goes down."

"Okay—owww!"

"Hold on, I'm almost done with the painful part. There. Let's get you bandaged-up now."

Brad taped gauze to Jesus's knees and elbows and applied ointment to his nose. He loaded Jesus's bike onto the top of his car and drove him home.

After bringing his bike inside, Brad said, "I'm going to call Martha and see when she can take you."

"Thank you."

"Take a couple of aspirin before you go to bed and you'll sleep better."

"Okay."

As he left, Brad said, "And pray that Martha is available to fix you up."

Jesus sat on the couch feeling each beat of his pulse as his body throbbed. Looking at his bike with hatred, he said out loud, "This is all your fault."

Going to the bathroom, every step was painful. As he returned to the couch, it occurred to him that praying might be a good idea. They didn't really pray on Gooberia, but since they did on Earth, he thought he would give it a try.

He couldn't get down on his knees because they were too tender, so sitting, he said, "Lord, please help me through this. I don't know why it happened, but I do know that I'm miserable right now. Please, make sure Martha is available and oh, help me deal with the emotions I'm feeling. Do I really have to feel this bad? Bless you, Lord, and amen."

He sat there a while in silence and then fell asleep.

"Pause," the fussy judge said. "That's enough testimony for today. Put him in the hole and we'll resume tomorrow morning."

Chapter 8 – Suicide

On Gooberia, "the hole" is a hole—six feet by six feet by six feet. There's no chance for escape. A Goobers' arms aren't strong enough to right themselves if they fall over, much less dig themselves out overnight. Prisoners are lowered into their dirt cell using a winch.

"Bring in the accused," said the fussy judge, banging his gavel. Jesus meandered to the bottom of the courtroom. He appeared serene and composed.

"I have a question before you continue your testimony," the fussy judge said.

"Yes, Your Honor?"

"You mentioned in yesterday's testimony that you prayed. To whom were you praying?"

"I beg your pardon?"

"Were you praying to Goob or their God?"

"What difference does it make?"

"It makes a big difference to me," said the fussy judge.

"It does? To be frank, I guess I was praying to their...our God."

Shaking his head, the fussy judge said, "Continue your story."

"Thank you, Your Honor."

Jesus struggled out of bed the next morning. Any movement that involved bending his knees or elbows evoked pain. He walked to work at a slower-than-usual pace and arrived late.

"There you are! My goodness, what happened to you?" Clara asked.

"Sorry I'm late. My bike and I had a falling-out yesterday...er, a falling-*down* to be precise. I'm moving slowly."

"Understandable. Are you up for this?"

"Oh, yeah, sure," he said, mustering as much bravado as he could, still oozing from half a dozen wounds.

Clara stood there studying him. Jesus responded by inhaling, standing as straight as he could and thrusting out his chest.

Sighing, she said, "Yeah, right, very convincing."

He exhaled, slumped and sat down. "I can do it, I swear."

"Well, I don't have much choice now, do I? I've got to get you trained as fast as possible. Let's get started," she said, handing him a binder. "Read the first section and then we'll have you verify your till and get on a register."

Jesus frowned, as the binder was rather thick. Clara responded, "Cashiering in and of itself isn't that difficult, but you're handling the company's money and that requires some dotting of i's and crossing of t's. I want you to take this home tonight and read through it. Be sure to sign this and return it to me," she said, pointing to a waiver.

"Okay." He read through the first section quickly. After a brief quiz, Jesus counted his till and they walked out to his register.

"George will be training you today."

"Hey," George said. "Let me lock my drawer up and we'll get started."

"Good luck," said Clara.

George returned, trudging back to the register. He didn't look any happier than the first time they met.

"Is everything okay?" Jesus asked.

"What do you mean?"

"You just look sad, that's all."

"I'm fine. Here's the trainee sign. Put it at the end of the counter." Jesus tried to engage in small talk, but George resisted any attempt at conversation.

The shift went smoothly until a customer, who apparently didn't see the trainee sign at the end of the counter, got agitated at Jesus's cautious, slow scanning. He wasn't doing anything wrong; some of the items had curved bar codes and were difficult to scan.

It was as if each beep from the scanner made the customer angrier. It was made even worse when the customer challenged a price. When George asked him if he was sure about the price he had seen on the shelf tag, the man exploded, "I'm right, I'm right, of course I'm right! I spend a lot of money here and I've never been treated this way before!"

Confused, Jesus asked, "You've never been through a price check before?"

"Don't you talk back to me!"

"I was just trying to understand why you feel mistreated," Jesus said.

"You tried to cheat me!"

George reassured him that they just wanted to solve the problem, and Jesus chimed in, "That's right, for a customer like you, who spends a lot of money here, we're just trying to be accurate."

"You condescending bastard!" the man said. "You wanna fight?"

With wide eyes, Jesus asked, "You mean like a duel?"

"What?"

"Are we talking fists?" Jesus asked. He had read all about boxing and he was curious to try it out.

The man began to stammer. Leaning over the counter and lowering his voice, Jesus said, "Hey, I had a bike wreck yesterday and I hurt all over. Would you be able to wait till next week, say Thursday? I could give you a much better effort by then."

The man quickly left, abandoning his groceries.

"That was weird," said Jesus. "He seemed like he wanted me to get angry."

A voice nearby said, "That's because anger attracts anger and love attracts love."

Jesus looked up. "Hey, Martha. How are you?"

"Outstanding, I am," she said. "Interesting transaction you had there."

"First day cashiering, too. Makes me wonder what the second day will be like," Jesus said.

Martha looked him over. "You look, you look...well, you look like hell. Can I give you a hug?"

"Please don't be too enthusiastic."

They hugged. "I heard you might could use some work," she said.

"Yeah, I guess so."

"Are you asking for my help?"

"Yes. Let's make it official. I'm asking for your help. When are you available?"

"Let's see...considering your condition, how about we squeeze you in tomorrow at noon?" she suggested.

"I can make that."

"Good," she said, writing her address on the back of her business card and handing it to him. Jesus rang up her items and she waved as she left.

In the meantime, George had put back the angry customer's items and they completed the shift without incident. Jesus tallied his cash and it was only off a few pennies. George congratulated him in a distracted, weary kind of way. Concerned about him, Jesus said, "Have a nice night, or even better—may each moment be better than the last."

As George left the office, he looked back and weakly said, "Thank you. You too," and shut the door.

Patsy, the head cashier, confirmed Jesus's concern. "He does seem kinda depressed, don't he?"

Neither of them had a clue as to what to do.

The next day, Jesus arrived at Martha's bungalow after a difficult night of sleep. Opening the door and hugging him, Martha said, "Welcome Jesus! I just love saying your name."

"Careful, I'm still sore."

"Okay, okay. I'll be careful. Get ready and I'll be right back."

There was a chair in the corner. Jesus sat down and took off his shoes. The room was small and neat with a massage table in the middle. Pictures from the Far East covered the walls. A large illustrated poster of the acupuncture points figured prominently. Middle Eastern music played on her computer. It felt peaceful.

Returning, Martha asked, "Why aren't you undressed?"

"Uh, uh..."

"Wait. You've never had a massage before? Jesus shook his head. "I just figured that with your name you would really be into, you know, the healing community."

"Nope."

"Okay, then. Get undressed and lie face-up on the table. Put this towel over your groin and I'll be right back."

Jesus did as she said and shortly she returned. "So, I take it you've never had acupuncture either?"

"Correct."

"Okay, the first thing I'm going to do is read your pulses," she said, placing her fingers on his right wrist. She stood there staring off into space for a minute and then went to the other side of the table and repeated the procedure on the left wrist.

Looking him in the eye, Martha said, "You must have led a very interesting life up until now."

"You have no idea."

"I'll bet I will soon," she smiled.

Alarmed, Jesus thought, *What is she going to find out from this procedure?*

Holding a small, thin, steel needle, she explained, "Acupuncture is the process of inserting needles like this at certain points in the body to balance the chi or prana. When someone goes through what you've been through, your energy can get out of balance."

"After what I've been through, I would surmise that my bicycle is out of balance," Jesus said. "Is it going to bleed? I've bled enough recently."

She laughed, "Well, I can't comment on your bicycle, and you might or might not bleed. Now, I want you to inhale and then as I insert the needle, exhale quickly."

They went through this process about twenty times. Most of the insertions didn't hurt at all, some hurt a little and one or two hurt a lot. He yelped after one and asked, "What the hell was that?"

"Liver point. Do you drink or do drugs?"

"If you mean alcohol, no."

"Do you smoke a lot of pot?"

"No, none."

"Huh. An agitated liver meridian would normally mean a poor diet, or alcohol or drug abuse. Are you angry a lot?"

"Define 'a lot.'"

"Ahhh, so that's it. You're having trouble dealing with your emotions. Join the group. Fortunately for you, young man, we can get you back in balance," she said.

"Balance does seem to be a problem of mine recently."

Martha laughed. "Yes, I see that now. The bandages were a dead giveaway."

"Let me ask you a question."

"Sure."

"How do I deal with my anger? I don't like it. I don't like it at all. It changes my behavior! I've acted in ways I've never conceived of before and done things that must have looked absolutely insane to an observer."

"Can you give me a ferinstance?"

Jesus told her about the bike wreck and his behavior afterwards. Martha seemed amused. "Nice! Way to fully express your feelings! That's downright bold. I'm impressed. Seriously."

Jesus frowned. "Great. You're crazier than I am."

"No. Well...possibly. In any event, expressing your feelings is an absolute must otherwise," she bent over so they were face to face and lightly touched his nose with her index finger, "the emotion builds up inside and comes out as something else...like a bike wreck. What was bothering you before the wreck?"

"Ohhh, several things. One that had bothered me from the beginning is my roommate, Jack. He said some stuff that irritated me, about the money I owed him...like I could get it any faster. I had to get my documentation to be able to access my..." Jesus said, his voice trailing off.

"Beginning of what?"

"Uh, since I arrived here."

"Arrived from where?"

Jesus told her he wasn't quite sure and related his amnesia cover story to her.

"That's a very interesting, very convenient story," Martha said, "Very interesting, indeed."

Feeling nervous, Jesus thought, *There isn't any way she can figure out anything about me from this procedure, is there?*

After twenty minutes, Martha removed the needles. "Roll over and we'll start with the deep tissue bodywork. Is there anywhere other than the bandages that I should be careful?" she asked.

"You know, my neck has been bothering me ever since my first night here."

"Uh-huh, first night here."

Her skepticism was easier to ignore after she started the massage. He couldn't believe how good it felt. The constant touch of her warm hands and the kneading of his sore muscles combined to relax him. He focused intently on each part of his body she worked on. It felt marvelous, and when she rubbed on a sore spot, it was a good pain. After about forty-five minutes, she patted him playfully. "Get up, sleepyhead."

Jesus cautiously made his way up to a sitting position, feeling a little light-headed. Martha handed him a glass of water. "How do you feel?"

"Somewhere out there, a boundary exists between crisis and healing. I just crossed over to the healing side."

"Good. How's your anger level?"

"Definitely reduced."

"Marvelous," she said. "Would you like some advice on how to further reduce it?"

"Sure."

"The key is balance. Being human," she paused, looking at him intensely, "is a juggling act. You have ten bodies you're dealing with and all of them are interacting with each other."

"Ten? I'm having enough trouble with just this one."

Martha laughed. "That's true for most people, and that's because they're trying to deal with the one they see, the physical. The general perception is that the mental body is for figuring things out and the emotional body is most often a nuisance. Another way to look at it is that the mental body is for listening and the emotional body is the map of your issues. Working on those will improve your relationship with God."

Jesus tried to digest all of this, but his mind wanted to calculate something, anything. Finally, he said, "That's three bodies. What are the other seven?"

"There's the pranic body; that's what we worked on today with the acupuncture. Prana is one form of spiritual energy necessary to maintain your physical body. There's the auric body, subtle body and others."

"How do I acquire prana?"

"A variety of ways. Breathing, meditation, yoga and food are all ways of bringing prana into the body. Right now, to maintain your body, you just need to remember a few things like drinking plenty of water, exercising, meditating on a daily basis, and remember always...the other person is really you. That could keep you busy for years."

Staring at her for a moment, Jesus said, "I don't understand that last one."

"Projection. Projecting one's thoughts, feelings and issues onto someone else. Look it up on the Internet, spacey boy, I've got another session."

"Yeah, yeah," Jesus said, his head swimming with all of this new information. He got dressed, thanked her, paid and left. On the walk home, he kept going over what Martha had said. This could be the information and techniques he needed to finish his mission. He must do some research on this. For the moment, it was enough that his next bike ride to the store was comfortable, enjoyable, and fairly pain-free.

Over the next few days, the cashier training continued. His patter with the customers had improved and Clara had noticed. She promised that she would bring up his probation vote at the next department meeting. The thought of joining a community, even one you get paid to be in, satisfied him at the deepest level. He wondered if joining the church would produce the same result.

He had a routine now—work, eat, do some research, make a status report, watch TV. But, every day on this planet, no matter how good he felt during the day, fear and loneliness crept in as he sat alone at night. He tried to ignore it. Maybe joining these communities would help.

On Friday before work, Jesus visited the pastor. He asked how things were going and Jesus told him of the past ten days.

"Why are you here, my son?" asked the pastor.

"I want to join the church."

"Splendid!"

"So, what do I need to do to qualify?"

"Qualify? I hadn't heard church membership quite put that way."

"Well you know, the gauntlet of paddles, blood sacrifice, tattoos, whatever it takes."

The pastor stared at him, unamused. "Hazing isn't a requirement to join the church."

"I read that there is usually some kind of initiation or ritual defining the moment and the intent when joining a community or an organization. What do you do here?"

"I think I remember that you haven't you been baptized. Correct?"

"Correct."

"Well then, once a month we have a service for new members to get baptized, if necessary, and then profess their faith and alignment with the beliefs of this church and take communion. The Tuesday before the new members ceremony, we have a one-hour class to prepare you. It just so happens that the class is next Tuesday."

"Excuse my ignorance, Pastor, but what is a baptism?"

"It is a sacrament of the church and removes the guilt and effects of Original Sin."

"How does it work?"

"I sprinkle holy water on your head."

"I see. Should I bring a washcloth and some shampoo?"

Frowning, the pastor said, "No. Very little water is used."

"Okay. Thank you, Pastor. I'll attend the new members class to get prepared," Jesus said.

On Monday, he saw Alice at yoga and told her he was joining the church. "Big whoop," she said.

"What?"

"Yeah, I'm not a big fan of churches. Remember? I'm an atheist."

"Why don't you believe in God?"

"It was the way I was raised plus some experiences I don't want to talk about. I think churches in general do more harm than good."

"So, I shouldn't join the church?"

"I didn't say that. This church does quite a few good things for the community, but you're wasting your time believing in God."

"Wasting my time? I disagree."

"So, you believe in an almighty deity that allows such pain and suffering and evil to flourish? How could a loving God allow that? Answer me that!" she demanded.

"Yes, I do."

"How? How could you think that? Isn't it much more likely that mentally and emotionally stunted mammals that only think of themselves cause all the pain and suffering? Why would a loving God allow us to do that to each other?"

"Yes and no," Jesus said, "but to answer your question about a loving God, maybe to understand that requires a paradigm shift on your part."

"A paradigm shift?"

"Yes. From my studying, I've learned that if $A + B = C$ and you know A and C are true and accurate, then you need to examine your assumptions about B."

"Explain."

"If A equals a loving God and C equals pain and suffering then what does B equal?"

"I don't know."

"In your paradigm, there is no conceivable B, and it's not possible for A to equal C, so therefore there is no God. For most people on this planet, since they don't know what B really is, they explain it as 'God being mysterious' or that 'God is vengeful.' In my paradigm, God isn't mysterious or vengeful."

"So, what's your B then?"

"From what I've learned so far, everyone on this planet must find their own B. And I'm starting to think that if you find the true B it actually cancels out C and leaves only A. Even though I'm pretty sure this is true, I haven't found mine...yet."

"Huh, interesting. I like talking to you about this stuff. You don't seem very judgmental."

"What would be the point?"

"Exactly. Hey, when can you start working at the soup kitchen?"

"How about next week?"

"Wednesday and Friday lunch shifts?"

"That should work," Jesus said, heading for the exit. "Oh, and you're welcome to come witness my baptism and communion on Sunday."

Laughing, Alice said, "No thanks!"

By the time Sunday came, Jesus was nervous and not really aware of it until Jack pointed out that he had left some tags on his new clothes.

"Quit fidgeting," said Jack. "I can't figure out how to tie this facing you. Take it off and I'll tie it on me and give it back to you."

"What's the point of a tie anyway? Servitude?"

"That's as good a description as any. Here."

Jesus put the tie on and went to look in the mirror.

"It may be uncomfortable as hell, but you look good," Jack said.

"I think I'd rather be initiated the way people were in the historical Jesus's day."

"How'd they do it back then?"

"Naked. They were naked when they were baptized."

"You really like showing off that handsome penis of yours," Jack said, laughing.

Jesus chuckled. "Thanks, I needed that. It means a lot to me that my friends are attending."

"Sure," Jack said, smiling. "Come on, let's go."

They arrived at the church to find Brad and Barbara waiting for them. They took their seats and Brad asked if Jesus was nervous.

"Yes."

"Just picture yourself naked," Jack said.

"What?" Brad asked.

"I'll tell you later," Jack said as the service began.

The baptism and communion went smoothly, though several times Jesus thought he would start laughing at the thought of being naked in front of the congregation. The pastor mistook Jesus's grin as joy. After the service, he and his friends lined up outside to thank the pastor.

Shaking Jesus's hand, the pastor said, "It was a pleasure to see someone filled with the Holy Spirit when being baptized. Usually people are so nervous. I've even had one throw up before."

"Thank you, Pastor. It's a genuine pleasure to be a part of this community. Thank you again."

69

As they walked to their cars, Brad asked, "Hey, are we on for a ride tomorrow?"

"Yup, I'm ready. Between yoga and a session with Martha, this body feels pretty good right now."

"How about meeting me at my place at one?" Brad asked.

"I'll be there," said Jesus, loosening and taking off his tie.

"Don't take it off. You look so handsome in it," Barbara said.

"Thank you."

"Come on, you goober, let's get home," Jack said.

"Bye," Barbara said.

Jesus turned and gave her a little wave as he got into Jack's car. "You know, I think she has a crush on you," Jack said.

"I had surmised that and I don't want to talk about it," said Jesus. He had been on the planet for two months now. He was sure that he could avoid the issue for the remaining ten months.

That night he couldn't get Barbara out of his mind, and struggled to fall asleep only for her to show up in his dreams. Awakening with a start, he tossed and turned before falling asleep again, followed by another dream featuring her.

Jesus woke up the next morning in a foul mood. He spent the morning doing research before starting the ride to Brad's place.

He zigzagged through a small business district when out of the corner of his eye he noticed something fall off the top of a nearby building. Getting closer, he saw a crowd gathering. Riding by, he could see that the object was a person, lying in a pool of blood. It felt like a two-by-four hit him in the chest.

When he arrived at Brad's, Jesus told him what he had seen. "Ew! That's terrible. Do you still feel like riding?"

"No, but maybe it'll clear my head."

It didn't. He had this weird feeling all day and couldn't shake it. The thought of someone committing suicide frightened him. He began to wonder if his own emotional issues became severe, that he might consider the same.

The next day at work, there was a buzz in the air. "Did you hear?" Clara asked, as soon as he walked in.

"Hear what?"

"George committed suicide yesterday."

"He...he didn't jump off a building, did he?"

"Oh, so you heard. Very sad. Very, very sad. The funeral is Saturday at 11 a.m." Shattered, Jesus sat down trembling. After a few moments, he stood up, got his till and headed to his register. A couple of hours later, Jesus called Clara over as she passed by.

"Clara, I need to go to that funeral, but I'm scheduled to work at that time."

"Were you friends with George?"

"No, not really. Yesterday though, as I was riding over to Brad's place, I saw someone fall. It must have been him, and I rode right past him lying on the sidewalk."

"Really? Oh, Jesus," she said and paused. "Both of you, that is. That must have been awful. Of course we'll find someone to take your shift or at the very least, cover for you while you're at the funeral."

There was a long pause. Jesus didn't know what else to say. He felt sad and guilty. He had seen something was wrong with George, but had made little effort to help. He didn't know how to deal with these emotions, but at least he knew what he was feeling.

Word quickly spread among the team that Jesus had seen George commit suicide, and everyone wanted to stop and talk about it. They seemed to be having as much difficulty dealing with it as he was.

Chapter 9 – Exhausted

Proud that he had been voted onto the front-end department, Jesus tried to focus on his mission, but thoughts of George kept creeping in. Someone at the store had learned that he had left a note—he couldn't take it anymore and he thought that death had to be better than living with the sadness and loneliness he felt. Jesus could see that it had upset everybody in the store, and he reflected on his own situation. Emotions were troubling— he wasn't sure if he could handle them. It amazed him that people didn't commit suicide more often. A more disturbing possibility arose in his mind—that everyone had suicide thoughts at one time or another. *What if I can't manage? What if suicide looks like an answer?*

His stress was intensifying, but Jesus had to complete his mission. It was his duty to do everything he could do to stay emotionally balanced. He was beginning to comprehend why people spent so much effort to distract themselves. Feeling pain, regret, guilt, sadness and loneliness could be dispiriting.

Jesus hoped his first shift at the soup kitchen would offer distraction from these thoughts, but it didn't. Working on the dishwashing detail with Burt and chatting about the weather, Burt abruptly changed the subject to George's suicide. "Did you hear about that guy who went splat on Monday?"

"Yes, I worked with him at Grains for Brains," Jesus said.

"Really? I'm sorry. Were there any signs?"

"He seemed unhappy the past couple of weeks. I asked him at one point if he was okay."

"Feeling guilty that you didn't do more?"

"Yes," said Jesus, glad that someone understood. "Yes I am."

"That's normal. I do know this—he's going to hell."

Walking up to the sink, Alice asked, "Who?"

"George," Jesus said.

"George Bush?" she asked.

"No—well, maybe. The George that I worked with at the store," Jesus said.

"Why would he be going to hell?" asked Alice.

"He committed suicide and that's an affront to God and his Ten Commandments. 'Thou shalt not kill'," he said. Jesus was sure Burt was trying to tweak Alice.

"Heaven and hell are just myths to keep people behaving correctly," she replied, making air quotes with her fingers. "We start training kids early with Santa Claus and his list of who's naughty or nice."

"Even with your beliefs, wouldn't committing suicide be giving up? Passing up the opportunity at life?" Burt asked.

"Yeah, maybe," Alice conceded.

Jesus interrupted, "But consider this: What if there is such a thing as reincarnation? I know this probably doesn't fit your beliefs, Burt, but throughout the Universe nothing is wasted. Everything is recycled. Why wouldn't souls be reincarnated? I mean, how many people have learned everything there is to learn in one lifetime? Is it possible that suicide and atheism are some of the things we must experience here at 'Earth University'? I don't think it's possible to understand what another person is going through. In the end, I'll leave judgment up to God, not a human interpretation of the Bible."

"Interesting," Alice said.

"And besides, if there is a God—which I do believe in—and He is omnipotent and omniscient, which is generally accepted by those who believe, then wouldn't He already know that the person is going to commit suicide? I mean it's not like God is going to be surprised. Right?"

"Yeah. I would have to agree we really don't surprise God by our behavior," Burt nodded.

"Exactly, otherwise He wouldn't have given Moses a whopping 613 commandments. He knew we'd make mistakes," said Jesus.

Alice seemed mesmerized. Finally, she said, "If you'll wipe down those tables, you can take off."

"Thanks for giving me this opportunity," Jesus said. She nodded and smiled. As he rode home, he realized service to others put him in a good mood.

Jack, however, was not in a good mood; he was sitting on the couch with a cloud of smoke around his head.

"Wow, I thought for a moment I needed to call the fire department," Jesus said.

"Ha ha."

"What's got you so upset?"

"George."

"Ah yes, George. May he reincarnate into a happier life. You and George were friends?"

"We were smoking buddies. He was a really good guy. I'm going to miss him," Jack said, getting up off the couch and going to his room.

Jesus observed the same cycle of emotion at work; small talk for a while, then somebody would bring up George. They would commiserate for a moment, then turn inward to deal with their own feelings—until they were ready to talk about it again. By the time the funeral came around on Saturday, Jesus recognized that everybody was eager to wish George well on his journey and return to their own pursuit of happiness, or probably more accurately, distraction from their pain.

Jack picked Jesus up at the store, bringing a change of clothes for him. They met Brad at the funeral home entrance. As they took their seats, Brad whispered, "No questions during the service."

Jesus whispered, "Yeah, I get it. I'll be a saint. I swear."

"Hey, I've heard you swear and you ain't no saint," Brad said. Jack shushed them loudly.

Jesus found the service pleasant. Several people got up and said nice things about George. One of them mentioned something about not seeing the signs of his depression, which affected Jesus immediately. He'd finally been able to squelch the feelings of guilt about not making more effort to help George, but they came flooding back now. Walking back to the car, Jack asked, "Did you see the signs?"

"I noticed he was unhappy and asked him if he was okay," Jesus said.

"I saw it, too," Brad said.

"It's too bad. Maybe we could have done something about it," Jack sighed.

That felt like a punch in the stomach to Jesus. He wished he could go for a ride and clear his head, but he had to go back to work.

Jack dropped him off at the store. As soon as he walked in, Barbara turned around and looked at him. She immediately walked up and put her arm around his waist and her head against his shoulder. His typical reticence dissipated and he responded by putting his arm around her and giving her a little squeeze. She returned to her register, saying nothing. Jesus went to the restroom to change, all the while thinking how much he appreciated her support.

The rest of the shift was pretty much a blur, as Jesus was lost in thought the entire time. Just as he was about to leave, Barbara came up and handed him her number. "If you need to talk, about anything, give me a call."

"I just might do that," he replied.

Sunday morning, Jesus skipped church. He thought a couple of times about calling Barbara but he didn't feel like talking, and spent the rest of the day watching TV before leaving for work.

Monday came and yoga helped settle him down. He had been experiencing a repeated cycle of thought...could he have done more, followed by yes, followed by feelings of guilt. The meditation at the end of class seemed to alleviate that, and he was looking forward to riding with Brad.

After class, Martha greeted Jesus. "How's the balance?"

Rolling his eyes, he said, "About the same, but different."

"Different how?"

Taking a deep breath, he said, "Same level of emotional upheaval, different reason."

"You think it's a different reason, but is it really?"

Jesus went on to explain the events of the past week. Martha was sympathetic, but closed the conversation with, "I want you to think about what I said. Is it really a different reason that you're feeling unbalanced?" He furrowed his brow and Martha chuckled. She left as Brad approached.

It felt good getting on the bike. Brad suggested they try a different and somewhat longer route. Jesus agreed and let him take the lead. They headed out of town. It was one of those Texas days where if you're in your car, you turn on the heater in the morning and the air conditioner in the afternoon. They cycled along, picking up speed going downhill and climbing steadily uphill. The cadence of the ride relaxed Jesus as he listened to the sound of his bike chain sync up with his breathing. Brad slowed down to talk with Jesus.

"So, what were you talking about with Martha?"

"She was checking in with me and asked me about my balance—or lack thereof. I thought I was feeling unbalanced because of the situation with Jack, and George's suicide. Her assertion is that I'm feeling unbalanced for a completely different reason."

"Really?"

"Yeah, and it's bugging me that I haven't figured it out yet."

Laughing, Brad said, "So, thinking about being unbalanced is unbalancing in and of itself?"

Jesus laughed, too. "Quite probably. But she may be on to something."

"Car coming," Brad said, accelerating out in front of him.

Slowing down again, Brad asked, "So, why do you think she might be right?"

"Well, she could be wrong, or the reason for this feeling of discomfort could be something that I have yet to identify. What I'm beginning to think, though, is that my discomfort could be due to my perceptions and beliefs rather than any specific experiences."

"You're making my head hurt."

"Fine, fine," Jesus said, sprinting out in front of him.

They eventually headed back towards town. Rhythmically, like a cicada call, the thought *How am I looking at this wrong?* buzzed through his mind. He decided that it was time to try prayer again. Aloud, he prayed, "Lord, I need an answer. I need an answer to the question 'How am I looking at this wrong'?"

At that moment, Jesus saw the drainage grate. Before he could swerve, he rode over it, his front wheel got stuck and over the handlebars he went, Superman style. He just barely got his hands out to avoid landing on his face, but badly scraped his elbows and left knee. He got to his feet and yelled, "Crap...I tore the scabs off my elbows! Oww! Sonuvabastard!"

Brad heard Jesus yell and turned around. "Yikes! That looks like it hurts."

"Sonuvabastard, sonuvabastard, son of a bas-turd!" Jesus yelled.

"Sonuvabastard?"

"Yeah," Jesus said, sitting down on the curb. "'Sonuvabitch' seemed derogatory towards women. Now I'm being derogatory towards all people whose parents were unmarried," he said, cradling both elbows and getting blood all over his t-shirt.

"Didn't you see me point out the grate?"

"Nooo, I did not," Jesus said, with more than a little irritation in his voice.

"Hey, don't get angry with me. I held up my end."

"Sorry, I'm frustrated."

"Weren't you paying attention?"

"Apparently not," Jesus said, through gritted teeth.

"Dude, there are dangers everywhere when you're on your bike," Brad said, sitting down next to Jesus. "You've got to stay focused."

Glaring at him, Jesus said sarcastically, "Oh, really."

"All right, I'll stop with the speeches for now. Do you want some water?"

"Yes, please."

Brad stood, yanked Jesus's bike out of the grate and grabbed a water bottle. "Your bike looks okay," he said, handing him the water.

"Of course it is. The bike is always fine."

They sat in silence for about ten minutes. Finally Brad said, "Are you working today?"

"No."

Standing, Brad said, "Good. It'll give you a chance to rest and heal. I, however, have to work, so let's get going."

Jesus groaned into a standing position, feeling very angry at crashing again. They got on their bikes and rode to his apartment. "Do you want me to bandage you?" Brad asked.

"No thanks. I could use the practice," Jesus grumbled.

"All right then. See you at work tomorrow."

"Okay," Jesus said, dragging his bike inside.

He heard explosions as soon as he walked through the door. Jack was playing his video game and smoking pot. Looking up, he said, "Ow! Not again?"

"Yeah, again."

"Come on over and take a load off," Jack said, patting the couch.

"Let me get some first aid first."

Jesus went to the bathroom, cleaned his wounds, patched up his elbows and knees the best he could and joined Jack on the couch with a grimace.

"You look like hell," he said, putting the game on pause.

"I'm exhausted—physically, mentally and emotionally."

Jack leaned over, picked up his pot pipe, lit it, and took a long drag. He offered it to Jesus. "You wanna hit?" he asked, while trying not to exhale.

"Yes," Jesus said, taking the pipe. "Anything to put me out of my misery."

He inhaled. The next few minutes consisted of coughing, watering eyes and some sneezes. He tried to hand the pipe back, but Jack wouldn't accept it. "Everybody coughs their brains out the first time. Take another hit and see if you can hold it in your lungs longer."

Jesus tried again and coughed, but not as intensely.

"Take another hit. We're gonna get you stoned."

He tried once more and this time he didn't cough. He started to say something, but his brain began to go numb. He sat there for a few minutes, watching Jack play the game. "Take one more hit. That should get you toasted."

Jesus did and sank back into the couch. His brain was now completely numb and he closed his eyes. That didn't last very long because dizziness set in. He sat forward and realized that he wasn't focused on his pain. He felt it; he just didn't care.

"You feeling it yet?"

"Yup, I'm feeling it."

"Wanna play?" Jack said, gesturing at the TV.

"Sure. What are we playing?"

"Call of Doody. You shoot people and turn them into various forms of excrement and then you shoot those. Since you're a newbie, we'll start at the easiest level."

"How many levels are there?"

"Three—Toilet Training, Regular, and Shitstorm. We'll start with Toilet Training," Jack said.

It was fun and distracting. After a while, they got hungry and ordered some pizzas. Jesus couldn't believe how good they tasted. They smoked some more afterwards and then listened to music. The pot seemed to accentuate all his senses. It was a distraction enhancer, he concluded.

"It's good to have a smoking buddy," Jack said, as he turned the game back on.

"So, this is basically what you do with your free time?"

"Yup. Smoke, play games, listen to some tunes, try to get laid, repeat."

"Not a lot of time for self-improvement with that schedule."

"I'm not into the career thing. I just want to enjoy myself."

"Well, I mean, self-improvement doesn't have to be about career. There's personal self-improvement, too."

"Hey, you're harshing my buzz, man," Jack said, turning a character in the game into a bubbling pool of diarrhea.

"Sorry, I can't help myself. Being a scientist, I'm always examining stuff, trying to improve things."

"A scientist?"

"Not a laboratory scientist. A scientist studying the human condition."

"A sociologist?"

"Yes, that's it. I view myself as a sociologist."

"Well, this guy has a social problem. I just turned him into a turd!" Jack said, laughing.

"You know, I have an urge to use a bidet after playing this game," Jesus said, standing and walking to his bedroom.

"Where you going?"

"I've got to get some sleep. Good night."

It was a dreamless night and Jesus woke up angry. He had to work the morning shift and he didn't feel up to it. He went to the kitchen where Jack was eating a bowl of cereal.

"So? How do you feel?"

"Crappy. And angry. And crappy. I thought pot was supposed to make you feel better."

"It does, while you're doing it."

"Well, I'm just as angry as yesterday," Jesus said, coughing. "I don't want to go to work today."

"Call in sick then."

"Eh, I don't want to let anybody down. I'm taking a shower," Jesus said, marching into the bathroom. The water felt good and he mellowed a little.

He made breakfast and since it was getting late, instead of walking he rode his bike to work...slowly and carefully.

He barely got there on time. After verifying his cash drawer, he headed out to the register. Barbara asked, "Are those fresh bandages? Did you wreck again?"

"Yes," Jesus said tersely.

"Okay, I won't ask any more about it."

"Thank you."

Feeling sorry for himself, he compared cashiering to one of the twelve labors of Hercules. Every time he picked up an item, his sprained wrist would complain. His knees and elbows were slightly swollen, and standing in one spot wasn't helping that. He didn't know if it was the customers or him, but tempers seemed short. One customer in particular commented on how slow he was and mumbled something disparaging about how he probably wasn't smart enough to be a cashier.

"Excuse me!" Jesus said. "What did you just say?"

The customer's eyes bugged out. She seemed surprised either that he heard her or was able to comprehend her meaning. "Nothing," she said.

"Lady, I'm going slower because of a bike wreck yesterday. I'm in pain. As for your comment about my intelligence, I've gotta ask myself, 'What would Jesus do?'" he said, pointing at his button. "I'll tell you what I'm going to do. I'm going to the office so I don't do or say something I regret." Turning to Barbara, he asked, "Would you please finish the transaction with this...customer, please?"

Barbara hurried over. Jesus thanked her and marched to the office slamming the door behind him.

"Aaarrgghhhh!" he yelled. "Please Lord, remove this anger." He tried some deep breathing from yoga class. It took ten minutes or so to begin relaxing. Embarrassment set in as he walked back onto the sales floor.

"Are you okay?" asked Barbara.

"Yes. I let her get under my skin. I should know better."

"None of us are perfect."

"Obviously." Catching himself, he said, "Sorry, sorry. I'm not in a good mood."

"That's okay. Let's see if you can get off early today," she said sympathetically, calling for the head cashier on the intercom.

Nodding, a wave of gratitude engulfed him. He rang up a few more customers and then was told to count his money and head home. He called Martha and scheduled a session with her.

He didn't have any obligations until the next afternoon, so he spent the rest of the day stoned and playing video games. When he woke up the next morning, he felt guilty. Watching TV, he rested until it was time to go to the soup kitchen.

Alice greeted him with, "What happened to you? Are you up for working at the steam table today?"

"Bike wreck, and yes," Jesus said. He got an apron and Alice handed him a hair net. "What's this for?"

"So your hair won't get in the food."

"Are we denying these people protein?"

Laughing, Alice said, "No. What do you do when you find a hair in your food?"

"I eat it. It's over 90 percent protein."

"You're so weird," Alice said, shaking her head and walking away.

It was hot working over the steam table. Person after person came through and Jesus smiled at each and every one of them. Few smiled back and almost no one said anything except what they wanted. Some even seemed embarrassed to be there. It was gratifying to help, yet sad at the same time.

He finished up his shift and went home. Jack was smoking away and, of course, offered him some.

"No thanks."

"Why not?"

"You know, it doesn't seem to solve anything. It just postpones the inevitable," Jesus said.

Blinking his eyes several times, Jack asked, "The inevitable?"

"Yeah, the inevitable. Inevitably, one must feel their emotions or they won't heal or dissipate...or whatever they do. I smoked twice over the last couple of days and today I'm just as angry and sad and guilty as I was before I smoked."

"Who wants to feel bad?"

"It's not a matter of want. If you don't deal with them, they build and grow into future problems."

"Whatever. You're not going to guilt me into quitting."

"I'm not trying to guilt you into anything. I'm trying to deal with my negative emotions and pot simply doesn't help. I'm sure alcohol is the same, too."

Jack ignored him and focused on his game. Jesus went over to the computer to prepare for the next night's roundtable.

The following morning, he felt better emotionally and less like he would explode at any second. His body felt a little better too, and he was looking forward to work.

Clara was in the office when he arrived. She asked if he was feeling better. "Yeah, I'm a little less stiff."

"And a little less angry?"

"Yes. You heard about that?"

"Of course I did. Logbook, remember?" she said, picking it up.

Jesus felt a little sheepish and it must have showed because she said, "You did the right thing leaving the registers. All of us get angry. Customers can be trying at times. Some of them don't treat us as equals or even like people. You showed great restraint in coming back to the office to vent, albeit a little too loud," she said, smiling.

Laughing, Jesus said, "Aarrgh," in a whisper.

"Better," Clara chuckled.

Barbara, Brad and Pete were all working the day shift and it was fun. Jesus was beginning to warm to Barbara. She noticed, but didn't fawn over him like she had initially. She asked him if he was going to go to the roundtable that night.

"Definitely. I've already got a list of things I want to talk about."

"Of course you do," Brad said.

"Pete, you ought to come along, too," Jesus said.

"It might be worth it just to hear you swear in church, but I think I'll pass," he said.

That night, Jesus got to the church a little early. Ralph and Juan were there. Jesus shook their hands and sat down. An elderly lady walked in and he went over to introduce himself.

"Hello, my name is Jesus."

"Beg your pardon?"

"My name is Jesus. Your name is?"

"Gertrude. Nice to meet you, Jesus," she said with a smile.

"Thank you. It's nice to meet you, too."

"What an unusual name," she said.

Jesus shook his head, "Well, I wouldn't have thought so, but apparently it is."

"Indeed. Maybe the world would be a nicer place if more men were named Jesus."

The pastor entered, followed by Brad and Barbara. Alice came in last and they began with the pastor's question, "Does anyone have a topic?"

Gertrude asked, "Why is everybody looking at Jesus?"

There were a few giggles around the room as he said, "I, uh, brought up a few controversial topics at the last roundtable."

"Oooh, I want to hear about that," she replied.

The pastor interrupted, "You can ask Hey-Zeus about that after we're finished."

As Gertrude gave the pastor an odd look, Jesus said, "Well, I do have a topic...hunger."

"Okay. Begin," said the pastor.

"Pastor, I think it's tremendous that this church runs a soup kitchen, but I can't figure out why humanity allows one in seven people to go hungry."

"There are a lot of impoverished countries out there that aren't as advanced as America and they suffer a lot," Ralph said.

"Actually Ralph, that number applies to America, too," said Alice.

A murmur went around the room. "The only explanation that makes sense to me is that humanity is still exhibiting animal pack behavior. You know, letting the weak and old die off," Jesus said.

"That's not entirely true, my son. There are plenty of examples of charity to help the disadvantaged," the pastor argued.

"I understand that's true, but it's not as widespread as it could be. It's not like the resources aren't available. They are. It seems very un-Christ-like to let people go hungry," Jesus said.

"Amen, brother!" said Gertrude, standing and slapping her hand on the table. "Pastor, I want to volunteer for the soup kitchen."

Chuckling, the pastor said, "All right Gertrude, talk with Alice about volunteering. She handles the schedule among other things."

"You know one in seven people worldwide amounts to a billion people. Who's going to pay for all that?" Juan asked.

"Cut out military spending, or at least reduce it," Jesus said.

"Yeah, right," said Ralph. "How can we do that when everybody is trying to bring our country down?"

"Everybody? I don't buy that at all," Jesus said. "A few groups around the world are angry at the United States. Is that a reason to spend 41 percent of the world's combined defense expenditures of $1.6 trillion dollars? Are we that fearful?"

"You've got to protect American interests," Ralph protested.

"Isn't one of America's interests that her citizens are fed? Isn't one of America's interests peace? Isn't that important to everybody? Can you promote peace and arm yourself simultaneously? Not according to Einstein," Jesus said.

"Are you sure you're being realistic?" Barbara asked.

It surprised Jesus that Barbara would ask such a question. "Realistic?"

"Yes, realistic. We do have to protect ourselves," she said.

"You don't believe in turning the other cheek? Does that not apply to governments?" Jesus asked.

"It doesn't apply in the real world," said Juan.

"What doesn't?" asked the pastor.

"You know, turning the other cheek, all that Jesus stuff. It doesn't work," Juan said.

Silence indicated that more than one of them felt the same way.

"If you ask me, that attitude is what prevents it from working for you. Have you practiced it, or are you afraid to?" Jesus asked.

Juan blinked several times. Stammering, he finally said quietly, "I'm afraid."

"Join the group. We're all afraid. Have you been successful at practicing this, Jesus?" Brad asked slyly.

"Good God, no. But I have set my intention to do so," Jesus said.

Laughing, Brad said, "Good save."

"Good save?" Barbara asked.

Brad told the story of Jesus's first bike accident and the angry driver and the table got a chuckle out of it.

"Yeah, I know. What right do I have to talk about non-violence after that? That's my point. After we eff up, we have a choice whether or not to change. When it comes to hunger, humanity has a choice whether or not someone dies of hunger every four seconds. It's all about choices and beliefs. For example, humanity has a choice when it comes to defending its make-believe boundaries: like a bunch of pack animals, or following the guidance of one of its greatest prophets," Jesus said.

"What do you mean 'make-believe boundaries'?" Ralph asked.

"They're not real. They're in our heads. Look, God is real, humanity is real, Earth is real. Countries, boundaries and money are all decisions. They're not real. You can't see the borders of the United States from space," Jesus said. "It wouldn't surprise me if Arizona ordered the National Guard to line up and whiz to mark their border."

Everybody laughed and then sat in silence for a while. Finally, Juan spoke up, "I still don't believe it's realistic to behave that way."

Brad said, "I have doubts at times, too. It does seem to be an ideal, but is it worth our lives, to live up to that ideal that God has set forth for us?"

Smiling, Jesus said, "It amazes me how many people are willing to die for their country...if they're allowed to kill someone else. However, they're unwilling to stand up for what's right through an act of non-violence as set forth by one of God's prophets. Not only are they willing to die for their country, they're willing to break the commandment 'Thou shalt not kill.' I mean, it's pretty straightforward. Children understand this." Jesus shook his head.

"I'm glad it is so clear to you, Hey-Zeus, but some of us still struggle with the simple things in life," the pastor said.

"So, I should show a little compassion then?" Jesus asked.

The pastor smiled and nodded yes.

"With the name of Jesus, you'd think that would come easier for me," he grimaced.

Frowning, the pastor brought the discussion to a close. Everyone filed out silently and made their way outside.

"You really have a knack for picking a topic," Brad said.

"Yeah, I'm going to go home and watch something on TV where I don't have to think...like *Jeopardy*," Barbara said.

Jesus took his time riding home in the cool night air thinking about what he had said during the roundtable. He wasn't gathering information or finding out how people feel as much as telling them what he found illogical about their culture and species. Why would he feel a need to tell them what he thought? He was here to gather information. *Maybe I'm beginning to identify with them a little too much.*

The next day, he rode to Martha's office. His body was slowly healing and he was looking forward to this session. Martha greeted him enthusiastically and squeezed him a little too hard for his shoulder. "Ow!"

"Sorry," she said. "Get naked and jump on the table face-up and we'll get started. I'll be right back."

By the time she returned, he felt fairly centered and relaxed. She busied herself reading his pulses and making noises every few seconds.

"So?"

"Interesting. Let me see your tongue. The underside, too. Anything I need to know about?" she asked, pulling out her needles.

"Right shoulder, right hip."

"How's the anger level?"

"High," Jesus said, relating the incident at the store.

"All right. That's a pretty good way to handle that. What was it specifically that triggered the anger?"

"Oh, I don't know. I don't really want to talk about it."

"If you want to be less angry, which I know that you do, getting to the root of the reaction that produced or triggered the anger would be beneficial," she said, moving her face within a couple of inches of his.

"You're irritating me."

"Okay, okay, we're all friends here," she said, getting out of his face and smiling.

Inserting a few more needles, she said, "You're doing great. You're letting that anger and energy move through you. Are you familiar with the chakras?"

"The what? Shark-ass? Is that an herb or a mineral?"

She doubled over laughing and stuck herself with the needle she was holding, "Ow, ow, ow."

"You know I just read about this thing called karma," Jesus said, enjoying her pain.

"Oh yeah, your mama," she said, feigning anger.

"I'm glad you could feel some of my pain...and not vicariously," Jesus said, hitching his eyebrows up.

"That's it. Feel the anger! What do you want to do right now?"

"I want to take a couple of those needles and pin your lips shut," he said, smiling through gritted teeth.

"Marvelous! I'm standing here and I can physically feel your pulsating anger. The more you let out, the emptier your emotional cup will be and the better you'll feel," she said.

Jesus snarled and barked at her. Laughing, she said, "Down boy! Hey," her voice getting quieter, "there are ways to alleviate your anger before it gets unmanageable."

He peered at her skeptically. "No, really. I swear," she claimed.

Jesus took a deep breath and closed his eyes. Any initial pain he felt when the needles were inserted was gone and he felt a surging sensation throughout his body.

Seeing him grin, Martha said, "Grooving on the energy, eh? Feels mighty nice, don't it?"

Jesus grinned even bigger and nodded yes.

"Okay, keep your eyes closed and just listen. You can, on your own, practice something that will help drain your emotional cup," she said.

"Balledherass!"

She let out a deep, throaty laugh. "No, no. It's balderdash."

"Oh. You know, that doesn't make any more sense."

She continued, "Anyway, it's called 'tapping.' Basically, you tap along your meridians and shark-ass."

Ignoring her mocking, he asked, "And what does that do?"

"It moves negative emotions out of the body."

"Really?" Jesus said, opening his eyes.

"Absolutely, and you can use it to work on more deep-seated issues, too. Though I don't really detect many of those in you," she said, giving him a funny look.

Jesus shut his eyes and imagined what life would be like on Earth without having to constantly deal with negative emotions. Would it be heaven or would it get boring? What would happen if he didn't have this constant challenge?

"Okay, one more thing I want to impart to you. There are no accidents. They're caused by your mental and emotional states. The key to becoming happier is learning to recognize what you're feeling or thinking, in the moment. You go back and evaluate your experiences according to what you're thinking and feeling at the time of the experience. Then you work to improve these states. That's the cycle. It is a lifetime or lifetimes process and God is there to help you in every moment."

"Wow, can you write that down? Are there any websites about tapping?"

"Yes, there are. I'll give you a list of my favorites before you leave."

Jesus closed his eyes again and imagined feeling better. He was willing to try anything to complete his mission.

Martha pulled the last of the needles out and had him flip over on the table. The deep tissue massage was magnificent. There was nothing on Gooberia that felt this good. After finishing, she suggested that he come back in a couple of weeks. He looked forward to it.

Chapter 10 – Jesus exposes himself

To Jesus's surprise, he saw Martha before their next session at the store. She asked how he was doing.

"I'm doing better. Thanks for asking."

"How's the emotional cup?"

"It's still fairly full, but it hasn't intruded since I last saw you."

"Are you doing any yoga and meditation?"

"In class, yes. At home, no."

"You might find it very helpful. Bringing prana or spiritual energy in, and practicing focusing the mind will definitely help with emotions. Did you look up those websites I gave you?"

"Yes, but I haven't put them into practice yet, though I have been paying attention to my thoughts."

"That's a good start. Keep it up. See you soon."

The rest of the shift, he contemplated how he could get yoga and meditation in every day. His days were full of work, the soup kitchen, church, bike rides, yoga class, studying humanity on the Internet and TV, and the nightly status reports. With difficultly, he tried to prioritize his activities. His mission was important, but so was his happiness. It seemed that without happiness, the mission could be in jeopardy and yet, it seemed self-centered. What was necessary, and how was he going to get it done?

His relationship with Barbara continued to grow. They worked together at least three times a week and he saw her every Sunday at church. More and more, he found himself having thoughts of her even when they weren't together. It felt like they were becoming friends.

Brad and Jesus rode almost daily. His speed and endurance while bike riding had improved and he could keep up with Brad now. He hadn't wrecked in over two weeks. They were riding through a busy neighborhood one day and had to pause at a stop sign. A car pulled up next to them with the passenger-side window rolled down. The passenger said, "Hey, get off the road, sissy pants."

"What?" Jesus said, aware of some anger.

"You heard me, sissy pants."

"Ignore him," Brad said.

"You heard him. I'm going to ignore you."

The passenger said to the driver, "What a loser!" and turned back to Jesus. "Get off the road before we run you over!" As they high-fived, Jesus was shaking. A white-hot heat rose up his body to his head. Through the open window, Jesus leaned in and punched the passenger in the nose.

Blood gushed. The passenger yelped, "You broke my nose!" As he opened the car door and started to get out, Jesus kicked the door as hard as he could. A fragile crack sounded as the door hit the leg of the passenger. Bouncing back, the door knocked Jesus into Brad, and they both fell down. The car sped away.

Jesus got up trembling, barely breathing, his legs weak with too much adrenaline. He let out a roar. Brad jumped to his feet. He reached out and touched Jesus, who spun around and raised his fist.

"Hey, it's me!" Brad said.

"What?"

"It's me. Calm down!"

Jesus lowered his hands, grabbed his brake levers and snapped them repeatedly. He was having trouble focusing and he felt like he was going to pass out.

Snapping his fingers, Brad said, "Jesus! Calm down. Focus on your breathing." Eventually, he started breathing deeper and deeper. Finally his shoulders relaxed, and he raised his head and looked at Brad.

"That's better. Dude, you can't let morons like that get to you. Sticks and stones, man. Sticks and stones," Brad said.

"What?"

"'Sticks and stones may break my bones, but names will never hurt me.' You've never heard that before?"

"No."

Shaking his head, Brad said, "Let's get going."

They returned to Jesus's apartment. Brad said goodbye and rode out of sight. Feeling ashamed, Jesus dragged his bike inside and sat down, head in hands. *I can't believe I behaved like that. I'm a scientist and I'm here on this planet to study this race of beings. I'm supposed to do that with dispassion. It doesn't make any difference if some of them are barely sentient. I'm better than that. What is happening to me?*

By now he was softly crying. *I don't know if I can do this anymore. Maybe George had it right. I'm failing in my mission and letting down my planet. I want to go find that guy and apologize.* Inhaling deeply, he realized this must be what overwhelming guilt feels like. *No wonder it's used so often to try to change the behavior of others,* he thought.

"Dear Lord," Jesus prayed aloud. "Please forgive me for my behavior today. Please help me understand why I am behaving this way. Please help me improve how I react to my emotions. Please help the man whom I wronged. Amen."

Exhaustion came and he fell asleep on the couch. He had a weird, disturbing dream. It took place in the time of the historical Jesus. In his Gooberian body, Jesus and the historical Jesus were being dragged up the hill of Golgotha to be crucified. The Romans tied historical Jesus to a cross and prepared to nail one of his hands in place. The centurion in charge interrupted, "You've got the wrong Jesus. This one's much worse," pointing to present-day Jesus.

The Romans tied him to the cross and the centurion in charge said, "Cut off that extra leg. He won't be needing that anymore." Jesus screamed as they severed his procreating leg. The centurion in charge laughed and said to nobody in particular, "A Roman circumcision." As Jesus bled, they nailed his right hand to the cross and he screamed again. Kneeling down in front of him, the historical Jesus said, "Forgive yourself," and he woke up.

The dream haunted him for several days and it was difficult to concentrate. Two days in a row, his till was off twenty dollars and Clara asked him about it. Before he had a chance to answer, Jack walked into the office and greeted him with, "If it isn't Jesus 'WWEFGH' da Vinci." Grabbing Jesus's right wrist and lifting it overhead, Jack exclaimed, "Winner and still champion, Jesus!"

Looking amused, Clara asked, "What's this all about?"

"He punched a moron in the nose for ragging on him," Jack said.

"Really?" Clara asked.

"Yes."

"That doesn't seem like you," she said.

"I don't know what's like me anymore," Jesus said dejectedly.

"We all screw up, dude," Jack said.

"Well, I don't," Jesus said angrily, walking out of the office.

A few minutes later he returned and apologized to Clara. "Don't worry, everybody gets upset now and then. I trust that you're working on it. Just keep that till accurate and who knows, you just might get a promotion in the near future," she said, twitching her eyebrows up and down suggestively.

"Yes, I am working on it and I will endeavor to improve my performance."

"Okay. Relax. Are you ready to work?"

"Yeah, yeah, I think so. Thanks for understanding," Jesus said, struggling to smile. He grabbed his cash drawer and went out to the registers.

The whole night was nothing but tales of violence inflicted, endured, or seen by the cashiers. Every story felt like a blow to his self-esteem. His coworkers weren't being malicious. They were trying to support him and show him that it happens to everybody, but he felt awful.

After work, Jack offered Jesus a hit from his pipe, but he refused.

"Why not?"

"It's not going to help me feel any better, Jack."

He gave Jesus a long stare and finally sighed, "Hey, sometimes feeling nothing is the best you can hope for." Jack went to his room and shut the door. That seemed sad to Jesus, but he derived some comfort from knowing at least he was making an effort to improve.

He sat at the computer to write his daily status report. Staring at the screen, he couldn't bring himself to start typing. After several minutes of wrestling with himself, he decided that shutting off his brain seemed the best course of action at the moment. The report could wait until tomorrow.

"Pause please," asked the curious judge. "Was this when you stopped making your daily status reports?"

"Yes, Your Honor."

"And you never made another one during your mission?"

"Correct, Your Honor."

"Why not?"

"I felt extreme guilt and was so ashamed of my behavior that I couldn't bring myself to report my actions to my project group."

"Why didn't you resume your reports later in the mission?"

"I felt like I needed to focus completely on the moment. It took monumental effort just to stay sane and keep up with my life that even writing about it seemed overwhelming."

"I see. Continue," said the curious judge.

The next day he rode his bike to the soup kitchen and hoped that working at the steam table would alleviate some of the guilt he was feeling.

Alice greeted him at the back door. "Hey Jesus, I think it would be a good thing if we all wore name tags. It'll help our patrons connect with us more, don't you think?"

Jesus nodded in agreement.

"I heard you punched somebody. It's good to know that you aren't as perfect as your name."

"Where did you hear that?"

"From Brad. I bet it felt good."

"No, it did not," said Jesus testily.

"Okay, okay. You're going to serve today," she said, walking away.

Serving didn't make him feel any better. These poor souls were so wounded; Jesus knew that giving them food would only temporarily relieve their condition. Person after person came up to his station—dirty, disheveled, some mumbling to themselves and few would look him in the eye.

Towards the end of his shift, one man walked up to his station and requested peas and carrots. Jesus didn't hit the tray quite right and some of the vegetables got on the man's meatloaf. Glaring at Jesus, he said, "You goober! You've messed up my tray! My food is touching!"

Slow to react and fighting anger, Jesus said, "I'm sorry."

"Sorry doesn't keep my food separate."

Jesus offered to get the man another tray, then filled it carefully and precisely. Carrying it around the steam table, he looked the man in the eye. Handing him the tray, he said again, "I'm sorry."

The man looked down at Jesus's name tag. He growled, "You ought to be crucified," and walked away.

Shattered, Jesus's brain went numb and his eyes watered. He made his way back into the kitchen and found Alice. Handing her his apron and hairnet, he said, "Here. I can't do this anymore today," and left.

He could hear her calling after him, "Jesus? Jesus, what's wrong?"

He cried on the way home. Walking in, he ignored Jack's alarmed "Dude, what's wrong?" and went straight to his room, shutting the door behind him. Knocking, Jack asked, "Is there anything I can do?"

"No."

Jesus rocked back and forth on the edge of his bed. *Nine months to go and it's getting worse. Getting worse!* He lay down on his bed and sobbed till he fell asleep.

He woke up ninety minutes later with his heart pounding and leapt to his feet. Grabbing a pen and paper, he began to write about the dream he just had.

A group of children were enjoying themselves on a playground. They looked so happy, and Jesus was standing off to the side watching them. A man giving off a glow from head to toe approached him and said hello.

"Hello."

"Rough day?"

"More than I can handle."

"You're not giving yourself enough credit."

"I don't need credit, I need peace. Peace of mind."

"Earth's an interesting place, isn't it?"

Jesus nodded in agreement.

"Let's sit over here and talk," the man said, motioning to a swing set.

They sat on the swings and rocked back and forth in silence for a while. Every few minutes, Jesus would look over at the man and he would be looking back with such a smile that the anger, guilt and sadness Jesus felt would subside a little.

Finally, the man asked, "You're on a mission, correct?"

"Yeah."

"Maybe it's not the one you think it is."

"What?"

"That's right. Maybe it's not the one you think it is. Every soul comes to this planet with a purpose and it varies widely from person to person."

"What's my purpose?"

Laughing a deep, hearty laugh, the man said, "Knowing that would take all the fun out of it."

"I'm not experiencing any fun."

"You'll have some fun soon, but that's not your purpose. Just know that you are loved and supported by God...or Goob...completely."

"Yeah, well, that's not really of comfort at the moment."

Smiling, the man said, "Maybe not right now, but it will be," and he faded from sight, the swing still rocking back and forth.

Jesus's hand cramped from writing so fast and intensely. Sitting back, he took a couple of deep breaths. He needed to relax more. He called Martha and they set a time for a session the following day. He planted himself on the couch in front of the television until he went to bed.

The next day, Jesus felt anxious all morning about his upcoming session with Martha. It didn't make sense, because he always felt better afterwards.

Given the previous two sessions with her, he expected Martha to give him an almost raucous greeting when he arrived. She didn't disappoint.

"Jesus! Whooooo!" she yelled, giving him a bear hug so hard he was sure he felt her liver.

Her exuberance irritated him. *What is she so excited about? My pain?*

"Hey! No fresh bandages. Congratulations!"

"Not externally."

"Oh really," she said slyly. "Do tell."

"So, you want to hear about my pain?"

"Yup. But first get undressed and get on the table. I'll be right back."

She returned shortly and sat in an office chair, rolled up to the table, put her elbows down, held her face with her hands and said with a big grin, "Tell me about this internal pain of yours."

She seems to be enjoying this too much, Jesus thought, but he took a deep breath and recounted the various things that had happened in the past week. He recited them in order—the punching, the crucifixion dream, the soup kitchen, the swing set dream.

"Wow! Wow, wow, wow! Anger and guilt, anger and guilt. You're definitely working some things out."

"I'm not working anything out."

"You don't feel guilty about punching that guy?"

"Well, yeah, but—"

"And you're having difficulty dealing with anger?" she asked.

"Yes, but—"

"And so far from what I've heard, these are fairly minor triggers."

"Minor? What do you mean minor?" he asked in an irritated tone.

"Well, this is stuff that you would normally work out as a kid or teenager."

"It's everything together."

"What 'everything'?" she asked, with a smirk.

Martha was getting on his nerves and she was punctuating her questions by inserting needles. "It just seems to be piling up. There's this Barbara thing. Ow!" he cried as she hit a painful point.

"What about Barbara?"

Jesus explained that Barbara seemed to want to be more than just friends. "Oh, that's heinous! A relationship with a woman! How awful! Oh, the humanity!" she said, mocking him.

"You don't understand!"

"Ohhh, the humanity!"

Something snapped inside of him. Pushing her away from the table, Jesus jumped to his feet, lunged at her and thrust a finger in her face. "You don't understand! Humanity is the problem. I'm doing the best I can and, and I want to finish my mission, but, but all these crazy... fucking emotions!" He was screaming by now and pacing back and forth naked, needles swaying every which way. "Where I come from it's either love or not-love, black or white. You people have more emotions than there are colors and how in the hell do you deal with that? There are so many distractions," he said, grasping his head. "Half the population are

90

medicating themselves so they won't feel and the other half are doing stupid stuff so they will feel. I can't have a relationship with Barbara. I'm a scientist. I'm not supposed to get involved. I'm just supposed to observe. And what if we had sex? I don't even know what species the offspring would be!"

Out of breath, Jesus saw Martha's eyes and her mouth was wide open. He realized he had gone too far and let out a yell that truly honored his frustration. Then everything went black.

"Jesus. Jesus, wake up," Martha said gently.

He opened his eyes. The ceiling seemed a lot farther away. Looking around, he realized he was on the floor. "What happened?"

"You passed out."

He tried to get up, but Martha pushed him back to the floor, "Relax, relax. Let's stay here for a moment," she said, coming into a cross-legged position. "I want you to close your eyes and take several deep breaths."

Her hand was still on his chest and her words felt soft and comforting. "Keep breathing deeply."

He sank into the floor, relaxing a little bit more with each breath. "Now, with your eyes still closed, focus on the Brow Point," she said, lightly touching his forehead.

"Okay," he murmured.

The next thing he heard was, "Jesus. Jesus, wake up."

"Did I pass out again?"

"No, you fell asleep. You relaxed quickly though. That's a good sign." Helping him to his feet, she said, "Get back on the table and I'll work some spots that will help you relax even further."

She began inserting needles again. "These points will not only help you relax, but will help your focus, too."

She sat back in her office chair, rolled up to the table and placed her hand on his chest and told him again to breathe deeply. "Close your eyes," she said. "Relax. Do you mind if I ask you a couple of questions?"

"Uh, no."

"So, just what species are you?"

Jesus tensed up immediately. "Relax," she said, taking an exaggerated breath for him to follow.

"What are you talking about?"

"Jesus, Jesus, Jesus," she said. "The cat's out of the bag. You're either insane, which I don't believe, or something else very interesting is going on. How can I help?"

She lightly slapped him on the chest and he realized he was holding his breath. "Jesus," she sang, "What's da buzz? Tell me what's a-happenin'. What's da buzz? Tell me what's a-happenin'."

"What's da buzz? What in the hell do you mean?"

"Sorry. I'm a fan of musicals." Then very slowly and deliberately she said, "Hey, I can help, and you can trust me."

"Look, you don't understand. This goes far beyond just me trusting you. Far, far beyond."

"I get it. I really do. You know," she said, sitting back in her chair, "humanity has been preparing for this the past sixty years or so."

"Fantasizing about something and then having the fantasy become real are two vastly different things. I'm not sure humanity can handle this."

"Maybe not all of humanity, but I can. Do I look freaked out to you?" she said, making all sorts of funny, distorted faces.

Jesus chuckled, "No. No you don't." He took a long, deep breath and looked her square in the eye. "All right then, here it is," he said, getting off the table, naked with needles still inserted. While he paced slowly back and forth, he told her about his planet, the discovery of the ancient sacred texts, the experiments, the space program, the transmogrification and his mission.

"Wow! I believe you."

"You do?"

"Yeah, I do. I've done a lot of acupuncture and read a lot of pulses in my day, but none of them were like yours. It's like the difference between a painting and reality. Your pulses had no depth and this explains why. You've only got ninety days in a human body."

Shaking his head, Jesus said, "Yeah, and I don't know if I can make it to the end."

"Oh sure you will. Can't you see God's hand in all this?"

"Goob. Goob's hand," he corrected.

"Goob, Goobers, I love it."

"I don't know what I see. This all seems so insane," he said, dropping his chin to his chest.

"Unimportant. Let's get you focused on your top priority right now—dealing with your emotions. Are you listening?"

"Yeah, I'm listening."

Martha grabbed both of his arms and shook him, "You can do this! You can do this! I swear! We just have to get you up to speed. It makes sense that you'd be having problems with your emotions since you've had no practice. It's like you're three years old. Actually, you're doing pretty good for a three-year-old. That must be because you have the mental body of an adult," she mused.

"Well, yeah. I have all my memories from my home planet."

"So, this transmogrification process left the mental body intact, but you came in with a new emotional body or maybe just an underdeveloped one. I would assume the rest of the human ten bodies are associated with your new physical body. Do you have karma on your planet?" Martha asked.

"You mean what goes around comes around?"

"A simple explanation, but yeah."

"Not really. Our civilization is so cautious it doesn't make sense that we would have karma. Things that have developed here on Earth took tens, hundreds, thousands of times longer on my planet. Why?"

Martha answered, "Working off your karma is part of the spiritual path on Earth. You have very little karma to work off and an advanced mental body. If you can learn to deal with your emotions, you might be able to move along your spiritual path quickly."

"Why is that important?"

"Think about it. If you can learn to deal with your emotions in the moment, work off your karma, do a couple of other things, you could become enlightened—the ultimate human experience."

Jesus stared at her uncomprehendingly for a few moments and then asked, "What other things?"

"Well, there's bringing more prana or chi into the body. That should be relatively easy since your body hasn't suffered a lifetime of abuse. You're already learning how to do that with Kundalini Yoga. Learning esoteric knowledge about how the world really works, you should have no problem picking that up easily. Lastly, enhancing your intuition to follow Divine Will or Divine Guidance. That takes practice, but it's definitely doable."

"Right now, not dying before the end of my mission would be the ultimate human experience."

Laughing, she said, "Understandable, but you have a unique opportunity here. Enlightenment is a lot more important than you think. It's the culmination of the process of growth for humans from animal to spiritual being. In the history of humanity, there have been probably less than a thousand beings that have made that leap. You've got a shot at doing it in nine months."

"Eh, I don't know. It almost seems like an insult to somebody, Goobers or humans, I don't know."

"Do you have something like enlightenment on your planet? Some ultimate spiritual goal?"

"No, we really don't have a next level of spirituality beyond the animal experience. Besides, we start off as plants," Jesus said, giving a simple explanation of the Goober birth process.

"Wow! From plant to animal to spiritual being in one lifetime. Holy Trinity, Batman! That's gotta be a first!"

"I'm not racing anybody. Boy, you humans sure are competitive."

Martha smiled. "Yeah, that we are. But look, the techniques I'm going to teach you will get you through your emotional upheavals, okay? Forget about the whole enlightenment thing. Let's get you centered and calm and then see what happens."

"I can get behind that."

Martha spent the rest of the session outlining a number of different spiritual practices for him to consider. "Remember, this process is interactive between you and the Universe. I can't stress that enough. And only one or two of these practices are absolutely necessary."

"Which ones?"

"Well, meditation for one. It's a must. Training the mind to be focused and still so you can hear God and Divine Guidance is the foundation of a spiritual practice."

"What's the other one?"

"Awareness. Awareness of your environment, what you think and what you emotionally feel. Some people call this spiritual vigilance," she said.

"How do I do that?"

"Meditate. The more you meditate, the more aware you become. The more aware you become, the more you see the clues that the Universe leaves for you to...meditate on. It is so completely wondrous and breathtaking, the adventure you've embarked on. It makes everything else look boring and insignificant."

"Okay, but I'm only doing this to be able to complete my mission."

"That's fine. But don't be surprised if your motivations change and well, frankly, everything you've thought is true, is not."

"Well that's comforting," Jesus said sarcastically.

Laughing, Martha slyly said, "Maybe not right now, but it will be."

Chapter 11 – Pissing off the pastor

Trying meditation the next day, Jesus's mind was all over the place. A thought would occur and he would invariably engage it and then add another conscious thought to it, followed by another and another until he had created a train wreck of thought. Examining these thoughts, he couldn't tell what was intuition and what was ego. Frustrated, he knew his only choice was to continue to practice even if there was no discernible improvement.

He had worked over ninety days at Grains for Brains and it was time for his review. Clara complimented him on his performance, and he was pleased that he was contributing his fair share. He stood up to leave, but she motioned for him to sit back down. "How would you like to move up to the next level?"

"What level? You mean head cashier?"

"Yes. It means more responsibility and more money."

His first reaction was to say no. There was no reason for him to do it and his mission didn't require it. Leadership and responsibility were interesting subjects, but not ones he was studying. But as he inhaled to respond, emanating from the center of his head, an unmistakable quiet, calm voice said, *Do it.*

Jesus had heard this voice before. Even when he wasn't focused on his thoughts as much as he was now, he had heard this voice. It was always right. Was this his intuition, the voice of God, or his inner teacher?

He held his breath as fear fought this new guidance. "Okay." Immediately, he relaxed. His decision didn't seem very scientific, but saying yes felt right.

"Excellent!" Clara said. "Let me work up a training schedule for next week. I'll put you with several different head cashiers. Okay?"

"Sounds good," Jesus said, standing up.

"Don't you want to know what your raise will be?"

"Don't I have to finish my training satisfactorily before I receive it?"

"Yes, of course."

"Then let's wait until I do."

"Fair enough," she said, "but whenever I'm due a raise I start dreaming about how I'm going to spend the money."

Jesus nodded and went out to the registers. Looking up, Barbara asked, "How did it go?"

Shrugging, Jesus said, "Well."

"Did she mention anything you need to improve on?"

Thinking about it a moment, he said, "Actually no, she didn't. She was almost flattering."

"Really? She doesn't treat me that way."

"Oh? Why?"

"My last review was almost all negative. In fact, I was put on probation. Thank God that's almost over. So, what else did she say?"

"Well, she offered me a promotion to head cashier."

"Seriously? You've been here a little more than three months and you're about to make head cashier, and I've been here two years and I'm barely holding on," she said, scowling and shaking her head.

"What can I say? I'm focused," Jesus said, wheeling around directly into a customer's cart. "Yeow!! Sonuva...female dog," he said, looking at the customer sheepishly.

"Oh, Jesus! Are you okay?" Barbara asked, half-giggling.

"I know, I know, I deserved that," he said, limping away. Spinning around, he said, "Hey, Barbara."

As she looked up Jesus stuck his tongue out at her. She laughed, furtively looked around to see if anyone was watching, and flipped him off. Chuckling, he went to clock in for his shift.

The rest of the day, his thoughts kept returning to money. What could he do with more money? He had plenty to do whatever he needed for the mission. Should he start considering what he wanted as well? Jesus didn't really know what he wanted, but to really experience humanity perhaps he should accumulate some possessions, beyond a bike and a computer. Maybe he should get a phone. He'd just need to be cautious so as not to become addicted. He didn't want to walk around with a glazed look and stooped shoulders—a malady afflicting many of the humans he had seen.

Barbara didn't help at all. She seemed to know what he was thinking. The second he refocused on the present, she would come over and ask what he was going to do with the extra money.

"You know, you could always get an apartment to yourself. Or, you could get a car," she said.

"Yeah, but why?"

"Cars can really come in handy. Vacations, shopping, family drives."

He frowned, "Great. Buy a possession so I can carry home more possessions that I buy. Seems insidious."

"No, no. It supports the economy."

"Maybe the economy needs a different foundation than consumption."

She looked at him as if he were crazy and walked back to her register. Since the next roundtable was coming up, he thought he would bring up the subject and get some feedback.

The next day at the soup kitchen, Jesus asked Alice what she thought about getting a car.

"Most people find it necessary, some don't. Are you thinking of getting one?"

"Yeah, I am."

"Why?"

"I don't know. Freedom?" he shrugged.

"In some ways yes, in some ways no. There's maintenance, insurance, and gas. With newfound freedom comes responsibility. Cars use up a lot of resources. Don't get one unless you really need it."

"Do you have a car?"

"Of course," she said, smiling and winking.

Rolling his eyes, Jesus said, "That's helpful."

"What's your reservation?"

"I've been reading online about sustainability. It's an intriguing subject and one that is about to get important very soon on this planet."

"On this planet?"

"Actually, on any planet. Every planet has finite resources."

She looked at him oddly. "What brought this up for you, other than the desire for a car?"

"I don't know. I guess I'm looking for balance in my life right now. I'm getting a raise and I've been thinking how to spend the extra money. I just don't want to fall into the consumption trap."

"I know what you mean. Filling the hole by buying things. I suppose that could be better than filling it with drugs and food."

Smiling, he said, "Just thinking things through."

"You don't know how rare that is," she said, walking away.

Talking with her felt good, but it didn't help much. As he watched hungry person after hungry person walk past his station, it occurred to him that possessions in and of themselves weren't a bad thing.

Where was the line though? When did possessions cross the threshold from necessary to extravagant? He wondered if, every once in a while, a little extravagance wasn't a bad thing. But how much comfort is one allowed? Was too much comfort lording it over others? Should he really be concerned, since he wouldn't be here that long? Contemplation yielded no answers.

At the church roundtable the next evening, Jesus announced, "I'm thinking about getting a car. Any thoughts?"

Everybody had an opinion—make, model, gas mileage, stereo system, rims, et cetera. Not one of them asked if he needed a car.

Waiting for them to finish, Jesus said, "Technically, I don't need a car."

"So? It's an American right to own a car," Ralph said.

"But what about the resources it uses to build and maintain? Not to mention how much it damages the environment, too," Jesus said.

"There are plenty of resources and the environment isn't that bad," argued Juan.

Everybody agreed, including the pastor. Jesus pressed, "Isn't acquiring something I don't need a form of greed, which would make it a sin?"

"It would depend on what you mean by 'need,' or what your needs are," said the pastor. "A car can serve many purposes beyond basic survival, like comfort and convenience."

"Okay, but it's not really that uncomfortable or inconvenient to buy necessities like food and carry them home on my bike," Jesus said.

"What if it rains?" Alice asked.

"Now, that would be applicable," Jesus said, nodding in agreement. "What if I wanted to get a better car than say, my roommate? You know, just to outdo him. To make myself feel superior."

"That wouldn't take much," laughed Brad.

"Heyyy!" Jack said.

"A girl would be embarrassed to get in that heap," Barbara said. There was a chuckle throughout the room.

Trying to deflect for Jack's sake, Jesus said, "So, to determine if I'm being greedy in my purchases, I need to look at purpose and motivation?"

"Those seem to be acceptable guidelines," the pastor said.

"I'll think about it some more then."

Gertrude brought up a new topic. "Did anyone vote in the primary?"

Most everyone said yes. Jesus couldn't let this opportunity pass. "From what I've read on the subject, it doesn't make much difference whether you vote or not. The political process is driven by money and the hunger for power...with occasionally a smidgeon of self-sacrifice and service."

"Not true, not true!" Ralph said emphatically. "Voting is the most important freedom we have!"

"Even before owning an assault rifle?" Alice quipped.

Several people snickered. Ignoring them, Ralph said, "This is serious. This is what America is about. We get to choose our leaders. Not everybody gets to do that."

"A sizeable majority of people in the world choose their own leaders, Ralph. But really, does the government affect you at all?" Jesus asked.

Scowling, Ralph said. "Well, of course, it does. It takes my money from me in taxes."

Nodding, Jesus said, "I know, and those taxes go up and down, but seriously, can you point to anything in your life where paying more taxes prevented you from say, going on vacation? Or stopped you from buying a new car? I think the only way the government affects the populace is when it's *giving out* money or starting a war."

Everyone thought about this for a moment before Jack spoke up, "What's your point?"

"The point is that the freedom of voting for your leaders is an illusion. You've got the Electoral College that dilutes your power. Indecent amounts of money are spent to mesmerize you to vote for a particular candidate. That Supreme Court decision to allow corporations to make donations allows them to donate money to further their own business interests, not what's best for you or the nation. Politicians lie to the public to get into office. They'll commit crimes to stay in office. They'll gerrymander to prevent a balance in representation. It's the powerful wielding their power. They don't want the people to have a say in their future; they wouldn't be able to feed off you. The United States is really an oligarchy."

"Well, that's a pretty dark assessment," said the pastor.

"Think it through. It's a farce, and the only way I see Americans taking back their power is if Congress overturns the Supreme Court decision...and that's not going to happen. A government by the people, for the people? I don't think so, not with non-human entities allowed to influence the process. You have to limit the power and greed of money as a basis of representation. Maybe an independent branch of government that runs elections. Maybe something like the Federal Reserve, only a lot more effective."

Brows furrowed around the table. Letting out an audible sigh, the pastor asked, "Is there anything else anyone wants to talk about?"

"We could talk about greed in religion. There's lots of material there," Jesus said.

"I beg your pardon," the pastor said.

"Yeah, Hey-Zeus, you may be going a little far there," Juan said.

"History is replete with examples of organized religion driven by power and greed."

"I think humanity and religion have advanced beyond that by now," the pastor said tersely.

"When did that happen? Take your religion, the Megalithics. Why, just recently—"

"Enough!" said the pastor, standing quickly, red-faced, and shoulders taut. "I will not have you bad-mouthing my religion...which by the way is your religion, too!"

"Really? You're censoring the subject? I'm just examining the issues of abuse of power and greed. Every institution on this world is infected with them to some degree."

"I will not have you questioning my beliefs, Hey-Zeus," the pastor said through gritted teeth.

"I wasn't. I'm just trying to figure out my own," Jesus said calmly.

"This meeting is adjourned," the pastor said, looking weary. After staring at Jesus for several seconds, he walked out of the room.

Nobody moved or said anything for several minutes. Then Gertrude asked, "What happened recently in the Megalithic Church?"

Jesus was just being the scientist he was. Feeling bad about upsetting the pastor, he didn't reply and got up and left.

"He went too far," said Ralph.

"Now, wait a second. If you're so interested in American freedoms then consider the freedom of speech. Why are we in this room if not to ask questions about things that concern us?" Brad asked.

"I've never seen the pastor act like that before," said Juan.

"Yeah. Jesus must have pushed a button. But what?" Alice asked.

Everybody shrugged and Barbara got up from the table. "Where are you going?" asked Jack.

"I'm going to go talk to Jesus."

She found him sitting on the steps at the side entrance. "Are you okay?"

"Yeah, sort of."

"You didn't do anything wrong."

"I know, but it wasn't my intention to upset him..." he said, falling silent.

They sat quietly for a while, then Barbara took his hand. Jesus looked into her eyes, smiled, and took a deep breath. Moments later, the rest of the roundtable filed out the door.

"Oooh," said Jack, smiling.

Jesus gave Jack a dirty look and let go of Barbara's hand. "Wait a few days and go talk to the pastor. I'm sure he'll forgive you," Brad said.

"For what?" Jesus asked.

"In his mind, you insulted him. I don't know why, but if you talk with him, you'll figure it out and patch things up."

"Maybe," Jesus replied. "I'll see you tomorrow." Riding his bike home, he wondered what his mistake had been. Had he been too insistent about his observations? Why had he missed the pastor becoming upset? The incident bothered him greatly.

The next day at work, Barbara was her usual concerned self. She asked several times if he was doing okay. Jesus felt conflicted about the handholding. On the one hand, it was comforting and it felt good. On the other hand, he felt uncomfortable with some of the roundtable group witnessing it. He wanted to forget about it, but Barbara wouldn't let it go and asked him why he let go of her hand.

"I don't know. Please, I don't want to talk about this right now. I need to concentrate on healing things with the pastor."

"Okay, but don't think I'm going to forget this," she said, sashaying away.

While waiting on his next customer, Jesus decided that he would try to speak to the pastor after church.

That Sunday, Jack offered to drive. Unfortunately, his car died just before reaching the church parking lot. On top of that, the church door slammed shut behind them and the whole congregation turned to see who was profaning God with this racket. Sheepishly, they took their seats in the last pew.

The sermon was about faith. The more the pastor talked, the more Jesus realized that he was talking about him, and that didn't feel good. He was sure that the pastor didn't fully understand what he was talking about at the roundtable. It made him all the more determined to talk to him after the service.

Afterwards, Brad asked, "What happened? Why were you guys late?"

Jack grumbled, "God didn't answer my prayer."

"You can't say that in here, Jack," Barbara said.

"Well I'm sorry, but he didn't. I prayed that we would make it to church on time and the car broke down. We had to push it about a hundred yards to the parking lot."

Brad broke out laughing. "Ah, the aroma of sweat."

"Maybe the pastor could say a little prayer over it," Barbara suggested.

"Wouldn't help. He could preside over a funeral though," Brad said.

Even Jesus laughed at that one. He was grateful for the kidding around. He wasn't looking forward to his conversation with the pastor and his dread increased as they filed out. The pastor shook Jack's, Brad's, and Barbara's hand with a two-handed handshake and a personal greeting. When it was Jesus's turn, he nodded and said, "Hey-Zeus," and walked over to another group of parishioners.

"Whoa! What a brush-off!" Jack exclaimed.

Frowning, Barbara said, "That seemed kinda rude."

"You might have to perform a miracle to get through to him," Brad said, shaking his head.

Jesus pursed his lips and sighed audibly. Breathing deeply to address his surging emotions, he sighed, "Maybe I'll have a chance to talk to him on Wednesday at the soup kitchen."

Chapter 12 – Jesus buys a sex van

Jesus's spiritual practice continued to evolve. His extraneous thoughts lessened and his breathing became less passive and more conscious. His increased awareness enabled him to pick up on more information from his surroundings. It felt like each day was longer, but not in a tedious way. Even his emotions felt more distinct and noticeable the moment they emerged. It had been several weeks since anger had gotten the best of him.

Still, he felt confused and he didn't like that. At heart, he was a scientist. He liked his ducks in a row and things tied neatly in a bow. Which was why his developing relationship with Barbara and the incident with the pastor bothered him so.

His discomfort must have been evident because one day, Pete asked, "Hey, what's that look on your face? Either you're constipated or somebody just kicked you in the groin."

"Both," Jesus said, smiling weakly.

Pete walked over and sat on the counter. "Tell Muslim Pete your woes."

Giving him a scornful look, Jesus said, "Under one condition...if you tell anybody about this you'll have to become a Methodist."

"A life of boredom and purgatory? You have my solemn oath," Pete said, raising his right hand.

Jesus told him about the handholding with Barbara and the pastor blowing up.

"Hmm, women and holy men. What's a guy to do?" Pete said.

"Yeah. Is this run-of-the-mill stuff?"

"Not really. Most people don't piss off their priest."

"Pastor," Jesus corrected.

"Pastor then. And what's the deal with Barbara? Do you like her?"

"Yeah, sure."

"Then what's holding you back? Go for it! Respectfully of course."

"It wouldn't be wise," Jesus said, walking away, leaving Pete perplexed.

Jesus hadn't taken three steps when Clara rounded the corner and called him into the office. She complimented him for his meticulous and accurate work as a head cashier. "So, I'm giving you a raise. Also, I've gotten permission to create a new position, Assistant Department Head, and you're one of the people I'm considering for the position."

Jesus was flattered, but for the rest of his shift, he kept thinking about the eventual return to his own planet. What kind of hole would he leave here when he returned? He realized his footprint was growing.

At the end of the shift, Jack asked Jesus if he wanted to go car shopping the next day. "You couldn't get your car fixed?" Jesus asked.

"The mechanic said it wasn't worth fixing. He offered $100 for it. I thought about it, but decided to place an ad on Gregslist. Did you decide whether or not you're buying a car?"

"Well, I've decided to decide, but that's as far as I've gotten."

"Maybe doing a little window shopping will help you with your decision."

"Maybe so. How will we get around? Are we going to ride our bikes to look at cars? Seems weird."

Mulling it over for a moment, Jack suggested Brad.

"That could work," Jesus said, noticing a small ripple of excitement spreading through his body. "Let's go ask him."

Brad agreed, and the next afternoon they all went to the first used car lot on their list. The dealer had some possibilities that caught Jack's eye. After several test drives, Jack settled on one he was satisfied with and began the ordeal of negotiating the price while Brad and Jesus perused the lot. Eventually, Jesus said, "Hey, what's that over there?"

Brad looked up to see Jesus trotting over to a van...with a mural of a bikini-clad woman superimposed over a mountain lake on the side. Jesus opened the driver's door and hopped in. Purple shag carpet covered everything, including the dashboard. The seats were covered with dark blue velour. Brad got in shaking his head, "This is unbelievable."

"Yeah! It's pretty fine, don't you think?" Jesus asked.

"No. No, I don't think," said Brad, shaking his head vigorously from side to side.

"What? It feels pretty comfortable."

"That's not the point."

"Enlighten me, then."

"This is a make-out van. You take women out and have sex in the back."

"Can't you do that in a car?"

"Well, yeah."

"Wouldn't this be more comfortable?"

"Yes," said Brad in a flat tone.

"Maybe we should test drive it. If this works out, we can get the gang together and go up to the lake. It'll be great!" Jesus said.

They got out of the van and were walking to the showroom when they saw Jack. Grinning from ear to ear, he feverishly told them what a great deal he had gotten. "With my down payment, my monthly payments will only be $120. I can totally afford that."

"That's great," said Brad. "Follow me. I want your opinion on what Jesus is looking at."

They zigzagged through the lot to get to the van. Jack glanced at Brad, then Jesus, then back at Brad. Pointing at the van, he began to laugh hysterically, "What, this? Seriously?" Brad cackled, too.

"What's wrong with it?" Jesus asked.

"Nothing at all, as long as you grow a mullet and get a wife-beater t-shirt and some cutoffs with the pockets hanging out," Jack said.

"Wait a second, let me write that down," Jesus said.

Brad playfully slapped Jesus on the back of the head. "Nooo, this is not for you. You're an adult, not a teenager. You're advancing at work.

You're about to get into a relationship. You need something more serious, more grown-up."

"I'm about to get in a relationship?" Jesus asked.

"Quit pretending. Everybody knows. Any time now, waves will be crashing on the beach," Jack said.

"If they haven't already," Brad added.

"We haven't even gone out on a date yet," said Jesus.

"And whose fault is that?" Jack asked.

"Look, it's complicated. All I know is that things have settled down for me some. I feel better, more confident, more comfortable in this skin, as it were. I think it's time to let loose, have some fun, live a little, maybe even live a lot. One never knows how long one will be on this planet."

"I was with you there until that last part. You say the oddest things," Jack said.

"Let's go talk to the salesman," Jesus said, marching off in the direction of the showroom. Brad and Jack exchanged glances as they followed Jesus. He found out the price and got some more information about the van. The salesman pulled out the paperwork and started filling it out. "I'm sorry, but before we get started I need to consult with my colleagues," Jesus said.

The three of them huddled in a corner of the showroom. "I think I'm going to do this, unless either of you can produce a reason otherwise," Jesus said.

His voice strained and gesturing wildly, Brad cried, "Nipples! The van has nipples painted on its side!"

"So what? They're covered up with the bikini top," said Jack.

"You're not helping," Brad said.

"I've really never understood the objection to the public viewing of the female areola. Seems rather nipplist to me," said Jesus.

"Nipplist? Really? You're not striking a blow for women's rights here," Brad said.

"He needs to loosen up, doesn't he Jack?"

"Amen to that, brother," Jack said.

"Time to negotiate. I've been studying up on this," Jesus said.

The three of them entered the office and sat. The salesman pulled out his pen with a flourish as if he were about to sign an historical document. "Alrighty then. Now, sir, have we agreed on the price you're going to pay?" the salesman asked.

"Aren't we supposed to haggle?"

"Do you have a counteroffer?"

"Yes I do. Zero."

"Zero? I don't understand, sir," the salesman said.

"Now you go, right? Then I come back with something a little closer. Isn't that the way this game is played?"

"Well, yes—but sir, the customer usually doesn't ask us to give him the car for free," the salesman said.

"Okay, let's try a different tack. How about you tell me the minimum amount you're willing to take for the van."

"Sir, that's for me to know and you to find out," the salesman said.

"That's not very helpful," Jesus said disappointedly. Brad leaned over and whispered a number to Jesus, who repeated the number to the salesman. The haggling began in earnest, and within ten minutes they had agreed on a price and Jesus had signed a contract to purchase the van.

"Yee-haw!" Jesus yelled, standing up to shake the salesman's hand.

Not quite knowing what to think, he replied, "And yee-haw to you, too, sir."

The three of them walked out to the lot and headed to their respective vehicles. It took them a moment, but they figured out how to get all three back home. Jack drove home in his new used car, and Brad followed with Jesus in the van. On the way, Brad mentioned that Jesus needed to immediately get some insurance before he learned how to drive, "if your driving is anything like your bike-riding...."

"That was a stability thing. Four tires are better than two wheels and one leg on a slick surface. And neither can match the tripod for stability," Jesus said matter-of-factly.

"Get the insurance first," Brad insisted.

"Will do."

On the drive home, all Jesus thought about were the things he could do and the places he could go now. All Brad thought about was what was going on with Jesus.

Leaving him in the parking lot, Brad got a ride back from Jack to get his car. Brad asked him what he thought of the van.

"It's tacky and sorta cool," Jack said.

"From what you know of Jesus, doesn't this seem a little out of character for him?"

Jack pondered for a moment. "Yeah, it does seem a little off."

While Brad and Jack were discussing the changes they saw in Jesus, he was sitting in the driver's seat of his new van. Adjusting the mirrors, he caught a glimpse of his face. It was hard to remember what he used to look like. An unknown feeling bubbled up. Was it guilt, or regret? Was it about the seeming disconnection from his mission, or losing his Gooberity? Was it about the fear to fully experience humanity?

Jack returned a couple of hours later to find Jesus still sitting in the van.

"Are you okay?" Jesus smiled and nodded yes. "Okay, well, I've got the morning shift tomorrow so I'm turning in early."

The next morning, Jack found Jesus asleep at the wheel. Rapping on the window, he yelled, "Dude! Wake up! Aren't you working the morning shift today?"

Jesus raised his head, a dazed look on his face. "Shit!" He dashed inside, showered, brushed his teeth, and got dressed in record time. He arrived sweaty, disheveled, out of breath, and ten minutes late for his shift.

"Everything okay? It's not like you to be late, Jesus," Clara said.

"I know, I know. It's a long story. I'd better get out to my register," he said as he quickly counted his till.

He hurried out the door, only to bump into a customer and drop his cash drawer. Change rolled everywhere. "Shii...zam!" he said, bending over to pick up the bills that had fallen out. Jack came over to check on the customer. As the customer walked away, Jack knelt to help Jesus gather up the money.

"Geez, dude! Focus," Jack said.

"I'm sorry."

"Hey, we all screw up now and then," said Jack.

Jesus grimaced and picked up his till. He took a deep breath and slowly walked to his register. Customers lined up immediately and it set the tone for the day. The pace was nonstop except when he knocked a jar of mayonnaise off the counter, breaking it. He almost swore then too, but was able to restrain himself.

Word of the new van, courtesy of Jack, made it around to the other cashiers. During a short lull, Wanda walked up behind him. "Jesus! You bought yourself a sex van? My oh my, is this a sign of the apocalypse?"

Startled, Jesus turned around and glared. She immediately backed off and went back to her register without saying anything further. The mockery continued at the end of the shift as he was tallying his till. He was the last one in the office when Barbara came in. "I heard about your van," she said.

Bracing himself for some more criticism, he asked, "What about it?"

"It sounds so cool! Will you give me a ride?" she asked, eyes sparkling.

Jesus did a double take. "That's nice of you to say. I've been getting a lot of grief over it."

"Really? I wonder why."

"I think it's the bikini-clad, erect-nippled woman painted on the side."

"I think that's kinda sexy," Barbara purred.

"That's what people are saying. That it's a sex van."

"So? What's wrong with sex?"

Jesus looked hard at her. He felt angry, scared, frustrated and curious all at once. "Nothing. Nothing at all."

Putting one hand to her head and another to her hip and giving a suggestive wiggle, Barbara said, "Maybe you should come up and try it some time."

Jesus stared at her, not comprehending her meaning.

"Don't you get it? Mae West!" she said.

"No. However, I've got to get some insurance for the van," he said, finishing his counting. Under his breath, he murmured, "And learn how to drive."

Barbara shook her head and went back to her register. Jesus clocked out and left to visit the insurance agent Brad suggested. It took about an hour to sign up for insurance. Now he had to get a learner's permit and driving lessons. Cycling home, a fleeting thought of the pastor came up and Jesus immediately changed direction and headed for the church.

It was late in the day, but the pastor was still there, going over paperwork. He reacted with surprise when he saw Jesus at the door. Standing, he quickly moved towards him and extended his hand. "My son, my son, please come in. I fear I owe you an apology."

The worry and tension plaguing Jesus's shoulders melted away. He sat down, a surprised look on his face. "An apology for what?"

The pastor hemmed and hawed for a few seconds before blurting out, "I'm afraid there *are* some problems with the church finances. I thought you were going to reveal that at the roundtable."

"How would I know anything about the church finances?"

"Well, you wouldn't, would you? I guess I was feeling a little guilty about letting the problem get this far along. You have nothing to feel sorry about."

Gazing at the pastor, he smiled and said, "Neither do you."

"Thank you," the pastor said. "There is something else I would like to talk to you about."

"Anything," said Jesus.

With a serious expression on his face, the pastor said, "I understand you have been dabbling in yoga and New Age philosophy."

"Who told you that?"

"Alice mentioned it offhand. I'm concerned that you've taken a wrong turn."

"Hey, I'm more comfortable and relaxed in this skin than I've been since I arrived here."

"Arrived from where?"

"Uh, since the police picked me up and brought me here."

"Hmm, yes, well don't let yourself be distracted from the one true path, my son."

"The one true path?"

"Yes. Jesus Christ is your Savior, as the Megalithic Church teaches."

"There are literally tens of thousands of interpretations of Jesus's teachings. What makes you think that the Megalithic Church has the correct interpretation?"

"It's simple—faith," the pastor said.

"Now, I understand trusting the path that God puts you on, but don't you wonder why God would create so many people just to send them to hell?"

The pastor blinked several times. "No, I don't."

Leaning forward and scooting to the edge of his seat, Jesus said, "Really? I do all the time. What would be the point? One lifetime to get it right and if you don't, you'll suffer for eternity? That doesn't make sense. What would you think of a human parent who treated their child like that? I mean, the story goes that He sent His only son to be the final sacrifice for our sins. It seems to me that God is perfection. He can only create perfection. He created sin, the devil and everything else in the Universe and if He didn't, He certainly would know that the beings He created would do so. It seems to me that He sent Jesus to show us the way to live—to be the Great Example. Love thy neighbor. Pray. Don't judge others. Turn the other cheek. Give to the poor. Wealth isn't important. Have faith in God. I know Christians do their best to live this, but it doesn't always come across like that."

"Are you the one judging now?"

Laughing, Jesus said, "Amen, brother! Father...I mean Pastor."

The pastor peered at Jesus, trying to digest everything he had said. Finally the pastor asked, "One lifetime?"

"Well, I've been reading about reincarnation, and it makes sense to me," Jesus said.

"My son, be careful."

"Why? Aren't Christian beliefs strong enough to withstand scrutiny?"

"Of course, but there are consequences for going down the wrong path."

"Like burning in hell?"

"Exactly."

Jesus paused a moment, staring at the pastor. What he had said felt like a threat. "That doesn't feel right at all. That sounds like fear and that's not what the historical Jesus taught. He taught love. That's why He came here."

Jesus stood up and walked to the door, turning around and looking at the pastor. He felt a mix of emotions—anger and compassion. "Good night. Or better, live long and prosper," Jesus said, with a faint smile.

"Good night, my son. I enjoyed our conversation. Stop by anytime." The pastor felt uneasy saying that. He wondered if Hey-Zeus was about to stir up some trouble.

Chapter 13 – Dating advice

Riding home, Jesus mulled over his conversation with the pastor, but as soon as he spied his van, he became preoccupied. He stayed up late studying the driver's handbook and was late for work again the next morning.

"Hey, Clara," he said, yawning.

"Are we boring you?"

"No. I was up late last night studying to take the driver's exam."

"Ohhh, I heard about your 'van'," Clara said, making air quotes. "There's quite a bit of talk about it around the store."

"Yeah, I know."

"Now, I haven't seen it and they're only secondhand accounts, but it sounds a little 'young' for a man of your years," she said, making air quotes again.

"'Young'? What does that mean?" he asked, his voice getting taut.

"For a man of your age, starting a family might be a priority. From what I heard about your van, you have something else on your mind."

"Like what?"

"Sex."

"Sex? Well, I have thought about it."

"Who doesn't? Though it's about what you're working towards in life, sexual experience or a family life."

"Really, it looked comfortable and I liked the painting on the side," Jesus said.

Bursting into the office, Barbara said, "Hey, you never answered my question yesterday. When are you going to give me a ride?"

Clara chuckled. Jesus, feeling uneasy, said, "I have to learn how to drive first."

"You can practice with a licensed driver in the car," Barbara said, fluttering her eyebrows. Clara laughed and went back to her spreadsheets.

As he and Barbara walked towards their registers, Jesus said, "When I get comfortable behind the wheel, I'll take you for a ride. I promise."

"All right!" Barbara said, practically skipping back to her register.

It was busy that day and when Jesus's break came, he checked out in Brad's line. "Hey, buddy!"

"Uh-oh. I know what that means," Brad replied.

"What *what* means?"

"You need a favor, don't you?"

Bowing his head, Jesus said sheepishly, "Yeah."

"What is it?" Brad asked, feigning annoyance.

"Can you teach me how to drive?"

Brad took a step back, eyes wide, a look of horror on his face. "Good God, no! I still have nightmares from watching you learn how to ride a bike."

Jesus laughed. "Yeah, yeah, I know. But driving isn't about balance. I'm sure I'll do much better. Really!"

Brad chuckled, "All right. Let me check with my insurance agent, file a will, say goodbye to some loved ones, and we'll go out driving."

"Perfect! How about tomorrow?" Jesus asked excitedly, ignoring the sarcasm.

"Okay, you goober," Brad said.

Moving over to Barbara's line, Jesus said, "Brad's taking me out driving tomorrow."

"He is? I bet you do very well."

"I think I will. We'll see."

Throughout lunch, his thoughts kept coming back to Barbara and it suddenly occurred to him that he might be going through puberty. How could that be, though? His human body was twenty-nine years old. Was there such a thing as *emotional* puberty? It didn't make sense...but then he wondered if that might not be the catalyst for the van purchase. He had learned that human behavior doesn't always match conscious thought but can be a sign of something deeper.

Lost in contemplation, he heard over the store intercom, "Will Jesus please return to his register?"

Ten minutes late, he apologized profusely to the head cashier. He did his best to keep focused the rest of the shift, which was difficult given his anticipation about his first driving lesson. That night, he studied some more.

Early the next morning, there was a knock at the door. It was Brad. "He's still in bed," Jack said, answering the door holding a cup of coffee.

"Geez. I expected him to be waiting in the van for me."

"I think he was up late studying."

"He does like to prepare," Brad said, walking back toward Jesus's room.

"You know, I never thought of you as a daredevil."

"You mean teaching him to drive? Come outside before we leave," Brad said, grinning.

He knocked on the door. There was no answer, so he opened it to find Jesus sprawled on his bed, snoring. "Jesus! Wake up, dude!"

Opening his eyes, Jesus felt disoriented, but suddenly remembered what today was and went from horizontal to standing almost instantaneously.

"Whoa! How did you do that?" Brad asked.

"Yee-haw! Let's do this thang!" He grabbed his clothes and dashed to the living room to dress.

"Aren't you going to shower and eat some breakfast?" Brad asked, following him.

"No. I'll grab an apple. Let's go!"

Laughing at Jesus's enthusiasm, Brad said, "Maybe I've forgotten the feeling of learning how to drive, but you seem almost too pumped up."

Jesus was already out the door and jumping into the van. Brad called out, "Let me get something from my car."

"Hurry up!"

As Brad climbed into the van wearing a motorcycle helmet, Jack watched from the apartment door. He laughed so hard he dropped his coffee cup.

"It's not going to be that bad, I swear, Jesus said, half-laughing, half-groaning. "I know I'll be a good driver."

"Okay, Rainman, let's see what you've got," Brad said.

Jesus proceeded to check his mirrors to see if they were properly aligned. Turning the key, the engine started. He released the parking brake and put the van in reverse. Checking both mirrors, he gently backed up, applied the brake and shifted into drive.

"Let's stay in the parking lot for a minute so you can get used to the accelerator and the brake," Brad said, taking off the helmet.

"Good idea," Jesus said, letting off the brake and slowly accelerating.

They drove around the parking lot for a minute before Brad said, "Good start. Let's get on the road." Before he had a chance to tell Jesus to signal a turn, he already had.

"I've only got an hour before work," Brad said.

"No problem. Jack agreed to take me out before his shift today," Jesus said.

"Man, you're in a hurry. Why?"

"I don't know. It's a rite of passage. Freedom..."

"Barbara?"

Smiling, Jesus said, "Maybe."

"I'm surprised that hasn't already happened."

"Well, a relationship with her wasn't important till recently."

"Going slow isn't a bad thing."

"You mean like with you and Martha?"

"What do you mean, me and Martha?"

"I've seen how you look at her."

"I didn't realize you picked up on such things."

"I'm getting better," Jesus said, stopping at a light. They drove for a few minutes in silence. "How am I doing?"

"Surprisingly well."

"So, do you have any advice for me?"

"Pick up your speed a little bit."

"Nooo. About Barbara."

"Oh, uh, treat her with respect. She'll let you know when she's ready to go to the next level," Brad said.

"Treat her with respect. That's good. And follow her cues?" Jesus asked. "Yup."

"Excellent. I can work with that." After a pause, he asked, "As opposed to what?"

"Letting your groin make the decisions."

Laughing, Jesus said, "Yeah, he's pretty insistent."

"Okay, let's head home."

Back at the apartment, Brad said, "That was perfect. The only thing I would suggest is to go a little closer to the speed limit, if not the speed limit. You don't want to get rear-ended."

"Gotcha. Increase speed. I can do that."

Brad grabbed his helmet and exited the van. Jesus honked impatiently. Jack appeared at the door. "Hold your horses, I'm coming."

Getting in the van, Jack asked Brad, "How did he do? Do I need your helmet?"

Shrugging his shoulders, Brad said, "Perfect. A little on the slow side, but not that bad."

"Thanks Brad!" Jesus yelled, putting the van in reverse.

Jesus drove out of the parking lot. Every turn he would flick the turn signal with a flourish like he was conducting an orchestra. He was clearly enjoying himself.

"You're doing pretty good. When are you going for your license?" Jack asked.

"If I practice every day this week, I figure first of next week."

"Next week? What's your hurry?"

Jesus turned to Jack and pumped his eyebrows up and down quickly a couple of times. "Ahhh, Barbara, eh?"

"You know it," Jesus said. "Got any advice for me?"

"Let her know you're interested and go for it. If she doesn't want to she'll let you know. Besides, she's been warm for your form ever since you showed up."

Jack's advice didn't quite agree with Brad's. Jesus felt he needed more opinions—three should be enough to reach a consensus on how to proceed.

They drove around for fifteen minutes or so in silence until Jack said, "I need to get a girlfriend."

Jesus didn't reply as he was paying attention to his driving, with intermittent thoughts about Barbara. "Earth to Jesus. I need to get a girlfriend," Jack repeated.

"Those are easy to get from the couch," Jesus replied.

"Ha, ha. I'm serious. I need to get a girlfriend."

Glancing at Jack, Jesus said, "No, you're not. You're not serious at all. You're only interested in sex. From what I've learned so far about women, they're supposed to be able to pick up on stuff like that."

"Like you're not interested in sex?"

"That's not what I said. Of course I wonder about sex, but I really want to know what makes her tick. What are her motivations? How does her gender affect her decision-making process? I'm studying her," Jesus said.

"Like a scientific experiment?"

Smiling at Jack's implication, Jesus said, "Yes, but with no dissection and only minor emotional scars. Oh, and I'll release her back into the wild when I'm finished with her."

A look of feigned horror crossed Jack's face and he pretended to scoot away. After a few minutes, he said, "Let's head back. I want to get a nap in before work."

Upon their return, Jack headed off to his room and Jesus to his. He surfed the Internet for a while then resolved to practice meditation. He easily got into a comfortable cross-legged position, but his mind was anything but calm. His brain would be momentarily serene, and then a series of thoughts would crop up like hiccups. When thoughts of Barbara and the van popped up, he had an even harder time refocusing. A flash of intuition concerning the pastor came up, so he finished the meditation and biked to the church.

He found the pastor in his office, head in hands, with a doleful look on his face. Looking up, he motioned for Jesus to sit down. "What's on your mind, my son?"

"I'm thinking about asking Barbara out and I wanted to know if you have any advice for me."

Straightening up in his chair, the pastor said, "Oh my. I don't get that question often." He leaned back. "It's been a long time since I've dated. Let's see. Abstinence, my son. You should abstain from sexual relations until you're married."

"Whoa there, Pastor. This is a first date. I'm not thinking about having sex on the first date."

"Well, we are talking about Barbara."

Leaping to his feet, Jesus said, "Hey! What kind of thing is that to say about Barbara?"

"Maybe I shouldn't have said anything, but unfortunately, it is common knowledge that she's slept around. You should be aware of that before getting into a relationship with her."

Jesus frowned and sat down. "So? She's got some sexual experience. I would think that would be better than not having any."

"Not from God's point of view. Only in marriage may one have sex. And I want to emphasize, that's a marriage between a man and a woman," the pastor said.

"I don't even want to get into the whole Biblical marriage nonsense. What is God's deal with temptation?" Jesus said, frustrated. He started to count on his fingers, "He gives us the equipment, the senses and the knowledge, and then He wants us to abstain? That doesn't make any sense. Why would we be here if not to gain experience?"

"Of course, we're here to gain experience. And serve God. But we do it His way," the pastor said.

"'His way'? You mean your interpretation of His way and it doesn't make sense to me. It's the judgment. We engage in an activity to gain experience. This experience is judged to be a sin. To absolve ourselves of the sin, we must accept the Savior, Jesus Christ, who died 2,000 years ago for our sins. What's to be learned? Blind obedience? Where's our responsibility to improve? Why judge the activity to be sinful and feel guilt and shame? Is that really necessary for us to learn and grow? I say, remove the judgment and guilt. If I make an error, I evaluate it, learn from it, and vow to do better.

I would believe in the teachings of Jesus whether He absolved me of my mistakes or not. His path of love is the only way, but human interpretation of the Bible to detect the sins of others, to me, is evil. Besides, I don't think Jesus died for our sins. I think He was demonstrating his greatest lesson—turn the other cheek. Even unto death."

The pastor's eyes grew cold. "I'm sorry you found my advice, uh, unappetizing. I have work to do. Please show yourself out," he said, returning to his work.

Jesus stood up and walked out, glancing back at the pastor as he left the office. The pastor didn't even look up. *Is he overly sensitive, or am I a jackass?* Jesus wondered. *Probably a little of both.*

Riding home, he thought about how he should proceed with Barbara—three opinions, three paths. He could just stay in the moment and wait for clues from the Universe, or he could commit to one of the three suggested paths. Of course, he hadn't even asked her out yet, but it seemed *that* wouldn't be a problem.

On Monday, Brad drove Jesus to take the driver's road test. He scored a 99 after a one-point deduction for talking. The examiner told him if he could take off points for the *amount* of talking he did, Jesus would have gotten a 60, but he could only give him a one-point deduction.

He drove the van to work the next day, eager to show it off. Everyone who saw it had a comment, mostly catty. When he showed it off to Barbara, she oohed and ahhed. "When do I get a ride?"

"How about after work tonight?"

"Let's," she said smiling.

Jesus could hardly think of anything else the rest of the shift. At the end of the night, Barbara finished counting her money before he did. "I'm ready..." she cooed.

Jesus grinned. He was trying to count and figure how to ask her out at the same time. Should he suggest something specific or just ask her if she wanted to go out? He couldn't decide. Finishing up, he passed his till to Brad. "You two have fun now," he said.

On the way to the van, Barbara asked, "Am I the first one to get a ride?"

"Yes ma'am, you are," Jesus said, helping Barbara into the van. He had been studying manners online again. "Where do you want to go?"

"It doesn't make any difference to me. Just take me for a ride."

"I don't have a lot of experience driving at night. Let's keep this trip short."

They drove around for a while in silence. Jesus noticed that Barbara seemed uncomfortable—had she taken his comment as a rejection? He didn't know what to do as he returned to the store to drop her off.

"Well, thanks for the ride," Barbara said disappointedly.

"Uh, let's do it again. Maybe this weekend?"

"Are you asking me out?"

"Umm, yes?"

Barbara's demeanor changed immediately. "Yes!"

"Good. What do you want to do?"

"Ohhh, um, um, how about a picnic?" she suggested.

"Yeah, that would be good. How about up at the lake?"

"Oooh, wouldn't that be romantic. I'll make us a picnic basket."

"What should I do?"

"Show up," she said, laughing.

"That's my strong suit."

Smiling, she grasped his arm. "This is going to be so great. See ya!" she said, bouncing out of the van.

"Bye," Jesus said. As he pulled out of the parking lot he thought, *that wasn't difficult at all*, but immediately the negative voices in his head took over. *What have I done? This isn't going to help the mission. I'm not ready for this.*

He felt excited and afraid at the same time. He got online and researched dating. It took several hours to get to sleep.

The next day, he decided to skip meditating before driving to his soup kitchen shift. He realized when arriving that he had no memory of how he had gotten there, such was the constant stream of thoughts about his upcoming date with Barbara. He gathered his gear and took his place at the steam table. Absentmindedly he served patron after patron, trying to evaluate how he had gotten to this point. Suddenly, one of the patrons slammed his tray several times. "How about some service here?"

Emerging from his reverie, Jesus apologized and served the man. Alice walked over to see what the commotion was. "Daydreaming, are we?" she asked.

Jesus smiled sheepishly. "Maybe a little."

Looking him over, Alice said, "It's a woman, isn't it?"

Jesus nodded yes. "You dawg! Who is she?"

"Barbara."

"From the roundtables? I didn't know anything was going on between you two."

"Got any advice for a first date?" Jesus asked.

"Trim your beard. Be polite. Listen to what she says. At least that's what I like," Alice said.

"What's wrong with my beard?"

"It's out of control. Have you even trimmed it since I met you?" Alice asked before walking away.

He wondered what else he might not know about first date preparation. Finishing his shift, he returned home and asked Jack what pre-date preparations he made.

"The usual. Floss, brush the teeth, shower, and trim the nose hair if necessary. Trim the fingernails and toenails. Oh, and trim the pubes, too," Jack said.

"Trim the what?"

"The pubes. Pubic hair. If you're going to have sex and you've got a jungle down there, trimming the pubes will make it more pleasant, for you and your partner. Especially where oral is concerned," Jack said.

"Oral Roberts?" Jesus asked.

Laughing, Jack said, "Oral sex, dummy."

"Oh. Oh yeah, yeah, I understand," Jesus said, but he didn't really. *I think it's time to research sex.*

He got dressed and left for work. It was a pleasant shift and Barbara was more than flirtatious. She managed to find an excuse to leave her register to come over and touch him at least a half-dozen times. Even though he liked it, Jesus felt a little awkward and wondered if she was going to want sex on their first date.

When it got slow and Barbara wasn't around, Pete came over and asked, "Barbara, eh?"

"Yeah, Barbara. We're going on a date tomorrow."

"Really? Well, good luck. Not that you're going to need it."

"Got any advice for me?"

"First date?" Pete asked. Jesus nodded yes.

"Well, she seems ready, but I've always taken it a little slower. I think getting to know someone is very important."

"I think that's important, too. Why do you think so?" Jesus asked.

"You never know about a person. They could be on antipsychotics, or a racist, or she might not know how to cook. You never know until you get to know them."

"That might be the best advice I've gotten yet, Pete," Jesus said, smiling. *This might be the answer to slowing down Barbara's advances,* he thought.

"Why, thank you," Pete said, walking away. "One more thing," he said, "Smell good. Women love a good cologne."

Jesus had read that on the Internet, too. "Do you have any suggestions?"

"Follow me to the body-care department," Pete said. He showed Jesus several varieties. "It's depends on what you like, and of course, what she likes." He had no idea what she liked, but after several minutes of sniffing, Jesus made his selection.

The day of the date, he was nervous. He followed most of the grooming advice he had received. Driving to pick up Barbara, it was all he could do to remember to breathe and what her address was.

When he arrived, Barbara bounded out the door carrying a big picnic basket and a blanket. Jesus got out to help her with it. "You look very nice. Let's put that in the back."

As he helped her into the van, she purred, "My, such a gentleman."

They drove up to Lake Travis, neither saying much on the way up there. After parking, they found a suitable flat spot, spread out the blanket and sat down. Barbara began unpacking the food.

"What are we having?" Jesus asked.

"Fruit," she said, revealing some strawberries and grapes. "Cheese and crackers, and, ta-da...wine."

Smiling, Jesus said, "Well done."

"What should we start with?"

"I don't know. I like strawberries."

Barbara reached into the basket and pulled out a container of whipped cream. Opening the top, she plunged the strawberry in. Scooting closer to Jesus, she said, "Open wide."

Is she trying to feed me? Jesus wondered. He opened wide and sure enough she stuck the strawberry into his mouth. He bit down hard and it was delicious. "Now do me!" Barbara said.

He obeyed and they swapped several strawberries. Then they moved on to the grapes. "Let's have some wine," she suggested.

Jesus hadn't had any alcohol since he had arrived on Earth. He knew little about it except that it could lead to a DUI. "Just a small glass please. I'm driving."

"Of course, sir," Barbara said, pouring two cups of wine and handing Jesus one.

"A toast," she said, lifting her cup, "to love and everything leading up to it."

"To love," Jesus said. Barbara smiled and banged the two cups together, spilling a little bit. She reached for a napkin to clean it up, but Jesus stopped her.

"Leave it. It's for the gods."

"For the gods," Barbara replied, finishing her wine.

"Let's have some crackers and cheese," he suggested.

They fed each other some more. They talked and laughed and were very much enjoying themselves until an audible grumble came from Barbara's stomach.

"Are you okay?" Jesus asked.

"Yeah, I'm fine."

"Hey, what did you do to your hair?"

"Do you like it?"

"Yes. It looks very nice. It looks longer," Jesus said.

"Thank you," Barbara said, getting a puzzled look on her face. "Are you asking me if I added in hair extensions? Because I most certainly did not."

"Oh, okay. So you just 'Gruyere'?"

"Did you just make a pun?" Barbara asked, frowning.

"Hey, don't make a 'Muenster' out of me," Jesus said, straight-faced.

"I hate puns," Barbara said emphatically, pushing Jesus in the chest with both hands and then farting.

Jesus's eyes opened wide. Pointing at her, he said slowly, "Ha-fart-i," and then rolled onto his back, laughing and holding his sides.

"I'm going to get you," she said, jumping on top of him. Their eyes met and Jesus felt a powerful and magnetic physical attraction he'd never experienced before. He tried to analyze the sensation, but his mind completely fogged up. They drew nearer and kissed. Her lips were incredibly soft; he had nothing to compare them to. Before he could process what was happening, she plunged her tongue into his mouth. Unable to control himself, he followed suit. He tried to copy her technique, but the kiss was sloppy and wet. When he got an erection, he pushed her away.

"What's wrong?" Barbara asked.

"Nothing. That was great, really great. I just think we should go a little slower and get to know each other better," Jesus said.

Sitting back, Barbara said, "I'm coming on too strong, aren't I?"

"Well, kissing is the next step. So no, you're not. I thought it best to let you know how I feel, and I feel like we should go slow."

"Okay," Barbara said in a quiet voice, her chin dropping to her chest.

Jesus put his arm around her. "You didn't do anything wrong."

Barbara looked up at him and smiled. She put her head on his shoulder and they sat like that for a while. It started to get dark, so they packed the food and loaded the van. Driving home in silence, he felt like he had done the right thing in bringing up how he felt, yet he didn't feel good about disappointing her.

When they arrived at her apartment, Jesus said, "I had a really good time."

"Really?" Barbara asked meekly.

"Really," Jesus said, getting out of the van to get the picnic basket. He walked her to the door and leaned over to give her a kiss on the cheek. Barbara looked surprised, as if she expected something else.

"Well, see you at church tomorrow," Barbara said.

"Definitely. Have a nice night," Jesus replied, walking to his van.

Disappointed, Barbara responded, "Yeah, have a nice night."

Jesus, on the other hand, felt triumphant. He'd had a taste of human sexuality and it was sweet. He could still taste her on his lips. It was unlike anything he had ever experienced before. He wondered whether it would be right to continue the relationship since she obviously wanted to take it to the next level. What if she got pregnant? The rest of the night, his thoughts see-sawed between how good the kiss felt and what repercussions might occur if the relationship went further. When he finally fell asleep, he had a smile on his face.

The next day at church, Jesus met up with Brad and Jack. Barbara didn't show up. Listening to the sermon, Jesus thought back to the evening before. He was pleased with the results, but wondered what Barbara's absence meant.

After the service, the three of them went to shake the pastor's hand. He asked where Barbara was.

"I don't know," Jack said.

"Jesus, you went out with her yesterday. Do you know where she is?" asked Brad.

The pastor, Brad, and Jack glanced at each other, then at Jesus. "I haven't talked to her today. I don't know where she is," Jesus said.

"Did the date go well?" asked Jack.

"Well yeah. I think so."

"What do you mean, you think so?" asked Brad.

"We had fun. We kissed. I asked her if we could go slow. End of story."

"What did I tell you about following a woman's cues?" Brad said.

"Don't I have a say in our relationship?"

"Not as much as you would think," Jack said.

All three looked at Jesus and nodded. "You look like bobbleheads," he said disgustedly, and marched off towards his bike.

Brad ran to catch up with him. "It's not over. You can overcome this." Jesus nodded and got on his bike. As he rode home, he decided he didn't want to think about it anymore. He'd talk with her tomorrow at work.

But Barbara didn't show up for work the next day, or the day after that or the day after that. Jesus meant to call her and find out how she was doing, but he kept getting distracted. He didn't see her again until Thursday night at the roundtable.

He arrived early hoping to talk with her. Each time the door opened, he straightened up with anticipation, but each time it was one of the other regular participants. By the time the meeting started, he felt disappointed.

"What shall we talk about tonight?" asked the pastor.

"How about dating?" Jack suggested.

Jesus flinched. "Ralph and Juan are married, but the rest of you are currently dating, aren't you?" the pastor asked.

Alice was seeing someone, the rest of the singles weren't. Brad was the first to speak up. "Jesus, why don't you tell us about your date this past weekend?"

Jesus scowled. "Hey, I'm just trying to help," Brad said.

At that moment, Barbara walked through the door. She looked stressed and under the weather. Jesus stood up immediately and sat down after she took her seat.

"My, how refreshing!" Gertrude said.

"What?" Jack asked.

"A gentleman standing when a lady enters the room," Gertrude said.

"What lady?" Jack asked, laughing.

"Now Jack, be nice," said the pastor.

"Yes sir," Jack said, lowering his head.

"Barbara, the first subject tonight is dating," the pastor said.

Barbara rolled her eyes and shifted uncomfortably in her chair. Nobody said a word. "Is there anything you would like to say about it?" the pastor asked.

Barbara shook her head no. The group began discussing a successful date from the female and male perspectives followed by proper post-date protocol. Barbara's face got redder and redder. Finally, she couldn't hold back. "Why didn't you call?" she yelled.

A hush fell on the room and all eyes turned to Jesus. Taking a deep breath, he said, "I thought I would see you at work the next day but you weren't there. Then I got distracted. Then you weren't at work the *next* day and I got distracted again. All of a sudden, it was today. Really people, is it mandatory to call right after a date?"

"Yes," everybody responded in unison.

Jesus slumped in his chair. After several moments of silence, he said, "Barbara, I'm sorry I didn't call you after our date."

This didn't mollify Barbara in the least. Standing and pointing at Jesus, she said loudly, "You should've called. You're a jerk." She walked up to Jesus and leaned over him. "Why don't you just disappear?" she said and then stormed out of the room.

Jesus, slumping even further in his chair, murmured, "Soon enough, soon enough."

Nobody said anything for several minutes until the pastor asked if there were any other topics to discuss.

"How about the Apocalypse?" Jack suggested.

That brought up some tension in the room. Everybody had an opinion. The pastor stood fast on Biblical teachings from the Book of Revelations. Other theories were proposed—a final war over resources, the earth going into an ice age triggered by global warming, a plague or plagues striking humanity, a great flood triggered by global warming, an alien attack, stressed plant life emitting spores that drive humans crazy and a few more.

Finally, Jesus could keep quiet no longer. "Egads, people, why do you worry about such things? You woke up on December 22nd and found that you still have the same problems you had on December 20th. Throughout human history, there has always been someone predicting an apocalypse. Why? Because it's easier to die than to live. We're here for one purpose, to bring light and love where there is none. God wants us to thrive and prosper, not to live in fear. Fear is darkness. Fear keeps us from being our true selves—children of God. There's nothing to worry about. I think if and when there is a judgment, it will be to take to the next level, whatever that is, those souls who have advanced to the point of truly understanding and practicing the historical Jesus's message."

"What about those people who don't really understand Jesus's message? They go to hell?" asked Alice.

"Why would God do that? Would you do that to your children? Or would you continue to love them? I swear, some of the behavior attributed to God in the Bible and in Christianity is ludicrous. If God was a parent on this planet, he would have been locked up for child abuse a long time ago," Jesus said.

"That's outrageous!" shouted the pastor.

"Is it? I find it outrageous that the first commandment of 613 commandments is 'Thou shalt not kill' and yet further on they permit genocide of the Canaanites. They even permit slavery. Does that make any sense at all, especially when you compare them to the historical Jesus's teachings of 'Love thy neighbor' and 'But whoever slaps you on the right cheek, turn to him the other also?' From what I've read, the Bible is replete with what man thinks God wants him to do from a human perspective. That perspective is based on being a predator, an animal, not a spiritual being. Is it just me or isn't that God's plan—to convert us *from* animals into spiritual beings?" Jesus said.

"Wow! I never thought of it like that," said Alice.

"Me either," said Brad.

Red-faced, the pastor said nothing. The conversation turned to other apparent inconsistencies in Christian teachings. The more the group got into the conversation, the angrier the pastor got. Finally, he could take no more.

"Enough! Christianity-bashing is the work of the devil! After all the church has done for you, you question its teachings? How dare you!" he said, standing and stomping out of the room.

After several moments of silence, Gertrude said, "You'd think someone confident in his views could handle a little scrutiny."

Jesus smiled, but deep inside he felt sick about Barbara. He yearned to heal things between them. He looked really tired.

"Jesus, are you okay?" Brad asked.

"I'm just worn out. I think I'll go home. Good night," he said, getting up from the table and walking slowly out of the room.

"Boy, these roundtables are sure getting exciting," said Juan.

"Too exciting. Shall we call it a night?" Ralph suggested.

The group agreed and filed out of the room, the events of the evening running through their minds.

Chapter 14 – Jesus gets sick

Jesus didn't feel very well the next morning. A dull headache led him to cancel a bike ride with Brad. By the time he arrived at the store, he felt worse. Barbara made it to work and avoided him as much as possible. When he came to her register to give her a break, she didn't touch him. He missed that.

After the shift ended, he finally had a moment alone with her.

"Are you still mad at me?" Jesus asked.

"I don't want to talk to you."

"Why not?"

"I'm still mad at you."

"For wanting to take our relationship slow? Why would that make you mad?"

"None of your business."

Jesus got up and sat down next to her. "Aren't I allowed to express my feelings?"

"It's not that," said Barbara quietly.

"What is it then?"

"A memory of my dad came up. He wasn't affectionate...at all."

"Hey, didn't we kiss? Passionately. You know, I really enjoyed that."

"Me, too. You just went from that to distant all of a sudden."

"Well, maybe there's some stuff from my past tied up in that, too. It's a shame you're not talking to me. I was going to ask you out on a second date."

"I would like that."

They hugged and Jesus planted a light kiss on her lips. "How about a movie after church on Sunday?"

"Awesome!"

"Yes, it is," Jesus said, smiling almost as much as Barbara. Leaving the store and going home, a feeling of relief spread over him...but the thought that she would eventually want sex overshadowed that. What was he going to do?

The next day, he felt worse. By Sunday, he didn't want to get out of bed. He was coughing and sneezing, sometimes at the same time. He wasn't sure, but he thought he might be dying, and even if that was the case, there was no way he was going to miss his date with Barbara.

He arrived at church just as the service started, and Barbara had saved him a seat. As he sat down, he let out a big sneeze that brought the pastor to a stop. Barbara leaned over and asked him if he was okay. He nodded yes, but knew otherwise. The pastor's sermon was about faith again, and again Jesus felt he was talking directly to him. He quoted Father Mulcahy from the TV show *M*A*S*H*, "A faith of convenience is a hollow faith."

That got Jesus thinking about his current situation. Was he eschewing Christianity because it temporarily wasn't working for him, or had God led him to a different path? He thought it over as he continued to sneeze, cough and one time...he farted. Barbara leaned over and whispered, "Havarti," causing Jesus to laugh-cough.

After the service, they went up to the pastor to thank him for his sermon. "My son, are you all right?" the pastor asked compassionately.

Jesus gathered himself the best he could and pronounced himself fit, only to cough several times on the pastor. Brad walked up then backed away as the coughing continued. "Time to go see Martha," he said.

"Good idea," Jesus wheezed.

"Who's Martha?" asked the pastor.

"She's a superb healer. She does deep tissue bodywork and acupuncture with some guided visualizations mixed in," Brad said.

"Wouldn't a doctor be more appropriate at this point?" asked the pastor.

Barbara concurred, but shaking his head no, Jesus said, "I don't follow that paradigm anymore. I follow the path of mental and emotional reasons as the basis of dis-ease."

"What are those reasons, then?" the pastor asked skeptically.

Jesus pointed at Barbara.

"You're blaming me?" Barbara asked incredulously.

"Nooo. It's my issues. My internal issues," Jesus said, sneezing loudly.

"I'm going over there to talk to some other parishioners before I catch something," the pastor said.

"That's not possible," Jesus said hoarsely, as Barbara led him away.

"Pause, please," said the curious judge. "I don't understand. What internal issues created your illness?"

"Your Honor, with humans, any sort of emotional upset can cause a reaction physically. I was having difficulty with my relationship with the human female, Barbara, and the result was catching a cold."

"Are humans sick all the time?" asked the empathetic judge.

"No, they adapt to their emotional bodies over time."

"So, they're sick more often when they're children?" asked the curious judge.

"Generally, yes. But adults get sick, too. For them, however, it's more likely that they have repressed their emotions to the point that it manifests as disease."

"Don't they realize that and make the effort to avoid repressing their emotions?" asked the fussy judge.

"Some do, yes, but few humans understand this paradigm. The majority of humans think that germs are the cause of all illness. I learned that emotions and repetitive negative thoughts produce an imbalance in a human's energy fields and that is when the germs infect them. They see the effect, but are confused about the cause."

"Continue," said the fussy judge.

"Are you sure you want to go to the movies?" Barbara asked.

Jesus nodded yes, doing his best not to cough. "Okay," Barbara said, happy that even in this state he wanted to spend time with her. But when they got into his van, the look on his face told Barbara that he really wasn't feeling well. "Maybe I should drive?" she asked, pointing to her car.

Jesus agreed. "What do you want to see?" Barbara asked.

"A return to good health."

"What theater is that playing at?"

Jesus laughed and coughed. "That's not a movie. It doesn't make any difference what we see."

"Oh. You're making a joke," Barbara said. "Let's go to the multiplex and see what's playing."

When they arrived, Barbara picked the movie. They found seats and she got up to get drinks. Jesus sat there trying to feel better. The previews had started by the time Barbara returned. The cold drink felt good on his sore throat. He tried to focus on her, but his body kept distracting him. As the movie started, he gently took her hand. She turned towards him and smiled.

Despite his best efforts, the next few minutes were filled with sneezing and coughing. After some shushing, dirty looks and one nasty comment of "Why don't you hurry up and die," Jesus leaned over and suggested they leave. Barbara helped him back to the car.

"Shall I take you back to pick up your van?"

"No. Just take me home."

When they arrived, Barbara helped Jesus inside the apartment. She recoiled as soon as they entered.

"Ewww! Digusting. What's that smell?"

"Believe it or not, it's better than it used to be."

She looked at him in horror. "Or maybe I've just gotten used to it," Jesus lamented.

"Where's your bedroom?"

"Back there," Jesus said, halfheartedly pointing.

Once in the room, he sat on his bed, groaning. Barbara looked around the room in surprise. "Hmm, a twin bed. No pictures. No drapes. It's kind of spartan in here."

"I don't need much."

"But it looks like a jail cell. It's not much bigger either."

Jesus agreed and closed his eyes. Barbara sat on the bed and felt his forehead—feverish. She went in search of a washcloth, but could only find paper towels. She wetted one and returned to place it on Jesus's forehead.

"That feels good."

"Is there anything else I can do for you?"

"Can you get me some vitamin C powder and two aspirin from the kitchen?"

"Of course," she said gently.

"Two packets please, and a glass of water, too."

Barbara had to clean a glass before getting the water, and she returned shortly. "Here," she said, kneeling at his feet.

"Thank you," Jesus said, putting the vitamin C in the water and gulping down the pills before falling back on the bed.

Barbara picked up his feet and helped him swing around to where his head was on the pillow, and then placed the damp paper towel back on his forehead. She sat on the edge of the bed and stroked his face.

"Do you want me to stay?"

"No. I think I'm just going to go to sleep," he murmured.

Barbara leaned over and kissed him lightly on the lips. "Good night."

"Mmm, good night," Jesus said, almost immediately falling asleep.

The next morning Jesus hadn't improved, and he called Martha and left a message that he badly needed her services. That wiped him out and he was glad that it was his day off.

Might as well try to be productive, he thought, as he tried to get on the web to continue his research. He didn't really have the energy for that and quit after five minutes, making his way to the couch and collapsing.

Jack came into the living room, bleary-eyed. "What's wrong with you?"

"I'm sick and probably dying," Jesus said. "And where were you yesterday? Why didn't you make it to church?"

Laughing, Jack said, "A woman. Besides, I didn't want to see you crucified in front of the whole congregation with Barbara hammering in the nails."

"Pfft. Barbara and I made up," Jesus said, sneezing.

"Dude! Get a hanky or put your hand over your mouth."

Jesus answered with another sneeze. Irritated, he said, "You won't catch anything."

"Sez you."

Jesus was too weak to argue and wanted to ignore him, but he had to ask Jack something. "Can you pick up my van at the church and drive it back here for me, please?"

Put out by the request, Jack managed a "Yeah, sure" and went to the kitchen.

"Thank you. I owe you one," Jesus said. Martha called and she could see him the next day, if he lived. In no mood for teasing, he huddled on the couch for the rest of the day and went to bed early.

Arriving at Martha's studio the next morning, Jesus knocked lightly on the door. She opened it with a flourish and exclaimed, "Blessed Jesus!" to which he responded with a sneeze. She gave him her trademark hug and ushered him inside.

"Strip and hop onto the table. We have a lot of work to do," she instructed, leaving the room. Jesus complied. Returning, Martha asked, "So, what's going on?" as she felt his wrist to check his pulses.

"I'm sick. Isn't it obvious?" Jesus said, coughing.

Laughing, Martha said, "Yes, I see that now. What's been going on in your life that might have brought this on?"

125

Jesus briefly went over the events of the past couple of weeks—learning to drive, upsetting the pastor, going on a date, upsetting Barbara, reconciling with her, and then getting sick.

"Hmmm. Well, there's plenty there to put you at dis-ease. Out of all of that, what stressed you out the most?"

"Barbara," Jesus admitted.

"Ahhh, women. What bothered you about her?"

"I don't know. We've had this connection from day one, but I've got my mission to consider. Anthropologically speaking, studying human interaction at this level would be important to my people. We don't have anything like this on my planet. On the other hand, I don't want to, as it were, love 'em and leave 'em. That wouldn't be fair to her, and then what about the consequences of the relationship going too far? I have no idea what the end result of that would be."

"What do you mean, 'the relationship going too far'?"

"You know, sex."

"You mean the natural next step in intimate human relationships?"

"Well, I'm not sure about the mixing of DNA if she got pregnant. There might be some three-legged Goober DNA mixed in. The child might turn out to be some sort of hybrid Human-Goober. And what if the child was male? If so, he would become an outcast, inevitably becoming a pawn of the porn industry."

After Martha composed herself, Jesus added, "And besides, leaving her after six months still seems rude."

"Maybe. Or maybe you could look at it like you bring each other six months of happiness. You know you could always tell her about your, um, status," Martha suggested.

"That would be insane. I'm not even sure about the consequences of telling *you*. When they find out that I've exposed our species to an alien being..." Jesus said, his voice trailing off.

"How would they find out?" Martha asked.

"When I make my report to my project group, of course."

"You could always withhold that information," Martha said, sticking an acupuncture needle into a particularly sensitive meridian.

Jesus winced and took a deep breath, then exhaled. "It's really not in a Goober's nature to do that." He thought about it a moment. "Maybe I could avoid bringing it up..."

He suddenly stopped talking and breathing, his body tensing all over. Martha immediately noticed and asked what was wrong. He pushed himself into an upright sitting position and hopped off the massage table, needles still inserted. Martha watched him pace back and forth muttering to himself for almost a minute.

"What's going on?"

He stopped and stared at her. "The evidence is there, the evidence is there."

"What evidence?"

"The only reasonable conclusion is that I'm turning into a human and might possibly be fully human by the end of my mission."

"Well, you've always been a little weird. What are you saying? You're completely weird now?"

"No, no, no! You don't get it! You don't get it at all!" Jesus cried out. "My essential nature is changing! When I got here my Gooberian personality, if you will, was intact. Granted it wasn't very complex compared to a typical human personality. Our egos and emotions are much less intense than humans. When I got here I had to, you know, fake some personality. But just now when I considered lying to my colleagues back home about the specifics of my mission..." Jesus said, shaking his head and slumping into a chair.

"Come on! Everybody lies."

"Yes. All humans lie, true. Goobers don't. It's not part of our nature," Jesus said, disgusted with this turn of events. Secretly, he had always considered Goobers superior to humans in many aspects.

"Let's look at this from some other angles," Martha said. "This might be good for your mission. It might make you feel better about sleeping with Barbara." Jesus smiled a little. "There's nothing that says this change is written in stone either. When you finish your mission and return and get re-trans...fatted, you may reabsorb the Goober personality traits. Wouldn't that make sense?"

"Possibly. It would have something to do with a magnetic field or even an unknown spiritual field that exposure to over time produces a realignment with the dominant species of a planet."

"Yeah, like that," Martha said, grasping Jesus's arm and leading him back to the table.

As Jesus lay back down, he let out a big sigh. "Thank Goob!"

Martha laughed. "That's right. Relax and breathe deep. You don't have to worry about being infected by us lowly humans."

"What?" Jesus asked, blushing.

"Intuition—a lowly, human method of communication with God. How's yours developing?" Martha asked.

"Not as well as yours," Jesus said, frowning.

"Goob," Martha said with emphasis.

"What about Him?"

"I just love saying that. I wonder what it stands for?"

"Stands for?" he repeated.

"Yeah. Some people on this planet think that God is an acronym and that the letters stand for Generate, Organize, and Destroy. What would Goob stand for?" Martha asked.

Without hesitation, Jesus said, "Well for Americans, it would be Generate, Organize, Obtain, Borrow."

They both laughed and Jesus felt better, but as the session continued the question of how much he might change kept cropping up in his mind. How long would it take to change back? And how was he going to fit back in when he returned to his home planet?

Chapter 15 – Explanation of enlightenment

Jesus was back at work the next day, feeling much better. It amazed him how quickly he recovered his health after a session with Martha. At one point, Pete came back to the office and offered to cover for him if he wasn't feeling well enough to finish his shift.

"Thanks, but I feel pretty good. Besides, it gives me something to focus on."

Walking into the office, Wanda said, "I need some quarters, please. Hey Jesus, rocked that sex van yet?"

Pete laughed and Jesus disdainfully said no.

"I can help you with that."

"Wanda, you need a chastity belt," Pete said.

"Plus a muzzle," Jesus chimed in.

"Oooh, you're into bondage!" Wanda said, wide-eyed.

"Oh, good grief!" exclaimed Jesus.

"Honey, I could show you fifty shades of black."

Laughing, Wanda and Pete went back out on the sales floor and Jesus returned to the monotony of counting money. His mind drifted to thoughts of turning human. Was it a good thing or a bad thing? What if he couldn't return home and had to stay? What if he didn't want to return home? His uneasiness began to get the best of him and when he went out to give breaks, he was in a foul mood.

Wanda was first and had some more catty things to say about bondage. Jesus didn't respond and noted the time she was supposed to be back from break. Fifteen minutes later, Martha came through his line.

"Hey, Jesus!"

"Hey, Martha," Jesus said quietly.

"Is everything okay?"

"No. You know that conversation we had yesterday? It's bugging me."

"How so?"

"Well, I can't really talk about it here."

"Yes, of course. How about we get some tea sometime in the next couple of days? We can talk about it then, okay?"

Jesus agreed and took a deep breath. They set a time and as Martha left, he observed his tension easing. *What would have happened on this mission if I hadn't had someone to talk to?* He was so grateful.

Jesus rode his bike to church the next day for his soup kitchen shift. Determined to approach the pastor about the last roundtable, he arrived twenty minutes early and went looking for him.

He was in his office as usual and Jesus knocked lightly at the door. The pastor looked up and took on a stern expression. "May I come in?" Jesus asked.

The pastor nodded yes and Jesus sat down. "Look, I didn't mean to as you put it, bash Christianity, Pastor."

"That may have not been your intention, but that was what you were doing."

"I'm sorry. I just have so many questions. Don't you have questions about your religion?"

"Don't you mean *our* religion?" the pastor said, opening his eyes wide and cocking his head.

"Well, yeah. I do honor Jesus's teachings. I wish I could believe like you do," Jesus said, his head bowing down.

The pastor, overcome with compassion, stood up, walked around and sat on his desk, placing his hand on Jesus's shoulder. "It's about faith, my son. I have faith in Jesus and the Bible."

"I understand that. What I don't understand is why that should preclude asking questions about it. I'm not out to mock you or your faith, but some of it doesn't feel quite right to me."

"I understand that now, my son. It just seems at times that you're trying to deliberately provoke me."

"No sir. I'm just trying to get a handle on all this."

Smiling, the pastor said, "I'll try to be more understanding in the future. Is there anything else?"

"No, I need to get to the soup kitchen for my shift."

"All right then. And thank you for donating your time. I understand that you work two shifts every week?"

"Yes. It seems like the right thing to do," Jesus said. They shook hands, looking each other in the eye. As he walked out the door, the pastor realized how much Jesus reminded him of his own son. Opening a desk drawer, he pulled out a picture of him. Staring at it, tears came to the pastor's eyes. He quickly put it away and returned to working on his sermon.

Jesus went downstairs to the kitchen and put on his apron. Alice gave him his assignment for the shift.

"Is everything okay?" Alice asked.

"I just talked with the pastor."

"How did it go?"

"I think he was still upset from the roundtable, but after talking, he seemed to understand that I wasn't trying to provoke him."

"Hey, you weren't the only one talking smack about Christianity."

"Yeah, but I started it."

"Well, I liked what you had to say. The pastor is a big boy. If he can't defend his faith, he must have some questions of his own," Alice said, walking away.

Have some questions of his own? Is that why he got angry? The rest of his shift, Jesus contemplated why people got angry.

Two days later, Jesus met Martha for tea. She was relaxed and smiling. Jesus was tight and serious. "So, what's up?" Martha asked.

"Issues with the pastor. At the last roundtable, he got very angry at me and accused me of Christianity-bashing and walked out."

"Really? Just walked out on the group?"

"Yeah. Alice suggested that he got angry because he had questions about Christianity of his own."

"Seems possible. What do you think?"

"I don't know. I'm still getting used to my own emotions, much less figuring out what's going on with other people."

"Emotions are great. It's almost always better to let them out than keep them in," Martha said.

"But why have them in the first place? What's the benefit of them?"

"They're signposts. You react with emotion—in this case anger—because of your beliefs."

"Oh. So it would be beneficial to monitor one's reactions to see what beliefs might need to be addressed or changed?"

"Exactly. You examine your thoughts, emotions and behavior so as to reveal what you really believe, and vice versa. Of course, we're talking negative emotions here."

"Not-love," Jesus said, nodding.

"Not-love?" Martha asked.

"On my planet, we only have two emotions. Love and not-love."

"Wow! No wonder you're having difficulty."

"Yeah. So, when people express negative emotions, it's a reaction to their beliefs being questioned?"

"That's one possible reason. It could be something from their past. Or you might not have a clue why they're reacting from the conversation or situation you're in."

"Oh, good grief. This sounds too difficult," Jesus said, putting his head in his hands.

"Nooo. That's what makes life here so interesting. It's at that point where you start paying attention to your intuition."

"Intuition? You mean the flashes of insight?"

"Yes, exactly. That's communicating with God."

"Goob," Jesus corrected, grinning.

Laughing, Martha continued, "It's not just those flashes of insight you need to be aware of, it's all of your thoughts. That's the path that leads to total awareness."

"The path? You mean a spiritual path?"

"Yes. It's really the only thing worthwhile to do on this planet. Everything you do, think or feel, whether you're aware of it or not, is about your spiritual path. At a point on that path, it will become important to know every thought. Of course, that takes a lot of practice. Meditation, yoga and prayer are the best practices," Martha said.

"To what end? What's the point? I'm here to study humans. I'm doing the best that I can. I just want to finish my mission and go back home," Jesus said.

"Why? Because as far as I know, only one other person in the ninety-plus billion people that have roamed this earth through history, has had the opportunity you have now."

"Who?"

"Jesus."

"What?"

"Nooo, not *you* Jesus, the historical Jesus," Martha giggled.

"Oh. Why?"

"Well, it doesn't parallel exactly, but it seems that the historical Jesus never disconnected from God as he grew up on this planet. I don't know if he reincarnated. Some claim it was his first time in a human body. I do know that he was *in* this world, but not completely *of* this world. And that's the connection I'm making between you and him," Martha said.

Jesus sat back in his chair and crossed his arms. He wasn't convinced. Noticing he wasn't breathing, he inhaled deeply. He got a quiet, one-word flash—*Listen*. Taking another breath and leaning forward, he said, "Clarify."

"Okay, I know I said something to this effect before, but maybe I can put it better this time. You know, I've been thinking a lot about your situation. It's unique and Goob put you here. So first, let's talk about karma and reincarnation. You said that Goobers don't really have karma. What about reincarnation?" Martha asked.

"Hmmm...we do believe in souls. However, we don't believe in—or are unaware of—reincarnation."

"Okay. Here on this planet, as I understand it, one continues to reincarnate until one has finished working off one's karma from all one's lifetimes, at which point, the soul moves on to another plane of existence or returns to serve the greater plan. So, what's the catalyst on your world for the soul to continue to improve?" Martha asked, hoisting an eyebrow.

"We don't have one."

Martha studied Jesus's face for a moment, wondering if she should continue. Taking a deep breath, she said, "I know I've told you this before, but with only six months of karma to work off from this lifetime and none, I think, from any previous lifetimes, you have a chance to become enlightened."

"What does that even mean? Am I too tan?" Jesus asked.

"Nooo. Enlightenment, enlightenment, enlightenment," Martha repeated, as if she wasn't quite sure what to say next.

Jesus noticed her uncertainty and trying to be helpful, he asked, "What's the definition?"

"There is no one concrete definition." After a couple of powerful breaths, she intoned, "Enlightenment is about your connection to God and your environment, both internal and external. Upon reaching enlightenment, you realize that there is no environment, there is no you, there is only God and there is only service to God. You have no other motivations. You still have ego thoughts, but your focus is not on that but on staying connected. You know, people think it's like a light switch. Once on, it will always stay on. Not true. It's more of a spectrum. You can trigger the energies, you can get glimpses of the big picture, but it requires constant effort until of course, you realize that it doesn't require any effort at all, but relaxation into the moment instead."

"So? What's the point?" Jesus asked. "Why is that important to my mission?"

"Would you agree with the point that the purpose of existence is to bring light to darkness?" Martha asked.

"Yes, definitely. I do agree with that."

"What's the easiest way to do that?"

"To be the best part of Goob that one can be?" Jesus asked.

"Exactly! And how do you do that?" She stood up with a flourish. "Treat everyone as if they were you. Identify your emotions and follow them back to the thoughts or beliefs that created them." Waving her arms as if she were conducting a symphony, she continued, "Meditate and practice yoga. Pay attention to all your thoughts. Bring more spiritual energy into the body. Release the Kundalini energy, the creative energy that God gave us. That's the spiritual path." She leaned over and whispered in his ear, "Follow the teachings of the historical Jesus. That's the key."

Jesus felt a wave of electricity surge through his body. His mind numbed. Time slowed down. An image of Barbara flashed in his mind. "What about love?"

"You mean physical love or emotional love or what?" Martha asked.

"Barbara."

"Ahhh, she's the lock!" Martha exclaimed.

"She's the lock? What the hell does that mean?"

Stiffening suddenly, Martha said, "Sorry, it's time to go." She got up and headed for the door. Twirling around, she said, "Meditate on that!" and left.

Confused, Jesus sat there. What did Martha mean by, "She's the lock"? "Historical Jesus is the key"? He thought that generally men of spirit avoided physical contact with women. Some of the stuff Martha said made absolute sense, like treating others as you would treat yourself. Transforming beliefs to change unwanted behavior by paying attention to thoughts and emotions made sense, too. Bringing in more spiritual energy was logical; he just needed to practice that more. But "Barbara's the lock"? Jesus was at a loss as to what that meant.

He got up, paid the bill, and went to work. During his shift, three different people mentioned something along the lines of "love is the answer." He couldn't ignore that. Towards the end of the shift, Barbara came in to shop. She checked out in Jesus's line.

She gave him a hug. Jesus was still a little uncomfortable with public displays of affection, but he squeezed back.

"How about trying to go to the movies again?" she asked.

"When?"

"Well, we both work the morning shift this Saturday. I was thinking afterwards, we could do a little shopping, grab a bite to eat and see a movie."

"Shopping? What for?"

"After seeing your room and apartment, it occurred to me that it could use a woman's touch."

"How will you touching my things help?"

Laughing and stroking his arm, Barbara said, "Trust me. Your room could use a little freshening up."

Jesus really didn't care about his room, but he said politely, "Dinner and a movie sound good."

"And a little shopping," Barbara added.

"All right. And a little shopping, too."

Saturday came and Barbara was downright ecstatic the entire shift. Jesus was looking forward to the date too, but he couldn't muster the same intensity as Barbara. They counted out their tills together at the end of the shift and Barbara was particularly focused and finished first.

"The winner and still cham-peen!" she exclaimed, jumping up and down, her arms raised.

"Yeah, yeah. What are you so excited about?" Jesus said, turning in his cash drawer.

Hooking her arm around his, she said, "I'm looking forward to this evening."

Jesus smiled, "Me, too," and they walked arm in arm to his van, ignoring their coworkers' teasing.

As the van rumbled to life, he asked where they were going. "How about the new home furnishings store on the east side?" Barbara suggested.

"Okay, what are we going to get?"

"I made a list," Barbara said. She recited her recommendations, "You need a new mattress and box springs, some drapes, sheets, a comforter, pillows, pictures, a desk and a throw rug for starters."

Not knowing how to respond, Jesus thought for a moment and asked, "What's a comforter do? Hug me?"

"That's my job," Barbara said, smirking.

"Gotcha."

When they arrived, Barbara began her shopping spree. She was enjoying herself immensely. But as the cart filled, Jesus grew tense. It was his room...now she's decorating it?

"Why do I need all this stuff? How do you know I can even afford all this?" he asked, even though he knew he could.

"Well, what are you spending your money on? It's certainly not furnishings," Barbara retorted.

"That'll be $1,358.58, without delivery," the cashier said. "Would you like the mattress, box springs and desk delivered?"

Jesus was incredulous and getting a queasy feeling in his stomach. "Deliver them here," he said, handing the cashier his driver's license and credit card.

Barbara loaded up the cart with all the bags. Jesus signed the receipt and followed her out to the van. She was bouncing along whistling, oblivious to how he felt. It just made him madder. As they climbed into the van, doing his best not to appear upset, Jesus said, "You know, I'm not feeling very well. Can we get dinner and see a movie on another night?"

She rubbed his arm sympathetically, "Ohhh, I'm sorry you're not feeling well. I understand."

She does not, Jesus thought. Then he remembered Martha's warning that his anger was a signpost and that got him thinking. As he started the van, he decided that he needed to work this out immediately.

When he dropped Barbara off at her apartment, she invited him in. He declined and she trudged to her door with shoulders slumped, looked back at him once, and went in. He felt incredibly guilty, but knew that he had to figure out what was going on with the anger that he felt.

As he drove home, he took stock of his feelings. The anger returned as he looked up in the rearview mirror. Was it because she didn't even ask him if he wanted all this stuff? Was it because she didn't ask whether or not he could afford it? Why was it important to her in the first place? He decided that he would seek out Brad and ask his opinion.

Brad was working as the head cashier that night, and Jesus drove to the store and found him verifying the cash drawers. "Hey, have you got a moment so I can run some stuff by you?" Jesus asked.

"I give my first break in ten minutes. What's up?"

Jesus explained the situation.

"Well, this isn't unusual. I'm assuming that eventually the relationship will get to the point where she spends some nights at your place?"

"I guess so."

"Women like to feel comfortable in their surroundings. Your room is probably worse than a cell in a monastery. She may be jumping the gun a little bit, but I think that she wants to feel relaxed when she visits. Besides, you only have a twin bed and that's not big enough if you have a girlfriend. You'll need a double bed at the bare minimum."

"Okay. That makes sense...but why did I get so angry?" Jesus asked.

"Hey, guys need a space to call their own. It's a territorial thing. If she takes over your space, you give up some of your power."

His heart racing, Jesus jumped to his feet. "That's it! I felt like I had no power." He walked over and gave Brad a big hug, "Thanks."

Squirming to get free, Brad said, "All right, all right. You're welcome."

Jesus let go of Brad and walked to the door. "Wait a minute, I've got something to tell you," Brad said.

Turning around, Jesus saw him take a deep breath and then slump. "In the interest of full disclosure...I've slept with Barbara before."

Jesus looked at Brad with a blank gaze, "And?"

Brad straightened up, "Well, some guys would be jealous. But then again, you're not like most guys."

"Should I be jealous?" Jesus asked innocently.

Brad cocked his head to one side, not quite sure how to take the question. "No, not really. Only if she sleeps with someone while she's dating you, but then you already know that," he said slyly.

"Anything else?" Jesus asked.

134

"Yes. She's slept with Jack, too," Brad said.

"How come you've waited till now to tell me this?"

"It seems it's about to get serious. I thought you would want to know."

Jesus thought for a moment. "Are you telling me this because she's slept with other people before or that she's slept with my friends before?"

"The friend one. I guess it really wouldn't make any difference, would it?" Brad asked thoughtfully.

"Not to me," Jesus said, shrugging and walking out the door. On his drive home, he thought about what Brad had said. He searched his feelings and couldn't find anything that could be termed jealousy. Why had Brad told him? Was it that *he* was jealous, and if so, of what? Was it that he didn't have a girlfriend? *A person could go crazy trying to figure such things out,* he thought.

The next day at church, Jesus sat with Brad and Jack in the last pew. Barbara arrived late and chose not to sit next to Jesus. He leaned over and whispered that he wanted to talk with her and she shushed him loudly.

After the sermon, the four of them lined up to thank the pastor. Jesus joined them last and asked Barbara if he could talk with her.

"I'm talking with the pastor. Wait your turn," she said.

Noticing this, the pastor asked if there was anything he could do for her. Barbara said no and walked off. Jesus thanked the pastor for his sermon and followed her towards her car.

"Barbara, wait a second. I want to talk to you."

Barbara spun around, "Maybe I don't want to talk to you," she said, doing an about-face and continuing marching to her car.

Taking several quick steps to catch up, Jesus said, "I know you're upset. Don't you want to know why I was a little upset?"

Barbara stopped and faced him. "What do you mean, you were upset? I was helping you out. What did you have to be upset about?"

"Look, I was upset because it was as if I didn't have any say about decorating my room. I admit it needs some work, but don't I get any input?"

Barbara's demeanor changed, "Like what input?"

"You know, on colors and patterns. Why don't you come over? We'll unload the van, and start working on the room. From there, I'll decide what to keep and what to return. How about it?" Jesus asked, smiling.

Barbara stood there for a moment. She really wanted to make this work. Finally, she said okay and they hugged.

They spent the next couple of hours cleaning the windows, dusting, and putting up some pictures and the curtain rod. She wanted to put up the drapes, but they were decorated with flowers, as were the comforter and sheets. On top of that, peach was not one of his favorite colors. They took what he didn't want back to the store and he picked out something more suited to his tastes. On the way back to the apartment, Barbara asked Jesus if he was hungry.

"Yes, let's put this stuff up and get some food."

Barbara bounced around to face him. "Yes! Maybe we could see a movie, too?" she asked.

Jesus smiled and nodded. They drove in silence, both of them feeling better about their situation. When they arrived at the apartment, they unloaded the van and took everything inside. Jack was on the couch, pursuing his favorite pastimes. "What's all this stuff?" he asked.

"We're fixing up Jesus's room," Barbara said.

Jack followed them into the bedroom. "Big deal," he said.

"It's taking shape. The desk and new bed arrive tomorrow," Jesus said.

"New bed? Oh, good grief. I'm going to have to put up with having a woman in the apartment? Nothing will ever be good enough," Jack said, returning to the couch.

Jesus looked at Barbara and raised an eyebrow; she quickly looked away. They hung the drapes and some more pictures and put down the throw rug. His room was definitely looking more comfortable.

Jesus sat down on the bed and Barbara quickly sat down next to him. They surveyed their work for a moment, then Barbara leaned over and pecked him on the cheek. Jesus put his arm around her and kissed her on the lips. She kissed back ardently. Jesus was enjoying himself immensely, but when she started unbuttoning her shirt, a wave of fear flooded his gut. He grabbed her by the shoulders and gently separated their lips. "Not yet. Soon, I swear."

Barbara was better prepared for his reticence this time. She sat back, looked into his eyes, and smiled. "Okay honey, I can wait," she said supportively. This caught Jesus off guard. He had expected her to be upset and she wasn't, and that made him feel weird. Something else besides fear was coming up and he wasn't sure what it was. "Can I ask you something?" she said.

Jesus looked at her nervously.

"Can I tell people that we're boyfriend and girlfriend?"

Jesus considered her question. *What would it hurt if others knew about it?* "Yes. You can tell other people that we're boyfriend and girlfriend."

Barbara put both arms around his neck and gave him a passionate kiss. His mind began swimming; the fear returned. Again, he pushed her away. She stood up smiling and took both his hands in hers. "Maybe we should skip dinner and a movie tonight. Walk me to my car?" she asked.

"Yes, ma'am. I can do that." Walking arm in arm through the apartment, Barbara gave Jack the bird as they passed by. She got into her car and rolled down the window. "Come here," she said.

Jesus leaned over and Barbara caressed his cheeks and gave him a gentle kiss, "Good night. And don't think I'm letting you off the hook for a dinner and a movie," she said, pointing a finger at him.

Jesus laughed and waved as she drove off. It was time to do some yoga and meditate. Barbara kept popping into his mind, and he did his best to focus but couldn't. *Meditation is like this sometimes*, he thought.

Monday, the bed and desk arrived. After the deliverymen left, Jesus put the new sheets, pillow and comforter on the bed and then placed the computer chair at the desk. He stood in the doorway to take in the full effect. A sense of pride spread through him. *Why would these things bring me any satisfaction?* he wondered. He needed to buy a television, too, he decided.

At work the next day, Jesus had to field questions about the relationship. Most of his coworkers assumed Barbara was exaggerating, but he confirmed her assertion that indeed, they were dating. Jesus wasn't sure why his coworkers would doubt her.

Jack was cashiering that day. When the action slowed, he jumped into the conversation Jesus was having with Pete.

"Pete, Pete, get this. He's letting her decorate his room," Jack said, laughing and slapping Jesus on the back. Pete lifted an eyebrow, but said nothing.

"The room was bare. A jail cell has more furniture. It's very comfortable now. I think I'm going to get a TV," Jesus said.

"We've got a TV. You can watch in the living room," Jack said.

"When Barbara comes over, we may want to hang out in a nicer environment," Jesus said.

Flushing slightly, Jack said, "Nicer environment? My environment is just fine."

"It stinks. It's dusty. It's messy. No woman would ever want to come over. It's disgusting," Jesus said, walking back to his register.

"Maybe that's the way I like it," Jack replied.

"Maybe that's what you think you deserve," said Pete, returning to his register.

Taken aback, Jack went to his register and didn't say another word to his coworkers the entire evening.

Jack and Jesus arrived home at the same time. Excitedly, Jesus dragged Jack back to see his room. The improvement was remarkable. Without a word, Jack walked to his own bedroom and shut the door. Jesus stood there, not quite comprehending Jack's reaction. He could tell Jack was upset, but he had no clue as to why.

Chapter 16 – Sign of the cross

Jack and Jesus didn't see each other again until the roundtable on Thursday. The session started with the pastor suggesting the first topic—commitment.

"What kind of commitment?" Alice asked.

"All kinds of commitments—relationships, work, health, religion. All kinds."

"How about adding self-improvement to that list?" Jesus asked.

"Doesn't that really cover all of those?" asked Barbara.

"Good point, honey," Jesus said, prompting Barbara's dimples to appear.

"Well, self-improvement is one thing and commitment is another. They do cross paths though," said the pastor.

"Isn't self-improvement a commitment to live life the best you can?" asked Brad.

The pastor tilted his head from one side to the other mulling over the question. "Yes, to varying degrees."

"I think a crucial element of self-improvement is to evaluate your commitments. If something is not working for you then find something that does," said Jesus.

"Ah! But that wouldn't be the definition of commitment now, would it?" asked the pastor.

"Why don't we look up the definition?" asked Gertrude.

"Good idea. Where can we find a dictionary, Pastor?" asked Jesus.

"There's one in my office. I'll go get it."

After the pastor left, the table exchanged glances. "Where do you think he's going with this?" Jack asked.

"Commitment to religion would be my guess," said Alice.

"That seems like a good guess," said Juan.

Moments later, the pastor reentered the room with a dictionary. "Ah, let's see. Commitment. Here it is. 'Dedication, application or a pledge or undertaking'," said the pastor, closing the book.

Everyone cocked their heads to one side, contemplating the meaning. "Is that the only definition?" Jesus asked.

The pastor, a little perturbed, reopened the dictionary. "Let's see. 'An engagement or obligation that restricts freedom of action'," he said rather slowly.

"Apples and oranges," said Alice.

"True. However, a pledge can restrict your 'freedom of action'," Brad said.

"Yes, but dedication or a pledge to an ideal, say your religion, is a moral duty," said the pastor.

"I agree that dedication to an ideal or a higher calling is a moral duty," Jesus said. "But everything we listed is based on self-improvement, including religion. The purpose of religion is to help humankind improve its relationship with God. What if the religion you've chosen is not working for you? If it's not fulfilling my needs then why wouldn't I seek some other avenue?" asked Jesus.

There was a pause as the pastor, with a strained look on his face, calculated his response. Alice chimed in, "You might abandon your religion or even...abandon your belief in a god. I just read something recently that among Christians, Protestants in the country number less than half now and Catholics number just over 20 percent. And 20 percent are unaffiliated."

"Maybe that's what's wrong with the country," Ralph said.

The pastor's shoulders lifted as he inhaled deeply. "A commitment to Jesus Christ as your Lord and Savior is your only hope for redemption."

"Jesus Christ's teachings were of the highest order," Jesus said. "I have chosen to follow His principles to the best of my ability. Why does that mean that I have to commit to a particular religion? Why can't I simply follow His teachings?"

The pastor gradually turned white and then red. Everybody expected another explosion of anger from him, but calmly he said, "It's helpful to receive guidance from a learned source."

"True enough. You know, I'm not advocating getting rid of churches or religion. They're an important part of the community and a way for people to practice service to humanity, like our soup kitchen. I just don't think any one religion has cornered the market on God."

"Stock in G-O-D up 1 5/8 due to increased demand," Jack said.

Everybody laughed—even the pastor. "Wouldn't it be a lack of humility to think that any one religion has all the answers?" Jesus asked.

"My son, Jesus does have all the answers."

"There's no doubt in my mind that living a life like Jesus would lead to all the answers. The problem is that man-made religion is not teaching that," Jesus said.

"Man-made?" Ralph asked.

"Yes, man-made by the directive of Constantine, emperor of the Eastern Roman empire. He supposedly converted to Christianity when he saw a sign of the cross in the sky during his battle to become the emperor of the Western Roman Empire. However, on the triumphal arch he built next to the Coliseum in Rome celebrating his victory, there was not a single Christian symbol on it, just pagan symbols, mainly of the sun god Apollo," Jesus said.

"What does that prove?" asked Ralph.

"He was a pagan Roman emperor and his internal support, even with his victory, was shaky. Jesus Christ's teachings had spread through much of the Roman Army officer corps and Constantine needed their support and thus the cross-in-the-sky story was invented. He later convened the Council of Nicaea to standardize the Christian religion between its various factions. Why? To consolidate his support. I don't know if the Council did this, but the major Christian holidays were moved to coincide with pagan holidays. Why? To create a consensus and to gather converts. It's an amalgam of a lot of different things and I think that Jesus's teachings have gotten somewhat lost in the practice of Christianity. You could call it Consensus-anity as it is practiced now," Jesus said.

With a look of utter exhaustion, the pastor said, "I admit that the Christian church's origins went through a lot of...of...fine-tuning for lack of a better word. I have faith that it was divinely inspired by God."

"I think a simpler explanation would be that God, through His prophets—I want to emphasize the plural—has given us guidance, but we shape it in a way that is human and therefore flawed. Most of that has to do with keeping power in the hands of the few. Religions would have us believe that we can only find God through them, in church. I'm learning that I can connect to God with each breath," Jesus said.

In unison, everyone inhaled deeply. Timidly raising her hand, Gertrude asked, "Prophets, plural?"

"Yes. Buddha, Confucius, the prophet of Islam, to name a few. They had valuable things to say, too. I don't know if any of what they said conflicts with what Jesus taught, but some of what they said touches on subjects that he didn't teach," said Jesus.

"Give us an example," said Juan.

"Hmmm, how about, 'In a country well governed, poverty is something to be ashamed of. In a country badly governed, wealth is something to be ashamed of.' Confucius said that."

"So are we well or badly governed?" Jack asked.

"Well in some ways, bad in other ways," responded Alice.

"In America, I think the same sort of thing has happened. The principles of democracy are exceptional, but it's developed into something else," Jesus said.

"Didn't Jesus speak about poverty?" Barbara asked.

"Yes, but he didn't directly tie it to governments. From my research, I'm assuming that he was strictly concerned with the kingdom of God and bringing about change in the Hebrew religion," said Jesus.

"Well, we're well governed. America is exceptional," said Ralph.

"Tell that to the 15 percent living below the poverty line," Brad argued.

"For a 'Christian nation,' I think we act a lot more like Romans than anything Jesus taught," said Alice.

"On that note, I think it's time to call it an evening. Thank you all for coming," said the pastor, looking directly at Jesus and frowning.

Barbara and Jesus planned their dinner and movie for Saturday. By the time date night rolled around, Jesus was in such a good mood he was whistling as he drove over to her apartment. Her home was immaculate and smelled Fa-breezy. There were lots of bright colors and every surface held some figurine or doodad. He wasn't quite sure what to make of the place.

"What do you think? Isn't it heavenly?" Barbara asked.

Nodding, Jesus said, "It's nice. It's very nice. You look pretty good, too."

"Thank you. Come back and see my bedroom," Barbara said, grabbing Jesus by the hand.

He was pleasantly surprised. It was in pastels, not as busy as the living room, and Barbara's perfume permeated the air. "Nice, huh?"

"Very nice. I really like it."

"I want you to meet my roommate. Go sit on the couch and I'll get her."

Jesus did as he was told and moments later, Barbara entered the room with a middle-aged woman with black hair. "Betsy, this is my boyfriend, Jesus."

He stood up and extended his hand. Betsy looked at Barbara and back at Jesus. "Your name is Jesus? That's an unusual name."

"What can I say, my parents were hippies," he said, hand still extended.

Betsy folded her arms, whirled abruptly and marched back to her room muttering, "That's not right, that's not right." She shut her door loudly.

Jesus pursed his lips and looked at Barbara, who shrugged apologetically. "Betsy's a fundamentalist."

"More like a judgmentalist, if you ask me."

"Yeah, she disapproves of anybody who's different from her."

Arriving at the restaurant, Barbara began asking a series of questions: Where are you from? What was that like? Where did you go to school? He was prepared for most of them until she asked what his parents were like.

"Well, from what I can remember my dad was a good guy. He ran a cheese shop."

"Did he approve of you leaving the family business?"

"Not really. But I needed to strike out on my own."

"I sort of know what you mean. My father ran a baking business, but when it started having financial difficulties, he left."

"He left?"

"Yes. My mother blamed me. She kind of lost it and was committed. I stayed with my aunt till I was eighteen and then came to Austin."

"Wow! Have you talked with him since?"

"Nope, I have no idea where he is."

"That's sad. Have you talked with your mom?"

"No. I talk with my aunt about once a year, but that's it."

"That must have been rough," Jesus said.

"Yeah, it was."

Nothing else was said until the food arrived. Then Jesus asked, "Are you still angry with your father?"

Barbara thought about it a moment. "Yes and no. I've done a lot of soul-searching about it, and there's definitely some anger still there. It was devastating." They hardly spoke the rest of the meal. Barbara declined the dessert menu and Jesus did, too. They paid and left for the movies.

Barbara wanted to see a romantic comedy, *Overused Premise*. She seemed to enjoy it, but Jesus was bored.

About halfway through the movie, she put her hand on his thigh. Jesus took the cue, put an arm around her, and took her hand in his. They sat this way for a while until a particularly poignant moment when their eyes met. Jesus couldn't resist the attraction; he leaned over and kissed her. She flung her arms around his neck and they kissed passionately. Several minutes went by and Barbara took Jesus's hand and placed it on her breast. Taken aback, Jesus broke off the kissing and sat back.

"What's wrong?" she whispered.

"Nothing. You took me by surprise, that's all," he whispered back, placing his hands in his lap.

"What? You don't want to touch me now?" she whispered angrily.

"No, no, no. My arm fell asleep. Let me switch sides." He stood and moved to the seat on the opposite side of her. After doing some arm stretches, he put his arm around her, leaned over and resumed kissing her. He grabbed her other breast and she pulled back.

"Don't do that," she said.

"I thought that was what you wanted."

"In the throes of passion, yes. Right away, no."

"Sorry. I'm unfamiliar with the rules."

"I'll teach them to you," she said with a giggle, as they continued kissing. Their breathing became labored and she took his hand and placed it on her breast. This time Jesus didn't shy away, but he didn't know what to do next. Barbara sensed that and unbuttoned her blouse a couple of buttons. She moved his hand under her blouse and pulled up her bra. As he cupped her breast, a wave of excitement spread over him and he became physically excited. She began to moan softly and the lights came on. The movie was over.

Barbara quickly rebuttoned her blouse. "I'll meet you outside the ladies room," and dashed off. Jesus tried to stand up, but he wasn't aimed quite right and his excitement was too noticeable. Still breathing rapidly, and his mind in a stupor, he put his focus on his third eye. He began to breathe long and deeply; in less than a minute he was able to comfortably stand and proceeded to the lobby.

While waiting for Barbara, he thought about taking the relationship to the next level. There was a part of him that yearned for it, but another part of him was still afraid. Maybe he needed to talk with Martha about this.

Barbara emerged from the restroom, cheeks flushed. "Everything okay?" he asked.

"Yes, honey. Everything is fine," she said and they kissed lightly on the lips. She took his arm and they walked out to the van. As they were driving home, Jesus said, "I really liked that. Can we do that some more?"

"Of course, but not tonight. My period just started."

"Ahhh, menses. I understand."

"Maybe next week?"

"Saturday?" Jesus suggested.

"I'll try to get the morning shift."

"Me, too," Jesus said. They drove in silence until reaching her apartment. He escorted her to the door and they engaged in another long, soulful kiss. Breaking the embrace, Barbara said, "That's enough. I don't want to get too wound up or I'll never get to sleep."

Jesus turned to walk back to his van. Barbara caught a glimpse of him in profile and cooed, "Oooh, I look forward to next week."

Jesus looked down and laughed, "Yup." He waved, got in the van and drove home. He was going to have a hard time getting to sleep, too.

Chapter 17 — This is my body

Time seemed to stand still for Jesus, consumed as he was with his upcoming date with Barbara. They were nervous around each other at work and their conversations were short and awkward. Several nights that week, he studied about sex online. He thought he knew what to expect.

In the middle of the week, he went riding with Brad. Jesus, full of questions, asked in the middle of an uphill section, "Where can I buy condoms?"

"What?"

"Condoms. Where can I buy them?"

"The drugstore. Where else? Haven't you bought condoms before?" Brad asked.

"No. No I haven't."

"Really? Huh, go figure. You're thirty, right?"

"Twenty-nine."

"You're twenty-nine and you've never bought condoms before?"

"Well, my past girlfriends all used birth control," Jesus lied.

"Weren't you afraid of STDs?"

"No. Should I ask Barbara if she is disease-free?"

"That's kind of a tough question the first time around. Once you've established intimacy, then you can ask a delicate question like that. Besides, you can never be sure that your partner is telling the truth or even knows."

Jesus knew that humans lied, but Brad's comment still surprised him. Lying was never a problem back home and it made him uncomfortable to think about it.

Saturday morning, Jesus and Barbara worked the early shift. During a lull, he went over to her register and asked how she was doing. She looked at him, face beaming. Jesus smiled back. "I look forward to tonight, too," he said.

Twice, Jesus gave out the wrong change to a customer and his till ended up twenty dollars off. He didn't care. His mind was on one thing and one thing only.

At the end of the shift, Barbara asked if Jack was going to be home that night. Jesus didn't know, but he told her that he would find out. As he turned around, there was Jack. "Yup. Working till close. Maybe I can get off early. Why?" Jack asked.

Jesus hesitated. Barbara grinned. Looking back and forth between them, Jack said, "Oh, I get it. Boom-chicka-now-now, ee-ee-ee-ee." He paused a moment. "Okay, I'll work till the end of the shift to give you two lovebirds some privacy."

Barbara gave Jack a big hug. Jesus said, "I'll pick you up at six thirty." He had two hours to get ready. First, he practiced a bit of yoga and meditation to calm his nerves. He performed his pre-date preparations and dressed in his nicest clothes. He still had thirty minutes to go. He started to get nervous again and got online to study some more.

As he drove over to Barbara's apartment, he thought, *How did I get to this point? Why is she so attracted to me?* He didn't have an answer, and when he filed his final report, he was sure that he would be asked about this. *Is this date really part of my mission?*

Barbara answered the door and his heart skipped a beat. "Come on in and have a seat. I'm almost ready."

"You look lovely," Jesus stressed, leaning over and giving her a peck on the cheek.

Jesus sat down and Betsy entered the room. She looked disapprovingly at him and went to the kitchen. Barbara returned with her purse and announced she was ready. Jesus was glad he didn't have to talk with Betsy.

"What are you in the mood for?" Jesus asked.

"Something light. How about Thai food?"

"Sounds good."

On the way to the restaurant, Jesus asked how Betsy became her roommate. "She used to belong to our church. When I first moved here I saw a notice for 'roommate wanted' on the bulletin board there. When I moved in she was much more pleasant, but she had a falling-out with her kids and since then she's changed."

"What was the issue?"

"I never did get a straight answer from her."

At dinner, Jesus asked Barbara some more about her childhood, and she asked him about his. He made up a few stories on the spot, with the excuse that he couldn't remember more because of the amnesia. It occurred to him that he ought to write them down so that he wouldn't contradict himself in the future.

Barbara didn't eat half her entrée, and she didn't want any dessert. Jesus ate everything on his plate, his yearning translating into gluttony. They paid the check and left.

Before Jesus could get his seatbelt on, he yawned. Barbara reacted quickly and began rubbing his arm. "I'm fine. I'm fine, really," he said, yawning a second time. For some reason, he felt exhausted. *Maybe it's from too much anticipation*, he thought.

Once they arrived at his apartment, Jesus plopped down on the couch. Barbara excused herself and went to the bathroom. When she returned, she heard Jesus snoring lightly. She sat down up against him and rubbed his chest. "Jesus. Jesus, wake up," she said in a singsong voice.

He snorted oddly and rolled toward the corner of the couch. Barbara sighed disappointedly. This wasn't the plan. She decided to drive Jesus's van home and pick him up for church in the morning. She wrote him a note and left.

Jesus awoke on the couch the next morning with a stiff neck. He was kind of groggy as he read Barbara's note. *Better start getting ready*, he thought.

Barbara arrived an hour later. She kissed him at the door. Just as they were leaving, Jack emerged from his room. "Hey, can I get a ride?"

"What's the matter with your car?" Jesus asked.

"It's getting worked on."

"What about your old car?"

"I finally sold it to some loser musician for $500," Jack said.

"Okay, but you'll have to get a ride back with someone else," Barbara said.

"Sure."

"Why?" Jesus asked.

"It's a surprise," Barbara said coyly.

Jack teased Barbara about the surprise all the way to church. They sat down in the last pew as usual and Brad arrived shortly thereafter. The sermon was about the Book of Genesis. The pastor went on and on about creating the heavens and the earth, man and woman. About how sacred it was and how humans needed to apply the same sanctity to their own creations. He emphasized that sex should be considered sacred, too—not as exercise or stress relief or an activity to alleviate boredom.

Jesus was considering these words carefully when Jack said, "So that's why he's so boring. He hasn't had any sacred activity lately." The four of them giggled, but Jesus wondered if he should consider what the pastor said.

After the service, Jesus made a point of sincerely thanking the pastor for his thoughts on the matter. Barbara pointedly said, "While sex is sacred, it's also a normal human experience. It sounded to me like you were judging people for having sex."

The edge in her voice surprised the pastor. "No, my dear. Well, yes, to some degree. As with any human activity, it should be practiced in moderation. I do think that it's special though, and should be treated that way."

Briefly considering the pastor's words, Barbara replied, "I agree with that. In fact, I think it was much better phrased than your sermon. Have a nice day."

Jesus asked Barbara about the surprise as they walked to the van. "We're going to the lake. I've prepared a picnic basket for us and it's in the back. Now drive, says Miss Daisy!" she exclaimed as she climbed in.

From Barbara's tone, Jesus inferred that he should laugh at the reference so he did. The drive up to the lake was meandering and beautiful. They entered the park and went to the same spot as their last picnic. Barbara jumped out of the van and went to the back to retrieve the picnic basket. Jesus got the blanket and spread it on the ground. They both sat down with a sigh. "What did you bring this time?" Jesus asked.

"A little wine, fruit, cheese and crackers," she said, unpacking the picnic basket. She had brought much less food than the previous time. Jesus opened the bottle of wine as Barbara opened the cheese and crackers. Barbara handed the wine glasses to Jesus to fill; he poured the wine carefully and handed one back.

"A toast. Here's to us," he said as they clinked their glasses together.

"Here's to not falling asleep," Barbara said, laughing.

They took sips of wine and gazed into each other's eyes. Jesus noticed he was slightly trembling and that Barbara was, too. She sat down her wine glass and spread some cheese on a cracker. She got to her knees and moved close to Jesus. "Open wide," she said.

He ate the cracker. He had tasted this cheese before, but for some reason it tasted so much better this time. "Ohhh, that is so good," he said. He prepared one for Barbara. "Your turn."

As she was chewing and making satisfied noises, Jesus noticed that the trees, grass and lake were more distinct, the colors brighter and the air crisper. *My senses must be heightened*, he thought.

After swallowing, she asked, "Was that your body?"

"Wait. You chastise me for puns and then you go and crack a Jesus joke?" he asked, half-laughing.

"I'm just teasing," she said sheepishly.

"That wasn't my body. This is my body," said Jesus, rising to his knees and striking a manly pose.

Barbara picked up her wine glass and finished it in one big gulp. Leaping at Jesus, she knocked him and his wine over. Before he could say anything, she began kissing him passionately. This went on for several minutes until Barbara suggested they get in the van.

It wasn't a comedy of errors, but the natural result of one partner being far more experienced than the other—especially with the condom. Nearing the conclusion, the van started squeaking, seemingly urging Jesus on. As he finished, he collapsed onto Barbara, but he couldn't feel her body. She couldn't feel his. With his eyes closed, he saw twinkling lights and it seemed like he was floating in outer space. Such a glorious feeling, he wished it would go on forever, but a loud banging on the side of the van interrupted his reverie. *What is going on?* he wondered.

"So, how do they procreate?" the curious judge asked.

"It's a simple pole and portal system similar to our own except for a few crucial details," said Jesus.

"And those details are?" asked the curious judge.

"The man's pole enters the woman's portal to inseminate her."

"Let me see if I understand this. The man's pole..."

"Penis, Your Honor. It's called a penis."

"The man's penis enters the woman and does what?" asked the curious judge.

"After vigorous stimulation, a fluid called semen shoots out and based on a number of factors, might or might not impregnate her."

"Vigorous stimulation?" asked the curious judge.

"Pumping, Your Honor. It can be a minute or thirty minutes or more depending on the man and the techniques used."

The curious judge contemplated this, using his hands to try to simulate the action. Suddenly, he began shaking uncontrollably and making an odd staccato noise.

"What are you doing?" demanded the fussy judge.

When the curious judge didn't respond, Jesus said, "I believe he is laughing, Your Honor, Goober-style."

"Stop that! Stop that right now!" yelled the fussy judge, which only provoked more laughter from the curious judge until he fell off his perch onto the floor. The laughter continued for several minutes until, breathlessly, he asked for help to right himself. When the court sentinels couldn't pick him up, a winch was brought in.

Once again on his perch, the curious judge apologized for his unusual behavior and promised that it wouldn't happen again.

"See that it doesn't," sneered the fussy judge. "Continue the testimony."

"Get dressed and come on out," said an unknown voice. Barbara whispered, "Oh my God, it's the cops."

Hurriedly, they dressed. They emerged disheveled from the van, beads of sweat rolling down their faces, shielding their eyes from the sun. As Jesus's eyes became accustomed to the bright sunlight, he was startled to see a crowd of people, fifteen to twenty in all, gathered around the van. Some of the people were smiling, but most of them had disapproving looks on their faces. Even more unexpected was the police car and the officer standing right in front of him.

"Don't I know you? Haven't I arrested you before?" asked the officer.

"I've never been arrested," answered Jesus.

"Where do I know you from?" asked the officer, a stern expression on his face.

Simultaneously, they both remembered and started laughing.

"Why are you laughing?" Barbara asked, nudging Jesus, her nervousness beginning to subside.

Smiling, Jesus said, "Honey, this is Officer Roy, who found me and took me to the soup kitchen."

Barbara's eyes opened wide. She grabbed Officer Roy's hand and shook it briskly. "Thank you! Thank you for taking care of him that night."

Amused by Barbara's gratitude, Officer Roy said, "You're welcome, young lady." Turning to Jesus, he asked, "So, how are things going for you nowadays?"

Seeing that the confrontation had turned friendly, the crowd began to disperse.

"Well, I've got a job at Grains for Brains and I belong to the Megalithic Church. I live in a two-bedroom apartment with a roommate. Most importantly, I have a girlfriend," Jesus said, putting his arm around Barbara and squeezing. "What are you doing all the way out here?"

"Exchange program. Well, I'm glad to see everything is working out for you. But catching you naked twice...." He paused. "If there's a third time, I'm going to have to arrest you," he said, returning to his cruiser.

Waving, Jesus replied, "Yes sir. I'll get the hang of wearing clothes, I promise."

Laughing, Officer Roy said, "Let's hope so." He pulled away slowly as Jesus and Barbara waved again.

"That was a close one," she said.

"He really wouldn't have arrested us?" Jesus asked, as they gathered the picnic supplies.

Loading them into the van, Barbara said, "He most certainly could have if he wanted to."

"How do you know?"

"It's happened to me before."

"You've been arrested before?" Jesus asked.

"Yes, for indecent exposure."

"It's indecent to be naked?"

"Not when you're little," she said, her voice trailing.

"So, if you have a small penis, it's okay?"

Barbara burst out laughing. "Nooo. Little meaning young."

"Oh. Yeah, I understand," said Jesus, starting the van.

They left the park and headed for Barbara's apartment. She tried to engage Jesus in small talk, but he was focused on some new feelings that were bubbling to the surface. He felt like he had done something wrong and he didn't know why. Making love was supposed to be the epitome of human interaction, yet there appeared to be some type of judgment on where it occurred. This feeling seemed to be similar to when he punched that man in the nose. This required some research.

When they arrived, Barbara asked him in but he declined. He gave her a peck on the lips and said goodbye. She felt like she needed some closure from the incident, but Jesus wasn't providing any. Their lovemaking was very satisfying, but right now she was feeling unsettled and she didn't like it.

Jesus got home and immediately got on the computer. He decided from his research that he was feeling shame. He didn't like it and he couldn't determine whether it was justified or not.

On his bike the next day, the feeling of shame gnawed at him. He sprinted several times to the point of exhaustion but couldn't get rid of it. He thought that maybe he should bring it up at Thursday's roundtable.

He thought about calling Barbara, but forgot and she didn't work the next day. Wednesday, she worked in the morning while Jesus was at the soup kitchen. He stayed late to help with some plumbing problems, making him late for work and missing her. She didn't work Thursday morning, so the next time they saw each other was at the roundtable.

Jesus arrived a few minutes early and as he turned the corner he saw Barbara and waved. Arriving at the entrance simultaneously, he opened the door and bowed. "After you, milady." She didn't respond. He tried to put his arm around her as they were walking, but she quickly shied away.

"You're upset I didn't call, aren't you?" he asked. Barbara didn't respond again and kept on walking. Jesus knew he was in trouble.

Barbara greeted everyone when she entered the room. Jesus walked in and sat silently, bracing himself for retribution. The pastor entered last and called for topics.

Jesus spoke first. "I would like to talk about shame. How did it start and why? What's its purpose in God's plan?"

The pastor began, "It was first mentioned in Genesis. After Eve took a bite of the apple, Adam and Eve lost their immortality, realized they were naked, and fashioned fig leaves to cover their nakedness. The bite of the apple cursed them with the knowledge of good and evil."

Brad spoke up, "So, even though God made them naked, which one would assume would not be evil since that's how God made them, they decided that it was wrong or evil?"

"There are theories that eating the apple represented disobeying God and that was, of course, wrong. They were then 'cursed with the knowledge of good and evil'," Alice said.

"Wait, I thought that God told them to be fruitful and multiply. Why would they cover up their genitals?" asked Barbara.

"Maybe they thought the snake was going to bite them," suggested Jack, producing a few snickers.

When it quieted down, the pastor continued, "Disobeying God is the greatest sin, people."

"But wouldn't God, being omnipotent and omniscient, already know that they would disobey him?" asked Jesus.

"Yeah, it's not like He hadn't already experienced that...with Lilith," said Alice.

"Who's Lilith?" asked Gertrude.

"Adam's first wife," said Alice.

"Adam's first wife? You're kidding me! Is that true, Pastor?" asked Gertrude.

Everyone looked at the pastor, waiting for a reply. "In the original version of Genesis, Adam did have a wife before Eve. But in the Christian version of Genesis, she was removed," he said.

"Redacting the evidence, as it were," said Alice.

"What did she do to get removed?" asked Juan.

The pastor didn't want to talk about this, but he slowly continued, "She refused to be on the bottom when they, uh, made love."

"Adam thought he was superior to Lilith and told her she belonged on the bottom. Typical male," said Alice.

"Doesn't make any difference to me whether I'm on the top or the bottom," said Barbara.

"You go, girl," said Jack, patting her on the back.

"What happened to her?" asked Gertrude.

Alice jumped in before the pastor could respond. "She said 'To hell with this' and left."

"Not exactly those words, but yes, that's basically what happened," said the pastor.

"So, God created *three* humans in the beginning?" asked Gertrude.

"A threesome! God is kinky," said Jack, with everybody laughing. "Man, I'm on fire tonight!"

"It seems to me that Adam and Eve, as male and female, represent two aspects of God. Why would he allow Adam to disrespect Lilith like that? That doesn't make any sense," said Jesus.

"Perhaps that's why early Christian leaders excluded her," suggested the pastor.

"Or maybe that was the early Christian leaders attempt to subjugate women to the will of men. Early man was insecure. Far be it to have a woman thinking for herself in the scriptures," said Alice.

"On top of that, God's wife, Asherah, was edited out, too," added Jesus.

"Are you serious? God had a wife?" exclaimed Barbara.

"Yes. She was worshipped as the 'Queen of Heaven.' However, over the next thousand years, the Hebrew religion became monotheistic and almost all mention of her was eliminated," said Jesus.

"Is that true, too, Pastor?" asked Gertrude.

"Yes. She was removed from the Old Testament long before Christians included it in their Bible."

"And what happened to Lilith?" asked Gertrude.

"She was included in several ancient civilizations' writings as a demon. But let's get back to Hey-Zeus's original topic of shame," said the pastor.

In unison, Gertrude, Brad and Barbara corrected him, "Jesus."

The pastor waved his hand dismissively and continued, "Shame is the human response to doing something wrong. It's God's way of correcting us."

Ralph finally spoke up, "Shame has made me the man I am today."

"But didn't Jesus teach against shame?" asked Brad.

"Well, yes," said the pastor.

"Jesus was sent by God to teach a better way. A great example is shame," said Jesus. I don't like this mixing of the teachings of the Old and New Testaments. It doesn't make any sense. If Jesus's teachings were the new and improved path, why would Christians even teach the Old Testament?"

"Yeah, what good is teaching guilt and shame if that's not God's plan anymore?" asked Barbara.

The pastor squirmed in his seat, uncomfortable with the direction of the conversation. He felt like the group was questioning his ministerial skills. "So, how would you teach your children to behave correctly?" asked the pastor.

Jesus immediately replied, "By love and by example. Just like the historical Jesus. It's tough enough learning all there is to know about the human experience, but to have to feel bad in order to learn that just makes it all the harder. Not to mention learning about the rich vastness of the human experience in one lifetime."

Slapping her hand on the table, Alice said, "Reincarnation. That's something else that was excluded from the Bible even though Jesus, the 'historical' Jesus, mentioned it."

Murmurs went up around the table. Gertrude asked, "Really, Pastor?"

Worn out, the pastor barely managed to answer, "He did say that John the Baptist was Elijah. Yes."

"Wow! You sure know a lot about early Christianity for an atheist," Jack said to Alice.

"I've never been satisfied with all the contradictions that I was taught as a child. It didn't make any sense to me. God seemed to do more evil than good. But maybe I need to take a different approach now," Alice said, glancing at Jesus.

Wearily, the pastor closed the roundtable for the evening. As everybody filed out of the room, Jesus felt better about the affair at the lake. He was deep in thought about the concepts of guilt and shame when something brushed the back of his neck. "Who touched me?" he said, spinning around.

Barbara jumped into view, laughing. "I'm still mad at you, but I wanted you to know that I liked the things you said tonight."

"You made some good points, too. I'm sorry I didn't call you. I don't have a lot of experience being a boyfriend," said Jesus.

"You'll get better," Barbara said, rushing off to her car.

"I will," said Jesus to himself.

Chapter 18 – Dark night of the soul

As far as Jesus was concerned, his mission had been a success to this point. He had integrated into human life fairly smoothly. He had a girlfriend, though she was frequently mad at him. He had a job, belonged to a church, served in a soup kitchen and had friends. His days were filled with work, exercise and eating right. He had reached the point where he practiced yoga and meditation daily. Fear-based thoughts were coming up less and less. Studying humanity through personal interactions and research on the Internet, he felt proud of the work he was doing and even daydreamed about being greeted as a hero upon returning to his home planet. He was satisfied, even fulfilled, and his life couldn't be going any better.

When Sunday came, Jesus went to church, took his customary seat in the last pew and waited for his friends to arrive. Barbara joined him, her perfume reminding him of their last picnic up at the lake. He put his arm around her and gave her a peck on the cheek. "Again, I'm sorry for not calling you. I'll endeavor to do better."

She smiled and snuggled up close to him. Jesus thought that this was the happiest he'd ever been, on Earth or on Gooberia. They sat in silence until Jack arrived. "Okay you two, break it up," he said, plopping down next to Barbara.

They talked quietly as the pews filled up. Brad arrived just before the sermon started. The pastor spoke on the story of creation. He was quite adamant that it was accurate and that to question it was to question one's faith. The four of them glanced at each other over and over again throughout the sermon.

After the service ended, the pastor took his customary position outside the church doors, greeting the parishioners as they exited. When it was his turn, Jesus asked, "Why did you refute everything discussed at the roundtable on Thursday?"

"Hey-Zeus, I put a lot of thought into my sermon. I know that several of you don't agree with me, but I believe the Bible is the word of God and nothing can shake my faith in it," he replied, looking at each of them in the eye one at a time.

"Okay. I don't think that the intent of the conversation was to shake your faith, but to get clarification on what we've been taught," Jesus said.

"If you find my position contrary to what you believe, you can seek out a church that aligns more with your beliefs," the pastor said.

Flinching, Jesus said in a concerned voice, "I'm not sure what I believe; that's why I ask questions at the roundtable."

Forcing a smile, the pastor said, "I'm pretty sure I know what you believe and it doesn't agree with the teachings of this church."

Jesus started to respond, but Brad jumped in. "Come on, let's go home."

The four of them walked away in silence. As they reached the van, Jack said, "What a dick!"

"He's not a dick, Jack. He's...he's confused," Brad replied.

"I don't know about confused. I think he feels insulted," argued Barbara.

"I'll talk to him later this week and see what's going on. I feel sort of unwelcome and it makes me uncomfortable," said Jesus.

"Me, too," said Barbara.

"He's a dick. Discussing religion is verboten at the roundtables now?" insisted Jack.

"It was a great place to find out what disparate people thought about things, to gather information," said Jesus disappointedly.

"He'll get over it. I think sometimes your conclusions...surprise him," said Brad.

Jesus and Barbara got in the van. He seemed dejected, so she suggested they get some lunch. Between breakfast tacos and Barbara's enthusiasm, he began feeling better and suggested they head to his apartment.

Jack met them at the door as he left, telling them that he would be gone for hours. He winked at Jesus. Barbara got the message immediately, but Jesus was thinking about church again.

Joining him on the couch, Barbara asked, "Whatcha thinking 'bout?"

"The pastor."

"Forget about him and give me a kiss."

He did, but his heart really wasn't in it. "You know we have the apartment to ourselves. For hours," Barbara said in a singsong voice.

Jack's comment finally clicked, and Jesus kissed her for real. They rushed to the bedroom in such a hurry that he didn't even take off his socks. His comfort level had greatly increased from their first time and he tried some new material he had found on the Internet. Lasting longer, they finished together, the sheets damp with sweat.

"Good God, that was incredible!" Jesus exclaimed, when he had caught his breath. "No wonder there's seven billion humans on this planet."

"Yeah, it was. And you're getting better, honey. You really are."

"Thanks, but additional practice may be needed," he said, rolling over and embracing her. They spent another hour cuddling and engaging in pillow talk before Barbara got dressed and left for work. After seeing her off, Jesus assumed everything was okay between them now. He spent the evening continuing his research on lovemaking techniques.

The yoga class the next day was particularly strenuous, and Jesus worked up a sweat. He was sitting down when he needed to adjust himself into another position on the floor. He made fists of his hands and was pushing down to lift his buttocks, when his right wrist suddenly collapsed. He let out a loud "Owww!" and sat there cradling his arm.

The teacher asked if he was okay. He assured her he was, but for the rest of the class, he found himself favoring the wrist. When class was over, he rode his bike home. The pain in his wrist had gotten worse and he had difficulty supporting himself with that hand. By the time he arrived, he was riding one-handed.

The pain put him in a foul mood. It was irritating that something as simple as adjusting his weight had injured him. He called Martha and left a message asking what he should do and then put ice on it.

The next day at work, the wrist was still bothering him. The angle he had to use to type on the register pinched it, so he switched hands frequently. He was deep in thought over why this had happened to him and finally decided that there must be some purpose to this and that he would try to be positive and not let it affect his work.

Just as he thought that, he looked up at his next customer. He looked familiar, but Jesus couldn't quite place him. The customer, recognizing Jesus immediately, yelled, "Ah-HA! Payback!" and punched him in the nose. Jesus took a step back with blood already beginning to drip. He looked at the blood on his hand and then at his assailant. It was the man he had punched on the bike ride.

Witnessing the assault, Pete rushed over and blocked the assailant's exit. The next customer in line also took a blocking position, trapping him. Taking a martial arts stance, the man said, "Come on! You want some more?"

Pete asked if he should call the police and quietly Jesus said no. He put up his closed sign and went to the front-end office. Pete moved aside to let the attacker go, and as he was leaving, he yelled back, "I knew you were a pansy. Ya freak! I'll be waiting for you outside."

Following him outside, Pete warned him never to return or the police would be called. The man made some more threats, but he eventually got in his car and drove off.

Clara was in the office when Jesus walked in with blood on his shirt. She exclaimed, "What happened?" and Jesus recounted the tale including the bike ride. "When you're ready, count out your till, and then you can go home and recover."

Driving home was difficult because his nose kept dripping blood. *At least I didn't ride my bike to work,* he thought. When he got home he prepared two ice packs, one for his wrist and one for his nose. Jack returned from running errands to get ready for his evening shift and found Jesus on the couch.

"What the hell is wrong with you?"

Jesus briefly described each ice pack's story in vague detail because he didn't feel like talking. "Karma's a bitch, dude," Jack said, walking to the bathroom.

Is that what's going on? Is that why I hurt my wrist? So I couldn't punch him back? If my wrist had been okay, would I have hit him? He turned on the TV so he wouldn't have to think anymore and shortly fell asleep.

He awoke the next morning with a headache, still on the couch. He tried to push himself up to stand and pinched his wrist. "Goddamn it!" he yelled. Today was one of his soup kitchen days and he didn't really feel like going, but he decided that service to humanity just might make him feel better. On the way there, he stopped by the bank. He wanted to buy a present for Barbara and needed cash.

He met Alice at the kitchen. Brad had told her about the pastor's most recent sermon, and she commiserated with Jesus about its implications. The soup kitchen shift went smoothly, though the headache never went away. As he trudged back to the van, lost in thought, someone slammed into him from behind, smashing his head against the van. Jesus crumpled to the ground, his nose bleeding again. "Give me all your money!" the attacker growled.

"What?" Jesus asked woozily.

"Give me all your money!" said the attacker, waving a knife at him.

Jesus's eyes were blurry and he couldn't make out the man's face. He fumbled around and pulled the cash for Barbara's gift from his pocket and handed it over.

"Give me your watch," said the assailant.

"I don't have one."

"Whaddya mean you don't have a watch?"

"I don't have a watch! Time's an illusion anyway," said Jesus.

"Shut up, ya freak! Lie face down and count to a hundred before you look up."

Jesus complied and heard the footsteps of the retreating mugger. His last thought before he passed out was, *Why is this happening to me, Lord?*

He became aware of someone nudging him. Turning over, he opened his eyes to see Alice, Burt and several other members of the soup kitchen crew standing over him. "Are you okay? What happened?" Alice asked.

"I got robbed. The mugger shoved me into the van and took my money. He had a knife," Jesus said, tenderly touching his swollen nose.

"There have been several robberies in this area in the last couple of weeks. Did he cut you?" Burt asked.

Struggling to his feet, Jesus said, "I don't think so."

"Are you sure? That's a lot of blood."

"My nose was already susceptible to bleeding since I got punched yesterday."

"That's a bad week. Let's get you inside and call the police so you can file a report," said Alice.

"I didn't get a good look at him. I don't think I'd recognize him if I saw him."

"Doesn't matter. The police should be made aware of the robbery. Come on, put your arm on my shoulder. Burt, get the other side," Alice said.

They helped Jesus inside and got him an ice pack. He asked Alice to call the store and tell them he would be late. The police soon arrived and took a statement. After a half hour, Jesus got to his feet wobbling slightly. "Are you sure you're okay? You might have a concussion," Alice said.

"Other than a headache, my sore nose and my aching wrist, I'm fine," Jesus said half-chuckling, making his way to the door. As he was driving to the store, he again asked God why this was happening to him.

156

He met Pete doing a carryout on his way into the store. "You look a lot worse than yesterday," Pete said.

Jesus told him about the robbery as they walked inside. Clara was making the schedule for the following week. "Are you okay? How did it happen?" she asked.

Telling the story again, Jesus became aware of his growing anger. He tried his best to ignore it, but the rest of the day it continued to present itself. Clara sent him home early, which was a good thing because he didn't feel like working at all. He drove home and prepared three ice packs—one for his head, one for his face and one for his wrist. Turning on the stereo, he eventually fell asleep on the couch.

The next day Martha returned his call about what to do for his wrist—and advised him on his nose as well. She couldn't see him right now and said she would call him when she could.

When he went to work, Barbara fawned over him and asked him several times if he wanted her to come over and take care of him. He put off answering until the end of the shift and then declined. He left the store as soon as possible to go home and heal.

After preparing three ice packs again, he was getting pretty good at keeping the ice from spewing out onto the floor. He slathered arnica gel on his nose and wrist and then covered himself with the ice packs. His body relaxed and he sank into the couch feeling somewhat comfortable for the first time in what seemed like days. He realized that nothing bad had happened to him that day. *Maybe this is one of those "bad things happen in threes" phenomena*, he thought.

On Friday, he awoke feeling nervous. It wasn't until he was almost at the church for his soup kitchen shift that he realized his nervousness was about the mugging. He scanned the parking lot when he arrived, then half-ran inside. After his shift, he went to see the pastor.

He was whistling when Jesus knocked on the door. Without looking up, the pastor replied, "I'll be with you in a minute."

Jesus sat down quietly. When the pastor looked up, he fell silent and his demeanor changed. "What can I do for you?"

Jesus didn't know quite how to begin. "Well, uh, I felt uncomfortable about your suggestion that I find another church. I owe you a great deal and I really like this church. I ask a lot of questions to expand my knowledge, not to insult you or shake your faith."

The pastor sat back in his chair and surveyed Jesus's face, moving his head from side to side, fixing one eye on him at a time. Finally, he sat forward, his elbows on the desk. "I don't quite believe you, Hey-Zeus. You constantly introduce the subject of Christian dogma, question it, and get the others riled up. Your intention seems to be to cause trouble."

"What? Because I ask questions about what appear to be inconsistencies? I'm just examining human beliefs. What are you afraid of?" asked Jesus.

His voice rising, the pastor said, "What am I afraid of? Nothing, with God on my side. The problem is that you don't respect me."

"Yes I do. That's why I'm asking you these questions. I would think that with God on your side, you'd be open to examining your beliefs."

"I believe in the accuracy of the Bible and how I was taught it," insisted the pastor.

"I'm sorry, but I think people evolve, gain knowledge, grow wiser. Things that happened two thousand years ago or more would be perceived differently by people today. The path of humanity is no different than that of a single life. You're born unable to even protect yourself. You learn what your parents and society want to teach you until you become an adult. At that point, you learn what life is really about. I think it's the same for humanity," said Jesus.

"That may be true, but I believe what I believe and you should respect that," stammered the pastor.

"I do. I really do. I consider you an expert on this subject. But even experts in a particular field continue to do research and test their theories. Is it that my asking you questions about your beliefs brings up doubt?" asked Jesus.

The pastor looked aghast. "You believe what you want, Hey-Zeus. You can come to this church if you want. You can work in the soup kitchen and you can come to the roundtables, but I will no longer engage in these diatribes against my religion," he snarled.

Stunned, Jesus slowly rose to his feet. He tried to say something, but he couldn't find the words. Walking to the door, he looked back. He tried to say something again, but still couldn't. He trudged to his van, feeling crushed. *What in the world is going on?*

He was so distraught he tried to unlock the van with his apartment key, which got stuck. He went back inside and called a locksmith. He called work, too, just to let them know that he was going to be late and why. About an hour later, the locksmith showed up and freed his apartment key.

Upon arriving at the store, he was greeted with several sarcastic remarks about his tardiness and he walked by the registers without commenting. He clocked in and headed for the front-end office. Looking up from her desk, Clara said, "There you are. Sit down, please."

Jesus slumped into a chair. He could barely look Clara in the eye. "I know times have been kind of tough on you lately, so it's better you hear this from me. I've decided to give the Assistant Department Head position to Brad. It was a tough choice, but I feel that Brad is somewhat more consistent than you, especially of late."

Since he was just visiting, this shouldn't have made any difference to Jesus. But it did and he felt hurt. He said he understood, thanked Clara for considering him, got his cash drawer, and walked slowly to the only open register. As the shift ground on, he began to wonder if God wasn't punishing him somehow. Maybe he wasn't following the right path. Maybe he should ignore the inconsistencies in Christianity and align himself with the pastor's beliefs. He didn't know and he didn't care at the moment. He just wanted to feel better.

Barbara visited his register several times when the lines thinned, but Jesus was distant. She wanted to know what was going on, but the thought of talking about it seemed overwhelming, even with her. Barbara took his remoteness the wrong way.

Later in the shift as Jesus waited on a customer, he kept hearing pieces of conversation from Barbara's line. It seemed like she knew the customer and was being overly complimentary to him. She gave him a big hug after the sale was over. Jesus heard her say, "Saturday, 7 p.m. I'll be there."

He finally had a chance to talk to her when they were counting their receipts. "So, what's happening Saturday at 7 p.m.?"

"There's a benefit. Bill asked me if I wanted to go. I said yes," Barbara said.

"Uh-oh," said Wanda.

"I don't understand," said Jesus.

"We're just friends now, Bill and me, so you have nothing to worry about," Barbara said.

Wanda jumped in again. "We're talking about your ex-boyfriend?"

"Yes," Barbara said in a bored manner.

Jesus numbly stared at her, unable to comprehend this turn of events. Barbara continued counting her money.

"Wait, I thought you two were dating," said Wanda.

"We are," Barbara confirmed.

"I don't understand," Jesus said again.

"And you're going out with your ex, on Saturday night? Jesus, are you busy Saturday night?" asked Wanda.

"No. No, I'm not."

"What's up with you, girl? This don't make no sense," Wanda said emphatically.

"I'm going to go to this benefit with my ex, Bill, end of discussion," Barbara said, in an "I'm Queen of the Universe" kind of way.

"Are you trying to make Jesus jealous? That's it, ain't it? You're just trying to make him jealous," said Wanda.

Jesus stood and quietly asked, "Is that true, Barbara? Is that why you're going out with someone else Saturday night?"

Barbara jumped to her feet and spun around. "YES! You're not paying enough attention to me!" she said, red-faced and stomping her foot.

Jesus could have explained his aloofness, but he felt too disappointed in Barbara's behavior to do that. "So, you decided to try to make me feel bad in order for you to get the attention you crave?"

Wanda and Julia had stopped counting. Barbara was now toe to toe with Jesus and furious. "What else could I do? Trying to get your attention is damn near impossible!" she yelled.

He stood there trying to think things through. His chest felt tight and heavy, and his shoulders sagged. All this was too much and nausea began to set in.

"Well?" Barbara half-yelled.

"I can't accept this treatment from you and I can't talk about it at the moment. I'm afraid the outcome of this will be the opposite of what you expect. Good-bye," Jesus said, walking out of the office.

"Hey, you forgot to finish counting your till," said Julia, her voice trailing off. She got up, grabbed his cash drawer and took a step towards Barbara. "You blew it." She sat, slamming the money tray on the desk.

"Yep. You fucked up, girl. That's all there is to it. You fucked up," Wanda said, her head down.

Turning to Wanda, Barbara said, "Mind your own business!" and sat down to finish counting.

Wanda responded, "Oh, I do. And my business remains private, not public."

By then, Jesus had reached his van. Getting in, he sat there unable to even put the key in the ignition. Over and over he analyzed the past week's events in minute detail, trying to find a reason for why they had happened. *Is this the result of karma? Is there something I could have done differently that would have changed the outcome in each of these situations?* A headache brought his attention back to the present. He realized that he had been sitting there for over thirty minutes.

He started the van and began the drive home, his stomach churning. The pain was unbearable and he began to cry. He didn't believe in victim consciousness, but he couldn't deny it was exactly how he felt—like a victim. He wiped the tears away and tried to focus on the road, but he had rubbed an eyelash into his eye. He tried to remove it, at the same time checking to see that the light was still green, but then everything went black.

Why is that siren so loud? Jesus wondered. *Good Lord, my head hurts. Why am I lying down?* He tried to open his eyes, but couldn't muster the strength to do so and slipped back into unconsciousness.

He snapped awake feeling the warmth of the sun on his face. He needed to pee and with difficulty got out of the bed. Looking around, he realized he had no idea where he was. His head and face ached. Hobbling into a hallway, he half-yelled, "Where am I?" A nurse quickly walked over, took him by the arm and led him back to bed. "You shouldn't be up, Mr. da Vinci. You've had a concussion. A grade 3 concussion."

Staring at her before responding, Jesus said, "Grade 3? I'm pretty sure I made it to middle school."

Laughing, the nurse said, "Thanks for making my point. Lie down, relax, and rest. You've had your brains scrambled."

"Scrambled? I like them sunny side up," Jesus mumbled, before falling back into unconsciousness.

Hours passed before he opened his eyes again. It took a minute to focus and remember where he was. A knock on the door got his attention. It was Brad and Jack.

"Hey, how are you buddy?" Brad asked.

"You look awful," Jack said.

"I do?"

"You gave us quite a scare," Brad said.

"I did?"

"Yeah. You've been in and out of consciousness now for four days," Brad said.

"The van is totaled," Jack said.

Jesus tried to put it all together, but his head and face hurt too much. "What happened?" he asked.

"Somebody ran a red light and you t-boned them good," Jack said.

"You smashed your face on the steering wheel. Nothing's broken, but they want you to stay in the hospital until you've been conscious for twenty-four to forty-eight hours," Brad said.

"My van is a total? A total what?" Jesus asked.

"A total wreck, dude. It broke the front axle. You're lucky you weren't hurt worse," Jack said.

"Amen, brother," Brad said.

"Excuse me, gentlemen. The patient needs his linens changed," interrupted a nurse.

"Take care of yourself. See you in a few days," said Brad.

"Yup. Take care," said Jack.

The nurse rolled Jesus onto his side as she began to change the linens. They made small talk as he began to assess the previous weeks' events. By the time she left the room, he was in a foul mood. It seemed to him that he must have done something wrong for all this to happen, but he wasn't sure what it was. The more he thought about it the worse he felt, until the only thing he felt was misery.

Chapter 19 – Pneumonia and the dreams

His condition improved enough the next day that the hospital discharged Jesus the following morning. He still had a headache, most of his face was bruised and his lower torso hurt from being thrown against the seat belt. Jack picked him up from the hospital. "Hey, how are you feeling?"

"Crappy. Thanks for asking," Jesus said, easing into the seat.

"Man, your face is downright frightening. It's hard to get used to."

"I haven't seen it yet."

"Didn't you take a look in the mirror when you went to the can?"

"No. The light hurts my eyes and makes my headache worse."

"Oh. Are there any errands we need to run?"

"No. Just take me home."

"How about food? Do you want some treats? Some snacks? Anything?"

"I need some more arnica gel and some snacks would be nice."

"Grains for Brains it is."

When they arrived, Jack asked Jesus if he wanted to go inside. He didn't want to, but Jack persisted, telling him that everybody wanted to see him. Jesus finally acquiesced. Wanda was the first one to spot him. "Oh my Lord!"

Hearing this, the rest of the cashiers looked up and each left their register mid-transaction and rushed over to him. He was greeted with a litany of "Oh my Gods," and "Dear Lords," and "How are you feeling?" They seemed to need to touch him for some reason.

He was as gracious as he could be and excused himself quickly telling them that he needed to sit down. Jack scurried off to do the shopping and Jesus went to the front-end office.

"Oh my God!" Clara said.

He hoped she didn't want to talk too much, but Clara began peppering him with questions. He wasn't sure, but it seemed to him that she felt guilty. At the moment, he didn't care how she felt.

"What did the doctor say?"

"I'm supposed to see him in a few days. I'll find out more then and let you know when I can come back to work," Jesus said, his eyes closed.

"Take your time and heal up. I've got all your shifts covered for the next week."

"Thank you. I hope it won't take more than a week."

"That was some day you had."

"You don't know the half of it."

"Well, I heard about your fight with Barbara. There wasn't more than that was there?" Clara asked.

"Yes there was, but I don't want to talk about it. Where's Jack? I need to get home," Jesus said irritably.

Clara nodded and returned to her work. The door flew open and Jack bellowed, "Done! I've bought everything you asked for."

"Shhh! Quietly, quietly," said Jesus, wincing. "Thank you. Now let's go home."

As they were leaving, they were serenaded with goodbyes. Jesus managed a halfhearted wave that morphed into a temple massage. As Jack helped him to the car, Jesus asked for quiet on the way home, and at home, too. Jack agreed, but wondered how long he was going to have to put up with this.

When they got back to the apartment, Jack put up the groceries as Jesus went to relieve himself. A very loud, "Great Goob!" came from the bathroom. Jack grabbed the arnica and went to see what was wrong.

The door opened slowly. "I'm a damn raccoon!" Jesus said as he carefully kneaded his face.

He had two black eyes, his nose was a light shade of purple and his entire face was swollen. Jack laughed and said, "Yeah, you are. It's amazing that you didn't suffer a fractured skull. Here's your arnica."

"Thank you," Jesus said, applying it from temple to temple and forehead to chin. He went to his room and retrieved a heating pad and then settled in on the couch. Turning it on, he gently placed it on his face. The warmth began to build and it felt so good, Jesus began to moan softly.

Walking in, Jack said, "Good. You're not masturbating. That would have been awkward. I've got to go to work. See ya."

Jesus mumbled something as the combination of pain and pleasure produced an odd sort of ecstasy. His face and body still hurt, but this was the best he had felt in days and he quickly fell asleep. Several hours later, he awoke from a dream. The details were foggy at first, but then it came back to him. The first thing he remembered was falling—from a great height. It was warm, like on Gooberia, and he was in a Goober body. As the ground rapidly approached, his fear level rose proportionally. SPLAT!

Still breathing, he had only one working eyeball and could see but a millimeter or two above the ground. He heard two people approach, but he couldn't make out who they were. One of them spoke, "Ew, what a mess! Let's get started."

It sounded like Barbara and the pastor, but he couldn't be sure. After a few minutes of strange sounds and sensations, he grasped what was going on. It definitely was Barbara and the pastor, and they were rebuilding him as if he were clay. They molded and shaped his body until he was a whole Goober again and propped him up.

"This isn't right," said the pastor, grabbing his procreating leg.

"I kind of like it," Barbara said, grabbing a saw.

"Wait, wait, what are you doing?" asked Jesus, as he watched Barbara adjust her grip and set herself to do some sawing. She commenced hacking off his procreating leg, ignoring his screams. As he fell to the ground, Barbara and the pastor stepped back to admire their work, but decided more changes needed to be made. They propped him up and started anew. It didn't take long until Jesus realized that they were now sculpting him into a human male.

"You know, we could make his package bigger," suggested Barbara.

"What is it with you women?" asked the pastor. "It ain't the meat, it's the devotion."

"What? A woman can't have both?" asked Barbara.

Again they stepped back to admire their handiwork. "Are we sure he needs those legs?" asked the pastor.

"Well, we want to keep the middle one, but we can get rid of the other two," said Barbara.

Smiling, the pastor said, "We certainly don't want him learning to walk on his own."

"Certainly not. I'll put him on a sturdy hanger and keep him in the closet. You know, for when I need him," said Barbara.

"Perfectly acceptable. That way he won't cause any more trouble." They quickly severed his two human legs.

Laughing, Barbara said, "So much for two sets of footprints in the sand," and then Jesus woke up.

He booted up his computer and wrote the dream down immediately so he could discuss it with Martha. Still feeling unsettled, he went to the bathroom and splashed water on his face. For the next three days, his routine consisted of kitchen, TV, computer, bathroom and repeat until he was ready for bed.

At that point, the headache and swelling had disappeared. The bruising was about half gone and his mood had improved. He called Clara to tell her he was ready to go back to work. It turned out that a new cashier had called in sick and she asked if he could cover a shift that night. "I'll be there," said Jesus.

The possibility that Barbara might be working made him tense. He wasn't sure if he was ready to face her yet. She hadn't called since the accident. The pastor didn't visit him in the hospital. Maybe this was all for the best, considering he had only four months or so left on his mission. Disconnecting from his relationships on Earth would make the transition easier for everyone concerned.

Then suddenly, it struck him that he might not be able to leave. The project team, in charge of the transmogrification process, had practiced changing simple life forms into different things and then back, but they hadn't tested changing a human back into a Goober.

Early in the project, this detail was brought up, but Jesus had dismissed it. The thought had come up a couple of times while on Earth and again he had paid it no mind. He had faith that the Universe—or Goob/God—had chosen him for this mission. But now, he came to the realization that it was easier to have faith in Goob on Gooberia. It was a safe and predictable planet, and Jesus missed it. Planet Earth may be fun to visit, but after a while the fear and pain got rather old. Thinking about all this tired him out, and he took a nap before work.

When he arrived, the cashiers greeted him with great concern. He got into the rhythm of cashiering quickly and seemed to suffer no ill effects from his concussion. On his break, he was eating his dinner in the front-end office when Barbara came in to get some quarters. She ignored him, and he was about to say something but decided against it. After she left, her attitude began to gnaw at him. She didn't seem to have any concern about his condition whatsoever. He didn't understand.

After the shift was over, Jesus finished tallying his till first and went outside and waited for Barbara. Finally, she exited the store and as she approached, she didn't seem sad or distraught at all. She appeared as happy as a vegan at a juice bar.

When she neared her car, Jesus said, "Well, you're in a good mood."

Startled, Barbara jumped back. "Who is it?"

"It's me. Who else? What is going on with you?"

"What do you mean?" she asked. "I'm just fine."

"Well, your boyfriend just had a serious van accident and missed a week of work—or more, I'm still not clear on that," he said, scratching his head. "Anyway, you didn't call to ask how I was doing or come by and see me or...anything! How could you do that?"

"Boyfriend? Boyfriend? You don't act like a boyfriend."

"What are you talking about?"

"You were ignoring me and being all distant. Something was bothering you and you wouldn't open up. That's a big issue for me."

"It's good that you know that about yourself, but why didn't you take that into account? Give me some space or help me out of my funk?"

"I tried, but you shut me out."

"I know I'm not always a good boyfriend. But I'm an introspective kind of guy. It had been a terrible day. A terrible week for that matter, and I was just trying to process it."

"You shut me out. I'm not going to stand for that." Pausing a moment, she asked, "So what happened that day?"

"I had another fight with the pastor. He, for all intents and purposes, ended our relationship."

"Well, I'm sorry that happened to you, but it doesn't change anything. I went out with Bill and he was wonderful. He's changed and you haven't. It's like you have secrets and won't share them. I'm happy with Bill. You and I are no longer boyfriend and girlfriend," she said, getting into her car and driving off.

Jesus stood there for a while and it started to rain gently, a perfect match for his mood. He unlocked his bike and started riding home. His heart hurt and his head throbbed. This wasn't what he wanted. He was pretty sure he loved Barbara and for his remaining time on Earth he wanted to be with her. Feeling rejected and unloved, despair began to creep in.

By the time he got home, he was soaked and there was a burning sensation in his lungs. Each breath he took was painful and it felt like he had a fever. *Great, I'm getting sick on top of everything else,* he thought. Taking some vitamin C, he went to bed hoping that it would do the trick.

It didn't. He awoke to a new kind of "breath of fire." Each inhalation felt like his lungs were burning and he only had about 25 percent of his normal lung capacity. He checked out the symptoms online; it might be pneumonia. He called Martha immediately and made an appointment for the next day.

He stumbled into the living room where Jack was eating a bowl of cereal. "What's up?" Jack asked.

"I'm sick. I think I have pneumonia."

"What is it with you? You're having a phenomenal amount of bad luck lately. It's getting pitiful."

"Thanks for noticing."

"Pause, please," said the empathetic judge. "Am I to understand you got sick again?"

"Yes, Your Honor. The stress of the events of the previous couple of weeks led to my illness."

"What is pneumonia?" asked the empathetic judge.

"An inflammation of the lungs, Your Honor. It's very painful to breathe."

"This must have been very difficult for you," said the empathetic judge.

"It was quite a test, Your Honor."

The empathetic judge started and stopped several times trying to ask another question when he began making an odd sound. Quivering and with a green, pasty substance oozing from his eye, the noise he was making got louder.

"What are you doing?" asked the fussy judge.

When the empathetic judge didn't answer, Jesus said, "I believe he is crying, Your Honor, Goober-style."

"Stop that! Stop that immediately!" shouted the fussy judge.

Holding up his hand, the empathetic judge said, "I'm all right. Excuse my lack of control."

Pointing at Jesus, the fussy judge said, "I'm beginning to think that you have something to do with all these unusual outbursts."

"Please continue," said the empathetic judge.

Jack finished his bowl of cereal and grabbed his car keys. As he walked out the door, he said, "You'd better call Clara and let her know."

Jesus felt like he was letting Clara and the department down and that made him feel worse. He made the call.

"Pneumonia? Jesus, you could be out a month. Jesus!" Clara said.

"What?"

"Nooo, that was an exclamation. You take care of yourself and go to the doctor. I'll try and get your shifts covered. Bye," she said, hanging up before he could say anything.

When he hung up, Jesus froze in place. He couldn't believe how exhausted he felt. He strained to inhale and then with absolutely no effort let the air escape, followed by concentrating his energy and intention to take another breath. It took fifteen minutes to plan how to get up off the couch to get something to eat. He had to get some food in his stomach so he could begin taking the massive doses of vitamin C that Martha had suggested.

He went to bed before Jack got home and had a decent night's sleep and that surprised him because he had wondered when he went to bed whether he was going to wake up at all. He'd had another weird dream. Sitting at his desk, his lungs caught fire, flames leaping out of his chest. He tried patting the fire out with his hands—it burned him slightly—and then it slowly dissipated. But another fire started up again at the base of his spine. The flames were internal, but he could see the glow from the fire in his mind when he looked down. In rapid succession, six more sets of flames spread through his body at the groin, navel, heart, throat, forehead and the top of his head. He would have to describe this dream to Martha, too.

He ate a little breakfast and called a cab. Eventually it arrived and as Jesus climbed in, he noticed the smell of disinfectant. The driver wanted to make small talk and Jesus did the best he could, but he was short of breath. The driver asked what was wrong and stated that he didn't look well.

"I think I have pneumonia."

"Pneumonia!" the driver yelled. Tires screeching, the cab lurched to a stop. "Get out of my cab! Get out of my cab right now!" the driver said, leaping out and putting his hand over his mouth and nose.

Jesus struggled to get out, perplexed by the driver's reaction. "How much do I owe you?"

"Nothing! Get away from me!"

Jesus walked to the sidewalk watching the driver rub, what appeared to be hand sanitizer over any exposed skin. As the cab sped off, he wondered if he could walk the remaining three blocks. Several times his legs almost gave way, but finally he reached Martha's bungalow.

She flung open the door and gave him a big hug and a kiss on the mouth.

"Should you be kissing me? What if I'm contagious?"

Martha laughed. "You can't make me sick."

Sitting down gingerly, Jesus said, "I feel terrible."

"Are those bruises under your eyes?"

"What's left of them," he said, outlining the events of the last two weeks.

"Wow! That's extraordinary."

"Yeah. But that's not what I want to talk about."

"Really? All that and you want to talk about something else?"

"Yeah, I've had some weird dreams lately."

"Considering your experiences of late, your dog probably died in one of them," she said, chuckling.

Jesus tried to laugh and then cough, but he didn't really have enough breath to do either. "Good one."

"Tell me about these 'weird' dreams," Martha said.

Jesus described the amputation dream and the fire dream while Martha hurriedly wrote them down.

"Wow! You are going through some shit, I tell you what," she said, shaking her head.

"Yeah, but what do they mean?"

"Get up on the table and let's get started."

"You're going to have to help me. I'm not sure I can even get my clothes off," he said pitifully.

Martha helped him off with his clothes and onto the table. Jesus was so tired that he immediately dozed off. The next thing he knew, Martha was shaking him to wake up. "Time to turn over."

Jesus promptly fell asleep again, but woke up gasping for air a few minutes later. The compression of his chest was making it difficult to breathe. Martha tried to make him more comfortable by putting pillows under his shoulders and head and it worked. He fell asleep again until Martha roused him.

"Nice nap? Turn over."

"Okay. Are all the needles out?"

"Yes, they're out. Here's a list of the herbs and vitamins you should be taking."

Jesus tried to read the list, but even that was exhausting. Martha admonished him for trying to make sense of it. "Go to the store and have Brad pick out the items for you."

"Okay."

"Now, let's talk about your dreams and everything that has happened to you recently."

"Okay."

"Have you ever heard of the 'Dark Night of the Soul'?" she asked.

Jesus shook his head no. "Is that a horror movie?"

Martha laughed and said, "No. The Universe has its ways of testing us. So, how does one advance on the spiritual plane?"

"By being tested?"

"Right, by passing tests. Imagine you believe in God. Imagine that you have a strong faith and that you feel supported by the Universe. Then everything you know is yanked out from under you. And I mean everything. In your case, it's been just your health, job, girlfriend and mentor. How strong is your faith now?"

"It's a little wobbly."

"Of course, but that's the 'Dark Night of the Soul.' You're being tested. Your first dream seems like it's about two of your strongest relationships and how you feel you've been treated. It's consistent with your experiences, but the second dream..." she said, her voice trailing off.

"What? What about the second dream?"

Martha took a deep breath. "Your description of where the inner fires on your body were corresponds to where your chakras are located."

"So?"

"Don't you get it?" she asked, moving closer until she was a few inches away from his face.

"No."

"You dreamed that your chakras opened...fully. The fires seem to indicate that the Kundalini energy will rise in your body and that you'll transform from man to spiritual man—that you'll become enlightened. It's very exciting," Martha gushed.

Jesus was having trouble comprehending this. "So, my chakras will be on fire when this happens?" he asked in a concerned voice.

"No, not literally. That's just a representation of them opening. You really do have a chance to do this before you leave. It's amazing!"

"Well, I mean I know where my chakras are, but I haven't felt any heat or anything."

"How about a buzzing feeling?" she asked.

"Oh, yeah. I've had a buzzing feeling in my crown, brow point, throat and heart chakras while meditating, but that's it. Usually my forehead goes numb, too, but nothing else from the other chakras yet."

"You're on your way. Eventually, you'll have those feelings even when you're not meditating."

"Huh, go figure."

"Now, when you get to feeling a little better, it'll be time to increase your meditation and yoga. To start with you want to do at least forty minutes a day of meditation. Don't ask me why, but forty minutes is some kind of threshold that will take you to the next level. Okay?"

"Okay. It's not like work will get in the way," Jesus grumbled.

"Have you ever heard of the resentment prayer?"

"No."

"You pray for someone you have an issue with. You pray for their health, happiness and prosperity. You pray that they get everything they need and everything you want."

"Why would they want what I want?"

"That's not the point. The prayer is for reducing your resentment. You'll notice that when you wish the things you want for someone who's irritating or bothering you, you'll react. Over time, the reaction will disappear and at least one layer of your resentment will be gone."

"So, wishing something good for someone I've got issues with will help me move out of resentment?"

"Exactly. Practice it. Practice it any time a negative thought comes up about someone. You can start with Barbara, the pastor and the guy who punched you in the nose. Oh, and the guy who robbed you, too. That will start cleansing your mental and emotional bodies."

"I can do that. I can do all of that. That is, when I feel better," Jesus said.

"All right! Whooo! Let's call you a cab. I have my next client in about ten minutes."

169

Jesus rested until the cab arrived and gave Martha a weak hug as he left. He felt woozy, but a little bit stronger. On the way to the store, Jesus avoided small talk with the driver. He arrived just after the morning shift had finished counting their tills.

Fortunately, Brad was able to take the time to shop for him while Jesus rested in the office. He put his head on the table and focused on each and every breath. He didn't notice the door opening or hear someone speaking to him until he was touched on the shoulder. Jesus looked up and focused his eyes to find Pete and Wanda looking at him with concern. "What?" Jesus asked.

"Are you okay?" Pete asked.

"You look half dead, honey," said Wanda.

"I'm just tired and weak."

"It's none of my business, but that girl treated you wrong," she said.

Nodding in agreement, Pete said, "She did. Maybe you're better off without her."

Jesus shrugged. He really hadn't given it all that much thought since he'd contracted pneumonia.

"Everything that's happened to you lately, you might be cursed," said Wanda.

"Wanda! Jesus isn't cursed," Pete said.

"Are you kidding me? How can you ignore everything that's happened to him? This smacks of a voodoo curse. It does. Jesus, do you want me to find out if Barbara is into voodoo? I'm very sneaky. I can find out," Wanda said.

"I'm sure you are very sneaky, Wanda, but I'm not cursed. I'm not a victim. Everything happens for a reason." Jesus laid his head back down on the table. "Everything happens for a reason."

Pete ushered Wanda out of the office despite her protests. Through the door, Jesus heard Wanda say, "Look I know a curse when I see one and that poor man is cursed." Jesus chuckled, followed by a painful cough. He gathered himself and refocused on each breath.

Brad walked in with a bag of vitamins, herbs and soups. "Do you need a ride home? I have the time."

"No. You need to work. Can you call me a cab?"

"Certainly. It's too bad you're going to miss the roundtable this week. I'm thinking of bringing up how the pastor is treating you," Brad said.

"Please don't do that. That won't make things any better," Jesus said, looking up. "However, I do appreciate the sentiment."

Brad smiled as he made the call to the cab company and then went back to work. Jesus laid his head down again and rested.

When the cab arrived, he had difficulty picking up the bag of groceries. Brad came to his aid and carried them out to the waiting cab. As he walked with Jesus, he said, "I'll visit you Friday and fill you in on the roundtable."

"I'm looking forward to it. Thanks," Jesus said, getting into the car and going limp. He didn't have the energy to support any part of his body.

When he got home, he slowly emptied the bag of vitamins, herbs and soups onto the coffee table and collapsed on the couch. There he stayed except for bed, the bathroom or the kitchen. Occasionally he would see Jack either leaving or returning from work. They rarely talked, because Jesus simply didn't have the energy to do so.

On Thursday at the roundtable, the pastor called the meeting to order. "Where's Hey-Zeus?" he asked.

"He's got pneumonia," Brad said.

"Uh-huh" said the pastor.

"Wanda thinks he's cursed," Jack said, half-laughing.

"We reap what we sow," said the pastor.

"Are you suggesting God is punishing Jesus?" asked Alice.

"Why would God punish Jesus?" asked Gertrude.

"Hey-Zeus did his best to question God and the Holy Bible. There are consequences to that," said the pastor adamantly.

"So, God punishes those who seek to understand Him and the Bible?" asked Brad.

"It wasn't apparent to me that he was seeking to understand. It seemed to me that he was trying to disparage the teachings of Christ," said the pastor.

"That doesn't make sense," Barbara chimed in.

"No, it doesn't make sense at all," said Brad. "Jesus of the Bible taught the love and compassion of God. He was the new way and He wasn't Old Testament. That's why you're not making sense, Pastor. You talk of the Old Testament God of punishment and the teachings of Christ in the same sentence. They're almost mutually exclusive."

The pastor shifted in his seat several times and then leaned forward. "Son, God does love us and sometimes He loves us by punishing us to help us understand our wicked ways."

"What?" Brad asked incredulously.

"I agree with the pastor," said Ralph.

"Me too," said Juan.

"I don't," said Barbara.

"Are you sure you understand Jesus's teachings? I mean no disrespect, Pastor, but you don't speak of them the way I understand them," said Brad.

"What do you mean?" asked the pastor angrily.

"I mean, I don't believe in punishment. Yes, God tests us. He doesn't punish us. When we reach a certain level of spirit, we're tested to see if we're ready to move to the next level, a higher vibration if you will. That's what I believe is happening to our Jesus right now. But then again, that's my belief."

"Well, you go against scripture then," the pastor said.

"Your interpretation of scripture, Pastor," said Alice emphatically.

"Fine, my interpretation of scripture. Is there anything wrong with that?" asked the pastor testily.

"Only if you're judging someone else," Gertrude said.

"It sounds like you're judging me," said the pastor.

"Yes, I am judging your judgment of Jesus. You judge him for asking questions and trying to figure Christianity out. Yes, I judge you for that," said Brad.

Jumping up out of his chair, the pastor announced, "Meeting adjourned," and hurried out of the room.

Chapter 20 – The pastor apologizes

True to his word, Brad visited on Friday before work. He called first to see if there was anything Jesus needed which, of course, he did. When Brad arrived, he set down a bag of groceries and hugged Jesus. "How you doing? Feeling any better?"

"A little. I'm still very weak," he replied, collapsing on the couch. It still took too much effort to stand for any length of time.

"Well, everybody at work says hello and wishes you a speedy recovery."

"Everybody?"

"Almost everybody," Brad said, followed by an uncomfortable silence.

"That's what I thought," Jesus said, when he had enough energy to speak.

"So, what have you been doing?"

"Eating, taking vitamins and herbs, pooping. Repeat three times and go to bed."

Again silence. Brad didn't know what else to say. He didn't want to bring up Barbara or anything else that had happened over the previous couple of weeks.

Finally Jesus spoke up, "It's been lonely. Thanks for stopping by."

"Of course. I'm here for you. If there's anything I can do, let me know."

"Can I run something by you and see what you think?"

"Sure. What is it?"

"Martha told me that I have a chance to become..." Jesus said, pausing.

"To become what?"

"To become enlightened in this lifetime."

"Really? Wow! That would make sense with the events that have happened to you recently," Brad said.

"It does? How so?" Jesus asked, though he already knew.

"From my understanding, you're going through the 'Dark Night of the Soul.' Nobody goes through stuff like this without it being an opportunity to move to the next level. Spiritually speaking, that is," Brad said. "That's even what I said at the roundtable last night."

"Ohhh, I asked you not to bring that up," Jesus groaned.

"Hey, I didn't. The pastor did."

"He did? How?"

"When he heard all the things that you had been going through recently, he said you were being punished by God."

"Well, I had wondered that myself," Jesus said, his chuckling causing him to cough.

"You okay?"

"No, but continue anyway," Jesus said, wheezing.

"I said basically what I just told you, and several other people kind of piled on. He ended the meeting early and walked out."

"Really?"

Brad nodded yes, and Jesus wondered how much of his situation he should reveal to Brad.

"So, how did you feel about being told you could become enlightened?" Brad asked.

Jesus sat up as best he could and leaned forward. "It kinda freaked me out."

Brad laughed. "Yeah, that could freak someone out."

"I've had time in the last few days to reflect on that and my life...here in Austin. I've generally been successful, but the situations with Barbara and the pastor have me stymied. I just want to be at peace and I'm not," Jesus admitted.

"Does that surprise you?"

"Not really. Here's the thing. I've done my best to be a good human being, to fit in, to live life fully, and somehow I've pissed these two people off without any intention to do so."

"Does being a good human being include punching someone in the nose?" Brad asked with a smirk.

Jesus snorted, coughed, and grabbed his chest. "No. No it doesn't, but karma fulfilled itself there. I'll make amends if I ever have a chance, but what about the pastor and Barbara? In both cases my intentions were pure."

Exhausted, Jesus sat back as Brad tried to formulate an answer. Finally he said, "This sort of thing is part of the human experience. Even pure intentions can produce actions that have consequences. Have faith that everything will turn out well. Getting yourself worked up about it isn't going to help. Give the situation over to God and in your mind surround them with white light. You'll get the opportunity to heal those situations."

Jesus had another coughing fit. He looked so tired that Brad knew it was time to leave and let him rest. He stood up, leaned over, and patted Jesus on the shoulder. "You're doing better than you think. I've got to go to work now, but I'll check in on Monday to see how you're doing. Take care."

"Thanks for stopping by," Jesus said, going limp. He turned on the TV, but thoughts kept exploding in his mind like popping popcorn.

Should he continue going to the church? The pastor certainly wasn't making him feel welcome. But was this church just about the pastor or was it a broader community? His friends attended, he loved working at the soup kitchen, and the roundtables were a splendid method of learning about humanity. Why shouldn't he attend just because the pastor was upset with him? Communities were important to the human experience, and Jesus decided he wouldn't let the pastor's issues sway him.

This ran through his mind for several days until he realized he was angry with the pastor and that he needed to say a resentment prayer about him. "Lord, I pray for the pastor. I pray for the pastor's health, happiness and prosperity. I pray that the pastor receives everything he needs and everything I want." Jesus practiced this over and over again every time a thought about the pastor came up, until a new thought began to pester him—Barbara.

Jesus was angry with her to the point that he felt rage. He caught himself several times planning to publicly chastise her for her behavior towards him. He hated and judged himself for these thoughts and finally asked for divine assistance. "How can I forgive Barbara, Lord?"

Later that day, it occurred to him to practice a resentment prayer about her, too. He felt stupid for not having thought about it earlier and asked that the Lord bring His love and light to his ego/lower self to heal any anger, guilt, judgment or shame about his feelings towards Barbara. He paid intense attention to any negative thoughts that popped up about her and when they did immediately interrupted the mental hurricane to practice a resentment prayer. *This must be what Martha meant by spiritual vigilance*, he thought.

It had now been nine days of dealing with pneumonia. Jesus was sick and tired of feeling sick and tired. He wanted to leave the apartment and go back to work. He wanted to see his friends. His anger level rose and he immediately asked for God's help out loud using one of the few invocations from his home planet. "Oh Great Goob, how can I resolve this imbalance I'm experiencing?"

No answer was immediately forthcoming, but he paid attention to all the thoughts that came up. By the end of the day, he had noticed a pattern of thoughts about Clara. He realized he was angry at her passing him over for promotion. He tried rationalizing his feelings about it—*It really didn't make any difference to the mission* and *Brad is more qualified*—but it didn't make him feel any better. Again, he applied a resentment prayer.

The effort seemed to work, because when he awoke the next morning, he knew he wasn't sick any more. The burning sensation in his chest was gone, though he still felt weak. He called Clara to give her the good news. She stammered and hemmed and hawed until she admitted that she couldn't provide him with full-time shifts at the moment.

"I understand. I'm still a little weak and cashier shifts would probably be too much for me right now. Are there any head cashier shifts available?" asked Jesus.

"I could give you two shifts in the next ten days, but that's all that's available. When I fill out the schedule for the following two weeks, I'll try to work in some more shifts for you. Can you work next Tuesday?"

Jesus said yes, thanked her and hung up. Anger began to rise and he quickly began another cycle of resentment prayers about her. He missed human contact and didn't have any idea what to do until he went back to work. He called Alice to tell her that he was available for his soup kitchen shifts.

"Great! We've missed you around here," she said. She proceeded to fill him in on what was going on, including the last roundtable meeting. Jesus was just happy to talk to someone, but then she said something that caught his attention.

"I'm creating a vision of what I want the soup kitchen to look like a year from now."

She continued to talk, but Jesus was no longer listening. His mind had begun obsessing on the phrase "creating a vision." After they hung up, he spent several hours reading up on it. Over and over again, he wondered, *What do I want my life to be like with my remaining time here? Should I travel? Do I really want to work at the store? Do I want to spend so much time on my spiritual life? What's next for me?*

Jack came home just as Jesus was about to go to bed. "Hey buddy, are you feeling any better?"

"I'm weak, but my lungs no longer burn."

"That's good. You going back to work soon?"

Jesus relayed his conversation with Clara, and Jack was about to respond with something negative when Jesus interrupted him. "Jack, what do you want your life to look like?"

"What do I want my life to look like? I've never really given it much thought."

"What do you want your life to look like, say in four months or a year or ten years?"

"Hey, you only live once, so get in as much pleasure as possible."

"Well, I believe in reincarnation, and that kind of takes the pressure off. I don't have to worry about failing because I'll get another chance to learn what I need to. It makes me more willing to try things," said Jesus.

A perplexed look crossed Jack's face and after a few moments he went into his room. Jesus sat there for a while, contemplating what his vision of his life should be. Before he went to bed, he asked for help. "Lord, how can I make the most of my remaining time on this planet? Please give me a sign." Feeling satisfied with this question, he fell asleep immediately.

He woke up to his phone ringing at 8 a.m. It was Martha. "How are you feeling?"

Jesus took a couple of deep breaths to clear his head. His lungs were still sore, but when he stood up, he felt steadier. "I'm better. I don't think I have pneumonia anymore. I'm still a little weak, though."

"Bravissimo! Maybe you should come in for a session today to help your recovery."

They set a time of four o'clock. He was very hungry and decided to have a normal breakfast instead of soup. He took his vitamins and herbs so he wouldn't have a relapse. His energy level was high, but not enough to ride his bike so he called a cab, ran some errands and got lunch at a restaurant. Afterwards, he returned home and napped until it was time to leave for Martha's.

As she opened the door, Martha exclaimed, "He's alive! Hallelujah!" They hugged and she left so Jesus could undress and get up on the table. He was almost asleep by the time she returned.

"Ten days to heal from pneumonia. Pretty good. You must have been diligent about taking your herbs and vitamins."

"I didn't have any energy to do anything else. I felt pretty good this morning and ran some errands, but that wore me out."

"What else has been going on?" she asked, checking his pulses.

"I've been repeating the resentment prayer ad nauseam for the last five days or so. It seems to be working. And the last couple of days, I've started my meditation again."

"Fabulous! What else?"

"Well, Clara can't give me full-time shifts for a while. I'm working only two shifts in the next ten days, so other than that I've only got my soup kitchen shifts."

"Perfect timing!"

"For what?"

"To put together a daily spiritual practice to get where you want to go."

"Where do I want to go?" he asked.

"Close your eyes and visualize the following. Let's say you live the rest of your life on this planet never to return to Gooberia. Goo-bear-e-a, I just love saying that. Anyway, what would be the highest realization of your life? Your greatest potential? The best part of Goob you can be. What would that look like?"

Jesus opened his eyes and stared at Martha for a minute. "You mean, as if my mission ended with my last breath on this planet?"

"Yeah. What if they can't pick you up? You said your mission was to observe. What if your mission is to *participate*?"

"Well, I'm doing that to a certain degree already."

"I know, I know. Let your defenses drop, okay? What would you like to do that you've been hesitant to try?"

Jesus thought for a minute and replied, "Nothing. So far I've tried everything I've wanted to."

"True, but has it been easy, or have you made it an ordeal?"

"Ordeal. Definitely an ordeal," he said glumly.

"And why do you think that is?"

"I'm cautious, so what? That's the way I am. That's the way...I was..." he said, pausing and contemplating his behavior on Earth.

Martha told him to turn over and lie on his stomach and she started the deep tissue massage.

"Oh, Great Goob!" he exclaimed, suddenly rising up onto his elbows. "I don't have to behave this way anymore?"

"Yes. Think about it. You've been reluctant to try new things and to immerse yourself completely in the human experience because, in effect, you've 'reincarnated' with at least some of your prior life's personality intact."

Slowly sinking back down onto the table, Jesus continued his reflection. "I wish I could have one of these every day," he murmured.

Martha finished up the massage and sat down next to him. "Okay, now what is really important?"

Jesus thought for a moment before answering. "I just want to help whether it be here or my home planet."

"Ahhh, service. Alignment with God's plan. Fairly tricky with an active ego."

"So, I should try to eliminate my ego?"

"Good God, no!" Martha exclaimed. "You need it. It's necessary to manifest on the physical plane. *Balance* is what's necessary. Not that you're all that out of balance."

"No, I'm not. I lead a pretty clean life. It's the cautiousness that holds me back, analyzing everything. I approach everything in my life using the scientific method."

"There's nothing inherently wrong with that. There are spiritual scientists out there. It's all about balance between thinking and feeling. You need both the head and the heart. It may have been a lot easier on your planet. Here, sometimes, you'll need to do something that your head just doesn't understand, but will be best for the heart."

"How does the ego play into that?" asked Jesus.

"The ego permeates everything in your life. Its agenda is survival and getting what it wants. But it's afraid. It wants to protect you from getting hurt. Yet, putting your heart on the line is sometimes the only way to grow. The key again, is balance. Balance between your higher self and ego."

"And so to reach this balance requires a focus on one's spiritual path?"

"Of course. It's selfish and yet it serves humanity, too," said Martha with a smile.

Jesus took a deep breath thinking this was all too much. Too much to consider, too much to attempt at the moment. *What would the outcome be? What would be the point?* Then he realized this was his ego asserting its agenda. "One day at a time."

"One day at a time indeed. Session's over. How about we get together again in a month or so?"

"That sounds about right," Jesus said. After he got dressed, he pulled out his wallet. "You know this work is worth a lot more than just a hundred dollars."

"Service. Besides, the Universe pays me, not you. You're just the conduit...this time. I never worry about money. It always materializes as I need it. Sometimes before."

She gave him a big hug and a kiss. Riding home in the cab, Jesus felt energized and wondered what he should do next, considering he didn't have anything planned except to go to church on Sunday. He needed to take care of his insurance from the wreck and he needed to buy another vehicle, but neither of those things seemed important at the moment. He decided to meditate when he got home and see what came up.

As he was meditating, an image of the lake flashed in his mind and he knew that he needed to go there, but he had no car. Then Brad's face appeared to Jesus as he finished the meditation, so he immediately called him.

"Hey Brad, how's it going?"

"Very well, thank you. You sound much better."

"I am. I just had a session with Martha and I feel great. Hey, I have a favor to ask. Can I borrow your car tomorrow?"

"Uh, yeah, but I would need to get picked up after work. I'm working the morning shift."

"Why don't you pick me up in the morning and I'll drop off the car when I'm done?" Jesus suggested. He explained about the lake flash and Brad agreed that it was the thing to do.

Driving up to the lake at a leisurely pace the next morning, Jesus wondered what to do when he got there. By the time he arrived, he still had no clue. After parking the car, he walked around the shore, occasionally picking up a stone and trying to skip it across the water. Even though it was Saturday, there were only a few people there.

He picked out a picnic table close to the water and sat down, feeling an urge to meditate. He closed his eyes and concentrated on his breathing. Each time his mind latched onto a thought and began expanding on it, he recognized the reaction and gently brought his attention back. But the same things kept coming up—thoughts about Barbara and the pastor.

That made him uneasy and he returned his attention to his breath. After about twenty minutes, the thought burst into his mind that he needed to make peace with both of them. Whatever their response, he needed to make the effort. The urge to do it immediately overcame him and he opened his eyes to end his meditation, but then he felt he was supposed to continue. Impatience drove him to do something, anything, but he resigned himself to continuing. The restlessness slowly dissipated and he relaxed. It occurred to him that he wanted to be friends with both of them, but they might not feel the same way. He resolved himself to accept whatever their responses were. He couldn't take it personally.

After fifteen more minutes, he opened his eyes and contemplated the arc of his life to this point. He loved and hated Earth. He wanted to go home and he didn't want to go home. Having so many unknown factors in his life made him feel uncomfortable and weak. Over and over again when those feelings arose, he reminded himself that Goob was actively watching over him and taking care of him.

Getting hungry and thinking about breakfast tacos, he got in the car and headed back to Austin. He had just driven past the city limits sign when he heard, "Go to the church, NOW!" Taken aback by the forcefulness and clarity of the thought, he decided to obey it. *Is this really the time?* he wondered. On the way to the church, he played out in his mind several scenarios about how the meeting would transpire. None of them ended well.

The church secretary was at her desk and said the pastor wasn't in. This surprised Jesus. Why would the Universe tell him to come to the church if the pastor wasn't there? Walking through the sanctuary, he pondered this. Suddenly the doors flew open and in walked the pastor. He stopped dead in his tracks as soon as he saw Jesus. Jesus stopped too, and they stared at each other for a few seconds.

The pastor broke the silence with, "Jesus, my son, come here," walking towards him with his arms open wide.

Oh my Goob, he pronounced my name correctly!

The pastor strongly embraced him and patted him on the back, saying over and over again, "I'm truly sorry. I'm truly sorry."

This was not one of the scenarios that Jesus had thought about. Grabbing his shoulders and looking into his eyes, the pastor said, "I hope you'll forgive me for my behavior, my son."

Jesus's mind numbed at this turn of events and all he could manage was, "Sure."

"Let's go to my office and talk," said the pastor, putting his arm around him.

When they arrived, he motioned for Jesus to sit down. Taking a seat, the pastor took a deep breath and looked Jesus in the eye. "Again, I'm truly sorry, Jesus. Truly sorry. I've been talking with some of my colleagues and a..." the pastor paused, taking another deep breath, "psychiatrist."

Jesus didn't know how to respond to this admission. The pastor seemed like he was embarrassed or ashamed and Jesus didn't understand. All people have problems, some people see psychiatrists. Big deal.

"Good for you," he finally said.

The pastor was surprised by this response and began to explain, "You see, from the moment I met you, you reminded me of my son. We're estranged. I, uh, misinterpreted your questions as defiance and it seems, fell back into to some old behaviors." His shoulders drooped and he seemed weakened by this disclosure.

Jesus could see that the pastor was upset and he wondered why. He asked, "So, you're upset because this happened?"

The pastor looked perturbed by the question. "Well, of course. I'm not supposed to behave in such a manner."

"So you feel guilty?"

"Yesss," the pastor emphasized.

"I've found that when I feel guilty, I punish myself by repeating the behavior so that I'll continue to feel guilty."

The pastor sat up straight in his chair with a quizzical look. He tried to respond several times, but stopped himself. Finally he said, "I'll have to ruminate on that one for a while."

Smiling, Jesus said, "Sure. You know, you're human and that means you're not perfect. We all have issues. Even pastors."

The pastor slumped again at that remark. He looked like he aged ten years in just a few seconds.

Leaning forward, Jesus said, "Look, perfectionism is a poor motivation for improvement. You're already perfect in God's eyes. Trying to be perfect is, in effect, denying that. All we can do is improve. In reality, that improvement is based on unlearning everything we've been taught that keeps us thinking we're separate from God." Jesus thumped on the pastor's desk for emphasis.

This last statement flew in the face of the pastor's beliefs. Responding slowly, he said, "Well, I don't know about that, but I do believe in your right to state it."

Jesus felt like there had been a breakthrough and a sense of peace spread throughout him. "Excellent!" he said, rising from his chair. "See you in church tomorrow?"

Smiling and nodding, the pastor said, "I'll be there."

"Me too," said Jesus as he left the office. He dropped off the car for Brad, called a cab, and went home.

He spent the rest of the day processing the meeting, replaying it over and over in his mind. He had confronted one of his two relationship issues, met it with grace, and it had worked out better than he possibly could have imagined. It was as if his willingness to deal with the possible pain and rejection were enough to ensure his success. *Would it go as smoothly with Barbara?*

He awoke feeling anxious the next morning. It didn't take him long to figure out that it might be due to the possibility of seeing Barbara. He got ready and Brad picked him up. They took a seat in the last pew.

Barbara arrived late and when their eyes met she hesitated, then sat down very quickly. Jesus's heart was pounding and he found it difficult to concentrate on the sermon. At one point, the pastor mentioned that perfectionism was a poor motivation for improvement, and Jesus's ego roared. He quickly tried to get his pride under control. He was glad he had contributed, but he didn't want to go overboard. Between that and thoughts of Barbara, he remained distracted for the rest of the sermon.

After the service wrapped up, he wondered whether he should initiate any contact with Barbara, but before he had an opportunity, she bypassed the receiving line and walked straight to her car. When Brad reached the pastor, he commented on how much he liked his perspective on perfectionism. Jesus was next. The pastor hugged him and they made small talk.

On the way to the car, Brad said, "So, it looks like you made up with the pastor."

"Looks like. One down, one to go."

"Did Barbara say anything to you?"

"Not a word."

"What are you going to do?"

"I don't know, but I do seem to have a lot more angst about talking with her than I did with the pastor."

"My advice would be to let it happen naturally. Don't force it. If you two are meant to make up, then the Universe will provide the opportunity."

"Would you be able to wait say, if you and Martha had a falling out?"

Brad laughed. "No way!"

"Good advice then," said Jesus, laughing also.

"When do you go back to work?"

"I have a head cashier shift on Tuesday."

"Great! I work that night. Come to think of it, so does Barbara. Wow! A shift and a show."

Jesus sighed as they reached Brad's car. As they got in, Brad asked Jesus if he wanted to go for a bike ride. "I'm still not 100 percent, but maybe later in the week?"

"Excellent. I miss our rides."

"Me, too."

"Do you need to borrow the car again this week?"

"I don't think so. I'm going to look for a car online and try to buy something by the end of the week."

"Another sexmobile?"

"No," Jesus said emphatically, "something mature. Something that gets good gas mileage. Something used."

"Keep the faith," Brad said, pulling in at the apartment. "See you on Tuesday."

Jesus waved and went inside to begin a session of spiritual practice. The next day, he called his insurance agent about the wreck. On Tuesday as he was researching used cars online, he realized he was becoming more and more tense. Practicing some yoga and meditation and then saying a few dozen resentment prayers, he managed to get into the right frame of mind for work.

When he entered the store, a cashier chorus greeted him. "Hey, he's back!" "Jesus returns!" He smiled warmly at his coworkers and waved as he walked to the front-end office. Clara hugged him as soon as he walked in. They went over the schedule for the next two weeks and Jesus saw that she had him down for several shifts in the coming week.

"I couldn't get you any more yet. How are you feeling?"

"Much better. I'm about 85 percent at the moment. I should be 100 percent by the end of the week."

"That's great. We've missed you around here."

Smiling, Jesus said, "I've missed all of you, too. It got pretty boring at home."

"Yes it would. Here's the logbook for you to catch up on. I've got to go see 'The Kernel' about something," Clara said, chuckling.

"Okay." He had missed the joshing-around and camaraderie. Sitting down, he read the logbook and started preparing for his shift. The evening cashiers filed in, got their tills and began to verify them. Wanda, Pete and Sonya were noisily counting their money. Feeling playful, Jesus crept up behind Wanda, grabbed her shoulders and growled, "I'm a voodoo zombie and I want to eat your brain."

Wanda screamed, "Holy Mother of God, Jesus! Don't do that! Are you making fun of me?" Wanda stood and started slapping at him before hugging him. "I've missed you."

"I've missed you, too!" he said, kissing her on the cheek. Just then Barbara walked in and the room fell silent. Wanda, Pete and Sonya left for the registers, leaving Barbara and Jesus alone. He sat quietly as she counted. Just as Jesus found the courage to say something, she left for her register. His chest feeling heavy, he tried to stay positive, but he was sure that Barbara was still mad at him.

When Jesus gave Barbara her break, she left the register without the usual banter. Saying a resentment prayer silently, he rang up customers. When he noticed he was getting low on quarters, he dashed to the office to get some more. Just as he reached the door, he heard Barbara angrily say, "You son of a bitch!"

He took a step back, not knowing whether to go in or not. He hoped that Barbara's outburst didn't have anything to do with him. He decided to go see if Pete had any extra quarters instead.

"Avoiding Barbara, eh?"

"Well, she's yelling at somebody. I think on the phone."

"Not surprising. From what I've gathered, things aren't going well between her and Bill."

"Well, she deserves her privacy." As Jesus walked away, he experienced a flood of mixed emotions. Barbara returned from her break red-eyed and red-faced. Jesus asked if everything was okay.

"Everything's fine. Just fine!"

He thought it best to give her some space. He went to relieve Brad, who had already picked up on what was going on. "Trouble in paradise? Maybe you two will have another chance."

Uncomfortable at Brad's implication, Jesus did his best to focus on serving customers. Throughout the evening, several of them commented that it was nice to have him back. His last customer was particularly flattering and Jesus finished the breaks feeling positive and wanted.

Plopping down in his office chair, he was overcome with exhaustion but determined to finish the shift. Pete was first off and asked about his recovery and they made small talk. "Don't worry. If it's supposed to work out between you and Barbara it will," he said, handing Jesus his till.

Jesus nodded but didn't respond. He wasn't sure he wanted things to work out between them. On the other hand, he wanted it desperately. *Dammit! Why can't humans experience one emotion at a time?* he thought.

The office got crowded as four cashiers entered. Nothing was said and all that could be heard was the tinkling of coins. Brad finished first and asked Jesus if he wanted to ride the next day.

"Not yet. I'm really tired. Maybe by Friday."

"Let me know when you're ready," said Brad.

The three women finished almost simultaneously. Wanda and Sonya gave him a big hug when they left, but Barbara didn't say anything. He finished up his paperwork and the squad leader verified that the totals were correct. That was a relief, because Jesus wasn't sure how focused he had been during his shift. He called a cab and waited outside for it.

He saw Barbara leaning up against her car; it appeared that she was crying. He debated whether he should do anything. Finally, he decided to go over and show some concern.

"Is everything okay?"

"I'm mad at my boyfriend. The jerk!"

"I'm sorry that things aren't going well for you."

"Thank you. Are you better?"

"I'm getting there."

"Do you need a ride home?"

"No thanks. I called a cab."

"Are you sure?"

"Yep. Oh, there it is. Take care," Jesus said, walking quickly towards the cab. As he was about to get in, he looked back at Barbara. She was still leaning up against her car and she waved. As the cab departed, he realized he was feeling something he hadn't felt in a while. Hope.

Chapter 21 – What do women want?

Jesus contemplated his interaction with Barbara when he got home. He was interrupted when Jack walked in, angrily stomping back to his room without even looking at Jesus.

"Hey! Are you okay?" Jesus yelled. Jack stomped back into the living room and began pacing. Several times, he stopped and inhaled as if he were about to say something, but instead he exhaled loudly and resumed his pacing.

Suddenly he blurted out, "What is it with women? What do they want?" he cried, as he threw his hands in the air.

"I don't know...unless it's security, commitment and loyalty." Thinking for a moment, Jesus said, "Yeah, those are three of the main ones, but I'm sure there's some more. Why don't you bring it up at the next roundtable?"

"That won't do any good. Look at the group. Barbara goes from man to man. You—you pissed off Barbara. Brad secretly has a thing for Martha. Juan just got divorced. Alice is straight, but she doesn't really like men, not so far as I can tell. I don't know what Ralph or Gertrude's deal is and why would the pastor know anything about women?"

"Maybe you don't know them as well as you think. Maybe someone will say something that triggers an insight for you. You can learn from anybody."

"Oh, never mind," Jack said impatiently, hurrying off to his room.

If Jack wasn't going to bring it up, Jesus thought he would. Maybe he could get some insight into Barbara, if that was possible. He chose to stay positive about the situation, and the best way to do that was working on his daily spiritual practice.

That was his focus for the next three days, plus shopping for cars. By Friday, he had bought a small compact. Returning home, he practiced yoga and meditation, ate, and then went to the movies by himself. Loneliness set in as he sat in the dark, and he looked forward to getting back to work on a regular basis.

The next day he was scheduled to work as head cashier. The office hummed with talk of a new cashier, Dave. The ladies, including Barbara, commented on his good looks and the fact that he played guitar in a band. Ignoring the conversation, Jesus went about his duties.

The morning shift filed in to count their money and the conversation started anew about Dave. A cash drawer dropped on the desk loudly and interrupted his thoughts. "Wake up, Jesus. No more daydreaming about Dave," said Wanda, with mock seriousness.

"What? Dave who?" asked Jesus.

"Dave the dreamboat, my new squeeze."

He didn't know how to respond, and his obvious confusion led Wanda to say that she was just kidding. The rest of the cashiers finished shortly and left Jesus alone with his thoughts about Barbara.

Break time came and he walked out to the registers. "Who's first?" The breaks flew by, and Jesus felt more comfortable and energetic than during his previous shift. Barbara's break was last. "Your turn. Be back at 7:45," he said, checking the clock.

"Yes, sir!" Barbara said in a friendly manner. Jesus ignored her attempt at humor and had to repress the urge to touch her.

She tried some small talk when her break was over. "How are you feeling?"

"Just fine, thank you."

"That's good. You gave everybody a scare there. We were all wondering if you were going to suffer from amnesia again."

"Nope."

"Are you going to church tomorrow?"

"Yes."

"Great!" she said, smiling. "See you there!"

Wonderful, Jesus thought sarcastically, *another opportunity to work on my Barbara issues.* Walking back to the office, he suddenly became aware of his negativity. He paused at the door reframing his thought into a more positive one. *Yes, this is another opportunity to heal my relationship with Barbara.*

"Is everything all right?" she called out from her register.

Jesus turned, forced a smile and nodded. He went in and sat down, wondering about the outcome of their relationship. After a quick resentment prayer, he continued his duties.

His focus was interrupted by the intercom. He had a call from Clara, who asked him if he could fill in for Brad as head cashier the next evening. He agreed and checked the schedule to see who would be working the shift. Jack was working, and also the new guy, Dave. *That'll be interesting*, he thought.

The cashiers started coming back to the office to verify their tills. Barbara was first. She prattled on about nothing in particular. Jesus did his best to maintain his concentration. Touching his arm as she left, she said, "Take care."

Her touch generated an electricity that circulated throughout his body and again, he repressed the urge to touch her. She smiled broadly as she exited the office and Jesus laid his head on the desk. *How am I going to get through this? How am I possibly going to get through this?*

As soon as he got home after work, he went to his room to meditate. Getting comfortable, he looked around the room. Everything reminded him of Barbara, and thoughts of her kept floating through his mind. Over and over again, he gently brought his concentration back to his third eye. Frustrated at his lack of focus, he was ready to quit when it occurred to him that he was afraid. He didn't want to get hurt again and he was still mad at her. Events had unfolded so quickly that he hadn't had time to process those feelings. If he was going to heal, he had to talk to her about how he felt, but he didn't know how. Composing himself and concentrating, he remembered what Brad had said about letting the Universe provide the opportunity. Holding onto that thought, after his meditation was over, he went to bed and fell asleep quickly.

The next morning, he arrived at church early and Barbara was already there. She appeared to be in a good mood and touched his arm as she said hello. Again, electricity spread through his body and his mind numbed. She asked if Jack was coming.

"I don't know. I didn't see or hear him as I was getting ready."

"Brad's sick."

"I know. I'm filling in for him tonight."

"Oh, that means you'll get to meet Dave, the new cashier. He's working tonight."

Jesus winced slightly. *Is she trying to make me jealous again?* The pastor began his sermon. It was on the prodigal son. The pastor got quite emotional and so did Barbara. After the service was over, Jesus and Barbara filed out to greet him. Before Jesus could get a word out, Barbara asked him if the parable could apply to women.

"Of course it could," the pastor said. "Many, many people, man and woman, have led 'wasted' lives only to return home. And that return should be celebrated."

"I thought you might be talking about me," said Jesus.

The pastor immediately replied, "No, my son, it doesn't apply to you. I was the one who was lost."

It surprised Jesus that the pastor was so forthright. Before he could say anything, Barbara took his hand. "Let's go."

As they walked away, the pastor waved. "Thanks for coming!"

Jesus felt uncomfortable holding hands with Barbara and broke her grip. He didn't trust her and he didn't trust himself around her. As they reached her car, she suddenly blurted out, "Maybe we can have lunch sometime."

He wasn't ready to talk about his anger even though this was an opportunity. Three times he tried to say something, and each time Barbara's shoulders sank a little bit. Looking down at her feet, she said, "I understand if you don't want to."

He could feel her sadness in his belly and he felt he should say something. Putting his hand on her shoulder, their eyes met, but still he couldn't muster a single word. He abruptly turned and walked to his car. As he drove home, the weight of their meeting stirred up his anger and pain. Tears began to well up and by the time he parked his car at the apartment, he was crying. He rested his head on the steering wheel, feeling like he had lost something—something important. *Did I just blow it with her?*

Eventually, he went inside. Some tapping, yoga and meditation helped. He had faith that somehow this would work out for the best, but as he was driving to work, the anxiety of seeing Barbara again caught up with him. Breathing through it helped some. He parked the car, recited a half-dozen resentment prayers and braced himself for the coming shift.

The front-end office was noisy as usual, and Jesus unlocked the cabinet so the cashiers could get their cash drawers. Barbara was the last to arrive. Her face was puffy and her eyes were red, but she stopped to ask Dave if he had met Jesus.

"You mean am I born again?"

"Nooo. Our head cashier, Jesus H. da Vinci."

"No, I'd remember that."

Barbara introduced them and they shook hands. "Jesus, eh? Can you go bless the water fountain? I feel like a drink. Make it red wine would you? I don't like white."

Jesus didn't respond and the other cashiers groaned. As they filed out onto the sales floor, Dave stopped and turned to Jesus. "I want to see you walk on the water first before turning it into wine."

Pushing him in the back, Barbara said, "Quit it Dave. We've heard all these before."

Immediately Jesus stopped what he was doing. Barbara had defended him! Before he could start obsessing on that, the cashiers getting off the morning shift came into the office. Pete asked him how he was feeling. It had been over two weeks since the pneumonia and Jesus pronounced himself fit.

"Have you and Brad been riding yet?" Pete asked.

"No, we haven't. It's been at least five weeks since we last rode and now he's sick. I'll have to call him tomorrow."

The morning cashiers finished their counting and left. Jesus gave breaks and Barbara didn't say anything when he told her what time to be back at her register. When she returned from her break, neither of them spoke and it made him uneasy. He returned to the office and began his routine of resentment prayers and breathing. When that didn't completely remove the uneasiness, he tried some tapping. That worked and he was able to focus on work again.

Barbara was the last cashier to get off her register. She quietly counted her till. The office emptied and they were alone. Jesus wanted to say something soothing and spent several minutes formulating the right thing to say. Hearing the door close, he looked up. She had left without saying anything. Haunted by the issue, later at home he prayed, *Oh God, please relieve my pain...and hers.*

The next day, he called Brad to see how he was doing. "What's wrong, buddy?" Jesus asked.

"Some sort of intestinal bug."

"Difficulty digesting things, eh?"

Irritated, Brad said, "Yes, that would appear to be the mental or emotional reason for my dis-ease."

"So what's up?"

"Oh, I don't know. I haven't got a clue. It'll come to me eventually," he sighed. "Hey, could you do me a big favor?"

188

"Sure, anything."

"Can you work my cashier shift tonight? I told Clara I would be in, but I'm not quite up to it."

"Of course," said Jesus, noting the time. "I'd better get going then. Take care."

He rushed to get ready and left for the store. As he clocked in, Clara was clocking out. "What are you doing here?" she asked.

"I'm filling in for Brad. He's not well yet."

"Thank you. Thank you for not leaving us short-handed."

Jesus smiled. "Of course, my pleasure." She gave him a hug and told him again how good it was to have him back. Wanda, Barbara and Dave were already in the office. Dave started in on the comments about his name again, but Wanda scuttled that. "Dave, you keep talking about my man here and you'll have to deal with me."

Barbara added, "Putting other people down is just a way of propping yourself up." She stood up, grabbed her till and leaned in close to Dave. "And it's as ugly as your face is pretty," followed by sticking out her tongue at him.

Shocked, Dave started grumbling to himself. He and Jesus finished double-checking their tills at the same time and headed for the registers. "Dude, you know I'm just kidding. They just don't understand guys. Guys rag on each other."

Coming to a halt, Jesus stared hard at Dave. "I was unaware of that." As he headed to his register, he could hear Dave resume his grumbling.

It was so busy that the shift passed quickly. A couple of times, it felt like Barbara was looking at him. When he checked, she had such a sad look on her face that it made his heart ache. He did his best to concentrate on his customers. They got off their registers and counted their drawers in silence. When they left the store, Jesus walked her to her car.

"I would be open to a lunch," he said.

Barbara looked surprised, then gleeful, as she tried her best to contain herself. Taking a deep breath, she said, "How about Thursday?"

"That would work," he said. "What time?"

"One o'clock?"

"Okay. Breakfast tacos?"

"I'll pick you up."

"No, let's meet at Blondie's. See you then," said Jesus.

He walked over to his car, and as he was getting in he looked back at her. She had the strangest look on her face. It was somewhere between winning the lottery and a prophecy being fulfilled.

Jesus had plenty of time to work on his spiritual practice since he had few scheduled shifts. His feelings ran the gamut from giddiness at having lunch with Barbara to feelings of abandonment and anger. Doing his best to forgive her, he asked God dozens of times to help heal their relationship, whatever that might look like.

Thursday arrived, and Barbara called him early to see if they were still on. Jesus said yes and arrived at the restaurant to find Barbara waiting for him. She had makeup on and was wearing a pretty dress and high heels.

As they walked to their table, Jesus caught himself gazing at her derriere several times. Barbara caught him once. After they sat, he immediately picked up his menu and pretended to study it. Barbara tried to get the conversation going.

"How are you feeling?"

"Fine."

"So, you've recovered from the pneumonia?"

Jesus nodded yes and went back to reading the menu. Barbara sighed and perused hers. They sat in silence till the waitress came back for their orders.

"Did they catch the guy who robbed you?"

"No."

"How much money did he get?"

"Two hundred dollars," Jesus said, without emotion. "The money was to buy that desk you liked so much at the flea market."

Beginning to cry softly, Barbara looked down and wrung her napkin. "Jesus, I'm so, so sorry. I, I—" she murmured.

Squirming in his seat, Jesus tried to think of something comforting to say. He couldn't, and sat there quietly.

Raising her head, Barbara said, "Look, obviously I'm not very mature, but I'm doing the best I can. It's just that I always felt you were hiding something from me and that's a big issue for me. I'm working on it and I hope you can forgive me."

Staring off into space, Jesus said, "Interesting. Your distrust of me has led me to distrust you. I know that anger attracts anger, but do emotions always breed the same emotion? I wonder..."

"You have every reason to distrust me, Jesus." She sat there not knowing what to say next.

"What about Bill?"

"He cheated on me...again."

"Well, I'm sorry to hear that. That must have been devastating."

"It's my own fault. I thought he'd changed."

They sat in silence until their food arrived. Barbara picked at hers and finally spoke up, "Jesus, I realize I made a mistake. I know that. Is there any way you can forgive me and we can get back together?"

He put down his fork and looked her in the eye. "I don't know. I really don't know. You tried to make me jealous. You didn't support me through my crisis with the pastor. You didn't visit me in the hospital," he said, his anger rising. "You didn't even call when I had pneumonia! I don't know if I can ever trust you again." He picked up his fork and started stabbing at his food. He didn't want to feel angry with her, but he couldn't help himself.

Barbara began crying again. Jesus dropped his fork and abruptly stood up. He reached for his wallet, pulled out a twenty and dropped it on the table. "I'm sorry. I can't do this anymore," he said and left.

Crushed, she was sure she had blown it with him. But then she did something she almost never did—she prayed...at the table...out loud. "Lord, I put this situation in your hands. I know I've hurt Jesus. I know I've hurt him a lot. Please help heal his pain. I don't mean for us to get back together again, but please help him to trust again. Bless you, Lord, and amen."

She felt better and dried her tears. She was determined to heal her own issues and as she drove home, she felt that she would be a better person from this, however things turned out. She was certain of it.

Jesus wasn't sure whether he had done the right thing by telling Barbara how he felt. He felt better letting things out, and then he felt worse because it had hurt her. He arrived home to find Jack sitting on the couch staring off into space.

"Do you know anything about dreams?" Jack asked.

"You mean dream interpretation?"

"Yes."

"Some. It's not an exact science."

"I had a crazy dream last night."

"Let's hear it."

"It was so weird. I'm listening to a lecture and I hear a car accident outside. I jump up and run to the window to see what happened. Three angry men get out of the wrecked SUV. I watch for a little while and then return to my seat. Then I hear the three angry men in the next room. I get up, cross the room and sit on the floor against the wall to listen to their conversation. I hear a woman trying to calm them down. Then the three men burst into the lecture room, talking about getting some payback. The woman, carrying a baby, follows them in, still trying to calm them down. Eventually, they all leave.

"I hear another loud crash outside and leap to my feet and run to the window. There's an old forties pickup truck that's fallen partially into some kind of industrial vat filled with water. It's teetering on the edge, with a little bit of the bed submerged. A man's in the water, holding onto the back of the truck. He's slowly sinking. I notice that the baby the woman was carrying is playing in the bed of the truck. Then the man starts talking to me."

"Weird," said Jesus.

"You know it. The man says, 'When I need a question answered, I ask the tater tot. You know those little bumps on them? They can be eyes. If you need a question answered, always look into the four eyes of the tater tot,' and then I woke up."

"Nice dream! I'm glad to know that I'm not the only one having really weird dreams."

Jack stood and paced. He walked up to Jesus and asked plaintively, "But what does it mean? It's got to mean something. It was the weirdest dream I've ever had."

Inspired, Jesus headed for the bathroom. "Follow me."

As they stood in front of the mirror, Jesus asked, "What do you see?"

"One average-looking guy and me."

"Nice, but let's get more specific. How many eyes do you have?"

"Two."

"How many did you have on the playground?"

Peering at Jesus, Jack said, "Are you calling me four-eyes?"

"Hey, it was your dream."

"Wait—I'm the tater tot?" Jack asked slowly.

"You, my friend, are the delicious tater tot."

Jack seemed to be having trouble processing this interpretation so Jesus said, "My take on the dream is this—the baby is your ego and it's playing around, you're easily distracted, and some part of your life is slipping away."

"What about looking into the eyes of the tater tot?"

"If you want answers, look yourself in the eye—or in this dream, eyes—and ask a question. You have all the answers."

"I do?"

"Everyone has all the answers for themselves. They just have to be brave enough to look at them. It's not easy, but self-reflection is necessary. If you don't look, the Universe will find a way to get your attention, rest assured."

Jesus left and Jack stood there, looking himself in the eyes. Every time he was close to formulating a question to ask, his ego reasserted itself and distracted him. Finally, fed up, he declared that this was bullshit and went to his room.

The roundtable was that night and Jesus prepared by doing his spiritual routine. During the meditation, the top of his head started buzzing. He had felt this before, but this time the chakra opening felt conical, ending in a point at his corpus callosum. It also felt as if someone were taking a scalpel and scraping the edges of the cone. Before getting dressed, he added it to his mental list of things to ask Martha the next time he saw her.

It was so pleasant outside that Jesus rode his bike to the church. He thought he was completely over the pneumonia, but found he was still a little weak.

When they were all gathered, the pastor asked for a topic and everyone looked to Jesus. "Why is everybody looking at me?"

"You bring up such great topics," Gertrude said.

Pondering what to suggest, he scanned the room and saw Jack looking at him nervously. Jesus took a deep breath and went ahead. "Let's talk about relationships. Intimate relationships."

Somehow, Jack summoned up the courage to speak, "Yeah, what do women want?"

The three women of the group, Alice, Barbara and Gertrude, looked back and forth at each other and simultaneously said...

Gertrude: "Security and responsibility."

Barbara: "Emotionally open."

Alice: "Pursuit."

The men of the group laughed. Jack said, "Of course. Women don't know what they want."

"I think it's a little more complicated than that, Jack," said the pastor.

"Of course it is," said Barbara. "It depends on the guy." Alice and Gertrude nodded in agreement.

Brad perked up. "What do you mean?"

"No guy has *everything* a woman wants, at least not in the beginning. She knows she'll have to smooth out the rough edges. But she does have a basic list," Alice said.

With frustration in his voice, Jack asked, "So, what's on the list?"

"Well, you know," said Barbara, her voice trailing off.

"No, I don't. That's why I'm asking," said Jack, through gritted teeth.

"Maturity," said Gertrude, raising an eyebrow and looking directly at Jack.

"Yeah, and stability," said Alice.

"He should have a nice appearance, you know, and keep himself up," said Barbara, looking at Jesus.

"Respect. Definitely respect. Ladies, if he doesn't respect you then dump him," said Gertrude.

"He should be creative, too," said Alice.

"He should be emotionally open and trust you with all his secrets," said Barbara again, looking directly at Jesus.

"You said that one already," said Jesus flatly.

Barbara frowned and then her face lit up with inspiration. "Oh! And, of course, fantastic sex!" That comment was followed by deep and throaty laughs from all three of the ladies.

"I've never had fantastic sex," said Gertrude, glancing at the pastor with a curious smile.

Caught off guard, the pastor, stammering slightly, said, "Jack, are you writing all of this down?"

Giving him the look of death, Jack said as politely as he could muster, "Yes, Pastor," repeatedly clinching his left hand into a fist.

Brad chuckled at Jack's reaction, but Alice's mention of "pursuit" was weighing on his mind. Jesus, on the other hand, was trying to stay in the moment. With Barbara across the table, his ego was responding in a physical manner.

Juan and Ralph looked at each other. "I think it's getting a little warm in here," Juan said. Ralph nodded in agreement.

The pastor jumped at this opportunity to ask if there was another topic anyone wanted to discuss. Brad spoke up and asked, "Who here sits down and listens for God?"

This question took everybody by surprise. Several moments of silence followed until Jesus said, "Well, I do."

"How often?" Brad asked.

"I meditate three times a day and I practice yoga twice a day...usually. I do my best to stay in the moment because I can't hear God if I'm focused on the past or the future," Jesus said.

"That's a lot," said Barbara. "I go to church on Sunday. I have recently prayed, but that's about it."

"I pray in the morning and in the evening before I go to bed," said Gertrude.

"I pray when I need something," said Ralph.

Sheepishly, Jack said, "I really don't pray."

"That's not a surprise, Jack," the pastor said, giving him a disapproving look. Turning to Brad, he asked, "Is meditation really praying?"

Brad and Jesus looked at each other and Brad said, "In the sense of communicating with God, yes, definitely."

"In some ways, meditation is better," said Jesus.

Except for Brad, this set the room atwitter. "How do you figure?" the pastor asked skeptically.

Jesus sat back and glanced at Brad. Taking a deep breath, Brad said, "Generally—not all the time, mind you—praying is about asking for something. Sometimes it's for yourself, sometimes it's for friends and family, and sometimes we pray for people that are...victims."

"So? What's wrong with that?" asked Juan.

"Nothing," said Jesus, "Nothing at all. Meditation, however, is about *listening* to God. You see, in the vast scope of the Universe, we can perceive but a fraction of what's really going on. Our viewpoint is very limited compared to God's. There are always answers that go way beyond what we can possibly conceive."

"How do you know that you've gotten the right answers? I mean, I understand your point and agree that we must listen for God and his answers, but history is replete with atrocities done supposedly in the name of God," said the pastor.

"Yeah. How do you know that you're not deluding yourself?" asked Alice.

"Has anyone here experienced that one voice in your head that's always right?" asked Brad.

Everyone nodded in unison. "I've always called that my common sense," said Alice.

"Does it make any difference what you call it?" asked Jesus. "Calling it God, the Great Spirit or the Universe doesn't affect its accuracy, does it?"

The group sat in silence, contemplating their experiences with the small, still voice. "That doesn't answer my question. How do you know that you're not deluding yourself?" asked Alice.

Jesus responded, "Meditation—the practice of meditation. Think how long your mind has gone untrained. And when I say mind, I mean ego. The ego is like the guy sitting behind you in the movie theatre who

194

wants to share the movie with his wife, disturbing everyone around them, yet has absolutely nothing interesting to say. The consistent practice of meditation—bringing my attention, my focus, back to the present, slowly but surely—calms down my ego. With my ego chatter reduced, it's much easier to hear God and get the answers I need. My guess is that the atrocities you mentioned weren't committed by spiritual people who meditated."

"I've tried meditation before," said Barbara, "and it doesn't work for me. My mind is all over the place, concerned about what I should be doing next, what I want to eat for dinner and so forth. I tried it and it didn't work."

"How many times did you try it?" asked Brad.

"A couple," said Barbara.

Laughing, Jesus said, "Thanks for making our point. Two attempts at meditation aren't going to undo a lifetime of mental anarchy. But with a daily practice, you'll start to see an improvement in mental discipline within a few weeks."

"And with continued practice, you'll improve your communication with God," said Brad.

"Well, this conversation has given all of us a lot to think about," said the pastor. "I think it's time to adjourn."

Chapter 22 – Enchanted Rock

"Would you teach me how to meditate?" Barbara asked Jesus as they walked to their cars. He stopped and looked at her skeptically. "No, really. I want to learn how to meditate."

Breathing deeply, Jesus said, "All right, but no hanky-panky. If you are truly serious about learning to meditate, I'll teach you what I've learned so far."

They decided that the next evening would work, and Barbara asked if he wanted to go to dinner first. Repressing a surge of testosterone, Jesus said no. He told her not to be late.

He awoke the next morning feeling bright and refreshed. Aware of an energy flowing throughout his body, he realized it was not of the physical kind, yet he felt it physically. He wondered what it was and asked the Universe for an answer. When he got distracted, he didn't notice the energy. But when there was a lull in his outward activity, and he could center himself and turn inward again, he was able to differentiate the energy clearly from other human sensations and stimuli. That didn't last long though, because thoughts of Barbara kept sneaking in.

When she arrived that night, Jesus led her back to his bedroom. Stopping in the doorway, she said, "It's just the way I remember it."

"I haven't changed a thing, or for that matter, added anything either. Let's sit here," he said, pointing to the throw rug she had picked out. "All right, sit cross-legged and get comfy."

They sat face to face, their knees a few inches apart. With a suggestive smile on her face, Barbara winked at him and wiggled her eyebrows. "Wipe that look off your face and take a deep breath."

"Yes, sir," Barbara said disappointedly.

"Now close your eyes. I want you to breathe deeply—first filling up the bottom of your lungs, then the middle and finally the top of your lungs. Fill them up completely and then ever so slightly pause. Exhale from the top of the lungs first, then the middle of the lungs and then empty the bottom of the lungs."

Barbara repeated this process a few times and told Jesus that she was feeling a little light-headed. "That's because you're bringing more prana into your body than you're used to. It isn't anything to worry about."

"Okay."

"Since you're a beginner, I'm going to show you a meditation that gives you something to focus on. Rest your left hand in your lap, take the four fingers of your right hand and locate your pulse on your left wrist. No need to press so hard. A light touch is all that's required. Sit up straight and don't curl your shoulders in. We're going to do this for eleven minutes, okay?"

Barbara nodded and Jesus started the timer. Almost immediately, Barbara giggled. Without opening his eyes, Jesus asked, "What?"

"A song keeps coming up in my mind and my pulse matches the beat."

"That's okay. When that happens or any thoughts come up, as soon as you recognize that you're distracted, calmly and without judgment, bring your focus back to your pulse."

She was quiet through the rest of the meditation, but Jesus's mind was not. Thoughts of them getting back together penetrated his consciousness over and over again. He hoped she didn't want another meditation lesson.

The timer on his phone went off, to his relief. "How do you feel?" he asked.

"Even though my mind was all over the place, I feel very relaxed right now," Barbara said.

"It shows in your face."

"Can we do this again?"

"You need to learn to do this on your own," he said. "And you could always take a yoga class...but I suppose we could have another lesson."

Barbara nodded and smiled. She stood up, stretched, and continued her stretching as she sat on his bed. Jesus sat down next to her and their eyes met.

It was as if two high-powered magnets joined with a powerful smack, and before he could think, they were kissing. Within seconds, they had stripped off each other's clothes and jumped into bed. His fingers explored her body and he began to run his fingernails lightly over her skin. As his hand reached her upper thigh, her leg involuntarily shuddered and she let out a low moan.

"Ahh, you like that, don't you?" he asked, letting out a husky laugh.

She nodded and closed her eyes as Jesus sat up to get closer to his target. "It's making my toes curl," she purred.

Jesus continued, gazing upon her, when all of a sudden Barbara yelled, "Cramp!" Jesus turned his head just as Barbara sat up to grab her foot. Their heads met in a loud crack and Jesus fell backwards off the bed, landing flat on his back, his head bouncing off the floor with a thud.

Barbara jumped off the bed and knelt next to him, alternating "Ow, ow, ow!" with "Are you okay?"

Jesus lay on the floor with his eyes closed, saying nothing as he tried to gather his wits. Finally opening his eyes, he asked, "Who are you?"

Hysterical, Barbara cried, "Oh my God! You don't have amnesia again, do you? Please, please don't have amnesia."

Jesus started laughing and Barbara yelled, "You bastard! How could you do that to me? How could you?"

Sitting up and still chuckling, Jesus said, "I'm sorry. How's the cramp?"

"I think you scared it out of me, you bastard," she said, slapping him on his arms and chest. He grabbed her wrists and slowly pushed her to the floor. Kissing her repeatedly, her cries of "You bastard" were soon replaced by subdued moans and sighs.

After indulging their passion, Barbara breathlessly asked, "When's the next lesson, teacher?" Jesus, still in a post-coital daze, didn't answer. She pinched him to get a response.

"All right, all right. Soon. Let me gather my thoughts."

"Okay," said Barbara, putting her arm across his chest and her head on his shoulder. *Why am I fighting this?* Jesus wondered.

He abruptly sat up, surprising Barbara. "Is everything okay?" she asked, leaning on her elbow.

"Are we back together?"

Barbara shot up into a kneeling position and grasped Jesus's hands. Her voice trembling, she asked, "Do you want to get back together?"

Jesus half-smiled, lowered his gaze and nodded. Looking up into her eyes, he said, "Yes."

Barbara bounded to her feet and jumped up and down yelling, "Yes, yes, yes!" Watching in fascination as her breasts bounced and jiggled, he wondered what was so mesmerizing about them.

Barbara collapsed onto him and they began kissing again. She suddenly stopped. "I can't stay here tonight. I have work in the morning and I've got no clothes here."

"I've got the evening shift tomorrow," he said.

"Shall I come over afterwards?" she asked.

Thinking for a moment, Jesus said, "No. Let's go to church together on Sunday and then get lunch afterwards. I'll pick you up. Oh, and leave the afternoon free."

"Oooh, special plans?" Barbara asked.

"Maybe. We'll see," he said, grinning and opening his eyes wide.

Barbara got dressed and Jesus put on his robe. He walked her to the door and they kissed.

"See you tomorrow," she said, sashaying to her car.

"Bye," he said, walking back to his room to finish his spiritual practice. His mind kicked into gear and he wondered what had just happened. *How did this start?* After a few moments of consideration, he thought, *To the heavens with this. I'm committing to this relationship. No more doubt. I forgive her for her past behavior and I forgive myself for mine.*

Jesus spent the next morning gathering up the items he needed for the date with Barbara. When they passed each other at work, she flirted with him to try to get him to reveal his plans. "You'll find out after church tomorrow. I'll pick you up at nine thirty," he said. She planted a quick kiss on him with Wanda watching, so that soon the whole store would know they were back together.

Barbara watched from her apartment window the next day as Jesus arrived. She checked herself one last time in the mirror by the door. Before Jesus could knock she flung it open. "Good morning, sir. How may I help you?"

Playing along, Jesus said, "Why madam, would you do me the honor of accompanying me to church on this fine fall morning?" He doffed an invisible top hat and with an exaggerated bow, almost fell over.

Barbara, acting faint and fanning herself with both hands replied, "Oh dear. This is a surprise. I suppose that I could possibly do such a thing."

Jesus offered his arm to Barbara, and within a few steps they arrived at the car. Opening the car door for her, their arms were still linked and it seemed that Barbara didn't want to let go. His puckish side took over and he spun her backwards around the door and onto the car seat, legs flying up in the air. "Jesus! What in the hell are you doing?" she yelled.

Laughing, Jesus bent over and helped her sit up straight. "Now milady, shall we repair to the church?" Barbara grabbed the car door and slammed it, narrowly missing Jesus.

As he got in, Barbara punched him in the arm. "Slapstick or politeness—choose one or the other, but don't alternate between them."

"Isn't that how we got started again?" he asked, grinning.

"No, that was *foreplay* and slapstick. I had to put on extra makeup to cover up the bruise on my forehead," she said emphatically.

"Awww, let me kiss your boo-boo," he said sweetly.

Barbara laughed and bent over so he could kiss her forehead. On the way to the church, she asked several times what was under the blanket in the back seat. Jesus would only say with an air of mystery, "It's for this afternoon's activities."

They joined Brad and Jack when they arrived. Seeing them holding hands, Jack said, "I thought I heard some boom-chicka-now-now, ee-ee-ee-ee, wink-wink nudge-nudge after I got home last night."

Looking at Jack with disgust, Brad said, "Really? I think you're trying too hard."

"That's what she said," Jack replied, laughing.

Brad shook his head and turned to the couple. "I'm happy for both of you."

They both beamed until the start of the sermon. The topic was forgiveness and Jesus listened intently. The pastor focused on forgiving others. Jesus thought the pastor left out forgiving oneself.

After the service, the pastor noticed Jesus and Barbara holding hands. "I see you two are back together," he said.

Jesus said, "Yes, sir. About your sermon, why didn't you mention forgiving yourself?"

Pausing, the pastor said, "Forgiving yourself? I let God forgive me."

Barbara, fired up for their date, saw what was happening and started dragging Jesus away. Half-stumbling, he yelled back, "How can you understand or feel God's forgiveness if you haven't forgiven yourself? They're not mutually exclusive!"

"Okay, okay, what are we doing today?" asked Barbara eagerly.

"We're going bowling," Jesus said, trying to repress a smile.

"Bowling? Really?"

He couldn't hold back and started laughing. "Stop that!" Barbara said, slapping him on the arm. By now they were in the car and she tried to peek under the blanket.

Jesus smacked her hand. "Patience, my dear. Patience."

Barbara grumbled and Jesus said, "All right. First we're going to lunch at Earth Mother's and then afterwards I'll tell you about this afternoon's activities."

As they got in the car after lunch, Barbara asked, "Okay, what's the big surprise, Jesus?"

He reached around and pulled off the blanket to reveal two backpacks. "Ta-da! We're going to Enchanted Rock."

"You expect me to go hiking in this dress?"

"Nope. That's why we're stopping at your place first and I have a change of clothes in the trunk."

"Oh, Jesus," Barbara whined.

"Hey, it's a beautiful afternoon. You'll get some fresh air. It'll be nice."

"But the sun hates me," Barbara said. "I get burned too easily."

"That's why your backpack contains sunscreen, which I will apply liberally all over your body."

Barbara smiled, but tried one last excuse. "But Betsy is home. She doesn't like you."

"I can deal with her," Jesus said.

They drove to her apartment and went inside. Jumping up off the couch with a look of horror on her face, Betsy said, "You brought that devil into my home?" She quickly ran to her room.

"I'm going to the bathroom to change," said Jesus, shaking his head.

After he finished, he opened the door to find a cross thrust at him. "Be gone, you devil!" Betsy yelled.

"Good Lord," Jesus said, taking a step back. "What is wrong with you?"

Betsy looked disappointed that her admonition didn't have a greater effect. "Excuse me," he said, as he pushed past her.

Barbara came out of her room. "Betsy, stop that. I mean it." Barbara linked arms with Jesus and as they walked to the car, she said, "I think she's getting worse."

It was a beautiful fall day in Texas and Jesus took the back way to get to Enchanted Rock. Barbara chatted constantly on the way there. Friends, Betsy, people from work, television shows—a constant stream of distraction. *How does she breathe?* he wondered.

"How much longer?" Barbara asked.

Jesus took a minute to answer so as to enjoy a moment of silence. "We're almost there, honey."

Cresting the last hill, Enchanted Rock came into view. The large pinkish-white rock looked like Mother Earth was about to give birth. "Oh my God! We're going to climb that?" asked Barbara.

"Yes. It's not that hard. At least that's what Brad told me."

The closer they got, the more enormous the granite dome appeared. Jesus pulled into the ranger station to pay their entry fees. As he got back into the car, Barbara said, "Honey, I really don't think I can climb that."

"Oh relax. It's only 500 feet above the surrounding plain."

"It looks like it will take hours to climb."

"Maybe 45 minutes. Probably less than that."

He parked in the closest lot to the base. They got out of the car and Jesus checked their provisions—water, granola bars and sunscreen. "We're ready," he declared.

"You forgot you need to lather me up," said Barbara with a wink.

Jesus pulled out the sunscreen and handed it to her. "I thought you were going to apply it," Barbara said.

Laughing, Jesus said, "We'll never make it to the top before dark if I do."

Barbara frowned and coated herself with sunscreen. Setting out for the summit, they left the parking lot and crossed the dry creek bed maneuvering over the concrete berms.

Jesus put his arm around her shoulder and they meandered down the path, nodding to other park visitors as they passed. They crossed another dry creek bed and began the climb upward, zigzagging along the trail until they reached bare rock.

Barbara stopped and looked up. She couldn't see the top. She was already slightly winded so they rested a minute and drank some water. It seemed quite steep to her and she had to stop to rest again after fifty yards. She still couldn't see the top. She looked back toward the parking lot and it seemed so small and far away. "This is scary."

Jesus snorted. "It's only scary when it's wet."

"What happens if I fall?" she asked pensively.

"You'll roll all the way to the bottom," he said, before recognizing her discomfort. "You walk in front and I'll walk behind you. If you fall, I'll catch you." That seemed to mollify her some and they continued on. They stopped again after another fifty yards and drank some more water.

"This is taking forever," Barbara said, even though it had only been twenty minutes.

They continued walking and slowly the slope eased. Finally, they reached the flat top of the big rock. It was dotted with small impressions filled with puddles and plant life. Jesus picked a spot and pulled out a blanket from his backpack so they could sit down. Barbara collapsed onto the blanket with a loud, "Ow! This is hard!"

"That's why you have a blanket and a towel to sit on." She stood up so he could arrange things. After drinking some water and eating a granola bar, Barbara relaxed. "This is some view," she said.

"It's beautiful, isn't it?"

Pointing, Barbara said, "It's raining over there."

"That must be near Llano to the north. That shouldn't bother us. So what do you think? Pretty nice, huh?"

"Yes, it's pretty nice. What kind of rock is this?" asked Barbara.

"Pink granite. This kind of rock formation is called a monadnock,"

"A monad-rock?"

Smiling, Jesus said, "Nock, nock. It's an old Native American term for—"

"Big rock?" interrupted Barbara.

"Probably. The Native Americans that inhabited this area thought Enchanted Rock had spiritual and magical powers."

"Are we going to perform some magic now?" asked Barbara, raising an eyebrow.

"Yes. We're going to meditate."

Barbara looked disappointed and so he quickly added, "This is a special meditation. We're going to look into each other's eyes. It is said that this will reveal one's deepest secrets to the other. Are you ready to expose your deepest, darkest secrets to me?"

"Are you ready to reveal yours to me?" she asked defiantly.

"Of course," Jesus said dismissively. "Scoot closer, but no touching. Place your hands on your knees, forefinger and thumbs touching, the rest of your fingers extended. Breathe long and deep like I taught you, and if you can, blink as little as possible. We're going to do this for eleven minutes." Jesus set the timer on his phone and they began.

Initially, Barbara giggled and had trouble sitting still, but then she got into it, gazing at him intently. After a few minutes, Jesus's face began to change and seemed to be distinctly separate from his head. Her breathing slowed. Her mind quieted. She felt his conflict, his kindness, his purpose. Then his face changed into something she didn't recognize....

"Omigod! Did you see that?" she exclaimed.

Jesus was disappointed that she had broken their gaze. "Right behind you. A lightning strike!" Barbara yelled.

"I didn't hear anything," said Jesus, noticing some other park-goers running towards them. He turned to look and saw two lightning bolts strike in quick succession about two hundred feet away. "Wow, that's interesting. No clouds, no thunder."

"Let's get out of here!" said Barbara.

"Calm down. Let the other panicked people go down first. We don't want to be in front of anyone rushing down the rock face," said Jesus.

They quickly packed and headed down. The descent was tricky as the surface was curved. It seemed like they were walking towards a cliff, and it scared Barbara. She clutched Jesus's arm and took baby steps. They went down a lot slower than they went up, and stopped at the bottom for Barbara to rest. She threw her arms around Jesus and looked him in the eyes. "Thank you for not making fun of me."

"I wouldn't do that. Well I do, but not as a general rule," he smiled, kissing her sweetly on the lips.

They saw several deer grazing as they made their way back to the parking lot. Crossing the concrete berms, Jesus saw that there were some people sitting on a blanket in front of the dumpster. As he and Barbara neared, it became apparent that they were eating. Jesus greeted them when he got close enough. "Great day for a picnic."

202

There were two women and a young boy of around four, sitting on a blanket and eating. They smiled and said yes it was and the first woman holding the boy implored him to say hello, but he was too shy. "You know, there are picnic tables right over there," Jesus said, pointing.

"I know, but we were so hungry we just plopped down..." said the second woman, stopping to wipe her nose. It was bleeding. The other woman reached into a backpack, pulled out a napkin and handed it to her friend. Dabbing her nose, she said, "That's odd. That hasn't happened in ages."

"I hope everything is okay," said Jesus, as he and Barbara walked towards his car. As they got in, Jesus noticed a small trickle of blood coming out of Barbara's nose. He handed her his handkerchief. "Here. Your nose is bleeding."

"Oh! I've never had a nosebleed. What do I do?" asked Barbara.

"Just lean your head forward and pinch your nose for five minutes."

"You don't think this is because of the lightning, do you?"

"I seriously doubt it," Jesus said reassuringly.

"Your voice sounds different."

"How so?"

"It sounds richer, or something."

"Nope. Still making a few dollars over minimum wage," laughed Jesus, but he could hear it, too.

On the drive home, he made several attempts to figure out what had just happened, but each time, the Universe threw a deer or an armadillo into his path, requiring him to return to the moment.

Barbara contemplated the day's activities also, but not the lightning and nosebleeds; she wondered what she had seen during the meditation. It was as if her mind couldn't quite comprehend it and was attempting to hide the image from her consciousness. She concentrated on trying to see the memory fully. Frustrated that she couldn't, she glanced at Jesus. He smiled at her and she forced a smile in return. This happened several times until she dozed off.

"Wake up, Barbara. We're home," said Jesus, nudging her gently.

"What? Okay," she said sitting up and blinking her eyes. He leaned over and gave her a peck on the cheek. She stumbled out of the car. He rolled down the window and told her he would call her the next day.

Unable to quiet his mind, Jesus took several hours to get to sleep that night and he woke up groggy to a phone call from Brad. He asked Jesus if he felt like a bike ride. He didn't, but they hadn't been riding together in so long that he said yes; maybe it would wake him up.

Brad showed up about an hour later. It was a chilly fall morning and they were slow to warm up. Brad asked him what was new. Jesus hesitated, mainly to catch his breath, and gave an account of the trip to Enchanted Rock.

"Whoa! You need to talk to Martha," exclaimed Brad.

Puffing heavily, Jesus asked, "Why? Does it mean something?"

"It could. I've heard about such manifestations before."

"And?"

"Just talk to Martha," Brad reiterated. By the time they returned to their starting point, Jesus was exhausted. He hadn't felt like this in a while. Brad asked about going on another ride soon.

"Give me a couple of days to recover," said Jesus. "I'm not in shape yet. How about this weekend?"

Brad agreed. Once Jesus returned home, he immediately started a yoga set, not even changing out of his sweat-dampened riding shorts. His concentration during meditation was superb. Only twice did his mind stray. He prepared some lunch and sat down on the couch to eat and watch TV, but soon dozed off.

He awoke with a start and the first thing on his mind was the store. Overcome by an urge to see Barbara, he made a shopping list and drove there. He slipped in the back so as to surprise her.

Quickly he selected the items he needed, said hello to some coworkers and went to the end of Barbara's line. It was after five and very busy, so she didn't notice him. The customer in front of him suddenly turned around. "Oh my, you can go in front of me. My nose is bleeding."

"Mine, too," said the customer behind Jesus. They both went to customer service for some tissues and Jesus felt their fear. *Am I the cause of this? What should I do?* he wondered.

"Jesus!" Barbara said ecstatically, running around the counter to give him a big hug. "What are you doing here on your day off?"

"I had a few items to pick up, but mainly I wanted to see you," he said.

Kissing him on the mouth, she asked, "Should I come over after work?"

Jesus hesitated, then pulled out his handkerchief and passed it to her. "What's this for?" she asked. Jesus pointed to her face. Wiping her nose, Barbara said disgustedly, "Damn lightning." She returned to work, and he stood at the end of the counter making small talk with her for a few minutes. Then he saw Martha get in Barbara's line.

"Martha, so good to see you," said Jesus, putting his arms around her. Barbara stood silently as she watched the two of them embrace.

"This is Barbara."

"Nice to meet you," said Martha, extending her hand. Barbara gave her a one-pump handshake and began ringing up her items.

Turning to Jesus, Martha asked, "What's new?"

"Lots. I want your take on what happened to Barbara and me out at Enchanted Rock yesterday."

"Did something happen out there?" Martha asked, as if she already knew. "I so love Enchanted Rock."

Martha paid for her groceries and she and Jesus moved a few feet away so he could tell her the story.

"Jesus, listen to me," she said, grasping his arms and looking very serious. "It's time to step up your yoga and meditation practice. Don't worry. This is just a phase and you'll get through it quickly, if you persevere. Let's have a session in the next couple of weeks. You'll know when. Sorry, but

I've got to go." She gave Jesus a big, long hug and noticed Barbara furtively glancing over at them. Forgoing her usual kiss on the lips, she took her groceries and left.

When he returned to the register, Barbara asked, "What did she say?"

"Nothing much. We're going to get together for a session in the next couple of weeks," Jesus said, not fully explaining because he knew Barbara wouldn't understand. "Hey, I've got to go," he said giving her a peck on the cheek. "Let's get together after work on Wednesday."

"Okay," said Barbara quietly.

Jesus knew she was upset, but he knew it was more important to focus on his spiritual practice. That night he even tried the one-breath-per-minute meditation—inhale for twenty seconds, hold the breath for twenty seconds and exhale for twenty seconds.

He put in two and a half hours of spiritual work the next morning and there was only one nosebleed that evening at work. He prayed that night for God to help him see the way and that his spiritual practice not disturb or harm anyone.

On Wednesday, he worked the lunch shift at the soup kitchen. Alice assigned him to the steam table. He had gotten used to the smells of the soup kitchen, but he was assaulted by a different odor when a disheveled, hunched man came up with a sheepish look on his face.

"Is everything okay?" asked Jesus, sniffing.

"I shit myself," the man said.

Jesus could physically feel the man's embarrassment. The smell made his stomach turn, but his compassion kept him from gagging. "Let's take care of that before you eat." He quickly walked around the steam table to see a dark wet spot on the rear of the man's trousers. "What size pants do you wear?"

The man told him as Jesus led him to the restroom. A commotion started, as patrons waiting to be served started banging their trays. Jesus ignored them and went to the clothing donations room. He quickly located a pair that was close to the size the man told him and hurried back to the restroom. He could hear Alice shout for everybody to calm down as he knocked on the restroom door.

The man let him in. He was naked. "Why did you take off everything?" Jesus asked.

"I didn't want to get shit on my shirt," he said dismissively, turning around and presenting Jesus with a behind covered in feces, some of which had run down one leg.

Trying not to gag, Jesus asked, "Why didn't you clean yourself?"

Half-turning, the man said, "I can't do it very good anymore. I have arthritis in both shoulders and it really hurts to reach back there."

Nodding, Jesus wetted several paper towels. Steeling himself and silently asking for strength, he gently rubbed the man clean. It took almost twenty paper towels. The man thanked him when he had finished, put on the clean pants and the rest of his clothes and left. Jesus picked up the soiled pants and took them to the dumpster. When he had returned, Alice was serving in his place.

"Where have you been?" she asked angrily.

"A man soiled himself and I got him a fresh pair of pants and helped him clean himself. Actually, I did all the cleaning," said Jesus, shuddering slightly.

"Did you wash your hands?" asked Alice, still angry.

"Yes. Of course," he said, surprised by her reaction.

"Look Jesus, every day someone comes in here who's shit in their pants. I know it's sad, but you can't get involved."

Looking at her as if she were kidding, he echoed, "Can't get involved?"

"Yes. If you're trying to get to heaven by doing good works, it ain't gonna happen," said Alice.

"Hmm," said Jesus. "I'm starting to think that Earth is heaven."

Chapter 23 – Jesus expresses his love

Barbara came over the next night after work. Wound up, she prattled on about her shift—what was said by whom, insolent customers, complaints about Clara. Jesus listened patiently until she asked about his day. He told her about his experiences at the soup kitchen.

"That was brave of you, helping that man."

"I don't know. I couldn't let him sit down at the tables in soiled pants. That would sort of ruin the ambiance," said Jesus, deflecting.

"I could never do that," Barbara said, stopping to reflect. "Of course, if I want to be a mother, and I do, I would have to do that with my baby."

"Definitely. It's no different."

"I wouldn't agree with you that Earth is heaven though," said Barbara.

"You wouldn't?"

"Absolutely not. War, poverty, crime, innocent people maimed and raped. How could that possibly be heaven?"

"Well," Jesus said, pausing to gather his thoughts, "let me propose a scenario. What if you were allowed to visit a place where you could create your own reality? Would you want to visit that sort of place?"

"Well, it depends. Could I be anything I want?"

"Yes, of course. Anything you want."

"I want to be able to sing, but I can't. That shoots a hole in your scenario, doesn't it?"

"Not really. You're thinking only of the present. What if you learned music theory in this lifetime? What if you took singing lessons to improve your voice? What if these skills carry over to the next lifetime and become talents?"

Her desire trumping her patience, Barbara sprung at Jesus and kissed him passionately. She was about to suggest that they go to the bedroom, when Jesus pulled back. "I've got to go and meditate. I'm sorry I didn't plan this out better," he said, standing up.

"Now?" Barbara asked irritably.

"Yes, now. I must get forty more minutes of meditation in today."

"Why?" Barbara whined.

"We'll save that conversation for later. Watch some TV and I'll be back soon," Jesus said, walking to his bedroom.

Barbara groaned, "You're keeping something from me again," as she heard the bedroom door shut. She watched an old sitcom rerun and by the time Jesus had returned, she was asleep.

He roused her gently and led her into the bedroom. They stripped and climbed into bed. Barbara fell asleep immediately, but Jesus lay awake thinking about what she had said. If they were going to be a couple he might have to be more open with her, especially about his spiritual path. He fell asleep asking for guidance.

The next morning they got up early. Barbara was grumpy while preparing breakfast and Jesus suggested that she come over again after his shift.

"Okay, but get your meditation in before I come over," she said pointedly.

"I'll do as much as I can this morning, sweetie," Jesus said, planting a kiss on her cheek. Barbara grimaced, but said nothing. They ate breakfast and Jesus saw her to the door. "Have a nice day!" he called out. Immediately, he went to his room and meditated.

He arrived at work a little early that afternoon and visited Barbara at her register before going to the front-end office. Clara, having seen them kiss, asked, "Are you two back together again?"

"Yes."

"For how long?"

"About a week."

"That's nice," she said, frowning. "But stay focused."

Smiling, Jesus said, "Yes ma'am!"

Clara shook her head. "And you'll have to be especially focused today. We're down a cashier and the other two cashiers are in the bathroom trying not to throw up."

"I will," he said, as he verified his till. He headed out to the registers and relieved Pete. "So, you and Barbara again?" asked Pete, winking.

"Yes. Me and Barbara again."

"You two were destined to be together," he said, walking to the front-end office.

The shift was hectic. As Barbara left, she came by Jesus's register and hugged him from behind. "Try to get off early, okay?"

"I'll try, but we're already short-handed."

By the end of the shift, the two cashiers who didn't feel well felt worse, so Jesus was the last one off the registers. He counted as quickly as possible, but when he got home, there was Barbara sitting in her car.

"What took you so long?" she asked impatiently.

"I was the last one off the register. I'm sorry, but two of the cashiers got sick. I had to stay. Now be patient, and in forty minutes I'll be kissing you."

Barbara groaned as Jesus went straight to his room to meditate. By the time he had finished, Barbara was fast asleep on the couch again. He roused her and they went to bed.

The following morning, Jesus awoke feeling dissatisfied. He searched his feelings but couldn't come up with a cause. Barbara woke up cranky again, and over breakfast, he made an effort to placate her. "How about I try to get my evening shift covered? If I can, I'll pick you up for dinner about six thirty. I'll have my afternoon meditation finished. We can go back to my apartment and have the whole evening together," he said.

Barbara's mood changed immediately. After she left for work, he made a couple of calls to arrange things, then left for the soup kitchen.

At the appointed time, he arrived at Barbara's and knocked on the door. She opened it with a flourish. "Let's get out of here before Betsy sees you."

As they were walking to the car, Betsy ran out into the parking lot shouting that Barbara was going to hell for dating Jesus. They ignored her and got into the car. As they embraced, Jesus said, "You look ravishing. Is that a new dress?"

Barbara smiled, pleased that he had noticed. "Yes, and new shoes, too."

"My heart's aflutter," said Jesus. He drove them to what was becoming their favorite restaurant, Earth Mother's. After they were seated, Barbara ordered a glass of wine and Jesus a hibiscus-mint tea.

"A toast," said Jesus, raising his glass as Barbara sipped her wine. "To a cramp- and head-butt-free evening." Barbara began choking on her wine. "Sorry about that. Let's add 'choke-free' to that list, too," he said, grimacing.

"Amen," Barbara gasped, raising her glass. Catching her breath, she asked, "Why do you meditate so much?"

"That's not really public dinner conversation. What I want to talk about is how radiant you look. How that dress accentuates your voluptuous figure. How your beautiful face and aroma, when placed next to a fully bloomed rose, would cause it to shed its petals in despair. How the gods blush at the sight of your beauty. That's what I want to talk about," said Jesus.

Her heart pounding, Barbara sat back in her chair, stunned. No man had ever talked to her that way. Stammering and with effort, she managed a quiet, "Thank you."

"Truth is truth is truth," said Jesus, looking lovingly into her eyes. He reached across the table and grasped her hand, squeezing it gently. Barbara became misty-eyed and she looked at her lap. "What's wrong, honey?" Jesus asked.

She took several moments to respond. "I've wanted a man to say those sorts of things to me for so long. I've tried so hard..." she said, beginning to cry.

Compassion overwhelmed him, and letting go of her hand, he stood up and walked around the table, hugged her and kissed her on the cheek. Her soft crying grew into sobbing as she stood up. Looking into his eyes, she said, "I love you."

The other diners had gone silent and all eyes were on them as Jesus said, "I love you, too." When they kissed, applause rang out across the room.

They sat down and the waitress walked over to the table, beaming. "Did you just propose? Because if you did there's a bottle of champagne in it for you," she said.

Jesus was taken aback by the question. Barbara said nothing. "A momentous occasion, yes—a proposal, no," he said.

"Too bad," said the waitress, walking away.

Perturbed at her response, Jesus remarked, "That was odd."

During their meal, he tried several times to initiate conversation. Barbara only gave one-word answers and sighed with a smile of utter contentment. Comprehending the depth of Barbara's satisfaction, Jesus was just grateful that she was happy.

They paid the check and walked in silence to the car. After they got in, Barbara snuggled up close. Jesus put his arm around her and they looked deeply into each other's eyes and kissed. On the drive home, no words were spoken; nothing needed to be said.

Once home, they sat on the couch and snuggled. Sitting up abruptly and wrinkling her nose, Barbara said, "Tomorrow, let's clean the apartment—all of it, including Jack's room. This smell ruins the mood."

Jesus had gotten used to it over time. He cleaned the bathroom and kitchen on a regular basis, but the smell permeated everything. "But we both work tomorrow," he said.

"Let's see if we can get our shifts covered," she suggested. They made a couple of calls and the plan came together quickly. "You know, you could buy a new couch," she added.

Jesus agreed to that quickly. "Speaking of couches, let's get off this one," he said. Going to the bedroom, they lit some candles and lay down on his bed. He began to slowly stroke her arm, up and down, over and over, his nails skimming ever so lightly over her skin. Barbara matched each caress. They went on this way for close to an hour and then ardently melded into one.

His awareness returned and Jesus rolled onto his back, catching his breath. Barbara rolled onto her side and placed her head on his chest, listening to his heart. Da-dum...da-dum......da-dum, and then a full three-second pause before a very loud DA-DUM. "Jesus! Are you okay?" she asked, sitting up on one arm.

Smiling, he said, "Sure, I'm fine," putting both hands behind his head.

"But it sounded like your heart stopped."

"Only at the sight of your beauty," he said, rubbing her arm reassuringly.

Slapping his hand away, she said, "Be serious. That was scary. What just happened?"

He drew a deep breath, knowing that the time had come. "I was seeing if I could control my heartbeat."

"You can't do that. You might be able to slow it down some, but you can't get it to stop."

"I have to meditate," said Jesus, sitting up and stretching.

"Why? We're cuddling."

"I have to. It's important."

"But *why* is it so important? There's something you're not telling me."

He got up from the bed, went over to his yoga mat and sat down. "I've got to get through this particular phase of my spiritual path as quickly as possible."

Confused, Barbara asked, "When is speed a consideration on a spiritual path?"

"Excellent question. It really is. That had some depth to it," Jesus said.

"Quit patronizing me and answer the damn question," said Barbara, grinning.

Taking a deep breath, he said, "I'm the catalyst for the lightning and the nosebleeds."

210

Staring at him, she moved to the side of the bed. "What?"

"You heard me," he said, coming into a cross-legged position and rubbing his hands together in preparation for his meditation.

"And just how did you do that?"

"Not intentionally, I assure you," he said. "Everything in the Universe vibrates. Every atom, every molecule, every cell has a vibration. When you advance on the spiritual path, your vibration rises. There's a phase where you don't synchronize as well with your surroundings, and that can cause some...unusual events."

"Like nosebleeds and lightning?" Barbara asked.

"Yes. I must keep up my meditation and yoga so I can move through this phase as quickly as possible," he said, closing his eyes and breathing deeply.

Barbara sat on the edge of the bed surveying the scene. She watched his chest rise and fall rhythmically. His face would momentarily contort or twitch and then completely relax. Other than that, he sat perfectly still. Momentarily, she saw a glow around his body. She chalked it up to being tired enough that her eyes were playing tricks on her. She was asleep by the time he had finished.

The next morning, Jesus made breakfast for the two of them. Jack walked into the kitchen, hung over. He ignored them as he prepared a bowl of cereal. "Good morning, Jack!" Barbara bellowed, startling him.

"Good morning, roomie," said Jesus. "How are you? Didn't hear you come in last night."

"Not so loud. Geez," Jack said, placing his cereal bowl on the table and sitting down. "New expansion pack for Call of Doody 3. It's called 'Know Thy Enema.' It's pretty cool. We played till four this morning. I'm exhausted."

"Wow! That must have been exciting," Barbara said. "On a different note, do you mind if Jesus and I clean the apartment today?"

"Knock yourself out," Jack replied, staring at his cereal bowl.

"Jack, I'm thinking about buying a new couch for the living room," Jesus said.

Jack stiffened. "Hey, I like that couch. I've had that couch since I've been in Austin."

"It's an old couch, Jack. It's dusty, smelly, torn, bug-ridden and some springs are broken. It's time to replace it," said Barbara.

Jack grabbed his half-finished bowl of cereal, sloshing milk on the table, and threw it in the sink. Stomping to his bedroom, he slammed the door. "I didn't know he loved that couch so much," said Barbara.

"I don't think it's about the couch," said Jesus. "So, I'm thinking we clean today and shop tomorrow. How does that sound?"

Her man was supporting her and making the effort to make her more comfortable...Barbara was in heaven. Making a list of cleaning supplies they would need, they also discussed other possible furniture upgrades. Barbara started cleaning and Jesus went to the store. Checking out, he went through Brad's line. It was slow and they had a minute to talk. "A Saturday afternoon of domestic bliss?" Brad asked teasingly.

"Yeah," Jesus replied halfheartedly.

"You okay? You seem kind of low-energy for you," said Brad.

"I've been having this vague, and sometimes not-so-vague, feeling of dissatisfaction. Everything is going great. I feel more peaceful every day. It's just that I feel like I should be doing, you know...*more*," said Jesus.

"Take my word for it, you're doing plenty. I'll bet it's another phase. Like cleaning with your woman," Brad said, chuckling.

"Thanks," Jesus said sarcastically, grabbing his items and leaving.

By the time he got back to the apartment, Barbara had a good start on the kitchen. Looking up, she said, "You can start on the bathroom. You'll have to drain the toilet so you can get to some of those stains."

"Sure thing, Frau Bossy." As he was sweating into the toilet bowl, Barbara screamed. "What's wrong?" he asked.

"Scorpion!" she yelled. "Come and kill it."

Jesus shook his head and marched into the kitchen, "I'm not going to kill him. What has he ever done to you?" He went to his computer desk and retrieved a large envelope. Walking back to the kitchen, he squatted a foot from the medium-sized scorpion. "Okay, little fella. I'm not going to hurt you. You're safe. If you want to go outside, I'll take you outside. Besides, there's more food out there." He scooted a little closer to the scorpion and opened the envelope about two inches away. "Do you want to go outside?" The scorpion answered by walking into the envelope and curling up in a corner.

Standing, Jesus shot a disgusted look at Barbara and went outside down to the sidewalk. He crouched, opened the envelope, and out fell the scorpion, which scurried down the sidewalk and into the grass. Walking back into the apartment, Jesus said, "There. Problem solved."

It took hours to finish cleaning the apartment. The stench was gone, replaced by the odor of ammonia. They stood arm in arm surveying their work proudly. "What about Jack's room?" she asked.

"I'm not comfortable cleaning his room without his permission," Jesus said. "Let's ask him at church tomorrow. I'm going to open up the windows to air the place out."

Barbara went home to get ready for dinner and a movie while Jesus spent the next hour doing yoga and meditation. They decided to see the controversial indie flick *Santa Claus Is Really Jesus*.

Afterwards, Barbara asked, "So what do you think? I thought you might really like this film."

Jesus, focused on his breathing, wasn't paying attention. "I'm sorry. What?"

"The movie. The movie we just saw. What did you think of it?"

"It was interesting. I was focusing on my breathing, mainly."

Barbara shook her head and decided to take a different tack once they reached the car. "Are you going to give me any presents, Santa Claus?" she asked coyly.

"Have you been a good little girl?" Jesus asked.

"Most of the time," said Barbara, as she got into the car.

Once inside, Jesus said, "We'll see what's under the tree when we get home."

Jack wasn't home when they arrived. The cleaning smell was almost gone and Jesus realized how much he had hated the odor of the apartment. Barbara told him, "Wait here!" as she dashed back to the bedroom. He sat on Jack's couch. He liked the old couch, too. He got an idea just as Barbara called him back to the bedroom.

He found Barbara suggestively posed on the bed with three strategically placed bows. Laughing, Jesus said, "Did you plan this out or what?" He stood there staring for a moment at her glorious body. She tugged at his hand and he crawled into bed. They embraced and kissed and stroked each other and it was heavenly. *This just keeps getting better and better*, he thought.

Satisfied, Barbara fell asleep immediately, but Jesus couldn't sleep. The feeling of dissatisfaction returned, manifesting as a stone in the pit of his stomach. He tried tapping it away and it did ease some, but finally he got up to meditate. It came to him that it was time to have a session with Martha.

When he was finished, he crawled back into bed carefully, trying not to disturb Barbara. She awoke anyway, mumbling, "Damn meditation."

The next morning they had to rush to get to church. They arrived and sat down next to Brad and Jack seconds before the pastor began his sermon on marriage.

Barbara listened intently as he talked about the sanctity of marriage and how it was necessary to fully understand God. Jesus focused on his breath and the rivers of energy pulsing through his body.

When the sermon was over, Barbara leaned and asked Jack, "After lunch, Jesus and I are going to buy a new couch. Do you want to come along?"

"No," said Jack tersely.

"What do you want us to do with the old one?" asked Barbara.

Before Jack could respond, Jesus suggested, "How about we move it into your bedroom? It should fit."

Jack thought for a moment and agreed. "While we're in there do you mind if we clean a little?" asked Barbara politely.

Jack tensed from head to toe. "Fine," he said, jumping to his feet and pushing past them. He dashed to his car, not even waiting in line to greet the pastor.

"He seems to be upset. Is it because you're moving in?" asked Brad.

"Well, we haven't talked about that, but it's impossible for Jesus to stay the night at my place," said Barbara.

"Ah, Betsy. How's she doing?" asked Brad, as the three of them walked out.

"She's worse than ever. I'm afraid she might lose it completely," said Barbara. She turned to greet the pastor.

Brad whispered to Jesus, "How do you feel about Barbara moving in?"

Smiling, he said, "Tremendous. I'm happy about it."

"Except for the feeling of dissatisfaction?"

"Yeah. In fact, I'm going to call Martha right now," he said, walking a few feet away to make the call. They set an appointment for Tuesday.

Just as Jesus got off the phone, he turned around to find Barbara standing there with her hands on her hips. "Who are you talking to?" she demanded.

"I was making an appointment with Martha."

"Why do you see her so much?" asked Barbara irritably.

Jesus didn't want to argue the point so he gave a one-word answer, "Lightning." Barbara quickly changed the subject to lunch. They had a nice quick meal, went couch shopping, and bought an inexpensive entertainment center, too.

Jesus, yielding to pressure from Barbara, skipped his afternoon meditation. How could he make her understand how important this was to him? After she fell asleep that night, he snuck out of the bedroom and meditated in the living room. All four of his upper chakras were buzzing. He was very focused, although some stray thoughts emerged. Each time, he gently returned his focus to his third eye, and by the time he had finished he felt deeply relaxed and peaceful.

Carefully crawling back into bed, he fell asleep almost immediately. He awoke in the middle of the night to a warm ball of energy at the base of his spine. In his mind's eye, it was yellow, almost golden and bigger than a grapefruit. He knew what it was—Kundalini energy—and he resolved to relax, focus on his breath and let happen what may. The moment he made that decision, the ball of energy rose slowly up his spine, expanded, and dispersed throughout his chest.

It felt better than an orgasm. He kept breathing in and out through his heart chakra, marveling at how extraordinary it felt. He felt so serene that he fell back asleep in a few minutes.

He woke up ebullient and bounded out of bed in one move, somehow avoiding Barbara. She roused slightly. He couldn't help himself and yelled, "Yee-haw!"

"What's your problem?" mumbled Barbara.

"Go back to sleep, honey. I'll fix us breakfast," he said soothingly.

He ate and then prepared breakfast in bed for Barbara. Jack didn't have a serving tray so Jesus put the food on his desk chair.

"Time to wake up!" Jesus said.

"Go away. I don't have to be at work till this afternoon," Barbara said, annoyed.

"But the furniture will be here by ten."

"All right," Barbara said, sitting up. She was astonished at the breakfast before her. "Wow! Looks scrumptious."

214

"Nothing's too good for you," he said. "I'm going to take a shower before the delivery men get here. Barbara munched on her breakfast absentmindedly, thinking about nothing in particular, when she got a flash of Jesus standing naked in front of Martha. Odd glints of light reflected off his body. She dismissed the thought and kept on eating.

Jesus finished his shower and returned to the bedroom to take the dishes to the kitchen. Barbara put on his bathrobe and watched him walk naked through the apartment. He put the dishes in the dishwasher and went to the bedroom to get dressed. She gazed at him from the doorway. "Has Martha ever seen you naked?" she asked.

Thinking that an odd question, Jesus replied, "Deep tissue massage is a lot better naked."

"Of course, but I mean have you ever stood naked in front of her?"

"Well there was this one time when I was really upset. I jumped up off the table and paced around. The acupuncture needles were still inserted," he said, laughing.

"Interesting," Barbara said, interrupted by a knock at the door. The couch had arrived.

Jesus went to the door and invited the deliveryman in, pointing out where the new couch was to go. "Do you want us to haul away the old one?"

"No. We're saving that for a friend," Jesus said.

"Is your friend a cockroach?"

Jesus started moving the old couch out of the way one side at a time. Barbara got dressed and came in to help. Once in place, the new couch looked great. Next, the entertainment center was brought in, and it needed to be assembled.

They thanked the deliverymen and started to take apart Jack's cinderblock and plank shelves. Jesus found a screwdriver and they started putting the new piece together. When they finished, Barbara remarked, "We make a great team, don't we?"

"Yes, we do. That was easy, wasn't it?"

Next they went into Jack's room. Barbara told Jesus to get some garbage bags. It took them two hours to clean the small bedroom. When they finally got the couch in there, Barbara dumped all the dirty clothes on it. There was no place to sit.

It was time for Barbara to go to work. They decided that she wouldn't come over afterwards since Jesus had an early-morning session with Martha.

Waking early the next morning, Jesus spent an hour on his spiritual practice. When he arrived at Martha's, he went through the usual process of greeting, stripping and hopping on the table. Closing his eyes, he concentrated on the delicate energy flowing throughout his body.

The next thing Jesus knew, Martha was waking him up. "You sure are relaxed. I think this is the most relaxed I've ever seen you."

"Yeah," said Jesus smiling, "My relationship with Barbara is going really well. But..."

"But what?"

"But I keep having this strong feeling of dissatisfaction. It even shows up after we make love and I'm not dissatisfied with that at all."

"You're getting to that point where nothing on the physical plane enchants you anymore."

"Then why are we here? What's the point of being on this magical playground called Earth, if we're just going to get disenchanted with it?"

"You come for a while, you learn what you're supposed to learn and then you move on. Think of the Universe like school. You don't want to stay in second grade all your existence, do you?" she asked.

"I suppose not," said Jesus somewhat dejectedly. "But I love Barbara and want to spend my life here with her."

"Of course you love Barbara, but obviously your path is different. Yours is not one lifetime after another on this planet until you're ready to move on. Have faith in your path, Jesus."

He took a deep breath, thought for a moment, then asked, "So when is this feeling of dissatisfaction going to disappear?"

"When it's supposed to," she said. "Have you had any other interesting manifestations of late? Any more lightning or nosebleeds?" she asked, while checking his pulses.

"No, those have disappeared. But I did have an experience of Kundalini rising," he said.

Martha stuck him with several needles, one at a time. There was no reaction from him at all. "Liver points are good. Tell me about the Kundalini experience." He described it in great detail.

"I think you're ready for this," she said, planting a needle in the middle of his chest at his heart chakra.

Immediately, a warm sensation began spreading throughout his chest until it was the size of a basketball. It seemed akin to a mild electric shock. "Oh my Lord!" he exclaimed, giggling. "What's going on?" He did his best to focus on his breathing, but it was an ocean of delight—and it was high tide. It almost overwhelmed him into unconsciousness.

"Just relax and focus on your breathing," said Martha, beaming.

"This is so stunning! Oh my God, my Goob, glorious creator in the heavens. This is better than the best sex I've ever had. Oh my God! Oh my God, oh my God, oh my God," he declared. He laughed and then thanked God and then laughed some more. "What just happened? What is happening?" he asked in wonderment.

"Your heart chakra opened up fully."

"Bless you, Lord. Bless you, Lord. Bless you, Lord. Thank you, thank you, thank you," he said effusively.

"Okay, settle down. I want you to close your eyes and go deep within. Just let the images come up," said Martha soothingly.

Jesus obeyed. Myriad images came to mind, some he didn't recognize and some he couldn't explain. Martha kept tweaking the needles and sat quietly, conducting energy work for his benefit.

216

"You seemed to go really deep. Are you ready to turn over?" she asked quietly.

Jesus murmured yes and with difficulty made his way onto his stomach. "Anything you want to share?" she asked.

"A bunch of weird things came up. Nothing specific."

"Okay. Let me ask you this again then. What is really important?"

He thought a moment before answering. "My relationship with God first and foremost, then how that is reflected through my life with my relationships, work and service."

"Great answer," said Martha, "Okay, how do you improve your relationship with God?"

"By listening mainly, though I ask questions a lot."

"Does God answer those questions?"

"Yes, but I have to listen for the answers over the usual mind chatter."

"And how do you reduce that chatter?"

"Meditation, of course. And doing my best to be in the moment."

"Why is that important?"

"You can't find God dwelling on the past or thinking about the future."

"That's right. Past regrets and worrying about the future belong to the ego. So what's the main distraction your ego has been feasting on lately?"

"Barbara. But it's not regrets or worrying. It's..."

"Sex?"

"No, not at all. She's having difficulty with my spiritual practice. She doesn't understand, and to try to please her, I have on occasion skipped my meditation."

Martha pondered this admission for a moment. "This is something that everyone has to go through. Balancing the spiritual path with an intimate relationship is about moment-to-moment decisions...usually based on guidance or intuition. Rarely in the moment will you see the wisdom or the eventual outcome of a decision, and sometimes it will require enduring the wrath of a partner. That's where faith comes in. Remember, faith comes before proof." Martha sat back, a brief flicker of exhaustion crossing her face. She closed her eyes, took a deep breath, and as if a light was switched on, her face beamed once again.

Jesus noticed this transition and promised to keep up his spiritual practice no matter what.

Chapter 24 – Secrets

After the session, Jesus went to work and that night Barbara came over afterwards. She found him sitting on his bedroom floor meditating and let out an audible "Humph," shutting the door none too quietly. Taking several minutes to refocus, he finished and then went into the living room. Barbara was splayed out on the new couch, watching TV.

Sitting down, he kissed her. She moved closer and they cuddled up. They said nothing and just enjoyed each other's company. Getting ready for bed, they made plans to have dinner before the roundtable on Thursday.

They arrived at the roundtable holding hands. It took some of the group by surprise. When the comments about the renewed relationship died down, the pastor asked if there were any topics. As usual, everybody looked at Jesus to start things off. "I don't have anything in mind," he said.

Several moments passed before Jack suggested, "Road rage. The other day, I had this guy who thought I had cut him off actually follow me all the way to the store. He even stopped his car on the street in front and pointed at me as I was walking in. He almost caused an accident."

Feeling everyone's anger rise, Jesus asked, "What did you do?"

"I pointed back at him, laughed and flipped him off," said Jack smugly.

"You know, that happened to me once," said Brad. "I was driving on the freeway and changed lanes to move into an open spot. The other guy was trying to do the same and we almost hit. He pulled even with me and I looked over and he gave me the bird."

"What did you do?" asked Ralph.

"I gave him the peace sign. He looked embarrassed," said Brad.

"I don't know...two fingers instead of one? That's twice as much effort," Jack groaned.

After the laughter died down, Jesus added, "Yes, but with 100 percent less negative consequences."

"Were you trying to embarrass him?" asked Juan.

"Absolutely not," said Brad. "I was trying—and have been trying—to demonstrate the concept that the other person is you."

"That doesn't make any sense. We're all individuals," said Ralph.

"That's what your ego believes, but we're all connected by spirit. Humanity is of one spirit," said Jesus.

"Amen," said the pastor enthusiastically, to the surprise of everyone.

"You can't possibly know someone else completely," Brad said. "Almost any interpretation about someone else and their behavior is based on what you know, your experiences, your thoughts and feelings. Your insight into them is really...all about you."

Several people brought up examples of why they thought this was wrong. One by one, Brad and Jesus introduced alternate ways of looking at their examples.

Lastly, Barbara spoke. "What about keeping secrets?"

Jesus replied, "You may be right about a person keeping a secret, but are you aware of their motivation? Possibly they're trying to protect you. Maybe they think you can't possibly understand."

Barbara gave an exasperated groan and said pointedly, "*Maybe* they could trust that this person will understand and support them completely."

"Maybe so, maybe so," Jesus said, his voice trailing off.

A few moments of silence followed before Gertrude said, "I've got a topic. Do any of you think there's life on other planets?"

The pros and cons were debated with half the table thinking yes and half the table thinking no. The discussion appeared to be winding down when Gertrude asked, "What do you think Jesus? You haven't said anything."

For a split second, he thought about telling them his story, but instead answered slowly and deliberately, "I think that an omnipotent, omniscient creator who has created more stars than atoms in our bodies would not be content to create only one experiment of life, just as he was not content to send just one prophet to uplift us."

"Are you an alien?" asked Alice.

"Ah-ha!" exclaimed the fussy judge. "So, you were exposed as an alien on their planet."

"No. My behavior, at times, wasn't quite aligned with cultural norms. That led to Alice's question. However, I was able to deflect her suspicion, sort of, and that was the only time during my mission that I was asked that."

"Humph. Continue."

Jesus took his time before responding. "Why would you ask me that?"

"If anybody at this table was an alien, it would be you," said Alice.

"Why do you say that?" Jesus asked.

"I understand everybody else at the table, but sometimes I just don't get you," said Alice.

Slyly, Jesus said, "Maybe spirituality is alien to you."

Jumping in, the pastor said, "I think that's a good place to end tonight's discussion, people. See you Sunday in church."

As they were walking out, Alice said to Jesus, "That was hurtful."

Stunned, Jesus immediately said, "I'm sorry, Alice. That comment was indeed uncalled for. I sincerely apologize."

As she walked away, she called back, "I notice you didn't answer."

"How could I possibly be an alien?" he cried out.

Not knowing what to make of this exchange, Barbara suggested, "How about we go home, watch some TV and snuggle?"

"Sounds good," said Jesus distractedly.

As they drove home, Jesus mulled over what Alice said. Was he that much different from everybody else? Was his pride hurt because he wasn't blending in as well as he thought? Was his cover blown? Barbara noticed his discomfort but said nothing. As soon as they got in the door, she hopped on the couch. Jesus stood fast, looking at her. "I've got to go meditate."

"Now? Let's snuggle," Barbara said.

"Nope. I've got to ask some questions of the Universe," said Jesus with determination.

Barbara's face flushed red, and jumping up off the couch, she yelled, "I've got a question for you! You're obviously upset, but you won't share with me. Why?"

Jesus slumped. He was conflicted. What could he tell her? It suddenly occurred for him to say, "Martha told me I have a chance to become... enlightened in this lifetime."

Standing there and staring at him, she asked, "Enlightened? You mean one day you're just going to disappear?"

Momentarily confused by Barbara's question, Jesus collected himself. "Nooo. You misunderstand. You don't disappear when you become enlightened," he said gently. "Come here. Sit down. Let me try to explain."

They sat down and Jesus took several deep breaths. He wasn't sure if he could explain the concept and centered himself as best as possible to listen to his intuition. "Enlightenment is when you become connected to all things—plants, animals, people, Earth, the Universe, God. Even rocks."

"You're trying to connect with rocks?" Barbara asked sarcastically.

Jesus laughed and said as compassionately as he could, "No. Enlightenment is the highest manifestation of the human race. It's the point where a human being transcends their animal nature and becomes a spiritual being."

"I thought what we have is the best that humans can do," said Barbara.

Jesus took her hand. "It is, for humans demonstrating their animal nature." She looked disappointed and Jesus added, "Hey, you're one of my best teachers." That didn't seem to mollify Barbara either, so he said, "It's not going to change anything between us."

Barbara began to cry, threw her hands around Jesus's neck and pulled him close. "I don't want anything to change between us. I love what we have."

"I love you, too," said Jesus.

After a few minutes, he broke their embrace and went to meditate. Barbara was okay with that, but as she sat there watching TV doubt crept into her mind. She pondered what he had said until soon she was asleep.

She awoke the next morning in bed, not remembering how she got there. Jesus was already up fixing breakfast. Jack came in, interrupting their conversation, to get a bowl of cereal. He spilled milk on the counter, but ignored it and sat down to eat.

Jesus got up to take his and Barbara's plates into the kitchen. "Jack, why didn't you clean up this spilt milk? Come on, man. Get it together."

"You know, you used to be a regular guy and now you've turned into some kind of neat freak. You're losing your manhood, man," Jack said.

"I don't think so," Barbara said pointedly.

Jack abruptly grabbed his bowl and marched off to his room, spilling more milk on the table and floor. "What's bothering him?" asked Barbara, cleaning up the mess.

"I'm not sure, but he certainly isn't happy. He'll figure it out eventually," said Jesus.

They finished cleaning up the kitchen and then kissed as Jesus left for work. They passed each other at the shift change, and the next day the pattern repeated.

Early Sunday morning, Jesus woke up to a call from Clara. The team was short-handed and she asked him if he could fill in. He agreed and had an hour before he needed to be there. He bounded out of bed, woke Barbara and explained what was happening.

Getting ready quickly, he arrived at the same time as Clara. She told him she wanted to talk about something before starting the shift. "What's up?" asked Jesus, closing the office door.

"As you know, the Assistant Unit Leader position has opened up, and I applied for it. It looks like I'm going to get it," she said excitedly.

"Congratulations," Jesus said, smiling.

"There's more," she said enticingly. "That, of course, means that the Front-End Department Head position is opening up. Brad, as Assistant Department Head, would be the natural choice, and that would mean..."

"Ah, Assistant Department Head would open up," said Jesus.

"Are you interested?"

"I'm honored, but why me?"

"You've really rebounded from your bout of troubles. You're steady as a rock again. People love you. Your line is always the longest. I think you've got real potential to move up in the organization."

"Can I think about it?"

"Of course. Remember, a couple of things have to fall in place for this to happen, but I'm 95 percent sure that they will. That's why I wanted to gauge your interest."

"Thank you."

Meanwhile, Barbara went to church. She sat with Brad and Jack as usual, listening to the pastor's sermon about interpreting the Bible, which was an argument for taking it literally. Barbara tried to concentrate on the sermon, but her mind kept recalling the conversation about enlightenment with Jesus. By the time the sermon was over, she had decided to talk with the pastor about it.

When it came her turn to greet the pastor, she asked him if they could talk.

"What about?" the pastor asked.

"A conversation I had with Jesus," she said.

"Wait inside and I'll come and get you when I'm finished here," said the pastor. After greeting the remaining parishioners, the pastor met her inside and suggested they go to his office to talk.

"What is troubling you, my child? Did you and Jesus have a fight?" he asked cautiously.

"No pastor, not at all. We're very happy. He even told me that he loved me," said Barbara.

"That's nice. I don't understand what the problem is."

Barbara told him what she knew about Jesus's path to enlightenment and the incidents at Enchanted Rock. Surprised, the pastor said, "It sounds like Jesus is dabbling in the occult. That's not a good thing. Not a good thing at all. If you want, I'll have a talk with him."

"Would you? I don't want him to disappear or anything," said Barbara, with some concern.

"I'm not sure that would happen, but this is certainly not the path of the Megalithic Church and I will have a talk with him."

"Thank you, pastor. Thank you very much," said Barbara, as she left. She wasn't confident that she had done the right thing, but she would do anything to make sure that Jesus wouldn't come to harm.

That evening, she didn't let on that she had talked with the pastor, but Jesus picked up that something was a little off and asked her about it.

"Nope. Everything's good," she answered quickly. He suspected it wasn't but didn't press the matter.

Jesus had the next three days off except for his soup kitchen shift; Barbara had to work all three days so they made plans to be together. He made breakfast for her the next day and saw her off to work followed by a bike ride with Brad in the afternoon. It was fall in Texas, which meant it can be eighty degrees one minute and in the forties the next. Since the latter was true that day, Jesus got a chance to wear his leg warmers. Brad commented on how sexy they looked.

Jesus ignored him and went to the front to set the pace. Eventually pulling even, Brad said, "You seem a little distant today. Anything going on?"

They hadn't talked for a while, and Jesus didn't know how much he should share. Finally, he blurted out, "I think Barbara is keeping something from me."

"Isn't that what *she's* always complaining about?" Brad said, puffing for air.

Slowing the pace, Jesus said, "Yeah. I guess this is an opportunity to learn empathy."

"Oh, you're empathetic. Maybe not on this subject, but you're empathetic," Brad said.

"Thank you. I try to be. She's been having a hard time accepting my spiritual practice. I don't think she's entirely comfortable with the concept of enlightenment."

"People raised or taught under traditional theology wouldn't be," replied Brad, finally catching his breath. "The concept of empowerment when it comes to one's connection with God is scary and forbidden to them."

222

"She thought I was going to disappear."

Brad laughed at the notion. "I'm sure that the more she hangs out with you, the more comfortable she'll become with the subject."

"Thanks. That helps." They rode the rest of the way in silence as Jesus contemplated how he could help Barbara become more accepting of his spiritual path.

He awoke the next morning after Barbara had left for work. It wasn't until he was preparing himself some lunch that he noticed he hadn't had a single conscious thought that day. Of course, that thought produced another thought, continuing ad infinitum but at a slower pace than usual. He would have to talk with Martha about this. He called her and left a message.

When Barbara came over after work, they fooled around on the couch until Jack came home. He had a look of disgust on his face but said nothing. Barbara asked him how he liked his room now that it was clean. He responded by slamming his bedroom door.

As they sat down to eat, Jack emerged from his room and left without saying a word. They quickly finished dinner and cleaned up so they could cuddle on the couch. Getting comfy, Barbara noticed his expression. "Why are you looking at me that way?" she asked.

"What do you mean?"

"Like you're trying to figure something out."

If he was to be open with her, he was going to have to say what he thought. "It seems like you're holding something back from me."

"Is this some kind of tit-for-tat thing?"

"Nooo. I got this feeling last night and it's lasted through the day. Since you asked—I told."

"Well, since you bring it up, I think *you're* still hiding something from *me*. I'm beginning to think that you don't have amnesia at all. What do you think of *that*?" she asked, crossing her arms and sticking her nose in the air.

Jesus flinched. This was the second time someone had questioned his amnesia. An idea popped into his mind. "Why don't we do the meditation where we look in each other's eyes? That way we can reveal ourselves."

Barbara slumped and sat back. "I don't want to," she said, looking down.

"Why not? I thought you were enjoying it until the lightning hit."

"I was until I saw something really weird. It was scary."

"Scary? How?" Jesus asked comfortingly.

"It was like a," she paused, "one-eyed monster."

Turning pale, Jesus stammered, "A one-eyed monster?"

"Yeah. It was disgusting," said Barbara. "It gave me the willies."

Jesus jumped up off the couch and ran to his bedroom. He grabbed a pen and paper and ran back. "Draw it," he demanded.

"I only saw it for a second," said Barbara.

"Draw it, dammit!"

Taken aback, Barbara did as he asked, and handed it back to him.

He stared at it for several moments before letting out a big sigh. He didn't really want to do this, but he felt like he had no choice. Dropping to one knee, Jesus said, "You know I love you and I don't want to lose what we have."

Clasping her hands at her heart, Barbara excitedly asked, "Yes, Jesus? Is there something you want to ask me?"

He slowly got to his feet and began to pace. "The one-eyed monster you saw during the meditation was...me."

"I saw into your soul and you're a monster?"

Stopping his pacing, he said, "No, no. It's not that." He took a deep breath. "I'm an alien."

"I thought you were born in the United States."

"I wasn't born in the United States. I wasn't born on this *planet*." Barbara's look of confusion turned to fright. Jesus quickly sat on the couch and took her hand. "I was born on another planet, the planet Gooberia."

Barbara stared at Jesus uncomprehendingly for several moments before she slowly asked, "You were born on another planet?"

Forcing a smile, Jesus said, "Yes. Yes I was."

"And you're here for what reason?"

"My mission is...was...to study humans and this planet."

"You're not going to probe me, are you?"

"I thought I had already done that on numerous occasions."

"Jesus!" Barbara whined, slapping him on the arm.

"Sorry. I know this is difficult to understand, but it's true," he said. "I'm not here to hurt you."

Barbara put her head in her hands and started rocking back and forth before curling up into a fetal position. Jesus sat there patiently, letting this new information sink in.

Bolting up to a sitting position, she asked, "So, what I saw in the meditation was really you?"

"Yes. That's what Goobers look like. Let me draw you a complete picture," he said, grabbing pen and paper.

When he finished, Barbara studied the picture. "You have three legs?"

Jesus nodded. "One for procreation, one for nourishment, one for expelling waste."

"I don't understand. How did you get into a human body?"

Jesus explained about his mission, the ancient sacred texts, the transmogrification process, even how Goobers transmuted from plants into animals. How their legs were connected to roots and when the three moons of Gooberia were in a certain alignment, they become conscious and their roots withered while their legs remained connected. How they had to break free of their dead roots to get nourishment from the soil or else die. He described his own personal struggle to free himself.

Barbara listened intently. Her mind swirled as she tried to gauge whether he was telling the truth or not. "When is your mission over?"

"It's supposed to be about a year total. I really don't know when or where the transmogrification will take place. I don't even know if the process is reversible. It should be; I just don't know for sure."

"This has been pretty brave of you," Barbara said.

Jesus nodded. "Yeah, it may be the most daring act ever by anyone from my planet. Goobers are not known for taking risks."

Trying to weigh Jesus's story versus her experience of him was confusing to Barbara. She sat there and wondered what to do next. She closed her eyes and asked for help in figuring this out. Was it even possible to figure it out? Suddenly, she said, "Let's get married."

Jesus jumped to his feet and stared at Barbara. "Are you serious?"

"Yes."

"After everything I've told you, you want to get married?" asked Jesus incredulously.

"Yes."

"For God's sake, why?"

"I don't know if what you told me is true. I doubt anybody does, but I do know this—you're the best man I know. I love you and I love what we have."

A buzzing began in Jesus's chest. This woman actually loved him even though he had just told her the craziest story he was sure she had ever heard. He was overcome with a feeling of acceptance that he had never felt before. With tears in his eyes he dropped to one knee and asked, "Barbara, will you do me the honor of marrying me?"

Barbara dropped to her knees, clasped his hands to her chest and looked him in the eyes. In a trembling voice, she said, "Yes, Jesus. I will marry you." They hugged and she started crying. For the first time, she noticed a buzzing in her chest. As Jesus inhaled, she exhaled and vice versa. The buzzing she felt got stronger. The warmth in her chest spread, and with her eyes closed it seemed like a golden light was spreading throughout her body.

The rest of the evening was filled with sweet nothings and tender caresses. As he lay in bed with Barbara curled up close, Jesus wondered if he could possibly be happier. He fell asleep resolving to never leave Earth.

They had breakfast together the next morning before Barbara left for work. Jesus called Martha and they scheduled lunch that afternoon at a juice bar. The place was small and funky with a chalkboard menu written in a rainbow of colors.

Martha arrived a few minutes late. She started singing, "What's da buzz? Tell me what's a-happenin'," several times while doing some sort of freestyle dance.

Jesus laughed and called her a Goober. "From what you told me, I'm nothing like a Goober. I would be the Anti-Goober," said Martha.

Chuckling, Jesus agreed. "What's happening are several things. Do you want them in order of occurrence or in order of importance?"

Still dancing, Martha said, "You choose."

"Okay. I suggested to Barbara that we do the looking-in-each-other's-eyes meditation and she didn't want to. I asked her why not and she said the previous time we practiced that meditation, she saw something scary."

Martha stopped dancing. "Do tell."

"I asked her to draw what she saw and she drew a picture of a Goober from the waist up."

"Whoa!" Martha exclaimed.

Jesus continued, "She had already said that she thought I was faking amnesia, so...I told her who I really am."

"You told her?" Martha gasped. "What was her reaction?"

"She suggested we get married and, and...I proposed."

Martha raised both hands in the air shouting, "Jesus, Jesus, Jesus!" and twirling in place. She ran around the table grabbed Jesus's face and kissed him repeatedly. "You did it, you did it, you did it," she said admiringly. "You committed to your path. Way to be the ultimate spiritual scientist."

"It's not about my mission anymore. I love her and I don't want to go back," he said emphatically.

"Wow, wow, wow. So what are you going to do now?"

"Plan a wedding, I assume. I guess I'll have to get online and look up what that's all about."

"Keep it simple," Martha advised. "I guess you chose order of importance. So what else is going on?"

"My line is longer than everyone else's."

"Your line?"

"Yeah, at the store. The other cashiers on my shift will have one or two people in their line while I have six or seven. It's very noticeable. At the same time, some of my friends are starting to pull away from me," Jesus said.

"Ah yes. It would be more pronounced if you had long-time friends. You see, your energy is changing rapidly and people you don't know, whether they realize it or not, are attracted to that energy, while the changes you're going through have your friends reevaluating their own lives. Someone making substantial change in their life can be threatening to an underdeveloped ego," Martha said.

"The attraction business has gotten me a possible promotion."

"Much success. I've got to go now. I've got a one o'clock appointment," she said, giving Jesus a kiss. "I love you."

Smiling, he said, "I love you, too."

Jesus finished his juice and drove to the store. He picked up some items for dinner. He looked for Barbara's line, but she was on a break. *Even better*, he thought, *Now dinner will be a surprise.*

Barbara didn't arrive home until six thirty. She had gone out with some girlfriends after work and arrived home deliriously happy after talking about their upcoming wedding. "Are we telling people now?" Jesus asked.

"Of course! That's one of the perks—making your girlfriends jealous."

He frowned and said nothing. He told her to sit down and brought out a scrumptious vegetarian meal. The entire dinner conversation was about planning the wedding. His only duty thus far: ask the pastor to perform the ceremony.

"What about setting a date for the wedding?" Jesus asked.

"The sooner the better."

"After sufficient time to flaunt your good fortune? How long will that take?"

"I think I'll be satisfied with that in about six weeks," she said, kicking him under the table.

"Are you sure you don't need a couple of years?" he said, tucking his legs under his chair.

Jack walked in and Barbara took it upon herself to announce, "Jesus and I are getting married!"

Jack stopped in his tracks. "Want to be a groomsman?" Jesus asked. Jack didn't answer, staring at them for a moment. He continued to his bedroom and shut the door quietly.

Barbara looked at Jesus and shrugged. "When are you going to ask the pastor to perform the ceremony?"

"Tomorrow, after my soup kitchen shift."

The rest of the evening, Barbara talked about nothing except the wedding. Jesus was bombarded with questions about color, style and cost, to the point he was sure this must be another test by the Universe. He felt tired. Standing up, he said, "I've got to go and meditate. You know, Martha said something interesting to me at lunch today. She said 'keep it simple' about the wedding."

"I am. You had lunch with Martha?"

"Yeah. We had lunch at a juice bar."

"What did you talk about?" Barbara asked suspiciously.

Jesus grimaced at her tone. "I told her about our conversation last night and some other things."

"You talked about our conversation?" she asked.

"Stop that. You owe a lot to her. If it wasn't for her I might not be here right now. This planet was driving me crazy and she helped me discover a spiritual path. She encouraged me to explore a relationship with you. She was ecstatic when she heard that we were getting married."

"Explore?" Barbara asked, starting to get angry. "What am I to you? An experiment?"

Jesus quickly sat down on the couch next to her. "Yes, maybe in the beginning, but it's not about my mission anymore. It's about our love. I don't want to go back to my home planet. I don't want to study humans as a disaffected scientist anymore. I want to live and love my whole life with you. I don't know how that's going to look or how long that will be, but that's my only mission now, period," he said passionately.

Stunned, Barbara quietly said, "I'm sorry, Jesus. I didn't know. This is all so new to me. I don't know what to say."

"Okay, but there's no need to be jealous of Martha. Seriously, if it wasn't for her we would not be sitting here right now planning a wedding."

Patting his hand, Barbara calmly said, "I understand, honey. Why don't you go and meditate?"

Chuckling at her tone and manner, Jesus said, "Yes, dear."

Barbara giggled and said, "And don't come out till you've connected to the Universe, young man."

Their banter relieved his fatigue and he felt centered as he began his meditation. It came to him that he needed to increase his focus on the moment, ask the Universe when he didn't know or wasn't sure about something, and address any thoughts or feelings that made him feel bad or brought up doubt. By the end of the meditation, he noticed that his four upper chakras—head, third eye, throat and heart—were wide open and buzzing.

Afterwards, he went back into the living room to find Barbara asleep on the couch. The rush of excitement and enthusiasm had worn her out. He picked her up and carried her to the bedroom. She went back to sleep immediately, but Jesus couldn't get to sleep for a while. Thoughts of *Is this the right thing to do?* crept in, but a flash of intuition reminded him of the guidance he had received during meditation. He recentered himself and soon fell asleep.

He saw Barbara off to work the next day. She could barely contain her excitement about telling everyone at the store that they were getting married. After his noon shift at the soup kitchen, Alice caught up with him.

"What are you smiling about?"

"Barbara and I are getting married," Jesus said.

"Congratulations! Off to make wedding preparations?"

"Yes. I'm asking the pastor if he'll perform the ceremony."

Grimacing, Alice said, "Good luck," and walked away.

Jesus ignored her reaction and went to the pastor's office. He was on the telephone and motioned for Jesus to have a seat. After finishing his call, he asked, "What can I do for you?"

Taking a deep breath, Jesus said, "I'm here to inform you that Barbara and I are getting married. We would like you to perform the ceremony."

The pastor smiled politely, but shifted uncomfortably in his chair. "Congratulations," he said halfheartedly.

The smile on Jesus's face disappeared. "I thought you would react differently."

The pastor rolled his head from side to side. He never liked this part of his ministry. "Last week, Barbara came in to talk to me about your path to 'enlightenment'," he said, making exaggerated air quotes. "She was quite upset and fearful."

"We had a talk and she understands now. Will you join us in holy matrimony?"

"My son, we have certain guidelines about marrying a man and a woman. Your attempt at this metaphysical nonsense hardly makes you a realistic candidate for marriage in this church," the pastor said.

Stunned, Jesus reacted, "Nonsense? What are you talking about?" Hearing the tone in his voice, he took a deep breath and calmed down. "I support this church financially. It's one of the communities I'm involved with. I work in the soup kitchen. You actually saved me when I was at my lowest point as a human being. Barbara has told me how important you've been in helping her. We would really like you involved in this. Please, won't you perform the ceremony?"

"I can't. You're fooling around with this New Age stuff and she's a fallen woman. I just can't."

"Fallen woman? Fallen woman?" Jesus repeated. "All humans fail. End of story. God gives us the opportunity to atone for our mistakes and continue learning. Why do you insist on judging us when there is but one judge in the Universe?"

"Because it is scripture," said the pastor angrily.

"Written by man, to be judged by God, not man," said Jesus. He stood up and walked to the door. Wheeling around, he said, "I feel sorry for you, Pastor," and left.

Chapter 25 – The pastor is chastised

Arriving home, Jesus found Barbara working on the guest list. "Who do you want to invite?" she asked.

"You're working on that already?"

"The invitations have to go out stat."

"Stat?"

"Stat," said Barbara.

"Okay, Dr. Wedding. If they need to go out stat, how can I help?"

"What did the pastor say?" Barbara asked.

"Oh, uh, he declined. We'll have to get someone else."

"He declined?" said Barbara, shaking her head. "I'll go talk to him. He's been sort of a father figure to me. He'll listen to me. Who do you want to invite?"

"My friends, your friends, people from the store, people from the roundtable. Is your aunt coming?" Jesus asked.

"No. I'm not inviting her. She reminds me too much of my childhood."

"How about your mother?"

"I did hear from my aunt that she got out of the institution a few years ago, but neither of us have made the effort to contact the other."

"That's kind of sad," said Jesus, "and speaking of sad, or mad, I'm just a little upset with you talking to the pastor about my interest in enlightenment."

Barbara set down her pen and faced Jesus. "I was worried. I didn't understand and quite frankly, I'm ignorant on the subject. I'm sorry," she said. "So, cut me some slack, Mr. Spaceman. I'm learning as fast as I can."

Jesus chuckled, "Maybe we should put that on the invitations."

"What?"

Standing at attention with an air of British nobility, Jesus pronounced, "We cordially invite you to the nuptials of Mr. Spaceman and Dr. Wedding."

Barbara laughed. "We'll need a special valet for the spaceships. Not just anybody can park those."

"After the wedding, we'll become superheroes bringing love to the furthest reaches of the galaxy. We'll organize weddings for anybody. Man-woman, man-man, woman-woman, whomever. We should probably limit it to same-species weddings though."

"Hey, we're not the same species."

"Good point. If you can get along without me for about forty minutes, I'm going to meditate," said Jesus, leaning over and giving her a peck on the cheek.

"Yes, dear."

Jesus was about to try, for the second time, the one-breath-a-minute meditation. He had burned a CD to prompt him every twenty seconds to breathe, to hold his breath, and to exhale. It was difficult at first, with his abdomen flip-flopping around as if his body thought it was going to die.

A couple of times he had to take an extra breath, but by the end of the meditation he had gotten comfortable with it.

Barbara walked in quietly to get a pen, trying not to disturb him. Before she shut the door, she watched him. He seemed so serene it didn't look like he was even breathing.

When he finished, he walked back into the living room exclaiming, "I am so buzzed! I'm as high as the moon."

"What was that meditation you were doing? It didn't look like you were breathing," she asked. He explained the meditation to her.

"Why on earth would you want to breathe just once a minute?"

"It helps one overcome the fear of death."

"And why would you want to do that?"

"The lifespan for humans is much shorter than for Goobers, who live for thousands of years. If I am to live out my life on this planet in this body, I want to be prepared."

"Prepared? You die, you go to heaven. Right?"

"I don't believe in heaven. It doesn't make any sense, and God always makes sense. Humans always say that God is mysterious. I don't think He's mysterious at all. I think that's just a way of saying that one is ignorant. I think He reveals himself in every moment. An omniscient, omnipotent intelligence that's been creating for at least fourteen billion years suddenly decides four billion years ago to create a planet, and only four million years ago He creates the animals that the human race is descended from. Then they live one lifetime and if they follow the rules that have changed umpteen times in the last five thousand years, they get to go to heaven for eternity. Obviously that's been written for a species not yet capable of understanding the truth," Jesus said breathlessly. "There's got to be more to it."

Barbara stared at him uncomprehendingly. "And what does that have to do with death?"

Jesus laughed. "Sorry, I digressed a bit there. My point about death is that it's an illusion. Energy doesn't die, and a soul is organized energy. It's not going to dissipate just because the material body it's connected to dies. One lifetime for a soul to practice with an ego and that's it? What a waste that would be! The basis of reincarnation is that when one works off all of one's karmic debt and masters the transition—death—back to unity, reincarnation is no longer needed. That is, here in this particular experiment of the Universe. So, feeling fear while dying will just generate another incarnation. That's why I did this meditation. I'm just not sure yet," he said, stroking his beard, "as to the purpose of the ego...." He began pacing. "Is it a way of organizing energy on the physical plane? Is it a way of creating new souls? Is it a process of bringing the eternal light and dark matter together to create life on the physical plane, or is it just a mirror for the soul to practice in? I'm not sure...yet."

These concepts were new to Barbara. She had never known anyone who would ask such questions or think in this manner. "Are you sure you should be questioning God like this?"

"I'm not questioning God, no way, no how. I want to *know* God. I look at my planet and its simple ways and then come here and see a whole different spectrum of life. It's amazing and wondrous, and while I'm here, I want to learn as much about it as possible," Jesus said passionately.

"You're not just a scientist, you're a spiritual scientist," Barbara said, resuming her work on the guest list. Jesus smiled at the thought and joined her at the table to help. They managed to finish just after midnight and went to bed.

Barbara didn't have to be at work till three, so she ran wedding errands in the morning and early afternoon. She had asked Jesus to order the invitations, even though the time and place were yet to be determined. After performing his morning spiritual practice, Jesus headed to the stationery store before his soup kitchen shift.

While driving, his breathing produced an effect that he hadn't experienced before. It felt as if the air flowing over the alveoli of his lungs carried manna from heaven and was absorbed and transported throughout his body. The result was an overwhelming feeling of peace and a physical sensation not unlike a mild orgasm with each breath. He wondered if it would get stronger.

After arriving at the soup kitchen, Jesus put on his apron and hairnet and took his place at the steam table, setting his intention on service. It wasn't long before his intuition intervened. He looked up just in time to see a patron try to cut in line. Dropping his ladle, Jesus dashed out to the dining room to see a hand raised, tightly gripping a shiny object.

"STOP!" demanded Jesus. The shockwave generated from his words parted the patrons and knocked the knife-wielding man to the ground. Quickly getting to his feet, he struck a menacing pose. Jesus approached him, looked him in the eye and calmly said, "Drop the knife, please."

The man tensed with anger and fear, and for a moment it appeared as if he would lunge, but when he saw his true self reflected in Jesus's eyes, he dropped the knife. "Aw, shit."

"What's your name?"

"Jerry," the man replied.

Two patrons who had dropped their trays started to clean them up, but Jesus said, "No need to do that. Jerry and I will clean that up. Please get back in line for some more food." The first patron in line waved the two to get in front of him and they were served first. Jesus went to get a mop and some rags as Jerry picked up the spilled food with his bare hands.

When they finished, Jesus and Jerry took the trays to be washed. "I'm sorry," said Jerry.

"Hey, you're doing better than you think."

"What do you mean?"

"Today you didn't stab someone, and some days that's the best one can do," said Jesus, smiling. With tears in his eyes, Jerry hugged him and turned to head for the exit.

"Where are you going?" asked Jesus.

"I don't deserve to be here."

"Nonsense. Everybody has their moments and makes mistakes," said Jesus, taking him by the arm and walking him to the end of the line. "Forgive yourself. God already has and He's in your life every single moment." Jesus returned to the steam table to serve.

"That was extraordinary!" Alice exclaimed. "How did you do that?"

Jesus thought for a moment as he plopped mashed potatoes onto a tray. "I guess I was in the moment."

"I'm going to go tell the pastor," said Alice, hurrying off.

Meanwhile, Barbara had arrived at the church and was sitting down with the pastor when Alice burst into the office. "Jesus just prevented a stabbing in the soup kitchen!"

Standing simultaneously, the pastor and Barbara both exclaimed, "What?" Alice reported the event in detail and Barbara asked, "Is Jesus okay?"

"Yes definitely. If it wasn't for him, we'd be cleaning up blood instead of spilled food," Alice said, leaving to return to the kitchen.

"Wow," said Barbara quietly, "and you don't want to marry us? Why not?"

Going on the defensive, the pastor said, "My child, as much as I love the both of you, neither of you qualify for marriage under this church's tenets."

Barbara scowled and stood up, leaning over the desk. She said through gritted teeth, "Pastor, at some point you're going to have to choose between the church's tenets and what Jesus taught."

"What Jesus taught? What has Jesus been teaching?" asked the pastor.

"No, no. Not my Jesus. The historical Jesus," said Barbara irritably.

"Oh," said the pastor, pausing and searching for an answer.

Barbara calmed down. "You've meant a lot to both of us, Pastor. We would like to get married in this church by you. Yes, we've sinned, but we've only hurt ourselves. Can't you get past that and forgive us?"

"I'll think about it," said the pastor passively.

Letting out a groan of exasperation, Barbara said, "There's going to come a time when you realize forgiveness is more important than rules, Pastor." She stood up and marched out of his office, not even saying goodbye.

Barbara stomped back to her car uttering phrases under her breath like "Damn him" and "Who does he think he is?" She got behind the wheel, lowered her head and took a deep breath. "Lord, I need help with that man. If *he* won't marry us, then someone better please."

She had calmed down by the time she arrived at the site of her next errand—a small bungalow. She walked up the driveway and knocked on the door.

Martha answered and quickly stepped outside, shutting the door behind her. "Barbara! How nice it is to see you again!" Martha exclaimed, giving her a hug. "I'm working on someone at the moment. What can I do for you?"

Surprised by the passion of Martha's greeting, Barbara nervously said, "You know that Jesus and I are getting married."

"Yes, that's so wonderful."

"You've meant so, so much to my Jesus that..." Barbara faltered, beginning to cry, "that I would like you to be a bridesmaid at our wedding."

Tears in her eyes, Martha hugged Barbara close. "Of course I will. I'd be honored," and then gave her three quick kisses on the forehead as if blessing her. Gripping Barbara's shoulders and thrusting her to arm's length, she asked, "Bridesmaid dresses? Will there be a fitting?"

Barbara, drying her eyes, said, "Good God, no. Just wear your most beautiful dress. Okay?"

Martha smiled. "Keeping it simple, eh?"

"Yes. Oh, and I want this to be a surprise for Jesus," Barbara said, heading back to the car.

"Will do," said Martha, waving.

Barbara drove home to get ready for work. When she walked in, Betsy was praying to a painting of Jesus on the cross. Barbara tiptoed to her bedroom to change clothes. Betsy was still praying as Barbara quietly tried to leave. Just as she turned the doorknob, Betsy jumped up and yelled, "Sinner! You're going to go see that devil, aren't you!"

"I'm going to work, Betsy. I won't be seeing Jesus till tonight," Barbara said coldly.

Betsy gasped and started pawing at Barbara. "Is that where you've been all these nights? You've been sleeping with him?"

"Yes. I love Jesus and we're engaged now. Stop touching me, Mom...I mean Betsy," Barbara said, pushing her hands away.

Dropping to her knees, Betsy said plaintively, "Please don't leave me. Please, please don't leave me."

"Stop it!" Barbara cried, stumbling out the door, her heart racing. She jumped in her car, put the key in the ignition and grasped the wheel. Then in a moment of anguish, she slumped forward, hitting her forehead on the steering wheel. The horn beeped, startling her. She straightened up and started the car with determination. As she was backing out of her parking spot, she swore aloud, "This is not going to happen to me again."

Driving to the store, she refocused on the wedding, ignoring her memories and feelings bubbling up from the past. As she walked into the store, Wanda left her register, rushed up to Barbara and asked, "Is there gonna be a bridal shower? Who are you inviting?"

Barbara laughed. "Of course you're invited, Wanda. All the women on the team are invited, plus a few others."

"When's it going to be?"

"I don't know yet. I'll let you know."

"Oh, goody-goody," said Wanda, rushing back to her register.

This scenario repeated itself about a dozen times during the shift. Barbara loved being the center of attention.

In the meantime, Jesus left the soup kitchen and went home, tired from his shift. He napped for an hour before his meditation.

Fifteen minutes in, it felt like his face was shrinking; not his head, just his face. When his focus on his brow point—his third eye—was solid and unwavering, it felt as if the physical manifestation of his personality, his uniqueness, his separateness, would be sucked in like a whirlpool to be liberated out his crown chakra, merging again with the cosmic ocean.

This happened over and over again during the rest of the meditation. Just as he seemed about to cross the threshold into unity, resistance came up, interrupting his concentration, until the final intrusion—a knock at the door.

Jesus slowly came out of his sitting position and went to answer the door. It was Brad, asking if he wanted to go for a ride. Jesus agreed and changed quickly.

"Let's ride the 360 loop over the bridge and then turn around," Brad suggested.

They went the back way to get there. Once they were on 360, Brad pulled up alongside and Jesus asked, "Would you be the best man at our wedding?"

"Of course! And as best man, it's my duty to throw you a bachelor party. I've already talked with Jack. We figured that one of us would be the best man. He wants to get you a stripper."

Jesus grunted in disgust. "I don't want a stripper. Something low-key, something manly, but tasteful."

"I know exactly what to do. Leave it to me," said Brad, pulling ahead just as they headed downhill. They sprinted down the slopes keeping pace with the cars, and then watched them pull away as they slowed on the uphill. At the end of the ride, Brad and Jesus parted ways after making plans for their next ride.

The next day at work, Barbara and Jesus were bombarded with the question—when was the wedding? She answered one of these, within earshot of him, that it was the pastor's fault they didn't know yet. Leaving his register, Jesus gently said to her, "Let's give him one more chance. We'll see him tonight at the roundtable."

"Good. We'll embarrass him into saying yes in front of the whole group." Barbara said with an evil grin.

"Really? You want to guilt him into performing the ceremony? Do you really want the pastor in that frame of mind?"

"Well, he hurt me...and you, too," said Barbara.

"I know, but responding in kind is not the answer. Let's let the Universe present the right situation."

"But we're running out of time."

"True. Let's give him one more chance and if he doesn't take it, we'll find someone else. Okay?"

"Okay," Barbara said disappointedly. She wanted to do battle, but Jesus would have none of it. She was calmer by the time they got off their shift but still had a lot of fire left, and it showed when they made love, as they rolled off the bed onto the floor, breaking a lamp. Jesus cut his finger on one of the shards.

"Wow, I needed that," Barbara said afterwards, panting.

Jesus agreed while catching his breath. Studying his bleeding ring finger, he knew that the cut represented unions and grief and that this was significant because he hadn't hurt himself in a while. He said nothing to Barbara and went to take care of the cut. She got dressed and began to clean up the broken lamp.

They met in the kitchen and she asked if he was okay. He said he was and that he needed to meditate. As she made dinner, Jack emerged from his room to make several comments about their noisy interlude.

"I thought you appreciated robust lovemaking."

"Not when I'm not involved, though to be honest, I did pound the pud after I pounded on the wall," he said.

"Jack," Barbara said, going into a full body shudder, "I didn't need to know that."

"I probably would have appreciated it more if I was seeing somebody."

"I thought you were seeing somebody."

"No. Me and Suzanne broke it off about six weeks ago. What are you cooking?"

"Dinner for me and Jesus," said Barbara. "Too bad about you and Suzanne. I liked her." Changing the subject, she asked, "Are you going to the roundtable tonight?"

Jack slapped his hand to his forehead. "I completely forgot. I'll nuke a burrito and take a shower. I suppose you two need to take a shower, too. I better go first so there's enough hot water left."

He went to take his shower and Barbara set the table and put the food out. "Jesus? Dinner's ready."

Jesus emerged from the bedroom looking serene. "Hey, it looks great."

"How's your boo-boo?"

"I'm fine. Let's eat."

They briefly prayed and ate quickly. "Let's save time and take a shower together," Barbara suggested.

"You think that will actually save time?" asked Jesus skeptically.

"We can try it."

Showering together was not a timesaver. They arrived at the roundtable ten minutes late. They walked in sheepishly and took their seats. "Sorry we're late," said Barbara.

Jack asked, "How was the shower?"

"Jack!" Barbara exclaimed.

"We're clean," Jesus pointed out.

"And spent, too, I imagine," Jack laughed, with the rest of the table joining in.

"People, people. Some decorum please," said the pastor. "We all struggle with our animal selves."

"It's part of the path," said Brad.

"What path?" Ralph asked.

"We've talked about this before. The path of dealing with our animal instincts to become more highly evolved human beings. You agree with me, don't you Pastor?" asked Brad.

"Of course. That's where religion comes in. To help us with our sense of right and wrong," he replied.

Unable to restrain herself, Barbara said, "But if somebody does something wrong in your eyes or in your religion, that's it. No redemption, no nothing. Once they've sinned, they're cooked."

"That's not entirely true, Barbara. That would only apply to mortal sins," said the pastor.

"What's the definition of a mortal sin?" asked Juan.

"Deliberately committing an act incompatible with the moral law," the pastor replied.

"The moral law?" asked Alice.

"The moral law set down in the Commandments and the Bible," said the pastor.

"The Christian 10 Commandments or the Jewish 613 Commandments?" asked Jesus.

"The Christian commandments, of course," said the pastor, beginning to get annoyed.

"So moral laws change?" asked Gertrude.

The pastor, feeling trapped, answered slowly, "Yes, they do."

"So for the Jews, it was okay to kill a Canaanite, but God changed his mind and then it was wrong?" asked Brad.

"This is turning into sophistry," said the pastor angrily.

"Why would God change?" asked Barbara.

"God didn't change; human beings changed," said Brad. "Think about it, the Old Testament was basically written between 1000 and 100 BC. Hasn't the audience—humanity—changed over the last three thousand years?"

"Of course, and that's because the Lord sent His only begotten Son," said the pastor.

"I'm sure He was sent to help facilitate that change, but I think the question is if you commit a mortal sin, then commit to a life living by the principles set forth by Jesus Christ, you still go to hell?" asked Brad.

"Yes," said the pastor.

"So, what's the point then?" asked Jack. "Where's the motivation to be better if you already effed up?"

"What about all the other religions that have different moral laws? What if they want to convert? Is it too late for them?" asked Gertrude.

"More to the point might be, what's more important—that someone finds God in their own way or by your way?" asked Jesus.

The pastor leaned forward, putting his head in his hands. "My children, it is gratifying that you have put so much thought into our religion." He sat upright. "However, nitpicking at minor inconsistencies is counterproductive."

"How is it nitpicking when you use these moral laws to refuse to marry Jesus and me?" asked Barbara defiantly.

A groan went up around the table. "Why won't you marry these two wonderful young people?" Gertrude asked pointedly.

Holding up his hand, the pastor said, "Please people, this is a matter of church doctrine."

"Instead of helping people to find the right moral path, you condemn them for making mistakes in their past?" asked Gertrude angrily.

"Though they might have atoned for some of them, there is evidence that they have no inclination to stop all of their questionable behavior," said the pastor quietly.

Furious, Gertrude stood up. "And just how are you going to help them overcome their questionable behavior when they leave the church because you rejected them?" She walked around to confront him face to face, hands on hips. "And another thing: Love, forgiveness and acceptance are the hallmarks of Jesus. You don't turn your back on someone in need," she said. Wagging a finger at him, she continued, "This is pathetic behavior for a holy man. Absolutely pathetic, hiding behind a bunch of rules," she said, heading for the exit. "Jesus Christ would be ashamed of you," she yelled, slamming the door behind her.

Silence washed over the room. The pastor was pale and sweating, and the group looked embarrassed. Breaking the silence, Jack said, "I thought you were the only one allowed to stomp out of the room, Pastor."

Chapter 26 – Oneness

The pastor slowly rose out of his chair and shuffled to the exit, noticeably hunched over. As he opened the door, he mumbled, "Meeting adjourned," then shut it quietly. In shock, everyone silently processed Gertrude's diatribe.

Finally, Alice rose to her feet. "I've got to work early in the morning, so good night." The group followed suit and filed out of the room one by one. Reaching the parking lot, Barbara asked Jesus, "Are you going to talk to the pastor?"

"I'll talk with him."

When they arrived back at the apartment, Jack was already home and sitting on the couch, lighting a joint and starting a session of Call of Doody. Jesus motioned Barbara to go to his bedroom and he sat down on the couch next to Jack. After taking a hit, Jack offered the joint. "Want some?"

"No thanks. Jack, I've got a question to ask you."

Setting the joint down and picking up his game controller, Jack said, "Shoot."

"I know you haven't been entirely happy with the changes going on with the apartment, but I've got another one for you to consider."

Jack set down the controller and asked in a flat tone, "What?"

"Is it okay with you if Barbara moves in?"

Collapsing back into the couch, Jack moaned, "Oh, dude! Why would you want to do that?"

"Hey, it wouldn't be for that long."

"It wouldn't? Why not?"

"In a couple of months, we'd be getting our own place."

Jack leaned forward, putting his elbows on his knees and rhythmically pounding his fist into an open palm. "Well, yeah, of course you two newlyweds would be getting your own place. That makes perfect sense...."

"She would be here for two or three months, depending on how quickly we can find an apartment after we get married. There's no time to look for one now while we're planning the wedding, so, you see...."

They sat in silence for a while until Jack relit the joint. He picked up the game controller. "Yeah, she can move in," he said quietly.

Jesus got up and began walking to his bedroom, but then turned around and came up behind Jack, placing his hands on Jack's shoulders. Leaning over, he whispered, "Thanks, man."

Jesus went to his bedroom and sat down on the bed, putting his elbows on his knees and his chin in his hands. "What did he say?" Barbara asked.

"He said yes."

"Are you okay?"

Forcing a smile, Jesus said, "Sure. So what's next?"

"Would you have enough time to go with me to get the marriage license tomorrow?" Barbara asked.

"It'll be tight," said Jesus, getting up and walking over to her.

Barbara stood up and embraced him. "You can handle tight, can't you?" she asked, grinding her hips into his.

Jesus almost didn't hear her over the sound of Jack's game. "Why don't we make a little noise of our own?" he suggested.

"Our own explosions?" asked Barbara, grinning.

"I'm thinking we'll play a game where I repeatedly attack your front," said Jesus, chuckling and kissing her.

Interrupting their kissing momentarily, Barbara said, "Don't forget to attack my rear, dear," and they fell on the bed laughing.

Barbara was already out the door taking care of more wedding details by the time Jesus got up the next morning. He performed his usual morning spiritual practice and then got online to study the intricacies of weddings. After grabbing a quick bite, he left for the soup kitchen.

Halfway through his serving shift, he felt a tap on his shoulder. It was the pastor. He was pale and his face looked like an overused, dried-out dish sponge. He asked Jesus if he could have a word with him for a moment.

"Alice! Can you cover for me for a minute? What's this about, Pastor?"

Jesus handed Alice the ladle and walked with the pastor into the hallway behind the kitchen. Facing the pastor, he clasped his hands behind his back. "What can I do for you, Pastor?"

The pastor took a deep breath and tried to say something, but then hesitated. Jesus put his hand on the pastor's shoulder. Looking at the floor, the pastor said, "I've decided to perform the marriage ceremony for you and Barbara...if you still want me to preside."

"Holy Goob!" said Jesus, momentarily forgetting himself. Hugging the pastor with gusto, he said, "Of course we still want you to preside. Of course we do! I've got to go call Barbara and give her the good news." After Jesus ran back to the kitchen, the pastor leaned against the wall trying to catch his breath. He slowly slid down until he was sitting on the floor with his knees propped up. Putting his head in his hands, he softly cried.

Barbara was ecstatic when she heard the news and Jesus returned to his steam table. "What was that all about?" asked Alice.

"The pastor agreed to perform the ceremony!"

Alice stared at him as if she wasn't quite sure what to say. "If that's what you want, I'm happy for you," she said, walking away.

Jesus thought her response was odd but continued his serving duties in a state of near bliss. As soon as his shift was over, he hurried to his car to drive to the county clerk's office. He felt a gnawing sensation in his stomach and assumed he was hungry and maybe too excited. When he got inside, Barbara was already waiting.

As they embraced, she said, "Okay, the license will only be good for thirty days, so we'll need to set the date."

Jesus thought for a moment. "Then how about four weeks from tomorrow? Do you want to get married at the church?"

240

"Yes and yes," she replied. "Now we need a place to hold the reception."

"Number fifty-eight," a clerk yelled.

Barbara and Jesus strode up to the counter, handed their application to the clerk and sat down. The clerk looked it over. "Your name is Hey-Zeus?"

"It's pronounced Jesus, ma'am."

"Uh-huh. And your middle name is Magdalena?" the clerk asked Barbara.

"Oh, good grief," Jesus said, shaking his head.

"Well, aren't you two just perfect for each other? Sign here. Do you have the fee?" asked the clerk. Barbara handed a check over as Jesus signed the form. The gnawing sensation he felt was getting stronger and heavier.

As they left the building, Barbara took his hand. Walking merrily along, she abruptly stopped and let go. "What's wrong with your hand?" she asked.

"I don't know. The tremor started when I signed the marriage license application."

"Don't you go getting cold feet on me now, Jesus H. da Vinci. I won't stand for it," she said, marching to the car.

"My feet are the same temperature as the rest of my body."

"You know what I mean. Come on, let's go. We've got to get to work," Barbara said.

Perplexed, he got into the car. On the drive, she went over what was left to be done, but Barbara's groundedness and in-control demeanor did nothing to alleviate the sensation in Jesus's stomach. He decided he needed to call Martha.

Barbara was hardly at her register the entire shift. First, she went to the prepared foods department to see if they could cater the reception. Then it was back to the front-end office to pick out a florist and look at wedding dresses online. Fortunately for Jesus, his line was long and he could focus on customer service rather than on how he physically felt.

After work, Barbara asked if they could have the reception at the soup kitchen. "I don't know. Let's ask the pastor on Sunday," said Jesus.

"No. We need to know as soon as possible. What if someone else books the soup kitchen for that Saturday? That's your job for tomorrow," she said.

"All right. Brad and I will stop by on our bike ride."

"What? You made plans without telling me?" Barbara asked in a strained voice.

"What are you getting upset about? We just made the plans this evening. I didn't have a chance to tell you yet."

"Jesus, listen to me. Not to be a bridezilla, but there are a million details for this wedding and reception and I want it all to go off without a hitch. I need you to be available to help out when necessary. Okay?"

Rubbing his stomach, Jesus said, "All right, all right. I'll check in every day to make sure I hold up my end."

They drove the rest of the way in silence. Once inside the apartment, Jesus collapsed on the couch. "Oh, one other thing. I left a message for

Martha to set up a session, hopefully on Monday. That's my day off so there should be plenty of time for errands."

Barbara sat down and put her hand on his cheek. "Thank you, honey." Giving him a peck on the forehead, she said, "I've got to get on the computer and check on some details. Are you going to be okay?"

"I'm fine. Go do your wedding stuff."

With Barbara in the bedroom, he would have to meditate in the living room. He sat down on the floor and tried to get comfortable. It took a long time, forty minutes at least, to get centered. The pain in his stomach kept distracting him, but by the end of the meditation it was almost gone.

The next morning, the gnawing pain returned and he tried to ignore it. Jesus realized he could simply call the church's events coordinator and see if the sanctuary and soup kitchen were available rather than make a detour on his ride. Fortunately, they were and he made the reservations. The feeling in his gut grew stronger.

Brad arrived shortly thereafter and they began their ride. It was a warm day for December, in the mid seventies. They wound their way through back streets and side streets and crossed the pedestrian bridge at Lady Bird Lake. Eventually they got to Loop 360 and began the main part of the ride.

His eyes squinting from the rushing wind, sweat quickly evaporating to cool him down, the noise of the gears and the change from going downhill so quickly to going uphill so slowly...it was glorious. *This is freedom*, he thought. When Brad caught up with him, Jesus asked him breathlessly, "Have you ever experienced a time when your feet were cooler than the rest of your body?"

Brad's face scrunched up. "What are you talking about?"

"Barbara made a comment about me getting cold feet, but my feet feel fine."

Laughing, Brad said, "No. It's not physical. It means shying away from your commitment."

"Yeah, that would upset her."

Brad laughed again and rode ahead. They crested a long uphill stretch and set off downhill. Jesus mulled over what Brad had said for the rest of the ride.

Later that day, as he and Barbara drove to work together, he told her about booking the church and soup kitchen. She responded, "Oh goodie! This is coming together just like I thought it would."

The shift unfolded much like the previous night's, with Jesus working hard and Barbara bouncing off the walls. Pete was cashiering, and during a lull Jesus asked him if he would be one of his groomsmen.

Stunned, Pete stammered, "Wow! Thanks. Sure. Yes, I'll be a groomsman. Why me? I mean we're friendly here at work, but we've never hung out outside of work. Not that I don't want to, but..."

"Pete, I don't have a lot of close friends," Jesus said, pausing to gather his thoughts, "but you've given me great, balanced advice. You're a spiritual person and I want you there when I commit to Barbara." As he finished talking, a sharp, stabbing pain echoed throughout his gut and he doubled over.

"Are you all right?" asked Pete, as he put his hand on Jesus's shoulder.

Straightening up, he forced a smile. "It's just my mind messing with my body. I'm okay." They went back to work, occasionally interrupted by a squeal or an "Omigod" emanating from the front-end office.

On the drive home, Barbara asked, "How was your day?"

Jesus sat there, saying nothing.

"How was your day?" she asked again. When he still didn't respond, Barbara asked, "Why are you so quiet?"

Jesus breathed deeply. "I'm just tired."

"What do you have to be tired about? I'm the one taking care of all the wedding details," she said.

Somewhat loudly, Jesus said, "Well, maybe I'm picking up the slack at work for someone who's not pulling her weight," and leaned over the center console, making several comical faces at her.

Barbara straightened up, her face twitching as she inhaled. She was ready to let Jesus really have it, but then she audibly exhaled and slumped back in her seat. "Yeah, all right. I'm getting to do all the fun stuff and you're doing the same ol' same ol'," she admitted.

Jesus chuckled to himself. In a deliberate Texas drawl, he said, "Well, shoot. I don't know how fun 'twere to pick out, you know, the color of the bridesmaids' underwear, which Tibetan chant to play during our walk down the aisle, and whether or not we should stiff the pastor on his honorarium."

"Are you making fun of me? You, you…Goober!" she said in a mocking tone.

"Uh, that's racist. You're a racist!" Jesus said, feigning derision and sticking his finger in her face.

"How can you call Goobers a race? Slogging along on three legs? Maybe I'm a *ploddist*, but I'm not a racist," Barbara said indignantly.

Jesus immediately pulled into a parking lot and began to tickle her feverishly. "Are you calling me slow? Are you calling me slow?"

Playfully slapping him, she said, "Stop it. Behave yourself."

Several times on the drive home, a giggle from one of them started the other one giggling, too. Eventually, Barbara snuggled up close, putting her head on Jesus's shoulder and wrapping her arms around his waist.

When they got home, Jesus asked if there were any errands for the next day. Barbara said no but told him to keep Wednesday afternoon open.

"Why?" asked Jesus as he sat down.

"We're taking dance lessons," Barbara said gleefully.

"We are?" Jesus groaned.

Sitting down on the couch and giving him a little tickle, Barbara said in a funny voice, "Don't you want to feel comfortable dancing in front of everyone at the wedding? Doesn't my Jesus want to be comfortable?"

Laughing, Jesus managed a, "No, no, no!" Jack emerged from his room. "If you two have sex in here, I'll record it and put it on the Internet."

Barbara winked at Jesus. "A sex tape! I'm in." She stood up and began unbuttoning her blouse. "Where do you want me, director?"

Jack shook his head and marched straight to the front door. "I'm outta here," he said, slamming the door behind him.

"Yeah!" Barbara said, continuing to unbutton her blouse. "We don't have to be quiet now." She grabbed Jesus's hand and dragged him to the bedroom. He went willingly.

The next morning, when they discovered that Jack hadn't returned, they decided to skip church and go back to bed. In the afternoon, they finalized the details on what was left to do and even outlined what days the errands needed to be done by.

After meditating the next morning, Jesus rode over to Martha's for a session. She greeted him at the door with her usual over-the-top greeting and enveloped him in a hug. "Jesus, how in the heavens are you? How are the wedding plans going? Come in. Sit down."

Jesus told her the wedding date while rubbing his stomach. "What's going on there?" she asked.

"I've been having this gnawing pain in my gut for the last five days," he grimaced.

"Has it been constant?"

"No. It comes and goes."

"When was the first time it appeared?" she asked, picking up her notebook.

"When Barbara and I went to get the marriage license. A tremor showed up in my hand, too."

Martha frowned slightly, stood up and approached Jesus. Leaning over to stick her face within inches of his, she said, "Really? Cold feet?"

"I know, I know," he said disgustedly. "Commitment issues. I'm working on it."

"Don't beat yourself up. You're not the first man to waver on commitment and isn't this just another symptom of it?"

"Yeah," Jesus replied. "Let's go over how to deal with this again, okay?"

"Acknowledge what you're feeling, face the fear, forgive yourself, and ask for help in overcoming it. Do that and you will master this just like you have everything else."

Jesus closed his eyes and concentrated. A kind of constipated look came over his face and Martha laughed. "You're not going to grunt this one out."

"I want what's best for Barbara. I'm not sure that I'm it," said Jesus.

"Hey, she's as scared as you are. Think about it. You told her you were an alien and she stuck with you. You told her that you might be beamed back. She stuck with you. Marvelous stuff," said Martha, shaking her head.

"Her father abandoned her family when she was eight."

"Father abandonment issues? Wow! And with that, she's still all in? Don't tell me she isn't on a spiritual path. Now get up on the table, and I'll be back momentarily."

Jesus complied, closed his eyes, and prayed. *Please Lord, don't let the physical manifestations of my fear get in the way. Please don't let me hurt Barbara. I want what's best for her. Bless you, Lord, and amen.* The gnawing feeling disappeared.

Martha returned to check his pulses. Her eyes opened wide. Jesus noticed and asked, "What? What's going on?"

"You're almost done," said Martha. "Your chakras are really buzzing."

"Yeah, the lower three chakras started up only recently. The Kundalini hasn't risen again, but it actually feels like it's building up at the base of my spine," he said and closed his eyes.

Martha proceeded to insert a dozen needles or so at various points on his body. The last one was at the heart center, and whoosh—like popping bubble wrap, every chakra opened wide. He could see in his mind's eye the colors of each chakra: red, orange, yellow, green, light blue, dark blue, and purple. His mind swirled, and he concentrated on his breathing.

"How's that feel?" Martha chuckled.

Jesus opened his eyes. Everything was so distinct and every color was intense. He could hear notes from the chirping bird outside that he had never heard before. "This feels extraordinary. I don't feel like my body is here."

"A higher vibration will do that," said Martha. "You'll get used to it. Some might say it's 'being in this world, but not of it.'"

"So, what now?"

"There may be some more...physical manifestations..." Martha said enigmatically.

"More? Like what?"

"I can't tell you."

"How long will this last?"

"Quit thinking. Go deep within," Martha commanded.

Jesus closed his eyes and went for a wild ride. Colors swirled, visions appeared that he didn't understand, but it didn't matter. He was just relishing the energy flow.

There was a knock at the door, and Martha stepped out. Jesus was so relaxed that he promptly fell asleep until she roused him. "I hope you don't mind, but I've got to cut our session short. Is that okay?"

The energy flow was still there and he was ready to get up off the table. "Sure, I think I'm done for today."

"I'll say," said Martha, giving him a big hug and kissing him on the lips. "If I don't see you before the wedding, take care. I love you!" she said, disappearing out the door.

Jesus took a few minutes to reenter the world before he got dressed and drove home. Immediately upon arriving, he went into meditation for an hour, so as to maintain the energy that had been liberated during the session with Martha. The physical sensation of the energy flow continued throughout the following day. Just like the previous times that he had graduated to a higher vibration, it became less noticeable as he got used to it.

Barbara and Jesus passed each other at the shift change and when she was finished counting her money, she made a trip to his register. It was starting to get ridiculous now. Almost three quarters of the customers ready to check out were in his line.

Barbara tapped him on the shoulder and he turned around. She said to his customer, "Excuse us for a moment, we're in love," and then began to passionately kiss Jesus. It took only seconds for the kiss to almost cross from PG to R before Clara ran out of the office.

"Stop it, you two! You're killing me. I already have to beg cashiers from the north store to fill in for your wedding."

Barbara and Jesus untangled. She curtsied and thanked the waiting customer, then ran out the front door. The customers began booing Clara. Wanda started chanting, "Long live love! Long live love!" The rest of the customers and cashiers joined in, almost drowning out the "Aaarrgh!" that Clara uttered as she threw up her hands and retreated to the front-end office.

The next afternoon, Jesus met Barbara at the dance studio. She had brought her iPod and was talking with the dance instructor when Jesus arrived. They started off with a traditional waltz. After a while, an entirely different type of music started blaring.

"What in the heavens is that?" a startled Jesus asked.

Fiddling with his collar, she said, "I've put together a little medley for our dance. Okay?"

"All right," Jesus said reluctantly.

"Beautiful," Barbara said, breaking the embrace, her hips shimmying and her hands waving. "We've got three more lessons after this one to get it right."

Jesus sighed. "Yes, maestro."

That night after dinner, Barbara got on the computer to work on the wedding stuff while Jesus went to the bedroom to meditate. He got comfortable, chanted the opening mantra and began. He didn't know why, but he was unusually comfortable and relaxed. In his mind's eye, he saw the chakra colors located at the appropriate points on his body and they seemed to be even larger than when he was at Martha's.

A new, physical sensation of vibration began in his legs. Slowly, it moved up his body until it engulfed him. It was as if each atom in his body were separate and vibrating at a very high rate. The only thing that was keeping them connected was his will, and if he wanted them to, they would disperse on the wind like dandelion seeds.

It was a little scary at first, but Jesus was determined to embrace the experience. His breathing slowed until he was taking just two breaths per minute. He concentrated intensely on his third eye. Suddenly, a vision of a beige-colored tunnel extending upwards from his forehead at a forty-five-degree angle appeared in his mind. A flimsy veil covered the far portal, flapping as if there were a breeze.

This isn't rational, Jesus thought, and the vision began to disappear. *No! I want to experience this.* The vision returned and became even more distinct and vibrant. Then in an instant, the veil disappeared and his consciousness launched through the tunnel and into space.

"Pause please," said the curious judge. "Am I to understand that you did become enlightened on their world? What was that like?"

"Your Honor, to go into detail would be meaningless, because each human being reaching this point experiences something similar, but different. Suffice it to say that I felt a complete and total connection to everything in the Universe and I felt a peace that I have never known."

"Interesting. Proceed."

A knock came at the door. "Jesus, are you all right? You've been in there for over two hours," Barbara said.

With difficulty, he stood up, walked over to the door and opened it. Taking a step back, Barbara repeated, "Are you all right?"

"Of course I am. Why do you ask?" he asked quietly.

"That's the longest you've ever mediated, that I know of. You're almost glowing. You could get a job as a nightlight."

Jesus took a deep breath. He knew this was the ultimate test—being able to maintain his centeredness and energy in the company of other human beings. "Ah, very witty," he said.

Barbara tried to talk to him about wedding details, but he couldn't focus. His ego was having difficulty coping with what had just happened. He felt tired. He said so and went to bed.

Chapter 27 – Other physical manifestations

Their existence until the following Monday consisted of wedding details and lots of meditation, interspersed with spirited bouts of lovemaking.

Barbara asked Jesus to bring Brad by her old apartment after their bike ride to discuss wedding clothes. When they arrived, Brad and Barbara stood on the stoop talking quietly as Jesus caught his breath in the parking lot. Spying him from the window, Betsy grabbed something, forced her way past Brad and Barbara and ran up to Jesus. She began spraying him from a bottle labeled "Holy Water" and yelling various epithets such as "Blasphemer" and "Satan," and made the sign of the cross over and over again.

Jesus stared at her, sweating profusely. He suddenly seized the bottle from her and unscrewed the cap. "That's not the way to do it. This is the way to do it," he said, emptying the entire contents over his head. "Refreshing. Thank you, Betsy. That felt really good."

Betsy looked upon him with horror. Jesus thanked her again and gently placed his hand on her shoulder. Betsy immediately dropped to the ground, writhing on the asphalt as if she were having a seizure, and grunting something unintelligible.

Taking a step back, Jesus didn't know what to make of this development. He asked his intuition what to do but received no answer. Finally, Betsy regained her composure, sat up and looked around, dazed. When she gazed upon Jesus, her face filled with awe. Shuffling on her knees across oil and broken glass, she grabbed his hand, kissed it and placed it against her cheek. "Thank you, Jesus Christ, thank you. You are the Son of God!" she exclaimed, continuing to kiss his hand.

"Betsy, my name is Jesus H. da Vinci, not Jesus Christ...and we're all children of God. All I did was behold you with compassion."

"Nonsense, nonsense! You ARE the Son of God, you are the Son of God!" she insisted, beginning to sob uncontrollably.

Barbara rushed to Betsy's side and lifted her from the ground. Her housecoat was dirty and stained with blood, and it stuck to her knees. They stood together for a few moments as Betsy regained her balance. She stopped crying and with the most peaceful look Barbara had ever seen said to Jesus, "My mind is clear again. Thank you."

As they walked to the apartment, Betsy repeated over and over to Barbara, "I'm so, so sorry about how I've treated you, my child." Barbara began to cry, and hugged Betsy fervently.

"You have nothing to apologize for. It's all right," Barbara said. They walked arm in arm into the apartment and shut the door.

Jesus, turning to Brad and seeing his mouth wide open, asked, "Is that a new filling? Come on. Let's go home."

Brad walked over to his bike as if he were in a trance. Jesus led the way for a while until Brad pulled alongside and asked, "What the hell just happened back there?"

"Apparently, Betsy healed herself."

"And you had nothing to do with it?"

"I was there. So were you and Barbara."

"And you didn't do anything?" asked Brad.

"I saw the state she was in. I felt compassion towards her. I projected love and light to her heart."

"And you projected nothing to her mind?" asked Brad insistently.

"Well..."

Jesus was already asleep by the time Barbara arrived home from work that night. She almost woke him up to ask about Betsy, but he looked so peaceful and content that she couldn't do it. The next morning went the same way. She had a million questions, but she let him sleep in and left for work.

By the time Jesus arrived for the late shift, the store was abuzz about the apparent miracle. He deflected questions as best he could, even complaining that he was losing count when verifying his cash drawer.

The questions had abated when, towards the end of his shift, Betsy came through his line. He had never seen her in the store before, and here she was, buying one inexpensive item. As he handed her change to her, she grabbed his hand. "Bless you, Lord Jesus, for the miracle you performed on me."

Seeing that the other customers in his line had overheard what she said, Jesus leaned over and whispered gently, "Betsy, my dear, please don't disrupt my work."

With a look of dismay, Betsy took her change and hurried out the door. Several of the customers asked what she had meant. Jesus patiently explained that she had been going through a tough time and was grateful for his help.

That night, he fielded all of Barbara's questions about Betsy. He had no explanation for the incident and hoped the matter was concluded.

But it didn't end there. Betsy showed up again during his Thursday shift, and again, Jesus calmly asked her not to disrupt his work. She dashed out of the store, and under his breath, Jesus asked the Universe what was going on, but he received no reply. A nagging feeling came over him that if he had known that this "miracle" was going to take place, he might not have been so ardent in his spiritual practice.

That night, all Barbara could talk about was how great Betsy was doing and how disappointed she was that Jesus was rejecting her.

"I'm not rejecting her. Not in the least. If she wants to talk, we can do it away from work. I'm willing to do that," Jesus said.

His irritation showed and Barbara asked no further questions. Immediately recognizing his feelings, he excused himself to go and meditate. Again he asked the Universe why this was happening, and again he received no reply. But by the time he had finished his meditation, he had resolved to continue on his path no matter what was to come.

The next day, Jesus called Alice to tell her he was going to be an hour late for his shift. When he showed up, the kitchen was empty. Everyone was clustered in the dining room. Approaching the crowd, he asked what was going on. Alice, in tears, told him that one of the patrons had just choked to death and there was nothing that the paramedics could do.

She told him that several of the staff had attempted the Heimlich maneuver without success, and when the paramedics arrived, they had worked on him for thirty minutes and even performed a tracheotomy. They were just packing up when Jesus arrived.

"Who was it?" asked Jesus, pushing through the crowd to see.

When he reached the body, he saw that it was Jerry. Jesus got down on his knees, put his hand on Jerry's chest and said a prayer for him.

A moment later, something hit Jesus in the forehead and fell to the ground in front of him. It was a large, gristly, half-chewed chunk of meat. Jerry coughed and sat up with a pale, disoriented look on his face. A gasp went up from the crowd. Jesus stood up and backed away from him, but his path was blocked.

"You saved him," said one patron.

"It's a miracle," said another.

"Save me, help me," said several others in the crowd.

Jesus fought his way to the edge of the throng only to find Alice standing in his way. With a confused look on her face, she asked, "What did you do?"

He tried to answer, but couldn't. He fled past her, ran to his car and drove home. His mind was swimming and his heart was pounding. *Did I do that? Why is this happening? Make it stop.* As soon as he got home, he went into meditation and had difficulty slowing his breathing. Again, no answers presented themselves.

Frustrated with the lack of response, he got ready for work. Repeatedly, he brought his focus back to the moment and to his breath. By the time he arrived at the store, his composure had almost returned.

The shift went smoothly until Betsy showed up again, and Jesus had no recourse but to finally address the situation.

Taking her by the hand, with at least a half-dozen customers in line, he said, "Betsy, I did not perform a miracle. If the Universe decided to work through me to help you, so be it. Take the gift you've been given and work on your issues and problems. Calm your mind and listen for God's guidance. He will show you the way to help heal yourself. Take responsibility for your path and your communication with God. You're not a victim. All of us have challenges to overcome, and you were ready to heal one of yours. I suggest that you go home and meditate. Plus, I need you to stop coming to my workplace. If you want to talk further, we'll set up a time and place outside of work. Okay?"

Bowing her head, Betsy said, "Yes, sir. I won't bother you anymore."

"At work; we can meet outside of work. Let go of any guilt or shame you feel about your behavior because—look at me, Betsy—you're doing better than you think. I love you," Jesus said, taking her hand.

Looking at him with a childlike smile, Betsy said, "Okay," and waved as she left.

His customers had heard everything he said and broke into spontaneous applause. When one of them asked what was going on, Jesus again explained she had been having some problems and was grateful for his help.

When he got home, Barbara asked him how his day was. Rolling his eyes, Jesus said, "I don't know if I can talk about it."

"Oh, come on now, Mr. Spaceman. You know you can tell me anything," she said, soothingly massaging his shoulders.

"Betsy came through my line again and I gave her a pep talk. She seemed comforted by it."

"Did you tell her that you didn't perform a miracle?"

"Yes, and my entire line applauded."

"Did you tell her that you would talk with her outside of work?"

"Yes, I did."

"And she seemed comforted by your explanation? Why is that difficult to talk about? It sounds like it went perfectly," Barbara said.

"That wasn't the only thing that happened today," Jesus said, and then related the soup kitchen incident.

Barbara sat down next to him. She struggled to say something. Taking his hand and putting it in her lap, she sat in silence.

Finally, she asked, "This guy was dead?" Jesus nodded yes. "For how long?"

"I don't know, but the paramedics were packing up."

"Huh. Wow. You don't hear that sort of thing every day."

"I know, I know. I just said a prayer for him and I certainly didn't think he would come back to life. I didn't have a thought of curing Betsy of mental illness. I don't know what's going on," Jesus said, shaking his head.

"Do you think this had something to do with your spiritual practice?"

"Well, obviously!" Jesus said, standing up. He started pacing, hands behind his back. "This isn't how it's supposed to go. I'm on a mission to study humans, not change their destinies," he said, throwing his hands in the air.

Barbara thought a moment. "How do you know what their destinies are? How do you know exactly what your path is?"

Jesus stared at her, searching for a response.

"You're getting bent out of shape because your mission, your plan, is not going as you thought. Honey, if you look at it objectively, your plans went out the window a long time ago," Barbara said matter-of-factly.

"Yeah."

"Cheer up! Come on, think about it. What if this is the path God chose for you? What if healing is your path on this planet? What if you can help more people? What if that's a good thing?"

"Frankly, I'm afraid. I'm feeling a lot of responsibility here," said Jesus, sitting back down next to Barbara.

"I'm afraid, too. But what are you going to do? Accept that God is working through you. That's all you can do. Right?"

"Goob," Jesus corrected, with a faint smile.

"Goob. Definitely Goob," she said, smiling and hugging him. She stroked his face and kissed him, her breath growing heavy.

Jesus stood up abruptly. "I need to meditate."

Pouting, Barbara said, "What? Doesn't Mama deserve some healing? Some sexual healing?"

Jesus burst out laughing. "Oh, good Lord!" Walking to his bedroom, he said, "Later," without turning around.

"Is that goodbye, or are we having sex later?" Barbara called out.

Jesus stuck his head around the corner and smiled, lifting an eyebrow. Barbara laughed.

He lit a candle, sat down on his yoga mat, and got comfortable. His mind easily slipped into stillness. Focusing on each breath, he waited until his brain waves were at the alpha stage before he asked the question, "Why is this happening?"

Again, he received no answer. The lack of feedback from the Universe continued throughout the next week. No flashes, no synchronicities, no chance meetings with strangers, no offhand comments by anybody that would give him some type of clue as to how to deal with these unusual phenomena. He slowly began to accept that things like this might occur occasionally in his life.

Eight days later, he was musing on that as he headed back to the restroom in the middle of his shift. Before he reached the double doors, he heard a loud scream from the meat-seafood department. He made his way around the counter to find Brian doubled over and holding both hands tight to his body. Jesus asked him what was wrong and Brian nodded in the direction of the floor to his right. There lay a third of Brian's left index finger, sitting in a small pool of blood.

Others arrived and the Squad Leader, Dakota, grabbed a clean cloth. She delicately picked up the severed piece of finger. "I'll find someone to drive you to the minor emergency center. Come on," she said firmly. "Somebody get a bag of ice."

"Minor! One third of my finger is gone!" exclaimed Brian. Jesus shuddered at the memory of a punishment on Gooberia that was similar. Instinctively, he asked Dakota for the finger.

"What? No! We need to get him to the minor emergency center now," she said.

Jesus smiled at her, and she complied. He took the finger in the cloth, walked over to Brian, and asked him for his hand.

Brian was getting a little shocky, so Jesus repeated firmly, "Give me your hand, Brian."

Stretching out his arm and turning his head away, Brian said, "Okay."

Jesus unwrapped the cloth. He held the severed finger and the bloody stump in his right hand and placed his left hand on Brian's chest. "Look at me, Brian. Look at me."

Nervously, Brian slowly turned toward Jesus and looked him in the eye. He relaxed slightly, taking his first real breath in almost two minutes. "That's right, relax. Everything is going to be okay," Jesus said soothingly.

Suddenly, Brian gasped and convulsed slightly. Gingerly, he removed his hand from Jesus's grasp and inspected his finger. It was still bloody, yet it moved properly. "Go figure," Brian said before fainting into the arms of his coworkers.

Turning to Dakota, Jesus said, "You can take care of him now. I've got to use the restroom and get back to my register. They're probably wondering where I am."

Speechless, the three people who had witnessed the reattachment simply nodded their heads. Dakota and a couple of employees helped move Brian to the main office.

About thirty minutes later, Clara came out of the office and stopped dead in her tracks. Four cashiers, seven or eight other employees and ten customers surrounded Jesus.

"What's going on?" she demanded.

"Jesus healed somebody. Again!" someone in the crowd said.

"That's it. This is no way to run a business. Jesus, come with me. Everybody back to wherever you're supposed to be," Clara bellowed, walking rapidly to the office. She opened the door. "Patsy, you and Jesus are switching places. Come on. I need you out there right now," she ordered.

Patsy went out to Jesus's register and he followed Clara into the office. "Sorry for the—" Jesus said, before being interrupted.

"Stop right there. I'm not mad at you. I need an orderly work environment. I don't know what is going on with you, but you seem to be having a profound effect on the people around you and it's disrupting the store. For the time being, I'm giving you all head cashier shifts. Okay?"

"Sure. I can do that."

Clara opened the door, looking quizzically at Jesus. "I've got to go talk with Bob. I'll be right back," she said slowly.

Jesus sat there staring uneasily at the piles of papers and uncounted tills from the morning shift. He liked talking with the customers and his fellow cashiers. Even though the head cashier position was considered a perk and position of responsibility, it felt more like he was being banished. He paused to ask the Universe to help him feel his feelings and then let them go.

He began his duties, but at one point, he had to go out to ask Patsy a question. Immediately several customers moved to Patsy's line. She distractedly answered Jesus's question as she observed the activity. When Jesus returned to the front-end office, there was a loud, collective groan from the customers.

Bob and Clara entered moments later. Bob asked irritably, "Am I to understand that you performed a miracle in the meat-seafood department today?"

Getting up and facing Bob, Jesus answered, "Apparently, yes."

Bob looked Jesus over. "Look, it would be best if you wouldn't bring your religion to work, okay? It's a disruption."

Taking a deep breath, Jesus said, "Bob, I understand what you're saying, but it's not about religion and it's not something I have any control over."

When Bob finally spoke, he insisted, "We can't have you disrupting work, okay?"

Jesus became very calm. "I know that this is hard for you to comprehend. It's perplexing for me, too. Lately, when I see someone in difficulty, I feel a great deal of compassion and without thinking, I comfort them. Then it happens."

After pausing a moment to let this sink in, Jesus said, "Hey, you can look at it this way...the store just saved a significant amount of money on a worker's comp claim. That's a good thing right?"

Unable to refute Jesus's logic, Bob stood there, silent. Abruptly, he left the office. Jesus turned his attention to Clara. Startled, she too rushed out of the office. Sitting back down, he asked the Universe for help and continued his work.

When it was time for him to give breaks, the customers were like lemmings headed to the sea as they lined up at whichever register Jesus was working. The other cashiers' calls of "I can take you at this register" were of no avail, so they helped out by bagging for Jesus instead. Even customers who were unaware of the miracles flocked to his register.

At one point, while helping bag, Dave said, "Dude, you're pulling all the women out of my line." Jesus ignored him, but Dave couldn't let it go. In a loud carnival barker's voice, he announced, "Step right up folks! Come to this line and get healed by Jesus! That's right! Make a purchase over $100 and have your affliction healed. One healing per customer."

Jesus stopped ringing and turned to Dave. Through gritted teeth, he said, "You're not helping. Go back to your register, NOW!"

The force of Jesus's words knocked Dave to the ground. He jumped up immediately and slowly backed away. "Don't curse me, bro. I'm leaving. Everything's cool."

Jesus returned his attention to his customer and began ringing up groceries again. "What was that all about?" she asked.

"Apparently, he's gone off his medication," Jesus said.

The woman looked at the line of customers and then at Jesus. He met her gaze and she said, "You know, I always go to the cashier that seems to have something to say to me that I might need to hear. I listen to my intuition and then follow it."

Jesus smiled. "I live my life like that, too."

"So, what information do you have for me?" the woman asked.

Simultaneously Jesus saw the phrase in his mind and heard, *Let go.*

Repeating that to her, she started crying. He immediately walked around the counter to embrace her. She was sobbing by now and they stood there for a moment, swaying back and forth. Looking in his eyes, she said, "Thank you."

A sense of peace filled Jesus and the feeling of foreboding left him. "No, thank you. I needed to hear that," he said, kissing her lightly on the cheek. When she had finished paying for her purchase, she reached out and grasped Jesus's hand. "Bless you. You're a godsend."

He smiled, and trying to look as wise as he could, said, "You're just projecting," and winked at her. They gazed at each other momentarily. Letting go of her hand, he placed his hand on his heart. She paused a moment and then left.

The rest of the shift went fairly smoothly until the store closed and the cashiers came back with their tills. Dreamboat Dave started the miracle talk and the rest of them piled on. Jesus played along in good humor until the last cashier finally left. Dakota came to the front-end office to confirm Jesus's totals when she took a call. It was Clara, and she wanted to talk with Jesus.

"I think it would be best if you took a week or two off and let everything settle down," Clara said.

"If you think that would be best."

"It would give you time for a honeymoon," Clara said.

"Yes it would, but we were going to wait a few months for that. We were going to find our own apartment first."

"Well, it would give you time to do that, wouldn't it?"

"Yes, it would. Thank you," said Jesus, without a trace of sarcasm.

He hung up and laughed. "What was that all about?" asked Dakota.

"I've been benched. Clara is giving me a couple of weeks off to let things settle down."

Shrugging her shoulders, Dakota said, "It might be for the best. We wouldn't want people coming here and praying to the Grains for Brains register shrine."

Jesus chuckled. "Yeah, I could see how that would hurt sales. Maybe Bob could set up a card table for me in the parking lot."

Dakota smiled uncomfortably. Jesus wondered how much his life would change now. He finished his duties and drove home slowly. A bit too slowly, as he was startled into the moment by the sound of a police siren. He pulled over to the side of the road and turned off the engine.

"License and insurance please," the officer demanded. Jesus did as he was told. The officer looked at the license and shined his flashlight in Jesus's face. "It's you. Well, at least you have your pants on this time."

Jesus laughed gratefully. "Yeah, I've made that a habit now."

"Do you know why I pulled you over?" asked Officer Roy.

"No."

"You were going twenty in a forty-five zone. That's way too slow. What's going on?" Officer Roy asked.

"Unusual day at work. I guess I was contemplating."

"Contemplating? About what?"

"Uh…" Jesus paused to determine the level of truth he should include in his explanation. "I reattached a man's severed finger today. In the previous two weeks, I healed a woman of mental illness and brought a man back to life."

"That was you? I heard about that from a paramedic buddy of mine. The guy was dead for thirty minutes and you touched him and he was alive again. Unbelievable," said Officer Roy. "I'm only giving you a warning, Mr. da Vinci."

Jesus nodded and slipped back into an introspective state. Officer Roy printed out the citation and handed it to him. "You know, healing people isn't a bad thing."

"It's gotten complicated," Jesus sighed.

"I'm no expert, but it seems to me that you ought to trust God on this. Have a nice night and speed up," said Officer Roy.

"Thank you," said Jesus, starting his car.

Chapter 28 – Godlines

Pondering his day on the drive home put Jesus in a funk. As soon as he entered the apartment, Barbara asked, "What's wrong?" He explained about the severed finger, the customer, Clara giving him time off, and getting pulled over.

"Wow! All I did today was get a fitting and check on the flowers. You have a knack for the extraordinary, don't you?"

"Yeah," Jesus said flatly.

"Honey, you need to relax. All I know about these things that have happened to you, is that I love you no matter what. God does too, so get out of this mood and go meditate. I'll give you a massage when you're through," Barbara said with an air of authority.

Jesus smiled. "Yes ma'am." On his way back to the bedroom he stopped. "You know, getting bossed around by you isn't helping any."

Barbara laughed and Jesus blew her a kiss. He went inside and got comfortable for his meditation. His ego was all over the place, constantly bringing up the miracles, and he had to repeatedly refocus on his third eye. Frustrated, he persisted. Suddenly, the word "grace" popped into his mind. He realized that he needed to respond with dignity and resolve no matter what was happening. He hadn't asked for any of this, from the mission to the miracles, but by God he would dedicate himself to accepting that this was Divine Will. He would not shirk from it.

After the meditation, Barbara's stimulating massage not only eased his tension, it aroused him, too. Some passionate fooling around ensued and Jesus had no trouble falling asleep. Waking refreshed and looking forward to church, he was getting ready when Barbara walked in to announce she had too many errands to join him. So Jesus went to church alone.

He sat down next to Brad and Jack and asked about the details of his bachelor party, but Brad wouldn't budge. "It's a surprise. You won't be disappointed," he said emphatically.

The pastor's sermon was on flexibility in one's beliefs. *Sounds like the pastor had an epiphany,* Jesus thought, and it prodded him to continue to evaluate his own beliefs.

Afterwards, he remarked to the pastor, "Excellent sermon. Very thoughtful."

The pastor grinned, and tried to appear modest when he said, "I'm learning."

Jack spoke up immediately, "Then how do you feel about abortion?" Stiffening, the pastor's grin disappeared.

"Can't you let things be? Do you always have to stir things up?" asked Brad, slapping Jack on the back of the head.

Jesus ignored Jack and shook the pastor's hand. "Thank you, Jesus," said the pastor.

Brad and Jack stopped their bickering and stared, shocked to hear the pastor's correct pronunciation. Jesus started for the parking lot, only to turn around and find Brad and Jack transfixed. "What?" Jesus asked.

Before Jack could say anything else, Brad grabbed him and they all headed for their cars. "So, what time tomorrow night?" Jack asked.

"After dinner, about 7:30. Meet at my place," said Brad.

After her shift the next day, Barbara went straight to her bridal shower. Jesus meditated, ate alone, and then got ready for his bachelor party.

When he arrived at Brad's, Pete and Jack were already there. Brad had called for a cab, and when it showed up they all piled in. Brad brought a grocery bag with him but wouldn't let anybody see inside it. It took about twenty minutes to arrive at their destination—Heavenly Tobacco.

"What is this place?" asked Jesus as they walked in.

"A cigar lounge," said Brad.

"Oh, so no strippers, but we're doing drugs?" asked Jesus.

"Lighten up, you goober," Jack said.

Brad picked out four fine maduro cigars from Nicaragua. "Those are thirty bucks apiece!" said Jack.

"It's on me, boys," said Brad, smiling. He paid and they walked back to the room Brad had reserved. As everyone sat down, Brad set the bag on the table, left the room and returned with four snifters.

With a loud "Ta-da!" Brad revealed the contents of the bag—a bottle of cognac. Jack and Pete oohed and ahhed, but Jesus sat silently.

"Where did you get that?" Jack asked.

"I had a friend overseas send it to me. With shipping, this cost a cool $500." He raised the bottle up and kissed it.

"Technically, I'm not supposed to *drink* alcohol," Pete said.

"You don't drink cognac, Pete. You sip just enough to get it on your tongue and lips. Then you take a puff off your cigar, followed by pontificating," said Brad.

Jesus laughed, "I definitely know how to do that last part."

Brad prepared the cigars, and handed them out, then he opened the bottle of cognac. After pouring four glasses, he raised his own. "To the groom."

"To the groom," echoed the group, raising their glasses and taking a sip.

"Okay, as I light your cigar, you'll want to rotate it for a nice even burn," said Brad, lighting his cigar. He got up and lit each cigar in turn. "You want to take a puff about once a minute, *without* inhaling," he emphasized, as Jack started to cough.

As the tobacco began to take effect, Pete said, "I believe this is kicking my behind."

"Hear, hear," said Jack, taking a sip of cognac.

"What do *you* believe, Jesus?" asked Brad.

Jesus blinked a few times. "I believe Pete is right."

They puffed and sipped quietly for a while. "Too much silence; not enough pontificating," said Jack.

"To the bride," said Pete, hoisting another toast.

"To the bride," everyone agreed.

Jack blurted out, "I really blew it with Barbara."

"Inappropriate, Jack. Inappropriate," exclaimed Brad.

"Let him be," said Jesus. "You did, but life will give you another chance, Jack. I didn't know what love was until I met Barbara. Literally."

"I believe that would be a *first* chance for Jack, not *another* chance," Pete interjected.

Jesus smirked. "Whatever. I believe Barbara truly gets me and I believe in love," he said pausing, "And God, but that's about it."

"Three beliefs? That's all?" asked Pete.

"Beliefs are like icebergs. Five percent is visible, but the 95 percent you can't see affects everything in your life," Jesus said, waving his arms and spilling a little cognac on the table. "As a child, you learn what your parents and society want you to know, like 'Don't run with scissors' and 'Look both ways when crossing the street.' But you're also indoctrinated with negative things like racism and greed. As an adult, it's your responsibility to examine your beliefs—what you've unconsciously absorbed, like hating people different from you, or disrespecting women. If you don't, they'll worm their way through your consciousness, infecting everything you do." He slugged the last of his drink and slammed the glass down on the table. "Hit me again."

"Great, another Jesus rant," said Jack.

"To Jesus pon-snift-icating," said Brad, raising the bottle and pouring Jesus another snifter as Jack and Pete laughed.

Jesus leaned forward, putting his elbows on the table. Pointing at Pete, he asked, "What do you believe in, Pete?"

"I believe in keeping it simple," Pete said, raising his glass.

"Hear, hear. And a toast to my friends," said Jesus.

They continued on for a couple of hours, until the cognac was almost gone and the cigars were in ashes. Brad called a cab and they headed home. Jesus walked through the door to find Barbara on the couch in a negligee. "Whoa!" he grunted.

"I've got a surprise for you...edible panties," she said, holding them up for him to see.

"I'm not hungry," he said, burping and running to the bathroom. Within moments, Barbara heard retching sounds. She sighed and placed the panties back in the gift bag, then followed him into the bathroom. When he was finished, she gave him a glass of water and an aspirin and helped him to bed.

The next morning, Jesus awoke with a hangover. The thought of food sickened him. He spent the morning and most of the afternoon on the couch with the TV volume on low. Finally, his appetite returned and he ate, followed by a meditation.

The next opportunity he and Barbara had to talk was at dinner Thursday. As they sat down and blessed the food, Jesus said, "You're running yourself pretty ragged here lately."

"I've got a massage scheduled tomorrow."

"Good for you. Smart."

Emerging from his room, Jack said, "Twenty minutes to the roundtable, people." Barbara and Jesus gobbled up their food and then the three of them left in Jack's car. They arrived just in time and sat down.

"The pastor is under the weather and will not be making it this evening," Gertrude announced.

Juan rose to his feet and Alice asked, "Where are you going?"

"If the pastor isn't here, why meet?"

"This isn't a formal church event. Why don't we go ahead and have a discussion?" asked Gertrude.

Juan slowly sat back down and Jack spoke up, "I have a topic—the Ten Commandments. I've been studying them."

"You've been studying the Ten Commandments?" asked Brad.

"Yes, I have."

"For God's sake, why?" asked Brad.

"Not important. But do you know how many versions there are? Dozens!"

"Dozens?" asked Alice.

"Well, maybe *only* a dozen, but there's a lot. There's a Jewish version, Catholic versions and a lot of Protestant versions," said Jack.

"Isn't that interesting! Do any of them change the basic concepts? Like 'Thou shalt not steal'?" asked Gertrude.

"No, but the wording changes in some are significant. 'Murder' in the Jewish version is changed to 'kill' in the Catholic and Protestant versions," replied Jack.

"I'm still having trouble with you looking all this up. Something is going on here," said Brad.

"It is interesting that humans routinely edit the Word of God," said Jesus.

"Maybe God is editing Himself through humans," Barbara suggested.

"An omniscient being needs to edit Himself? Did He make a mistake, or has His audience matured?" asked Jesus.

"There are a lot of things that were considered acceptable in the past that are no longer—genocide and slavery, to name a couple," said Brad.

"Maybe we should write our own," suggested Jack.

Ralph, who had been sitting quietly, jumped out of his chair and bellowed, "Rewrite the Ten Commandments? That's blasphemy...and in a church no less! I'm leaving!"

"Sit down, Ralph," said Alice. "We don't have to call them commandments. We can call them guidelines."

"No, no. We'll call them Godlines," laughed Jack.

"That's good, dude. You're really bringing it tonight," said Brad, slapping Jack on the back as Ralph unhappily sat back down.

"I'd just as soon call them guidelines, thanks," said Alice.

"It'll be up to each of us to call them what we want," said Gertrude.

"That leads me to suggest the first one. 'This Universe is one of free will'," said Jesus.

"You mean THE universe, don't you?" asked Juan.

"Not in some interpretations of quantum physics," said Jesus.

"Everybody has free will? I don't think so," Ralph asserted.

"I disagree, Ralph. It's the prize in every womb. True, there may be consequences to your choices, but ultimately you have free will to act and think as you please," said Jesus.

"Okay, that's the first one. What's next?" said Jack, writing furiously.

Gertrude spoke up. "I talk with God every day. There should be something in there about that."

"Yeah, I never got that either. Every day is holy, not just Sunday," said Barbara.

"How about 'Cherish your relationship with God'," Brad said, then looked at Alice, "Or the quantum field for you atheists—'every day, not just on Sunday.'"

"I could live with that," said Alice.

"Is this just for Christians?" asked Juan.

"Don't we want to write something for everybody?" responded Gertrude.

"Yeah, it should be for everybody," echoed Barbara.

"Then how about, 'I am known by many names'," said Brad.

"And I have no favorite religion," added Jesus.

"So, get over it, people," said Jack, laughing.

"There shouldn't be any humor in this," said Ralph.

"God invented humor," argued Gertrude.

"Yeah, haven't you ever seen your face while climaxing?" asked Alice.

"Once. In Vegas," admitted Ralph, red-faced.

Everybody laughed heartily, including Ralph. Beginning to loosen up, he suggested, "What about killing?"

"And stealing?" added Juan.

"I think we can simplify that," said Jesus. "How about 'Doing intentional harm to someone, whether it be mental, physical, emotional or spiritual, is wrong.'"

"And will be judged by a jury of your peers," added Gertrude.

"What about *un*intentional harm?" Barbara asked.

"That could find its way onto the docket, too," said Jack.

They sat for a moment reflecting what had been said. "What about honoring thy mother and father?" asked Ralph.

"Too limited. How about 'Honor thy family'?" said Gertrude.

"That includes thy snotty little brother," snickered Jack, to several pairs of rolled eyes.

"Examine your beliefs every day," Brad said.

"Why?" Juan asked. "Your beliefs are your beliefs. Why would you want to change them?"

"But that's the point, Juan. Beliefs change all the time. The only constants in life are love and change," said Alice.

"We definitely should add that in," said Barbara, "but first we've got to add something about how hurting yourself hurts others."

"How does that work?" asked Jack. "Me smoking pot every day hurts every one of you?"

"Yes," everyone said in unison.

"Really?" asked Jack.

"Consider that science has already proven that every quantum particle in your body is connected to every quantum particle in the Universe," said Jesus.

"Experiencing life is okay, Jack, but when you hurt yourself, you hurt everyone," said Brad.

Jack groaned, "Okay, let me write this down...'Experiencing life is okay'..." Everybody waited for Jack to finish writing.

"Good one, Barbara," Jesus said.

"Thank you," nodded Barbara. "How about coveting?"

"It's so insidious, isn't it?" responded Brad. "I mean, it completely takes you out of being yourself. Why would I want to be somebody else or wish I had a better car than someone else? What's the point? Unless, of course, I was Jack and owned that old heap of his."

"Hey, I upgraded," groused Jack.

"Back to topic, how about 'Be grateful for who you are and strive to be the best part of God you can be'?" Jesus suggested.

"Encouragement! I like that. There's no encouragement in the Ten Commandments," said Gertrude. "Isn't that sad?"

"How about judgment?" asked Alice. "Let he who is without sin cast the first stone, yadda yadda. I've always thought that was good enough to make the top ten."

"We're already at eight, people," said Jack.

"Right—something about examining your own behavior first before judging someone else," said Brad.

"Unless, of course, you've been called to jury duty," said Jesus.

"Man, you beat me to it," said Jack.

"We should have something specific about killing," said Ralph, "It's numero uno and should be in there separate from the harm one."

"Yeah," agreed Alice. "What do you think it should be, Ralph?"

"I just want to say, I like how positive these are," acknowledged Ralph. "Maybe this one should be something along the lines that all life is sacred."

Gertrude spoke up, "How sweet! How about 'All life is sacred. Killing humans is wrong, whether it be by another human or any government'?"

Everybody thought that was perfect. Jack read them back and a few suggestions were made as to how to word them better. It looked like they were finished, when Juan spoke up. "Hope. We don't have anything in there about hope."

The group thought about that for a few minutes. "You mean being uplifted?" asked Jesus.

"Yes. I mean, sometimes I think about all the people in the world who are without hope. Don't you think that God's word should inspire them? And shouldn't there be a commandment about living well, too?" asked Juan.

"Hear, hear," Brad said. "Enjoy the opportunity you have."

"Make your life count," said Alice.

"Anything is possible," said Gertrude.

"Serve humanity," said Jesus.

"Dance as if no one was watching. That song always makes me cry," said Barbara.

"Those all take care of living well, but what about hope?" Juan asked.

"To me, hope is about second chances," said Brad.

"The Universe is all about second chances," said Jesus, pausing. "And the only constants are love and change."

"One more," said Ralph, "Work hard. Play nice."

And with that, they were done.

The next day, Barbara worked the morning shift, got a massage and wrapped up wedding preparations with her bridesmaids. Jesus spent the day alone. He drove up to Lake Travis and hung out at Windy Point, contemplating his life. The point was indeed windy and the water had worked up into a froth. The siren for boats to get off the lake sounded. A few raindrops fell, but Jesus sat there picking at stones on the ground, selecting several and peering at them intently. A loud crack of thunder startled him and rain started coming down heavily. By the time he got back to his car, he was soaked.

Lightning flashed again and again as he drove out of the park. As he was about to pull out onto the main road, a tree exploded and nearly hit his car. Twice more on the drive home, lightning hit trees in front of him. The second time, part of the tree fell onto the road and he had to swerve into oncoming traffic to avoid it, narrowly missing a car with horn blaring.

He hadn't been nervous about the nuptials, but this was definitely getting on his nerves. Pulling over to catch his breath, he asked out loud, "What in the name of heaven is going on, Lord? You've got my attention."

His intuition said, "Be calm. Everything will work out as it's supposed to."

What does that mean? Jesus wondered as he sat there trying to focus on his breath. As the rain poured down, his attention on the driving conditions became so intense that he soon forgot about the message.

When he got home, he got into dry clothes and meditated. Afterwards, he wandered into the kitchen, but preparing dinner was unappealing. He thought about calling Brad and then realized that in a way, this would be his last evening alone and that he should celebrate it alone.

He got dressed, went to his favorite restaurant, and had his favorite dish—Barbecue Tofu. While eating, he thumbed through the local newspaper for movie listings, but instead decided to go buy his favorite movie, *Groundhog Day*, a superb allegory on reincarnation. He went home and settled on the couch with some popcorn, thoroughly enjoying himself.

As the movie finished, Barbara arrived home. She dropped her backpack on the floor and fell back on the couch with a thud. "How was the massage?" Jesus asked.

"Not enough. I need at least two more to wind down," she said, picking pieces of popcorn off Jesus's shirt and eating them. "How was your day?"

"I enjoyed my last day as a bachelor," he said, describing it for her.

"That sounds nice. Was the movie good?" Barbara perused the DVD case. "I've never seen it."

"It's sublime and inspiring. I've got an idea. Why don't we go meditate together?" Jesus asked.

"Okay," Barbara said, following him to the bedroom. "You may not believe this, but I've meditated twice this week on my own. I'd be a lot worse off if I hadn't."

"Good girl," he said, lighting a candle and sitting down.

They got comfortable on their mats and began. A couple of times, Jesus caught himself listening to Barbara's breath while holding his own. He finally let go of that and went deep within. The next thing he knew, the timer went off. They got up, crawled into bed, embraced, and quickly fell asleep.

Chapter 29 – The dance

Barbara was already gone by the time Jesus walked into the kitchen to find Jack munching on some cereal.

"What was that sound I just heard? Was it a chain dragging a ball?" Jack asked.

Not comprehending Jack's meaning, Jesus ignored him and foraged in the refrigerator. He asked Jack when Brad was picking them up. "A little before one." They sat silently eating until Jack asked, "Nervous?"

"I don't know what I feel. There's a whole bunch of things coming up, but I have this sense that they have nothing to do with marrying Barbara."

Jack shrugged his shoulders. "Whatever. I'm going to get nice and toasted before we have to leave for the church. Want to join me?"

Jesus shook his head. "I think I'm going to go for a walk." He cleaned up, put on a coat and left. A front had come through and it was a crisp January morning with the sun shining brightly. He did his best to examine his feelings, but couldn't seem to separate them out. He finally gave up on that and went over his vows for the wedding, mentally noting a few changes he wanted to make.

An hour later, he returned to the apartment and walked through a cloud of pot smoke to shower and trim his beard. He got out his wedding clothes and laid them on the bed. Naked, he sat down to meditate. He focused quickly and went deep within. Out of the blue, a loud distinct voice intoned, *Be calm. Everything will work out as it's supposed to.* His reaction to that insight wasn't to calm down. It was vaguely foreboding, and in the past it would have been a little disturbing. He refocused, and the message came up two more times. Feeling frustrated that he didn't know what it signified, he finished his meditation and checked the time. After getting dressed, he went to the living room and found Jack still smoking.

"Open up some windows, Jack! I don't want to reek of pot at my wedding," he said.

"What? Is it time to go?"

"Fifteen minutes. Now, open up some windows," Jesus said pointedly, walking back to his bedroom.

"All right, all right," said Jack.

Jesus sat at his desk, looking at a photo of Barbara. The buzzing sensation in his chest grew stronger, the feeling of foreboding disappeared and the next thing he knew, Brad was knocking at his bedroom door. "Jesus, are you ready?"

He opened the door with a flourish and a big smile. Brad was caught off guard by Jesus's appearance. He was almost glowing. Brad smiled. "Yeah, you're ready. You're definitely ready. Let's go."

They exited the apartment together with Jack running after them and arrived at the church about forty-five minutes before the ceremony was to begin. Pete soon joined them and they were waiting in front of the open church doors when Barbara and her bridesmaids rode up in a limo. The bridesmaids came running up the steps while the bride waited in the car. Suddenly, it dawned on Jesus what Barbara had orchestrated for the wedding.

Jesus was all in white, Brad in purple, Jack in indigo and Pete in light blue. Martha was there in green, Betsy was in yellow, and Sunny, Barbara's friend from college, was in orange. He had peeked inside the church when he arrived and saw that each pew had attached to it a small spray of flowers with the same colors, plus red. Jesus choked back tears.

Martha greeted him in her usual way—a hip to shoulder hug. "What's going on?"

"Barbara asked you to be a bridesmaid?" Martha smiled and nodded.

Jesus gestured inside toward the flowers and then at the bridesmaids and groomsmen. "Ahh, the chakra colors. She didn't tell you? She's good at keeping secrets. She must have learned that from you. I love these dresses, too. Straight out of the forties. You can dance in them," she said gleefully, going into her signature freestyle dance.

Jesus smiled and walked inside to greet the guests for a few minutes before heading back to the pastor's office. He was putting on his cassock. "Are you ready, my son?" the pastor asked.

"Yes, I'm ready."

Betsy appeared at the door in a panic. "The music guy isn't here. What are we going to do? Barbara's out in the limo, crying."

Jesus looked at the pastor and then at Betsy. Inspired, he whispered instructions to her. Grinning, she said, "Okay!" and tottered off.

"Don't tell Barbara! Just tell her that I took care of everything," Jesus said.

"No music? What are you going to do?" asked the pastor.

"Not a problem," said Jesus, winking. "Two can play the surprise game."

They waited a few minutes and then proceeded to their places. Jesus scanned the crowd and did his best to look each person in the eye.

The pastor gave the sign for Betsy to go get Barbara. The bridesmaids and groomsmen then proceeded to their places...in silence.

Barbara entered the sanctuary and paused. She looked beautiful and her red dress accentuated her hourglass figure. Her head was bowed down and her shoulders sagged. The guests stood up and Brad said, "Okay, everybody. One, two, three, four."

In unison, the guests sang, "Da, da, da dum...da, da, da dum..."

Taken by surprise, Barbara began to cry again. Then she took a deep breath and dabbed her eyes, raised her head, threw back her shoulders and smiled. Gracefully, she walked up the aisle.

Jesus took her hand, whispering, "We can make our own music," as they turned to face the pastor.

The pastor began, "Dear Lord, bless the union..."

Barbara leaned over and whispered, "Goob."

Jesus, suddenly overcome with nervousness, giggled. The pastor frowned but didn't miss a beat. Finishing the prayer, he said, "Be seated, please. I must say, this has to be the most colorful wedding I've presided over, not unlike the bride and groom." The guests responded with laughter.

The pastor recited three scripture readings from the Bible and gave his viewpoint on marriage. He asked their intentions, and when it came time for their vows, Jesus cleared his throat. "I, Jesus H. da Vinci, take you, Barbara Magdalena Kaminski, to be my partner, in good times and in bad, in sickness and in health. I will love you and honor you all the days of my life and beyond. When I arrived here...in Austin, about all I knew was my name and I certainly didn't know anything about love. You have been my teacher in all matters pertaining to the heart and I look forward to further illumination with your guidance."

Steadying herself, Barbara said, "I, Barbara Magdalena Kaminski, take you, Jesus H. da Vinci, to be my partner, in good times and in bad, in sickness and in health. I will love you and honor you all the days of my life and beyond. You've helped me mature faster than I thought possible and you have taught me what it means to be truly human and I am better for it."

They blessed and exchanged the rings, and the pastor asked for the guests to intercede on behalf of the couple. He performed a nuptial blessing followed by the Lord's Prayer. After a solemn blessing for the union, he said, "I now pronounce you man and wife. Jesus, you may now kiss your bride."

As Brad handed Jesus a sailor hat, Barbara smiled and said, "*The* bride, Pastor, *the* bride."

Prompted by Brad, Jesus donned the hat and embraced Barbara, bent her backwards and kissed her passionately, imitating the iconic World War II photograph in Times Square.

The pastor introduced the new couple as "Mr. and Mrs. da Vinci."

"Ms.," Barbara said pointedly.

Sighing, the pastor continued, "Go in peace to love and serve the Lord and one another." Jesus and Barbara marched down the aisle to the applause of the guests, followed by the bridesmaids and groomsmen. They gathered outside in front of the church exchanging hugs and handshakes in the bright sunshine until Dreamboat Dave came running up to them out of breath.

"And just where have *you* been?" demanded Barbara, grinning from ear to ear.

"My car broke down. I had to fix it to get here," Dave said, wringing his greasy hands.

Looking over at the parking lot, Brad asked, "Is that your car?"

"Yes," said Dave.

"You sold him your old car?" Brad asked Jack.

"Yup. For $500," Jack chuckled.

Punching Jack in the arm, Barbara said, "Dave, go get cleaned up and head to the reception and start the music. The rest of you, go gather up the sprays lining the aisle and take them to the reception for the centerpieces.

Jesus and I are going to take a moment alone, and then we'll all meet back here in ten minutes for pictures."

There was a pause before everybody dispersed. Turning to Jesus, Barbara said, "It's over. We did it."

"Nope," Jesus said, "We did it and now it begins. How do you feel?"

"Wound up and tired at the same time."

"Me, too. Our dance ought to get rid of some of this excess nervousness."

The photographer joined them and the rest of the wedding party returned. Barbara told Jack that if he goofed off during any of the pictures, she was going to kick him in the *cojones*. "And these shoes are pointed, too! No children for you!" she exclaimed.

They finished up the pictures without incident and went down to the soup kitchen for the wedding party introductions. Barbara and Jesus visited each table, thanking the guests for attending. *The guests seem to be enjoying themselves,* Jesus thought. Betsy was smiling and having an animated conversation with the pastor. Juan and Ralph were sitting together, looking morose as usual. Clara, Alice and Gertrude were sitting together; Alice appeared a little tipsy.

Jack was slurping on his soup when a well-dressed man walked up to him and asked, "Jackson Beauregard Moses?"

"Beauregard?" asked Brad.

"It's a family name," said Jack testily. "Yes?"

"You've been served," said the man, handing a summons to Jack and quickly walking away.

"What's that?" asked Jesus.

Jack opened up the folded document and immediately went pale.

"Well?" asked Pete.

"It's a paternity suit. I'm required to call this lawyer to set up a test," Jack said.

"You could be a daddy!" said Barbara gleefully.

Jack looked up from the letter and tried to say something. Jesus attempted to deflect attention away from the situation by pointing to the wall. "Hey, isn't that a copy of the Godlines on the wall?"

Returning to the moment, Jack said, "Yeah. I framed a copy of it as a wedding present, too. Don't tell the pastor I put it up there. I wanted to see how long it took him to notice."

"Well, you know what they say," said Brad.

"What?" Jack asked.

"Thou shalt wear a condom..." Brad replied, setting off a round of laughter at the table.

"My life is ruined...so, fuck you," said Jack, getting up from the table and running out of the room.

Brad got up immediately to follow him, but stopped when Dreamboat Dave announced it was time for the couple's first dance. Barbara extended her hand and Jesus took hold of it, twirling her to the middle of the dance floor with her red swing dress swirling elegantly.

268

The music started...and it was the wedding march. Pete and Brad wadded up their napkins and threw them at Dave, who apologized profusely. He got things sorted out and soon a waltz played, with the happy couple beginning their dance.

About a minute in, the music abruptly changed to Benny Goodman's cover of "Sing, Sing, Sing." As the trumpets blared, Barbara and Jesus held each other close. Then Jesus reached across her body to her opposite hip with his right arm and with his left arm behind her legs lifted her into a back flip.

The crowd responded immediately with applause and as a tom-tom solo began, the applause turned into rhythmic clapping. Leaving their seats, they ringed the dance floor to cheer the couple on. Even Jack joined in when he returned.

Gaining confidence, Jesus and Barbara continued their frenetic dance. At one point, Barbara went into a handstand in front of Jesus and he grabbed her ankles. Her skirt slid down to reveal matching red panties. Jesus's eyes opened wide and he quickly mouthed a kiss towards her nether region as the crowd laughed. After a half dozen more swing dance moves, the pair were sweating and tired. As they stood panting, hands on hips, a buzzing began to emanate from the speakers.

Jesus picked up on it first and waved at Dave. After fiddling with the dials on his soundboard, he shrugged his shoulders. The feedback got louder and louder, and Dave pulled the plug on the music. But the sound continued increasing and then morphed into a deep, metallic, scraping noise. Some of the guests put their hands over their ears. Abruptly, the lights went out and the sound changed to a continual, blaring *wonk-wonk-wonk-wonk*.

In the darkness, an orb of white light began materializing around Jesus. With the ground vibrating, most of the guests panicked and stampeded out as pictures fell off the wall and shattered. Pots and pans hit the floor in the kitchen. Glasses on the tables fell, spilling their contents. The pastor and Betsy kneeled and began praying. Gertrude passed out. Barbara began to cry and sank to the floor. Waving, Martha yelled over the racket, "Come back anytime!" and then went to comfort Barbara.

As the ball of light got brighter and brighter, Jesus could see the room. He called out, "Lord, please don't let them take me. I want to stay. I want to stay here. Please!..." and then he fell silent, his lips still moving. He scanned the remaining people in the room until his eyes met Barbara's. He gave a halfhearted wave. She waved back and mouthed the words, "I love you."

Jesus put his hands on his heart and mouthed, "I love you, too." The ball of light collapsed in on itself and he was gone.

The lights came back on and one last pot fell to the floor in the kitchen, startling everyone remaining. Barbara continued to sob as Martha helped her get up off the floor and onto a chair. Betsy ran out of the room claiming, "It's a miracle! It's a miracle! Jesus has been resurrected! Glory be!"

269

The pastor got up off his knees, assisted Gertrude and sat down next to Barbara. Brad, Jack and Alice joined them. The only sound to be heard was Barbara crying and Martha telling her everything would be okay.

"What happened?" asked Gertrude. "Where's Jesus? Is he in the restroom?"

"Are you okay, Gertrude?" the pastor asked, patting her hand. Gertrude nodded yes. His head bowed, the pastor said, "I think I'm going to go call my son." He stood stiffly and shuffled out of the room.

"I thought he was estranged from his son," said Jack.

"Things change," Brad said, as Barbara's sobs got louder.

"Where's Jesus?" asked Gertrude again.

Throwing her hands in the air, Barbara cried to the heavens, "Why, Lord, why? Why did you take him from me?"

As Martha hugged Barbara close, Gertrude repeated, "What just happened? Where's Jesus?"

"I knew he was an alien. I knew it," said Alice.

"I don't know, but he's gone," said Brad.

"Well, that shoots my theory of him being a criminal on the lam... unless the Mob has gotten more technologically advanced," said Jack.

Alice stood unsteadily. "Don't you get it? He was beamed back to... wherever."

"Are you really saying he's an alien?" asked Gertrude. "How can that be?"

Brad wondered out loud, "Humans don't have the technology to do that. Does anybody else have a reasonable explanation?"

Jack spied the video camera on the floor and got up to get it. "Hey, it's still on." He began narrating, focusing on Barbara, "Here's the bride. Her husband has just been beamed out. Let's get her take on this extraordinary event. Barbara?"

"Shut up, Jack! Why don't you turn that camera on yourself and ask 'Whose daddy are you?'" said Barbara.

"That was uncalled for," Jack said quietly.

Barbara stood abruptly. "I know what I'm going to do. I'm going to the hotel and take a long, hot bath and cry some more and then meditate," she declared. All eyes were on Barbara as she left the room.

"I'm going to miss him. He was so...interesting," said Gertrude.

"That he was," said Brad solemnly.

"Yeah," mumbled Jack, as the room fell silent.

Clara broke the silence. "I guess I'm going to have to find another Assistant Department Head."

"Some of the things he said are starting to make sense to me now," said Brad. "Like, 'One never knows how long one will be on this planet.' What do you think, Martha?"

"That's true. One never knows."

Haltingly, Brad asked, "Would you like to go for a walk, Martha?"

"I feel like some swinging, myself."

"What?"

"Don't they have a playground here?" asked Martha.

"Yes."

"Then let's go play." She grabbed Brad's hand, giggling, and off they went.

Jack picked up his summons, grimaced, and stuffed it angrily in his pocket. "I'm going to go home and get wasted."

"Now, Jack, is that really necessary? Why don't the rest of us go and get a nice lunch and talk about all this some more," said Gertrude.

"I'm not driving," said Alice, standing up unsteadily.

"I only have a cat to go home to," said Clara.

"All right, but let's go somewhere I can get a margarita," said Jack sullenly. As the four of them walked out, he asked, "Do any of you know how to change a diaper?"

Chapter 30 – Jesus's last day in court

"And that is my story. The transmogrification back into a Goober body was obviously successful, and within hours I was back on Gooberia," said Jesus.

"That's enough for today. We'll reconvene in the morning to carry out your punishment. Put him in the hole," said the fussy judge.

"*If* I'm found guilty, correct?" asked Jesus as he was led up the ramp.

He was escorted to the hole, where the court sentinels attached the winch and slowly lowered him to the bottom of the pit. Pacing from one side to the other as best he could, he reflected on his life up to this point.

He missed Barbara so and wondered how she had fared these past three months. He was overcome with not-love, but it was more than that, it was sadness and grief. *How is it possible that I'm able to distinguish individual feelings here?* As he pondered that, memories of the wedding flashed through his mind.

The vision of Barbara walking down the aisle as the wedding guests serenaded her choked him up. The vows…"for as long as you both shall live." *Maybe we should have added "unless I get transmogrified,"* he thought. The dance…they had worked so hard on those moves. The best day of his life, interrupted.

Why was I chosen for this mission? He felt like the Universe was teasing him by showing him a better life and then cruelly snatching it away. Pounding the wall in despair, he yelled, "Why, Lord, why?"

Immediately, a flash of inspiration prompted him to formulate a plan for his last day in court.

There was only one punishment on Gooberia—"pruning," the severing of the procreation leg. The purpose wasn't just to prevent the convicted Goober from procreating; without the correct alignment of the feeding leg to the planet, the Goober would slowly starve to death. The percentage of leg taken determines how long the Goober would live. Ten to twenty percent, and the Goober would live a "normal" life—as an outcast. More than that, and they would die. This had never happened before.

The next morning, the court sentinels winched him out of the hole and led him back to the courtroom. The doors opened and Jesus walked in on two legs, his procreating leg thrust high. This type of hazardous behavior was unheard of and broke the first Gooberian commandment, "Do not take risks." With the onlookers either gasping or grumbling, he proceeded confidently down the ramp.

If he was to be pruned for doing his best to survive his mission, Jesus was determined to live on his own terms. When he arrived at the defendant's perch, he sat down, lowering his procreation leg.

Trying to quiet the crowd, the fussy judge hurt his hand banging his gavel. When the courtroom finally quieted down, he asked in a loud, firm voice, "Do you wish to change your plea?"

"No, Your Honor, I do not. I am innocent, and if you were in my position, you would have done the same thing, by Goob," Jesus said defiantly.

"I'm not in your position. I would never have attempted anything so foolish," sneered the fussy judge. "Let us pass sentence. You have been found guilty of treason. The panel of judges has determined that *all* of your procreating leg will be severed. Do you have any final words?"

Jesus, shocked at the severity of the punishment, stood and raised his procreating leg high. "I understand the verdict and I am willing to submit to it. But let me say this: I feel sorry for you, that you are unable to understand or empathize with what happened to me on my mission. The key to any society maturing and evolving is its ability to identify and sympathize with others' misfortunes. I have endured more than you can possibly conceive and I have compassion for your ignorance. I trust God's will in this matter. I know that you think my actions were foolish, but don't you trust that Goob has led me down the correct path *for me*, albeit an unconventional one?"

The fussy judge responded by ordering the court sentinels to bring in the pruning device. They opened a door on the defendant's floor and rolled out something similar to a guillotine. As they positioned it near Jesus, he offered his procreating leg. It took the court sentinels several minutes to secure his leg in the device because it wasn't designed to accommodate a whole leg. Because of this, one of the court sentinels advised him that it might take more than one attempt to complete the amputation.

At that moment, a buzzing noise began. It grew louder and louder until it transformed into a deep, metallic, scraping noise and then a continual, blaring *wonk-wonk-wonk-wonk*. The lights went out and the ground began shaking as an orb of white light formed around Jesus.

"No, NO!" Jesus cried. "I'm willing to take my punishment! I'm willing to take their anger and ignorance."

Through the energetic mist, he could see the frightened court sentinels scuttling up the ramp and the fussy judge, overwhelmed with anger, banging his gavel repeatedly, yelling, "Get back down there! Don't let him get away!" With difficulty, he got up from his perch and slogged towards the ramp.

By now, pictures were falling off the walls, including the Gooberian Commandments. With the judge approaching them, the court sentinels changed directions and scurried back down the ramp. Jesus watched as the fussy judge suddenly stopped, the intensity of his emotions appearing to shatter his internal structure. Oozing a green, pasty substance from his pores, the judge sank to the ground in a heap, his legs flaccid and splayed. Hysterically, he cried, "Help me, help me!" before abruptly falling silent.

The orb of white light grew more intense, and before he disappeared, the last thing Jesus said was, "Thy will be done."

Am I alive?

About the author

Age 6 – Attended Bible classes at a Methodist church in Houston, Texas.

Age 8 – Took Communion and was given his first Bible at a Methodist church in Boise, Idaho.

Age 10 – Parents had become atheists and the family joined the Unitarian church, in Salt Lake City, Utah.

Age 24 – Had become a confirmed agnostic.

Age 26 – His mother became a Unitarian minister, which had a significant effect on him.

Age 27 – Started on a conscious spiritual path triggered by having the first prayer of his life answered while in rehab.

Age 33 – Was introduced to Kundalini Yoga and got sober.

Age 37 – Visited India for the first time and prepared to take Amrit—the vows to become a Sikh. While there, he had an amazing meeting with Yogi Bhajan, who popularized Kundalini Yoga in the U.S. beginning in 1968. It was an enlightening experience, but he nevertheless decided against converting. On the same trip, he met the Dalai Lama and recognized that he aligned more with Buddhism than Sikhism, while still being a Christian.

Age 52 – Certified as a Kundalini Yoga teacher and wrote *"Plus-Sized Yoga: Beginners Yoga for People of All Sizes."*